# Shadows of the Past
A Pride and Prejudice Variation
MJ Stratton

**Shadows of the Past**
A Pride and Prejudice Variation
Copyright 2025 by MJ Stratton
Cover design by Pemberley Darcy
All rights reserved.

Amazon Edition
ISBN:

This book is a work of fiction. Any person or place appearing herein is fictitious or is used fictitiously.

All rights reserved, including the right to reproduce this book, or portions thereof, in any form. No portion of this book may be reproduced in any form without written permission from the publisher or author, except as permitted by U.S. copyright law.

**NO AI TRAINING**: Without in any way limiting the author's exclusive rights under copyright, any use of this publication to "train" generative artificial intelligence (AI) technologies to generate text is expressly **prohibited**. The author reserves all rights to license uses of this work for generative AI training and development of machine learning language models.

This eBook is licensed for personal use only and may not be re-sold or given away to others. If you would like to share this book with another person, please purchase an additional copy for each person. If you're reading this book and did not purchase it, or it was not purchased for your use only, then please purchase your copy.

Thank you for respecting the hard work of this author.

# Contents

| | |
|---|---|
| Dedication | V |
| About This Book | 1 |
| Prologue | 3 |
| 1. Chapter One | 6 |
| 2. Chapter Two | 16 |
| 3. Chapter Three | 24 |
| 4. Chapter Four | 33 |
| 5. Chapter Five | 42 |
| 6. Chapter Six | 49 |
| 7. Chapter Seven | 57 |
| 8. Chapter Eight | 65 |
| 9. Chapter Nine | 75 |
| 10. Chapter Ten | 85 |
| 11. Chapter Eleven | 96 |
| 12. Chapter Twelve | 105 |
| 13. Chapter Thirteen | 115 |
| 14. Chapter Fourteen | 124 |
| 15. Chapter Fifteen | 133 |

| | | |
|---|---|---|
| 16. | Chapter Sixteen | 142 |
| 17. | Chapter Seventeen | 150 |
| 18. | Chapter Eighteen | 159 |
| 19. | Chapter Nineteen | 169 |
| 20. | Chapter Twenty | 180 |
| 21. | Chapter Twenty-One | 189 |
| 22. | Chapter Twenty-Two | 200 |
| 23. | Chapter Twenty-Three | 211 |
| 24. | Chapter Twenty-Four | 220 |
| 25. | Chapter Twenty-Five | 229 |
| 26. | Chapter Twenty-Six | 234 |
| 27. | Chapter Twenty-Seven | 246 |
| 28. | Chapter Twenty-Eight | 252 |
| 29. | Chapter Twenty-Nine | 262 |
| 30. | Chapter Thirty | 270 |
| 31. | Chapter Thirty-One | 279 |
| 32. | Chapter Thirty-Two | 289 |
| 33. | Chapter Thirty-Three | 300 |
| 34. | Chapter Thirty-Four | 309 |
| 35. | Chapter Thirty-Five | 317 |
| | Epilogue | 322 |
| | Other Books by MJ Stratton | 325 |
| | Acknowledgements | 327 |
| | About The Author | 328 |

# Dedication

*For Dr. Kayla Goodman-Millett*
*Thank you for keeping me grounded as I juggled writing*
*and doing a doctorate!*
*Love you, friend!*

# About This Book

**E**lizabeth is not a Bennet. The circumstances that brought her to Longbourn are shocking. Darcy might be the only person who can help her.

Her past is shrouded in mystery. Having been discovered wounded and wandering a lonely road in Derbyshire twelve years ago, Elizabeth remembers nothing of her life before the Bennets took her in. Whatever shreds of memory she has are hazy and unclear. Content with the love of her adopted family, she never could have imagined the turn her life would take when Netherfield Park is let at last.

Fitzwilliam Darcy is pleased to assist his good friend Charles Bingley as he learns estate management. That is, until Bingley begins acting peculiarly around one of the daughters of the neighboring estate. He is baffled by Mr. Bingley's strange fixation with one sister even as he courts another. Darcy, too, finds Miss Elizabeth fascinating, but feels he cannot fully court the lady whilst Bingley is behaving so oddly.

When her past identity is revealed, Elizabeth must reconcile her past with the life she has come to know. The mystery of what happened in her father's house haunts her, and an unknown enemy seeks to finish what he started twelve years prior. Unable to resist her pull, Darcy joins Elizabeth as she learns to navigate her new life. As the danger mounts, he must protect her at all costs or risk losing the lady he loves forever.

*Shadows of the Past is a Pride and Prejudice Variation of medium angst. In this multi-trope, clean, Regency Darcy and Elizabeth story, Elizabeth is not a Bennet and has more exalted connections than she knows.*

# Prologue

*Yorkshire, 1799*
*Elizabeth*

Elizabeth crouched beneath her father's desk, the contraband clasped tightly in her little hands. She knew it opened—Mama had shown her its secret last week. *If only I could remember how to do it,* she thought.

The clock on the mantel chimed the hour, making Elizabeth jump. She needed to go back to the nursery. Papa would come searching for her soon, for it was nearly bedtime. Harry was already asleep—Nurse had put the lad to bed an hour ago before returning to her home.

*I must return this to Mama's jewel box before she discovers I have taken it. Besides, I left the other piece there.* Oh! Maybe that was the key! Perhaps she could sneak back into her mama's room, retrieve it, and finally unlock the secret. Elizabeth moved from her sitting position to her hands and knees, ready to crawl out from underneath the desk. A door slammed nearby, and voices became louder. She paused, holding her breath in fear of discovery. Surely, someone had not discovered her misdeed already!

"You are drunk!" Her father came into the room. He sounded very angry. Elizabeth crouched low, moving around the side of the desk and peeking out. Papa stood with another man in front of the fireplace.

"It matters not, Henry. I shall be at work tomorrow and no worse for wear." The man's slurred voice sounded indifferent. He waved his hand dismissively as he swayed with drink.

"I know it all! How could you? We built this company together—I fronted the costs! And now I have learned that you purloined funds to pay gambling debts! No, it will not do. I have enough surplus income to buy you out. If you will not sell, I shall take all that is mine and start fresh. And you know our other partner will agree. He is an intelligent man with an acute business acumen. When I tell him what you have done, he will jump at the chance to break with you."

The man gasped and stumbled. "You cannot. No, Henry, give me another chance. I shall pay it all back."

"You have had far too many chances. For years, I have made excuses for your actions. When you used your own earnings for your habits, I did not care, but taking from the company funds is too much. I shall not sit by and watch you destroy everything that I have built. I have a son. I wish for him to inherit all I possess someday. And what of Elizabeth? She is in need of a dowry. No, it is better we part ways now before there are too many hard feelings."

Elizabeth watched her father turn away from the intoxicated man in disgust and saw the exact moment he caught sight of her hiding by the desk. His eyes widened in shock, and his expression implored her to stay hidden.

Her gaze went to the man standing behind her beloved papa. His face was wreathed in shadows, but she could see his arm rising. Before she could speak a warning, the man brought some unknown object down hard on her father's head. Papa crumpled to the ground without a sound.

"You will not take my life from me," the man seethed darkly. He stumbled from the room, the heavy object still clutched in his hand.

Elizabeth crept out from behind the desk, crawling to her father's side. He lay still, his chest unmoving. "Papa?" she whispered. She shook him, but he did not stir. Elizabeth sat by his side, his hand in her own, silent tears streaming down her cheeks.

After some unknown passage of time, a noise came from behind her. She turned—something hard struck her head and everything went black.

# Chapter One

*Derbyshire 1799*
*Mr. Thomas Bennet*

"It will be good to be with our children again." Mrs. Fanny Bennet patted her husband's leg affectionately. He put his hand over hers, squeezing gently. The carriage swayed back and forth, the spring wind buffeting the sides.

"I have missed them," Mr. Bennet confirmed. "And it was generous of Madeline and Edward to stay with them whilst we journeyed to Hertfordshire."

An express had come three weeks past to their lodgings in Lambton, Derbyshire. Thomas Bennet's father and elder brother had died, leaving him—once a second son—the unexpected heir to the family estate. He had never thought Longbourn would be his. At the time, he had established himself as a country solicitor, working closely with Archibald Palmer, the father of Madeline Gardiner. She was married to Edward Gardiner, Mrs. Bennet's younger brother.

"My brother and sister will be eager to return to London. Their Easter visit extended long past what they expected." Mrs. Bennet smiled at her husband. "How long do you suppose it will be before we can depart for Longbourn?"

Mr. Bennet pursed his lips in thought. "I imagine we can be gone in little more than a fortnight. Madeline wrote she began packing soon after we left. We have only our personal effects; the house in Lambton was let complete, so everything within it must remain."

"We shall need two carriages and a wagon to transport everything." Mrs. Bennet frowned. "I do not suppose our servants will wish to come to Hertfordshire. They have family here."

"Now that their children are married, the Hills may wish to accompany us. I believe their daughter lives in Hertfordshire." Mr. Bennet patted his wife's hand soothingly. "Molly and Martha will remain here. They are still young, and their father leases a farm near Lambton."

"Longbourn's cook seemed competent. I think it is best to retain her." His wife's brow wrinkled in concentration. "There is so much to do! I was not raised to be the mistress of an estate. Oh, Thomas, what if I cannot do it?"

Mr. Bennet leaned down and pecked his wife on the lips. "I shall be there to assist you. My father taught me estate management, but I never thought to use that knowledge. We shall learn to be master and mistress of the estate together."

His wife beamed her gratitude. "It is very good that we already have a son. The entail will end with him."

"And this inheritance will help us provide dowries for the girls. They must be looked after, too."

Mrs. Bennet nodded in agreement. "Would it be too much to ask to redo the mistress's chambers?" she asked eagerly. "Will we have the funds?"

Mr. Bennet chuckled. "Yes, we can see it done as soon as we take residence. Heaven knows those rooms have not been refreshed since my mother came to Longbourn as a newly married lady. You will not mind sharing my chambers whilst the work is done?" He winked mischievously at his wife, pleased with the blush that appeared on her cheeks.

"Thank you, husband. I confess, I hardly know what to do with myself. I have always been forced to live frugally. Though the interest from my dowry helps with our finances, I know it is not much."

"We shall have two thousand a year, Fanny. All will be well."

Fanny shook her head. "You misunderstand me. I am frightened that I shall forget all I know about frugality and prudence. It will be very easy to find things to purchase. I do not wish to beggar the estate. Little Thomas needs something to inherit."

"It speaks well of you to be cognizant of the danger more money could bring." Thomas pressed another kiss to the side of his wife's head. "We shall exercise caution. I am certain there are things I could do to increase Longbourn's income."

The carriage lurched to a sudden stop. The coachman shouted something unintelligible. Thomas shared a worried glance with his wife.

"I shall just go and see what the fuss is about," he murmured.

Fanny clasped his hand. "Oh, do be careful! I could not bear it if something befell you now!"

Mr. Bennet pushed the carriage door open and climbed down. "Jones?" he called. "What is the meaning of this delay?"

"This here child, sir." Jones, the coachman, pointed a thumb toward a little waif standing in the middle of the road.

Thomas stepped forward to get a better look at the girl. She was petite, with dark brown curls plaited down her back. Her gown was pale blue and splattered with mud. His gaze traveled to her face. Dried blood stained her cheeks and forehead, and a bloody gash was prominently visible in her hair.

Stepping forward, he crouched down and took her hand. She looked at him vacantly, her eyes dazed and confused. "What is your name, lass?" he asked softly.

"Lizzy." She whispered her short reply. It seemed as though she looked right through him.

"What happened to your head, Lizzy?" Mr. Bennet pulled out a handkerchief and tried to dab at her wound. The child cried out in pain and collapsed on the road. She curled into a ball and let out a plaintive cry.

"We cannot leave her here, Jones." Mr. Bennet straightened. "Let me apprise Mrs. Bennet of the situation. The girl will come with us."

Jones frowned, but nodded. Mr. Bennet returned to the carriage. He opened the door and spoke briefly with his wife. Mrs. Bennet had a big heart and would agree with his decision to bring the girl along with them.

"Oh, the dear child!" Mrs. Bennet climbed down from the carriage amidst her husband's protests. "She will need a mother. Let me go to her."

The girl lay where Mr. Bennet had left her. Her arms and hands were curled beneath her chest, and her legs and knees tucked up under her chin. She shuddered, her sobs rising and falling like a child too tired to cry properly.

Mrs. Bennet crouched down next to the frightened girl and placed a tender hand on her back. "There, now," she whispered soothingly. "It is a little chilly out here. What say you to coming into the carriage? We have some bread and cheese. Does that sound nice?"

The girl—Lizzy—lifted her head and blinked owlishly. "I do not know if I like cheese," she murmured. Slowly, she sat up, keeping her hands clenched tightly in her lap.

"Let us find out." Mrs. Bennet stood and offered her hand to Lizzy. Slowly, Lizzy took the extended hand and rose to her feet. Her other hand came to her chest. Mr. Bennet noted the tightly clenched fist and wondered if the child held something. He said nothing, content to let his wife work her wonders. *She has always been an exemplary mother,* he thought proudly.

Mrs. Bennet led the timid child to the carriage. They both climbed aboard, and Mr. Bennet followed behind.

They settled onto the bench, and the carriage lurched forward. His wife drew a basket of food from beneath the bench and uncovered it. She broke off a piece of cheese and held it out to little Lizzy, who took it and popped it into her mouth. Bit by bit, Mrs. Bennet fed her bread and cheese, waiting patiently as she chewed in silence. At last, Lizzy's weary eyes closed, and she leaned against the squabs, drifting into sleep.

"What are we to do with her?" Mrs. Bennet whispered. "Surely, something dreadful has occurred. Did you notice the gash on her head?"

"Perhaps a carriage accident?" Mr. Bennet speculated. "We can send out inquiries when we arrive in Lambton."

"And if we do not discover her family? Then what? We cannot just put her in a home for orphans. It would not be right." Mrs. Bennet folded her arms stubbornly. He recognized that stance. His wife had already decided her course and would not be swayed.

"How are we to explain her presence to our children?" he asked, perplexed. Mrs. Bennet's motherly instincts had always been strong, but he sensed something more now. She looked at the girl sleeping on the bench across from them. There was steel in her eyes.

"She is our cousin. Her parents died in a carriage accident. She will remain with us until another family member claims her." Mrs. Bennet paused. "I wonder at her wound. If not a carriage accident, then what could have caused it?"

"I do not know." Mr. Bennet shook his head sadly. "I only hope we can do what needs to be done for her."

"As of this moment, she is one of our own. I shall be her mama, and you will be her papa. No one in Hertfordshire need know any different."

He nodded in agreement. "She looks of an age with Thomas. Maybe a little younger. Do you think she will be able to tell us how old she is? We only know her name."

"Lizzy. It is a pretty name. Miss Elizabeth Bennet." Mrs. Bennet smiled in satisfaction and snuggled next to her husband's side. "How do you feel about having six children, sir?" she asked cheekily.

"I would gladly have seven or eight if it were possible." Mr. Bennet kissed his wife's upturned nose. After their youngest, Lydia, was born, they had been told there would be no more children. Maybe little Miss Lizzy was a blessing.

The girl stirred a few hours later. She slept so soundly that she barely moved. Even the bumpy carriage ride did nothing to disturb her.

Mr. Bennet watched as Elizabeth's eyes fluttered open. She sat up and looked around in confusion. When her gaze landed on the couple sitting across from her, she gasped. Fear stole across her expression, and she whimpered.

"Papa," she whispered. "Papa."

"Who is your papa?" Mrs. Bennet asked tenderly.

Elizabeth blinked. "I do not remember," she replied. Her brow furrowed. "Why do I not remember?" One hand rose to touch the gash on her head. "What happened?"

"We are not certain." Mrs. Bennet replied gently, moving to sit beside her. "We hoped you could tell us."

The child closed her eyes, face drawn in concentration. When she opened them, they filled with tears. "I cannot recall," she said miserably. "I only remember walking for a long time."

Mrs. Bennet exchanged a glance with her husband. "Well, you may stay with us. I am Mrs. Bennet. This gentleman is my husband. We are going to fetch our children before we go to our estate. When we reach our destination, we will see if we can find your family. Can you tell us how old you are?"

Elizabeth frowned. "I believe I am eight. I had a birthday recently, I think."

"That is something." Mr. Bennet spoke for the first time. His words caused their young charge to squeak in terror and shrink in on herself. His wife gave him a confused look and then patted the child's hand.

"Mr. Bennet is not so very frightening," she said soothingly. "You will like him very much. He plays with his children and reads them stories."

Elizabeth cowered into Mrs. Bennet's side, burying her face in the lady's shoulder.

"There, there, now. You will see in time." Mrs. Bennet kissed the child's head. "Will you let me wash your face and clean the wound on your head?" She pulled a handkerchief out and held it out. "See? Nothing but white cloth. I have some water here in this flask." Pulling a metal vessel from the basket, Mrs. Bennet opened the lid and poured clear, cold liquid onto the white linen. Carefully, she turned Elizabeth's head and dabbed at the blood on her cheeks and forehead. Her efforts revealed a pale face with a smattering of freckles on her nose. Elizabeth's confused eyes held intelligence, and Mr. Bennet wondered what horrors had rendered her so skittish and fearful.

"That is much better." Mrs. Bennet put the soiled handkerchief into the basket. "We shall have to order you a bath when we reach our lodgings. I fear there is nothing I can do about the mess in your hair for now."

She exchanged a glance with her husband as Elizabeth leaned back into her side. The child drifted off to sleep, her fist still curled protectively around whatever secret it held.

When they arrived in Lambton, Mrs. Bennet gently shook her charge awake. "We have arrived, Elizabeth," she murmured. "Shall we go inside?" Elizabeth nodded wearily, taking Mrs. Bennet's hand as they stepped down from the carriage. Mr. Bennet followed behind, aware that the child feared his presence. He did not wish to frighten her.

"Mama!" Their son, Thomas, greeted them at the door, a broad grin on his face. "We thought you would be here hours ago! Who is that?"

The boisterous lad pointed at Elizabeth, who cowered behind Mrs. Bennet.

"Let us in the door, son." Mr. Bennet walked past his wife and ward to enter the house. He extended his arms to his heir, hugging him fiercely. "This is our distant cousin, Tommy. She will stay with us for now."

"What is your name?" Tommy broke away from his father and came toward the newcomer.

Instead of answering, Elizabeth whimpered and pulled further away.

"Her name is Elizabeth." Mrs. Bennet patted her son's head. "Perhaps you should go find Jane and Mary. I assume Lydia and Kitty are abed?"

"Aunt Maddy is with them now. And Uncle Gardiner went to the inn." Tommy bounded away, calling over his shoulder, "I shall go get Jane!"

"Will you order a bath, Thomas?" Fanny turned to him. "I shall take Lizzy upstairs. Mary has outgrown several gowns. We can use those until I can visit the shops."

Mr. Bennet nodded. Mary had inherited her father's lanky form. She was as tall as Jane, despite being three years younger than her oldest sister. Elizabeth's stature contrasted sharply—she was petite and not much taller than five-year-old Kitty.

Mrs. Bennet took their charge away, and Mr. Bennet did not see her again until the next morning. Still skittish, Elizabeth was at least clean. Once washed, her head wound did not look so terrible, and her hair was styled to hide the worst of the damage. Her hair fell to the middle of her back and was escaping its plait. She sat quietly at the table, her hands clasped in her lap and glancing nervously at the other children seated beside her. Kitty and Lydia remained in the nursery, but the Bennets had traditionally had their three eldest children take breakfast with them.

The reason for Elizabeth's presence was given again, and the children accepted it without question. Mr. Bennet resolved to pen a few inquiries directly after breakfast. Should they discover the child's family before they departed for Hertfordshire, she could be delivered into their hands when they commenced their journey.

*And if you cannot find them?* The voice of reason in his head begged him to consider the potential consequences—good and bad—involved in raising another child. *Fanny will treat her as one of her own,* he reasoned. *She has a big heart. I must be prepared to do likewise.*

# Chapter Two

*Nottinghamshire 1799*
*Lady Maude Montrose*

"My lady!" Jameson rushed into the room, foregoing his usual respects. He looked panicked and wrung the hat in his hands. Jameson was Lady Maude Montrose's most faithful servant, the only one she trusted to keep her informed of any developments concerning her second son.

"Jameson, what has you in a dither? What could possibly cause such alarm?" She set her teacup aside and smoothed the front of her gown.

"They are dead, madam!" He collapsed to his knees before her.

Lady Montrose froze. "Who is dead?" she whispered, her throat suddenly dry.

"Your son, madam. And his family. They were discovered this morning." Jameson looked up at her, his face wreathed in despair. He had been Henry Montrose's valet before his father, Lord Arthur Montrose, disowned him.

*No! It is not possible. Elizabeth is only eight. And Henry—the boy is only four years old.* She stood slowly, a strange sort of numbness spreading over her body. "I do not believe it. We must go at once. His Lordship is already in London, so we need not fear his reprisals."

"I ordered the carriage before coming to you." Jameson stood shakily.

"I shall delay long enough to pack a valise." She strode from the room, masking her fear and panic lest her husband's faithful servants suspect that anything was amiss.

Lady Maude Montrose had married forty-year-old Lord Montrose at the tender age of sixteen. The match had been arranged by her father, a minor baron with a head for business. Her fifty-thousand-pound dowry had been enough of an inducement for the much older Earl of Montrose to take a child bride. She gave him two sons in short order before locking the door between their rooms.

Their firstborn son and heir to the earldom, Harold Montrose, Viscount Marston, resided in London with his father. He had not married and had no intention of doing so whilst his father lived. Furious that the earl had disowned his younger brother, Marston resolved to see his father in his grave before siring an heir.

"Just the thing to torment him," he told his mother. "How could he do such a thing to my brother?"

The earl had disowned his younger son when, instead of taking orders, he used part of his inheritance to establish a profitable textile mill in Yorkshire. It was ideally located near the point where three counties met, with the family estate, Marston Hall, twenty miles to the east in Nottinghamshire, and Derbyshire an equal distance to the west.

Refusing to abide by her husband's wishes, Lady Montrose maintained contact with her younger son, Henry. She attended his marriage to Miss Amelia Lindon, the wealthy daughter of a tradesman.

Her dowry of forty-thousand pounds propped up Henry's growing business and urged it into greater prosperity.

When her granddaughter was born, Lady Montrose went to her daughter-in-law as soon as she could. Her husband had gone to London and ordered her to follow in a month. She used his time away to visit Yorkshire and her family. Amelia gave the baby her grandmother's middle name—Elizabeth.

There were no more children for four years before Henry's son was born. Amelia Montrose gave birth to little Harry Montrose on a cold winter's night. Unfortunately, Lady Montrose was required to wait some months before she could sneak away to see her grandson.

*"The succession is assured,"* she told Henry.

*"Has Harold not married yet?"* her son replied, affectionately caressing his son's cheek.

*"He maintains he will do nothing until our father dies. You know how he is."* She made cooing sounds at the baby. *"May I hold him?"*

Henry handed her the child. *"He strongly favors you,"* she murmured. *"How is Amelia?"*

*"She is well. She is resting upstairs. Elizabeth is with her."*

*"And how does my granddaughter like sharing her mother's attention?"* Lady Montrose smiled pleasantly and winked at her son. *"I imagine she has a few things to say about her new brother."*

*"Elizabeth is in love with Harry. She begs to hold him as soon as she wakes each morning. I have no doubt that she will be a perfect older sister."*

*"That is well. I have something for Amelia—a small token in honor of the babe."* Lady Montrose bounced Harry in her arms, pleased when he granted her a toothless grin.

*"I shall inquire."* Her son moved out of the room, and she turned her full attention to the boy in her arms.

*"You will be just as well-favored as your papa. I see him in your smile."*

*Amelia came in on Henry's arm. Lady Montrose turned to her, smiling broadly. "He is perfect, my dear. Congratulations."*

*"Thank you, Mother." Amelia smiled happily. Her brown curls bounced as she walked toward her mother-in-law. "I am pleased he takes after his father so well."*

*"And Elizabeth grows like you more each day." Henry kissed his wife's cheek. "I could not be happier to see your beauty mirrored on her face."*

*"I have brought you a present." Lady Montrose nodded to the little velvet box on the table next to her seat.*

*Amelia picked it up and opened it. "It is lovely!" she cried. Henry's personal crest had been carved into ivory and set in gold filigree. It was an amalgamation of the Montrose coat of arms and Lady Montrose's father's crest. Her son had commissioned and created it after he had been disowned.*

*"It is a peculiar piece of jewelry. I saw it in a London shop and knew it would be the perfect gift. The jeweler said he could put whatever I wished in the ivory. If you press down where the necklace attaches to the pendant, it will open."*

*Amelia picked up the necklace and pressed where Lady Montrose indicated. The front of the pendant popped open, revealing a cavity inside.*

*"It is a locket!" Amelia exclaimed, delighted. "I shall commission miniatures of the children at once."*

*After a moment's examination, she carefully detached the chain. A small gold pin slid from the back of the piece, still affixed to the chain. It was decorative in its own right and could be worn alone when not attached to the pendant. The locket could not be opened without the chain and its fitting.*

Lady Montrose roused herself from her reverie. The carriage rushed along the road, the well-sprung conveyance handling the ruts with ease. Within three hours, they slowed as they entered the small town where her son had once made his home.

The carriage came to a halt before a modest house on a row. Henry could have afforded a larger abode for his family, but he insisted that if he wished to leave a prosperous business to his heir, he must practice frugality now. And so, he chose simpler accommodations. They kept a cook and a maid, though neither lived in.

The door opened, and Jameson helped her down. She climbed the steps and entered the house without knocking.

"Who is there?"

A gangly red-headed man came out of the study. He wore a black armband and a sorrowful look.

"Lady Montrose." She stepped forward. "Who are you, and what are you doing in my son's home?"

"My name is Robert Bingley. Henry was my partner. Well, one of them."

"Where is he?"

"The family is laid out in the drawing room, my lady." Mr. Bingley turned and left the room, beckoning her to follow. "The maid found them this morning. They are still searching for Miss Montrose."

"What?" She spoke sharply. "What do you mean?"

They entered the drawing room. Three bodies lay before them. Her heart seized as she recognized her son, her daughter-in-law, and their only son. *Elizabeth! She is not here.*

"It appears that they were bludgeoned to death. Pardon my blunt speech, your ladyship."

"A burglary gone wrong?" she asked. Surely, only that could explain this senseless tragedy.

"That is what the magistrate believed, but other than Miss Montrose, nothing is missing."

She nodded slowly. "What is being done to find my granddaughter?" She felt numb, as if her feelings were just out of reach. Maude knew she ought to be wailing and weeping at the moment, but everything seemed locked away and untouchable.

"We have searched the house. We believe she may also be wounded. Two bloodstains in the study suggest that more than one person was present. However, only Henry was found."

"I wish for them to be interred at Marston Hall," she commanded. That was their rightful place. Something in her chest began to ache, and her eyes prickled uncomfortably.

"Forgive me, your ladyship, but I am aware that your husband has not looked favorably upon my friend for many years. Will the earl protest?"

"He is in London. I shall simply not tell him until it is too late. Jameson will see to the arrangements. I shall also order that their belongings be crated and sent to Marston Hall. Now, I shall inspect the house myself."

Determined to save her despair for when she was alone, she walked down the short hall to the stairs that led to the chambers her son had shared with his wife—such was the nature of their happy marriage. Nothing seemed out of place there, though there was a dark spot on the rug she suspected was blood.

Mr. Bingley had been correct. The jewel box on the dressing table appeared undisturbed. It was not large; a thief could easily have taken it in its entirety. That it remained suggested robbery had not been the motive. Moving closer, she noted the chain for the pendant she had given her daughter-in-law upon the birth of her son—part of it was missing. Frowning, she rifled through the box in search of the missing piece, but found nothing. *Strange,* she thought. *Amelia wore the pendant almost every day.* Indeed, from the moment the miniatures had been secured inside, Amelia had worn the pendant unceasingly.

She left the room, suddenly feeling unequal to walking through the rest of the silent house. Oh, how she wished to hear Elizabeth's excited cry or Harry's happy chatter. *Where is my granddaughter?* she wondered. The pain in her chest grew, and she drew a steadying breath.

Mr. Bingley awaited her in the study. "I know it may seem too soon, your ladyship, but I have found Henry's will. He left everything to his son but indicated that his daughter would inherit if Harry…" he trailed off. "What is to be done?"

"Elizabeth is not dead." She spoke firmly, a resolve settling over her. Maude pushed the fear and sadness away. *I must be strong—for Elizabeth.*

"But where is she?" Mr. Bingley raised his hands helplessly.

"Wherever she is, I shall find her. She is my grandchild. For now, gather any pertinent information regarding the disposition of my son's assets. Everything will be placed in trust for Elizabeth." She would use her connections to see that her granddaughter's inheritance was secured.

"What of the business? Will you sell Henry's shares?"

Lady Montrose paused, considering. "No, I think not. I shall arrange for a portion of the interest to be redistributed for the company's needs. Despite my lofty marriage, I admired my son for seeking his own fortune. Others of my station scorned him, but I felt only pride. I would hate to see his efforts go to waste."

"We can arrange quarterly expense reports if it suits you." Mr. Bingley nodded solemnly. "I had great respect for Henry, madam. He made me a partner based on nothing more than a few sound business decisions. I have not taken his belief in my abilities for granted."

"Then it is settled. I shall remain in the North long enough to see my family transported to my home and to begin the search for Elizabeth. Jameson!" Her faithful servant came from the hallway. "You are to remain here until everything is resolved. I shall go back to Marston Hall and see...see to everything..." She choked on a sob. "Then we will go to town."

"Very good, madam." Jameson bowed. His usually expressionless face was creased with sorrow.

In just a few hours, she had arranged wagons to carry her loved ones home to Nottinghamshire. Lady Montrose followed in her own carriage, lost in sorrow. The tears, once they started, did not cease. *Where is Elizabeth?* She pondered the situation during the entire ride, determined to send letters to the Bow Street Runners as soon as she reached Marston Hall.

# Chapter Three

*Hertfordshire, 1799*
*Mrs. Bennet*

"And here is the nursery, madam." Mrs. Smith, Longbourn's soon-to-be retired housekeeper, pushed open the door and stepped aside. "We have had it refreshed and aired—new mattresses on the beds and the like."

Mrs. Bennet stepped into the room and nodded in satisfaction. Her dark mourning dress contrasted starkly against the bright colors in the room. The large window illuminated the space with natural light. Standing before the glass, one could see trees and flowers. There were six little beds lining one wall, and a chest filled with toys on another. A door led to chambers occupied by the nurse and governess.

The younger children, who had accompanied the matron upstairs, squealed in delight and poured into the room. The three eldest entered more sedately. *My children will be well looked after,* she thought, *including Lizzy.*

Mrs. Bennet paused as she watched the girl looking curiously around the nursery. *Oh, Elizabeth.* Mr. Bennet's inquiries had yielded nothing. He searched Derbyshire for news, but no carriage accidents had been reported. Indeed, no one searched for any missing children.

*"I fear something nefarious befell her family,"* her husband told her in a hushed voice one evening as they sat before the fire in their Lambton chambers. He fingered the black armband he wore, his expression clouded with concern.

"We cannot send her away," Mrs. Bennet protested.

"I do not intend to do anything of the sort. You told me when we found her we would not consign her to an orphanage. Besides, the children have taken to her. Jane especially." Her husband pressed a tender kiss to her lips. "We are to depart for Longbourn tomorrow. The neighbors there will not know any different."

"She does not look like any of the other children," she reminded him. And indeed, she did not. The girls all had fair hair of varying shades of blond. Little Thomas had brown hair, but it was soft and warm in tone—more like chocolate. Elizabeth's curls, by contrast, were a deep brown with hints of red.

"We shall say she favors your grandmother. No one has met the lady, other than you."

Mrs. Bennet nodded. "Very good. I have secured her possessions in a small box." They discussed the strange piece of jewelry the girl had been clutching when she was discovered on the road, wondering whether it might have belonged to her family. The front bore a crest, though it was unfamiliar to both Mr. or Mrs. Bennet. Inquiries into its origins and locating a copy of Debrett's would have to wait until they settled in at Longbourn.

Coming back to herself, she addressed the nursery maid. "We shall hire a governess as soon as an acceptable candidate can be found. For now, do not hesitate to bring me any of your concerns."

She and Mrs. Smith left the room and went downstairs. Mr. and Mrs. Hill were waiting in the housekeeper's office, and they made their way there.

"I shall leave Mrs. Hill with everything she requires before I go to my daughter," Mrs. Smith told Mrs. Bennet. "My records are in good order, so I expect the transition will be smooth."

"Then I shall leave you to it." Mrs. Bennet went to her husband's study and found him poring over the estate books.

"Are the children settled?" he asked without looking up.

"They are." She came around the desk and put her hands on her husband's shoulders. He leaned back, relaxing in the chair as she rubbed the soreness away. "Tommy has found your old toy soldiers and is lining them up along the windowsill. He is launching pillows at them in a mock battle."

Her husband chuckled. "Such a rambunctious boy." He reached unconsciously for the black band situated on his arm, and Fanny wondered what memories danced in his thoughts. Mr. Bennet rarely spoke of his departed family, for the grief was still too near.

Mrs. Bennet ceased her ministrations and moved to her husband's side. "I wish to send out inquiries for a governess," she said. "I told the nursery maid I would do so. Besides, Jane and Thomas are too advanced for my help anymore." The admission rankled. Mrs. Bennet had been educated like many young ladies and given just enough knowledge to manage a household. She wanted more for her girls, though. Young Thomas especially needed more education than she could provide.

"Elizabeth seems more knowledgeable than Jane or Thomas, despite being younger." Her husband glanced up. "She reads and writes very well."

"Yes, though the particulars of her background are unknown to us, it is evident her education was not neglected." Mrs. Bennet moved around the desk and sat in the chair that faced her husband. "Did you know she went on and on about cotton textiles the other day? I could barely follow the conversation."

"It is peculiar." Her husband frowned. "Worry not, my love, we shall see to her well-being." The gash hidden by Elizabeth's hair was a daily reminder that she had suffered horrors they did not know. Her memory had not returned. True, she could read and write and speak. She remembered her Christian name, and that she had recently turned eight, but everything else about her life remained lost.

"I know we have only just taken possession of Longbourn, but already there is much to be done." Mr. Bennet gestured at the book in front of him. "Father relied on antiquated farming methods. I intend to make immediate changes. Spring planting is only just beginning, which makes it an ideal time to introduce improvements this season, with more to follow next."

"Is there a steward here?"

Mr. Bennet shook his head. "No, Father never hired another after Mr. Simms died. I plan to send out inquiries today—and shall include one for a governess." He picked up another sheet of paper. "My father meant to purchase three farms adjoining Longbourn. They are part of the Purvis Lodge estate. I believe I shall see the transaction through. The additional income may be invested for our daughters' dowries."

She nodded. "Very good. Will you have time to review the household accounts with me later? Hill is looking them over at present, but she has not your experience."

"Yes, we can do that after tea."

And so, the Bennets settled nicely into a new routine at Longbourn. Their new neighbors came to call, expressing their pleasure at making the acquaintance of the family, and offering condolences at the loss of Old Mr. Bennet and his eldest son. The sentiments were graciously received, and in time, Mr. Bennet began to heal from his grief.

The children adjusted to their change in circumstances with ease—the young are often more resilient than adults. Even Elizabeth seemed to settle comfortably into her place at Longbourn. She at first addressed her benefactors formally, but within six months, she began calling them 'mama and papa.' This pleased both Mr. and Mrs. Bennet greatly, and soon they resolved to forget that she had ever been anything but their own dear child.

There were a few instances that caused alarm during the first year at the estate. The four older children engaged in a game of *apodidraskinda*, an activity Mr. Bennet taught them after reading of it in one of his Greek tomes by Julius Pollux. One child would hide and count to one hundred whilst the others hid themselves somewhere in the house. The seeker would find the others. The last person found would win the game.

Mrs. Bennet could hear Elizabeth counting in the hallway outside the parlor. She smiled happily, listening as the child counted first in English before reverting to French at fifty. Finally, she reached one hundred and cried loudly, "You have had your time–now I shall seek you out!"

There were giggles echoing in the hall. "Found you, Tommy!" Elizabeth cried. Her adopted brother shouted, "No fair!" but came to the drawing room anyway, the place designated as where those who were 'out' would wait.

Tommy played with the drapes as he waited for his sisters. Mary joined him next, and they played with a basket of blocks at Mrs. Bennet's feet.

Suddenly, the peaceful atmosphere was shattered by a terrified scream. Mrs. Bennet jumped up, heart racing, and ran from the room. She made her way down the hall toward the study. Pushing open the door, she stepped inside. Jane stood in front of Elizabeth, patting her cheeks and crying. The other girl stood frozen, the horrible vacant look from when they found her back in her eyes. Mrs. Bennet put her hand on the child's shoulder, and she promptly collapsed.

"What happened?" Mrs. Bennet asked after lowering herself to the floor, Elizabeth in her arms.

"I do not know! I was hiding under Papa's desk. Elizabeth came in looking for me. She became very quiet. I peeped out because I thought she had gone, but she had not. She saw me and went stiff—just froze! I do not know what happened, but then she was screaming! Oh, Mama, is she well?"

"I believe she will be. Run Jane, fetch your father."

Mr. Bennet came quickly, having just returned home for tea. He carried the still unconscious Elizabeth to her bed in the nursery, instructing Nora and the governess, Miss Lynd, to inform him when she awoke.

Mrs. Bennet stayed by Elizabeth's side, holding her hand until she woke.

"Mama?" she asked timidly. "Where am I?"

"You are in the nursery, Lizzy." Mrs. Bennet brushed a curl from Elizabeth's forehead. "Oh, what a fright you gave me, child! Are you well?"

"I hardly know." Elizabeth pushed herself into a sitting position. "I do not recall what happened."

Mrs. Bennet related Jane's tale. Her adopted daughter frowned in confusion. "What could have possibly caused me to behave in such a manner?" she asked. "We were only playing a game."

"Perhaps it caused you to remember something," Mrs. Bennet postulated. "Tell me, do you? Is there anything?"

Elizabeth closed her eyes in concentration. "I see a man's face," she whispered. "He wants me to be quiet. He did not seem angry... That is all."

Mrs. Bennet struggled to hide her emotions. *Surely, this man has a connection to my daughter,* she thought. *But why did she scream? What is there to fear from him?*

"Well," she said aloud. "All will be as it has been. Let us just stay out of Papa's study when we play our games, hmm?"

Nodding, Elizabeth agreed. Mrs. Bennet asked if she would like some tea and called for a tray when the girl agreed.

Later that night, she told her husband what Elizabeth had remembered. "Do you think she went through something very dreadful?" she asked.

Her husband wrapped his arms around her. "It seems that way," he murmured into her hair. "Whatever she endured in the past, we shall ensure her future is immeasurably better. Elizabeth will want for nothing, least of all love."

Another strange occurrence came during their first winter in Hertfordshire. Snow fell just before Christmas, and the children squealed in delight as they stared out the window.

"There is not very much snow at all," Elizabeth remarked dismally. "Not nearly enough to play in."

"Hertfordshire is further south than Derbyshire," Tommy reminded her. "I do not like the cold, so I do not mind."

"Have you never ridden in a sleigh?" Elizabeth asked, turning to the boy. "It is such fun! You can fly over the snow!"

"I have never. When did you do that?" Tommy looked expectantly at Lizzy. Mrs. Bennet watched it all curiously, wondering what she would say.

Elizabeth's face held a dazed expression, and she blinked in confusion. "I think I did it once. We had warm bricks at our feet and a thick woolen rug on our knees. I sat on someone's lap..." she trailed off, distress flickering across her countenance. "Maybe I dreamed it," she murmured finally. "I think I should like to lie down." Without another word, she left the room, the same dazed expression clouding her features.

When she told her husband of their daughter's confusion later, Mr. Bennet expressed hope that perhaps her memories were returning. But when Elizabeth said nothing more, they let the matter rest.

In the year 1800, they observed Elizabeth's ninth birthday. Not knowing the exact date, the Bennets based their decision on the information she had imparted to them the day they found her. Thus, they designated the eighth of March and celebrated accordingly. Cook prepared all her favorites, and Mr. and Mrs. Bennet gifted her a new book and gown.

The following years saw Elizabeth flourish. Her head wound had long since healed, the scar now well disguised by her hair. All evidence that anything untoward had befallen their young charge seemed to be eradicated. Yet, certain sights and sounds, smells and words, seemed to encourage memories to surface. There was never anything clear or certain; they were always shrouded in mist and blanketed with confusion. Elizabeth always became very quiet when they occurred, often retreating to her bed for the remainder of the afternoon.

Mrs. Bennet worried about her adopted child. Her love for the young girl was equal to what she felt for her own children, and she feared that someday someone would appear and take her away. Evidence suggested that Elizabeth's past was not a happy one, and she refused to allow her to go back to whatever misery had preceded their finding her wandering along a road in Derbyshire.

With each passing year, no one came to claim her, and Mrs. Bennet grew easier. Elizabeth blossomed in both beauty and intelligence, her desire for knowledge pushing her to read and study far beyond what her adopted brother and sisters were wont to do. She loved them all, both elder and younger, and could often be found playing with Kitty and Lydia in the nursery each afternoon. Her example inspired Jane and Mary, and the five girls became nearly inseparable.

Tommy joined in their games until the time came for him to attend Eton, but he wrote faithfully, and his bond with his sisters remained strong and unwavering.

Mr. Bennet worked diligently to restore Longbourn to full prosperity. He invested with Mr. Gardiner to ensure that each of his *five* daughters had a modest dowry for their future needs. His investments saw excellent returns. By the time Jane came out at eighteen, her dowry had reached ten thousand pounds. The other girls had less, but by the time each of them married, he hoped that their dowries would be at least equal.

# Chapter Four

*Nottinghamshire, 1806*
*Lady Maude Montrose*

"It has been seven years, your ladyship. Forgive me, but perhaps the time has come to have your granddaughter presumed dead—for the sake of settling the matter of the inheritance." Mr. Silas Winters stood before Lady Montrose, his hat clasped in his hands. He worried the brim unceasingly. "I, too, miss your son. Henry was the best of men and an excellent business partner. But he is gone, and so too, I fear, is his daughter. There has been no sign of her these seven years."

"And what do you mean to do if I capitulate to your desires?" she asked testily. "What purpose does having Elizabeth declared dead serve *you?*" She was no fool. The man wanted something.

"Well, a considerable portion of my company's assets are tied up in the trust you so diligently prepared for your granddaughter. If I wish to expand, I must access more than the funds you presently release for expenses."

"Expenses which seem to have grown excessively these past two years. And tell me, pray, why have you not yet expanded? Surely, there is enough income being generated to allow it."

"Some investors require ready capital," he said calmly. "I shan't bore you with the details. The intricacies of trade can be of no interest to such an exalted personage as yourself."

"Do not patronize me," she snapped, rising. At her full height, she could look him in the eye, and she hoped the quelling glance she leveled in his direction put paid to his ridiculous sycophantic behavior.

"I meant no disrespect. If you could but see my purposes…"

"Enough! I shall not declare Elizabeth dead, and shall use every connection at my disposal to ensure you do not attempt anything to the contrary. Send your business matters to Jameson. He will see that you receive sufficient contributions from my son's estate to manage his portion of the affairs."

"Perhaps you could simply allow me to purchase his shares of the company," Mr. Winters declared beseechingly. "Then you would never have to see me again."

"Unfortunately for both of us, the trust was arranged such that Elizabeth's consent is required to dispose of any assets. I had it specifically drawn up to prevent unscrupulous trustees from making decisions of which I might disapprove. And if you possess the means to buy my son's shares, then you surely have the funds to meet your business expenses."

With a wave of her hand, she dismissed him. Winters withdrew sullenly, his displeasure plainly writ upon his face. *He will not give up easily*, she mused. Thus, it was no surprise to her when Mr. Robert Bingley appeared at her door a week later.

"Lady Montrose." He bowed deeply. "It has been many years since we last spoke."

"That fool Winters sent you. Speak quickly, that I may disabuse you of whatever notion you carry and send you on your way."

"Yes, Mr. Winters did send me. These are the expenses and reports he says you requested." Mr. Bingley placed a sheaf of papers in her hand. "It is a favor for a friend. I have sold my shares to Winters and invested elsewhere."

Lady Montrose blinked. "You are no longer in business with Mr. Winters?" she asked. "Why?"

"My reasons are my own, madam," Mr. Bingley said stiffly, refusing to meet her eye. "Be that as it may, I believe this is the best course of action for my family. We have removed from Yorkshire and are presently bound for Bedfordshire. My wife has family there who will receive us whilst I seek lodgings in town."

She nodded slowly. Curiosity urged her to press for answers, but she held her peace. "I wish you the very best, then," she murmured. "Henry always spoke fondly of you."

"I thank you, your ladyship." He bowed again. "For what it is worth, I support your efforts to search for your granddaughter. She is of an age with my own child, and they played together often. Caroline misses her."

With that, Mr. Bingley departed, leaving Lady Montrose to her thoughts. "Jameson!" she called, summoning her faithful servant to her side. "Has there been any news?"

Jameson bowed low and took a seat next to his mistress. "I received a note from the Runners this morning, madam," he said quietly. "They advise it is foolish to continue searching after so many years. They think all hope is lost."

"No." She slapped her hand against the arms of her chair. "Elizabeth is out there somewhere. I must find her."

"Mistress." Jameson took her hand. She allowed the familiarity in honor of his dedication to her and her son. "If she is still alive, it is likely that she is in an orphanage or has gone into service somewhere. How can we find her?"

Pulling away from his touch, she buried her face in her hands. "I cannot simply give up," she said, sobbing. "How could I betray Henry's memory?"

"I shall never give up, my lady," he replied. "There is one Runner still willing to search. His name is Marks. You might hire him away from the Bow Street Runners."

"See it done." Wiping her tears on a hastily procured handkerchief, she dismissed him, wishing only for solitude. Today, the fourteenth of March, was Elizabeth's birthday. The gloomy spring day perfectly matched Lady Montrose's mood.

Feeling unequal to life at the moment, she retreated to her chambers. In two weeks, she would travel to town where her husband awaited her. The old fool was one-and-ninety now and resided in town year round. He left her to her own devices, but required her to come to his side for the second half of the season.

How he managed to live so long baffled her. His lifestyle, whilst not dissolute, was hardly conducive to a long life. Lord Montrose ate rich, sumptuous meals and lived indolently. Their son, thirty-seven years of age, had taken over his father's duties in the House of Lords years ago. Despite his age, Lord Montrose still had all his faculties. Even so, he had happily ceded parliamentary responsibilities to Viscount Marston.

Before she could depart for London, an express rider arrived, bearing a letter edged in black. Her heart clenched with anxiety as she broke the seal.

*Mother,*

*Father is dead. I shall see you at Marston Hall within a week. His will demanded he be interred there.*

*Marston*

"He is gone," she murmured to the empty room. She did not know what to do with the information. Her husband had commanded her life for so long...

Well, one thing was certain. Her searches for her granddaughter no longer needed to be clandestine. Lord Montrose had decreed that his second son be cut off for sullying the family name. His edicts had not ceased when he learned that Henry had died.

"Who cares about the girl?" he had said, scowling. "Her mother is nothing but the daughter of a tradesman. Leave her to her fate." She recalled his cold demeanor when she had seen him in town that year. Furious, she had feigned obedience whilst continuing the search for her granddaughter behind her husband's back.

*And now he is gone. He can do nothing to stop me.* Her dowry had remained largely untouched for many years, for she did not have cause to venture into town for longer than her husband required her. The fifty thousand pounds had grown significantly, and now she was free to do with it as she wished.

*I shall find Elizabeth,* she vowed.

Marston—now Lord Montrose—arrived before the week's end, his father's body following in a wagon behind his carriage. They interred him in the family crypt with little ceremony. Most of Lord Montrose's friends had died long ago, and the only family he had left were his son and his wife. "What will you do now, Mother?" Harold asked as they ate a quiet dinner following the funeral.

"I believe I shall go to London," she mused. "This is your home now." *And I shall never grow used to knowing you as anything other than Viscount Marston.*

"I would never cast you out," he protested. "Marston Hall has a fine dower house if you wish to vacate the manor."

"Harold," she said calmly, "I mean to find Elizabeth."

Her son fell silent. She continued speaking when he did not reply.

"Your father kept a tight rein on my pin money," she confided. "I had enough to meet my needs, but no more. Despite our separate residences, he still had a hand in my life these many years. Now that I am free to do what I will, I mean to expand my search for your niece."

Her son sighed. "I would only caution you, Mother. You may not find her. And if you do, you may not like what you discover. Elizabeth will be fifteen now—a young lady."

"She was eight when…" Lady Montrose paused to compose herself. "She should remember us, should she not?"

"I met her only twice. Father kept me too occupied to get away. And are your words not further evidence to proceed cautiously?"

She nodded. "I need to know," she whispered. "I cannot bear not knowing."

Harold patted her hand and changed the subject. "Now that the old man is gone, I suppose it is time for me to search for a wife. At seven-and-thirty, there is no time to delay."

"If you live as long as your father, then there is no need for concern." She chuckled. "He married me at forty."

"I need an heir, Mother. A daughter will do as well as a son, thanks to the nature of the earldom's charter." The earldom was old, and as such, daughters could inherit in the absence of sons.

Lady Montrose smiled sadly. "I would like another grandchild," she murmured.

Marston—for she could not think of him as Lord Montrose yet—stayed in Nottinghamshire to oversee the spring planting. Lady Montrose wasted no time packing her trunks and making her way to London. She took up residence in her London home, Montrose House. According to her marriage settlement, she had lifetime use of the residence. The earldom had another property, Marston Manor, that her son and his future bride would occupy whilst in town. Within a fortnight, she had gone through her husband's belongings, sorting what ought to remain with the earldom and be sent to her son at Marston Hall, and setting aside the rest to be donated to charity. Her own chambers she resolved to refurbish. But first, she had a task to perform.

The day following her arrival, Lady Montrose spoke to the Bow Street Runner who was still in her employ, making arrangements to post a reward for information in the London papers. "It is impossible for a child to disappear without a trace," she said impatiently when he brought up the years that had passed since Elizabeth's disappearance. "Had you not been incompetent, then my granddaughter would have been found. I do not care how long it takes. You *will* find Miss Elizabeth Montrose."

Satisfied that he would take her seriously, she returned to her home. She felt a little regretful of her outburst, attributing it to her constant state of worry for Elizabeth. As she disembarked from the carriage, she noted a gentleman on the curb, ostensibly returning to his own residence.

"Lady Montrose. It has been an age."

"Mr. Darcy. It is good to see you." She curtsied.

George Darcy was of an age with her. He had lost his wife, Lady Anne Darcy, some years ago. Seven or eight, if she recalled. Mr. Darcy had mourned his wife at the same time Lady Montrose mourned the loss of her relations.

"I understand that condolences are in order," he said kindly. "Lord Montrose was a force to be reckoned with."

"My son will be even more so than his father." She smiled affectionately. "Thank you for your kind words." They parted ways, he to his home next door and she to hers.

The next weeks passed slowly, with no news from Mr. Marks. She grew impatient but tried to keep occupied with refurbishing her chambers. When they were finished, she moved to the public rooms.

In June, Mr. Marks finally came to Montrose House with information.

"I found an innkeeper in Derbyshire who remembers an inquiry that came through his establishment around the time in question," he said. "Some cove was searching for news of a carriage accident and a lost child. The innkeeper did not remember much else."

It was the best lead she had been given in a long time. "Did he not give you a name?" she pressed.

"No, my lady. He said it were something like Barnett. Maybe Bartlett. But he could not say for certain." Marks bowed his head regretfully.

"It is worth investigating," she muttered. "Where was this inn?"

"It were very near to the county border," he replied. "Not thirty miles from Marston Hall."

"The location fits. How far from my son's home in Yorkshire?" She leaned forward eagerly.

"Around twenty miles. A long way for a child to wander." He shrugged.

"There is no saying whether Elizabeth wandered that far. We only know that this mysterious Mr. Barnett sent inquiries there. Which means the letter must have originated somewhere closer."

"I shall do me best, m'lady." Marks looked doubtful, but schooled his expression when she gave him a hard look.

"Be off with you, then." She waved her hand dismissively, and he backed out of the room. Wearily, she rose and went to her chambers. Pulling a wooden box off a shelf in her closet, she took it to her bed. Sitting slowly, she held the box on her lap and opened the clasp.

Inside there were four miniatures. On her last visit, before everything had happened, she had commissioned portraits of her son and his family. They were immortalized in oils, their happy expressions captured forever. Amelia's fine eyes laughed from the painting. Elizabeth's eyes were very similar. *She likely favors her mother even more now,* she mused. *It is a shame that your parents did not live to see you grow into a young lady.*

Carefully, she put the mementos back into the chest. After returning it to the closet, she ordered a tray. No longer a young woman, she preferred to retire early. Though it was not quite six in the evening, she felt unaccountably tired.

*Rest is all I need,* she told herself. *I shall be well in the morning.* Yes, for the first time in many years, she had a direction. Elizabeth would be found soon; she knew it deep in her heart. *And when she is safely back in my arms, I shall make her my heir. Elizabeth will have everything that should have been her due, and more.* It never occurred to her that her grandchild might wish for anything different. After all, family was everything to Lady Maude Montrose. Would it not be the same to anyone who shared her blood?

# Chapter Five

*Hertfordshire*
*October 1811*
*Darcy*

"Really, Bingley, an assembly? I have barely set foot in the house!" Mr. Fitzwilliam Darcy cast his friend a mildly irritated look. How very like Charles Bingley to schedule a social event the evening his guest arrived from town.

"You will have six hours to rest before we depart." Bingley nudged Darcy in the ribs. "Now, let us take tea and then I can give you a tour!"

"Are your sisters in residence?" Darcy liked Bingley's sisters well enough. The elder, Mrs. Louisa Hurst, had lately married a gentleman of some means. Mr. Reginald Hurst owned an estate in Surrey. They shared a marriage of convenience, and he tolerated the pair when needed—for Bingley's sake.

The younger sister, Miss Caroline Bingley, had at first annoyed Darcy with flattering words and attention. Then, her affections were won by Sir James Blackwell, a decorated military officer and second son of a wealthy country gentleman. Sir James received a knighthood in recognition of his prowess on the battlefield. Darcy's cousin,

Colonel Richard Fitzwilliam, was acquainted with the gentleman and lauded his bravery.

"Louisa and Hurst will arrive in a few weeks. I believe she wrote that they intend to leave Surrey on the first of November, stopping in London for a day or so along the way. That should put them in Hertfordshire by the fourth." Bingley led the way down the hall to a large, well-appointed parlor. "Nicholls will bring us tea," he said, plopping down into an overstuffed chair. He slung one leg over the arm and grinned cheekily. "Caroline and Sir James are in Cheshire until December. He wished to introduce his future bride to his family. Her companion is with them, of course. I understand that he has purchased a house in town and means to purchase an estate in the future."

"I am very happy for them." Indeed, he was. Darcy despised fawning and false flattery. Miss Bingley had not been the worst artful woman he had ever encountered, but she certainly had been amongst them. Since becoming engaged to Sir James, however, she had revealed more of her true nature—and to Darcy's surprise, it was not entirely disagreeable.

Despite being born to trade, Miss Bingley dressed, walked, talked, and acted just like a gently born lady. At first, she had annoyed him with her flattering words and attention, but after meeting Sir James and falling in love, her manner had changed entirely. Where once she had disguised insults to look like compliments, Miss Bingley spoke sincerely, offering friendship and kindness to everyone, regardless of station. Her genuine manner impressed many higher-born ladies seeking honest friendship, opening doors that might otherwise have remained closed. Somewhere along the way, she had grown tired of artifice, disliking the woman she saw in the mirror and resolving to change her ways.

Darcy wondered if Sir James would have fallen in love with the Caroline Bingley that had fawned over *him*.

"You will dance tonight, will you not?" Bingley swung his leg off the arm of the chair and leaned forward, putting his elbows on his knees. "These are my new neighbors, and I want them to think well of me—and my friends."

"And my behavior will be a reflection upon you. Very well, Bingley, I shall dance. No more than three dances, however, and with ladies of my choosing. I shall not be pushed toward any particular woman."

"I shall only agree to that stipulation if you promise to dance at least two dances with unmarried ladies." Bingley folded his arms triumphantly.

Darcy laughed in surprise. "How well you know my habits. Very well, I shall dance two dances with unmarried misses. I shall even agree to dance an additional set with another married woman, bringing my total performances to four."

"Done." Bingley extended his hand, and they shook to seal their agreement. "Look, here is Mrs. Nicholls with tea!"

A middle-aged lady with silver gray hair placed a tea tray carefully on the table next to Bingley's chair. She curtsied and departed, leaving Bingley to pour the tea.

"Cream and sugar, Darcy?" his host asked.

Darcy nodded and accepted the cup Bingley offered. He sipped, savoring the pleasant blend. "The estate appears sound from the outside. Did you tour it in its entirety before signing the lease?"

"I did. Mr. Morris, the agent, said that the owner recently repaired a leak in the roof. There were also a few drainage issues addressed, from what I understand. The park is only four miles around—nothing to Pemberley, but it is a good size for me to test the waters." Bingley grinned and picked up a little sandwich from the tray and popped it whole into his mouth.

"And the owner has agreed to allow you to learn alongside the steward?" Darcy, too, picked up a sandwich, though he did not eat his in one bite.

"He has. I am allowed to make decisions as long as it will not jeopardize the prosperity of the estate. Your agreement to assist me convinced the owner to grant me the liberty to try my hand at it all."

Darcy smiled. "I assume you regaled him with tales of your prominent, land-owning friend from the North with five years' experience managing his own estate?"

"Do not forget that it is more than twice the size of Netherfield. Yes, he was convinced by just that logic." Bingley stood and placed his empty cup back on the tray. "Are you finished? I would love to show you the house. It is a good thing Caroline will not be my hostess. She would want to redecorate every room."

"Your sister is a lady of fashion."

"There are ten bedrooms in the family wing," Bingley said, leading his friend from the room. "On the opposite side of the staircase is the guest wing, with ten additional rooms. Both sides mirror each other. The third floor holds the nursery, rooms for the governess and nursery maids, and a few additional chambers. Servants reside in the west attic and below stairs. The east attics are for storage."

Bingley rambled on as they walked. Darcy admired the portrait gallery and peeked into a few guest chambers before Bingley showed him to his own. "There is a sitting room through there," he said, gesturing to a door on the opposite side of the chamber. "Your valet can stay here or with the servants—it is your choice. Now, I know you wish to refresh yourself, but I simply must show you the ballroom downstairs. I have plans to hold a ball there before Christmas."

Darcy groaned. "You and your dances, Bingley. Please tell me you have planned other forms of entertainment."

Bingley laughed. "We shall hunt and ride to your heart's delight, my friend. I promise I shall only request you dance once a week."

"What of other social excursions? Surely, the denizens of the area will wish you to attend all their functions. Am I to be paraded alongside you?"

Bingley chuckled. "You have a dismal view of the world, do you not? How can you have so much and still be so displeased with life?"

Darcy sighed. "I feel as though I am always on display. Ever since I inherited, ladies have thrown themselves at my feet—quite literally, I assure you. I detest walking into a room and being sized up for the amount of money in my bank account and the extent of my estate."

"That would certainly make socializing more tedious." Bingley frowned. "I shall do my best to keep the matchmaking mamas off your scent."

"And I shall do *my* best to be an amiable companion." In truth, Darcy had only agreed to come to Hertfordshire because his sister had practically begged him to go. Georgiana had experienced a disappointment that summer and had yet to recover her spirits, and now resided with her aunt, Lady Matilda Matlock. Darcy's aunt assured him that the time away from him would do Georgiana a world of good.

"She thinks you are ashamed of her," his aunt had confided. "Go with Bingley, Darcy. Keep writing to Georgiana and she will recover her spirits eventually."

And so Darcy had departed London after bidding his sister a fond farewell. Georgiana had barely looked at him as he said goodbye. *Would that I could take all her pain away,* he thought. *It is my fault. I failed her.*

Bingley's exuberance proved to be a balm to Darcy's dark mood. By the time they were dressed for the assembly, he felt more inclined to enjoy the evening. Bingley rambled on about the gentlemen he had met and the calls he had returned as the carriage made its way down the drive and onto the main road that led to the little market town of Meryton.

"Sir William Lucas is a jovial fellow. He is the master of ceremonies tonight, or so I have been informed. You will like him. He speaks of St. James with great fondness."

"I do not attend St. James regularly. Tell me, does he have any daughters?" Ever cynical, Darcy nudged his friend with his foot and raised an eyebrow.

"Two. The elder is Miss Charlotte Lucas. She is seven-and-twenty. His younger daughter is but sixteen—Maria, I believe her name is." Bingley paused. "Do not give me that look, Darcy. A man is not to be suspect simply because he has daughters to marry off."

"If you think for an instant that this Sir William does not see you as a potential mate for his offspring—"

"Oh, stop. I intend to enjoy myself fully tonight. If you cannot do the same, I shall send you back to Netherfield in the carriage."

Darcy drew in a breath. "I am sorry, Bingley. It seems I cannot shake the dark mood that hovers about me like a cloud. I shall do my best not to disappoint you."

Bingley nodded sharply, then continued describing his neighbors as though he had not just thoroughly chastised his old friend. "The Gouldings have a son and a daughter. Their daughter is not out, and their son is away at school. Then there are the Longs—Mr. and Mrs. Long do not have children, but they do have the care of their nieces. I met them when I returned Mr. Long's call. Oh—and then there is my closest neighbor, Mr. Thomas Bennet."

The name sounded familiar, but Darcy could not place it. "Has he an estate?" he asked instead.

"Yes. Longbourn lies south of Meryton, whilst Netherfield is just to the north of the market village. It is a prosperous little estate. I suspect the income is some thirty-five hundred pounds."

"And he has how many daughters?" Darcy tried to keep his voice level but failed miserably.

Bingley frowned. "Come to think of it, I do not know. Mr. Bennet said only that his son had recently returned from university and was now assisting him with management of the estate."

*Perhaps he has no daughters,* Darcy thought. *Surely a man with female children would wish his new and very eligible neighbor to know that they exist. Expounding on their charms would be top priority.*

"I look forward to meeting your neighbors," he said aloud, and none too sincerely. "I am sure it will be an enjoyable evening."

# Chapter Six

*October 1811*
*Meryton Assembly*
*Darcy*

Bingley's carriage slowed to a stop before a rustic assembly hall. Heavy timbers supported an awning over the door. Lanterns had been hung, casting a brilliant light across the entrance.

Gathering his fortitude, Darcy followed Bingley out of the carriage and into the building. The room was illuminated by what seemed to be hundreds of candles. Mirrors along the walls reflected the light, enhancing the brightness throughout the space. The first dance had yet to be called, and nearly every eye in the room turned toward the two gentlemen from Netherfield Park as they entered the room.

"Mr. Bingley!" A portly, cheerful-looking gentleman approached, bowing to Bingley in greeting. A plain lady who looked to be at least five-and-twenty trailed behind him.

Darcy assumed the gentleman was Sir William Lucas. The lady must therefore be his elder daughter, the one nearly on the shelf. He refocused his attention as Bingley offered an introduction.

"Mr. Darcy is my very good friend. He will be staying at Netherfield Park for some time to assist me." Bingley grinned. "We are both looking forward to the evening."

"As you should! Nowhere else will you find such agreeable company or beautiful ladies. Meryton boasts the jewels of the county, you know. Ah! I see Mrs. Bennet. Come, allow me to introduce you to her and her lovely daughters."

"Of course. First, let me solicit Miss Lucas's hand for the first set." Bingley, ever eager to please, smiled cheerfully at the lady. She accepted graciously, with none of the simpering or fluttering of eyelashes Darcy might have expected.

*She may not be a trial to stand up with,* he reasoned. "I, too, would be honored to dance a set with you, Miss Lucas," he said solemnly. *Best be done with Bingley's strictures as soon as possible.* "Do you have a set free?"

"My second is available, Mr. Darcy," she said politely. With that, her father led the small party toward a matron standing with two ladies some distance away.

"Mrs. Bennet," Sir William said in greeting. "How do you do this evening? Miss Bennet, Miss Elizabeth, you are both looking lovely."

"Thank you, Sir William." The elder girl, Miss Bennet, smiled shyly at the master of ceremonies. Darcy glanced at Bingley. His friend's mouth hung open ever so slightly. He wore a dazed expression, as if he had been struck on the head.

"Mr. Darcy, Mr. Bingley, may I present Mrs. Frances Bennet and her two eldest daughters. This is Miss Jane Bennet, and this is Miss Elizabeth Bennet."

Darcy bowed, but something in Bingley's expression caught his attention. The stupefied look that had overtaken his friend when he first saw Miss Bennet had changed into something more perplexing as he greeted the lady's younger sister.

Bingley's brow furrowed, and his eyes narrowed. His perpetual grin froze, and his mouth turned down slightly. "Miss Elizabeth *Bennet,* did you say? Have we, perchance, met before?"

Miss Elizabeth flushed and dropped her gaze to her slippers. "I have never strayed further from home than London, sir, and I visit town but rarely."

Darcy observed the entire exchange with keen interest. Never had he seen two sisters more different in appearance. Miss Bennet was the perfect example of fashionable beauty. She was tall, willowy, and had hair the color of wheat ready for harvest. Her blue eyes were kind and spoke of gentleness. The younger sister, by contrast, was petite. Her light and pleasing figure suggested she was of an active nature. When she raised her gaze from the floor once more, Darcy's attention was drawn to her fine eyes. They sparkled with good humor and a touch of mystery. *Curious,* he thought.

"Perhaps the Misses Bennet have a dance to bestow upon our guests?" Sir William asked.

"Indeed!" Bingley snapped out of whatever stupor had momentarily possessed him. "Miss Bennet, may I have your next free set?"

"The fourth is yours, sir." Miss Bennet smiled kindly, her eyes twinkling. "Elizabeth, have you a free set for our new neighbor?"

"I do. Mr. Bingley, my second and my last have not yet been claimed. Perhaps one will suit you?" Miss Elizabeth smiled, her eyes sparkling merrily.

"I shall have the second," Mr. Bingley declared. An unfathomable look flashed across his countenance before his easy smile reasserted itself. He turned to Darcy and raised an eyebrow.

"Mrs. Bennet, if I may be so bold as to claim a set?" he asked. Mentally, he stuck his tongue out at his friend. *I did tell him I would not be pushed into asking,* he thought.

"You are a flatterer, sir." Mrs. Bennet smiled kindly. "I would be pleased to accept your offer, provided it is a less vigorous dance. I am not as young as I once was."

The lady made no attempt to press him to speak to her daughters. Instead, she turned to them as the orchestra struck a chord to signal the dancers. "Jane, Lizzy, here are your partners. Off you go."

The ladies curtsied and departed with two local gentlemen. Mrs. Bennet turned back to Sir William. "You must have many others to meet," she said to Mr. Bingley.

"I do; however, I am engaged with Miss Lucas for this set. Pray, excuse me. Darcy, will you dance or remain here?"

"Mrs. Bennet?" he asked, turning to the lady who still stood beside him.

"Oh, the first set is always a reel, sir," she said. "I am content to wait until there is a slower set. But perhaps you would like to stand with me? I am eager to speak to you of Derbyshire. We lived there many years ago, before my husband inherited."

He blinked in surprise. "Really? Pray, where did you reside?"

She smiled. "We lived in Lambton, sir, very near the church. My husband worked with Mr. Palmer."

A memory stirred. "Bennet! The solicitor!"

Mrs. Bennet laughed merrily. "Yes, sir. My husband—on behalf of his employer—came to Pemberley more than once with papers for your father. Mr. Palmer may have been a country solicitor, but he handled many of Pemberley's smaller, local legal matters."

"I hardly know what to say. I remember when your family left the area. Mr. Palmer was not pleased to lose Mr. Bennet's aid."

"A series of sad events drew us south. I cannot repine Providence's hand in our lives, however. My girls were raised as daughters of an estate just as they ought to have been, and my son will inherit Longbourn and all that is his father's. I *do* miss the North." Mrs. Bennet kept her gaze on the dance floor, watching her daughters as they danced a Scottish reel. "How time passes. I can scarcely believe it has been twelve years." Her voice held a wistful tone and was touched by something more—something he could not name.

"Your daughters are very lovely," he said sincerely. And they were. Whilst Miss Bennet's fair looks were everything fashionable, it was Miss Elizabeth's darker coloring that drew him in. Her dark curls glistened in the candlelight, strands of red shimmering with every dance step. Her eyes were laughing, and her wide smile held no malice or deceit.

He remained with Mrs. Bennet for the better part of an hour, escorting her to the dance floor for the third set. After that, she crossed the room to visit another matron, leaving Darcy brooding against one wall.

Despite his best efforts, he could not keep his attention from settling on Miss Elizabeth. He found her attractive; that much he could allow. But she was the insignificant daughter of a country gentleman and not at all suitable to be mistress of Pemberley.

*Mistress of—what am I thinking? How very rapid is the imagination, jumping from admiration to matrimony in but a moment. I am no love-struck fool.*

"Come, Darcy, I must have you dance!" Bingley appeared at his side. "You have been standing here in this stupid manner long enough."

"I have danced two sets, Bingley. I shall dance two more before the night is through." Darcy kept his gaze on Miss Elizabeth, watching her as she made her way to seating arranged very near his present position.

"I have never met with prettier or more amiable ladies in my life," Bingley said fervently.

"You are dancing with the handsomest woman in the room," he reminded his friend.

Bingley beamed. "She is an angel!" he cried enthusiastically. "But look, there is her sister sitting there." He faltered, that strange look crossing his face again. Bingley shook his head. "She is very pretty and an agreeable companion. If you recall, I asked her to dance myself."

Darcy glanced at Miss Elizabeth Bennet. She sat near enough to hear their conversation; he felt certain. Annoyed as he was at Bingley's probing, he bit back the vitriolic reply that threatened to burst forth. "I shall ask her, Bingley, but she may not have a set left."

"If she does not, you will have to look elsewhere for a partner." Bingley nudged him. "Go on."

Sighing with restraint, Darcy approached the young lady. "Miss Elizabeth, I recall. Have you a set that I might claim?" His smile felt more like a grimace. It must have looked the same, for Miss Elizabeth raised an eyebrow and appraised him.

"My last is free, sir. Feel free to withdraw your offer if that set will discompose you." Her lips quirked.

*She is laughing at me,* he realized. He did not know whether to be impressed or dismayed. He cleared his throat and glanced away. "No, I do not believe I shall. Withdraw my offer, that is."

"Then the last set is yours, Mr. Darcy." Miss Elizabeth nodded and returned her attention to the dance floor.

Intrigued, he lingered for a moment longer before retreating to the safety of his wall. He stayed but a moment before resigning himself to find one more dance partner. Noting another wallflower, he prevailed upon Sir William for an introduction. The lady in question, Miss Victoria Bates accepted his offer to dance enthusiastically, beaming from ear to ear at his attention. Instead of putting him off, her genuine pleasure warmed his heart. They danced the fifth together, and whilst the lady did not seem to know the steps very well, her constant chatter spared him the need to search for conversation.

He strolled around the room as he waited for the last set. If he were honest with himself, he greatly anticipated those dances. Miss Elizabeth's liveliness drew him in. He watched her dancing, strange feelings of jealousy rising as she bestowed her attention upon other gentlemen.

At some point, he noted that Bingley, too, could not keep his eyes off the lady. His friend's attention drifted from his partner to Miss Elizabeth frequently. With each distracted glance, Bingley's confused expression reemerged.

Miss Elizabeth noted his friend's behavior and asked Darcy about it as they began their set.

"I cannot begin to explain what has got into my friend," he replied when she posed her query.

"I do apologize for being forward," she said haltingly. "It is only that I find his intensity somewhat disconcerting. I wondered if you knew the cause."

"Bingley is typically a happy fellow, eager to please and be pleased by all he meets. His manner tonight goes against everything I have ever known of him." Darcy glanced down the line of dancers. Bingley smiled at his partner. The same smile stayed in place until Darcy and Miss Elizabeth passed under the raised arms of Bingley and his partner. The former's gaze fell to Elizabeth's face and at once his smile vanished.

When they were safely away, Darcy turned to Miss Elizabeth and said, "I must apologize for my friend."

"His behavior is not your fault," she murmured. "Perhaps I remind him of someone."

They spoke of other subjects throughout the rest of the set. Darcy learned that Miss Elizabeth loved books and had read widely. She teasingly said she could not discuss books in a ballroom.

Smirking, he replied, "Then I shall have to call upon Longbourn to pursue the subject." His boldness surprised even him, and he found that whilst he spoke in haste, he meant every word.

The set ended, and they parted ways. Bingley's carriage was one of the first to be called, and the exhausted gentlemen clambered aboard. They sank back into the squabs as the conveyance lurched forward.

"You cannot tell me you did not enjoy the evening, Darcy," Bingley said after some minutes of silence.

"I confess, I enjoyed it more than I thought I would." Darcy grinned in the dark. Images of Miss Elizabeth and her fine eyes danced in his mind. "You seemed pleased with Miss Bennet."

"She is perfection itself, is she not?"

"I find her sister more to my tastes, to be honest."

Bingley fell silent. Darcy waited for him to speak, and when he said nothing, he nudged his friend's boot.

"There is something about her, Darcy," Bingley whispered. "It is as if a ghost from my past has arisen. But it cannot be so. She is not..." Bingley's voice faded.

"Not what?" Darcy probed.

Bingley sighed. "Nothing, Darcy. It is nothing."

# Chapter Seven

*October 1811*
*Longbourn*
*Elizabeth*

"Charlotte! Welcome." Mrs. Bennet greeted the Lucas ladies as they entered the parlor. To the youngest lady, she said, "Maria, Kitty and Lydia are upstairs waiting for you."

Maria Lucas bobbed a quick curtsey and rushed from the room. At just sixteen years of age, the younger Miss Lucas had been allowed to attend the first half of the assembly the night before. Kitty and Lydia had begged their parents to allow them to go as well, but Mrs. Bennet firmly reminded them that all her girls were required to wait until eighteen before attending even local events.

"You will have time enough to enjoy yourselves," she said. "Perhaps you might walk into Meryton and pick a pretty ribbon."

This had pacified the youngest Bennets, and they reluctantly agreed to bring the matter up no more.

Nineteen-year-old Mary had stayed home the night before. Having caught a cold three days previously, she did not feel up to attending the assembly. "I can barely breathe as it is," she reasoned when Mama tried to convince her to go. "It would not do for me to swoon on the dance floor." She looked much improved that morning and now sat at the pianoforte, playing quietly in the corner.

Papa and Thomas had also remained at home. Neither liked assemblies, preferring the peace of the library to the noise of a ballroom. And though Mrs. Bennet often tried to cajole her husband and son into escorting the ladies to events, they more often than not refused.

*"How did I marry a lady so fond of society?" Mr. Bennet teased his wife with a twinkle in his eyes. "We are very much the opposite, my dear."*

*"They say that opposite temperaments attract," Mary would reply. "Perhaps Mama is just different enough from you to keep things lively."*

Elizabeth greeted Charlotte warmly. She looked very well that day, dressed in a new blue day gown that Elizabeth had never seen before. "You look lovely, Charlotte," she said.

"I thank you, Eliza," she replied. "Mama has convinced Papa to take me to town for the season. This is one of the new gowns we ordered. Good morning, Jane! What a pretty shawl!"

Jane, too, hugged their friend, thanking her for the compliment. The three ladies seated themselves on a settee by a window, far enough from their mothers that they could speak with privacy.

"Mr. Bingley paid you a good deal of attention, Jane," Charlotte said. "What a triumph!"

"He danced the first with you, Charlotte." Jane tapped their friend's hand.

"But he danced two sets with *you*," Charlotte countered. "We all know where his attention will fall; you are quite the prettiest girl he will ever meet, with a gentle temperament, too."

"Mr. Bingley has been to town. Surely, he has seen other ladies that surpass my physical features."

"They may be lovelier in looks, but I doubt he has ever encountered a lady whose inner goodness is a match for her outward appearance," Elizabeth insisted. "You, the golden-haired goddess, make us all appear inferior by comparison. Oh, you cannot deny it, my dear sister. I, for example, am far too judgmental to ever have your goodness."

Charlotte and Elizabeth teased Jane a bit more before the subject turned to Mr. Darcy. "What do you think of Mr. Bingley's friend, Eliza? He watched you a great deal." Charlotte raised an eyebrow appraisingly. "I have never seen a more handsome man."

"Yes, he is very well favored. And so tall! His towering height makes me seem more diminutive than ever. And as for his attention, I am certain you are imagining things," Elizabeth demurred. "He watched the dancers and the other guests. That is all."

"He was kind enough to dance with Miss Bates," Jane observed. "I do not recall the last time she stood up for a set. The smiles his attention prompted were the most genuine I have seen in some time."

Yes, Elizabeth had noted his patience with the spinster. Miss Bates's father had been a solicitor in London before he died. After his passing some ten years ago, she had been shipped to Hertfordshire and was now dependent on the goodwill of a relation. Her aunt, Mrs. Norris, was a hard, bitter woman, who hardly embodied generosity. No effort had ever been made to secure a match for her niece.

Jane rose and left the room to seek her work basket. After her departure, Charlotte slid next to Elizabeth.

"Mr. Darcy was not the only gentleman to watch you last night," she said quietly.

Elizabeth sighed and asked, "Did you notice Mr. Bingley's strange behavior? I found his attention oddly unsettling." His inscrutable looks had haunted her dreams last night.

"His admiration of Jane is obvious," Charlotte added. "What is more confusing is his fixation on *you*. Perhaps he cannot decide which sister he favors more."

"I saw nothing of that in Mr. Bingley's gaze." Elizabeth shook her head. "No, it is likely that I have a face that reminds him of another. I know for certain that we have never met."

"Whatever the cause, you have the attention of two eligible men. Do not throw away this chance at marriage, Eliza."

She laughed. "Oh, how very rapidly you predict their motives! We have only just become acquainted. Surely, you would not have me throw myself at them in hopes of a proposal."

"Whilst I would not have you behave with anything less than perfect conduct, I would encourage you to secure a match as quickly as possible. Remember, I too, was once a hopeful young lady." Charlotte smiled sadly. "Papa is taking me to London in the spring. It is my last chance. My dowry is not as impressive as yours, you know."

"You will know success, dear Charlotte." Elizabeth clasped her friend's hand. "You are sensible and kind."

"If only a man could see it." Charlotte frowned before hiding her despair behind a smile.

The Lucas ladies left after tea. Feeling at odds with herself, Elizabeth donned her bonnet and pelisse, intending to take a long walk to clear her thoughts.

*I do have a dowry,* she thought to herself. *But it ought not to be mine.* Dismally, she recalled her come out nearly two years ago. Papa had called her into his study.

*He gazed at her solemnly, his hands on a wooden chest in his lap. Elizabeth approached cautiously, sitting in the chair next to him as he directed.*

"My dear Lizzy," he said tenderly. "Do you recall when we came to Longbourn?"

"Yes. "It was a great change for all of us."

Her papa had taken his duties as the new master of Longbourn seriously, increasing the estate's annual income until it exceeded three thousand pounds. Mama, too, had adapted to life as mistress of an estate with ease. She stumbled here and there, but overall, she became a consummate hostess and a competent mistress.

"What do you recall from before that?" he asked gently.

She froze. "There is nothing before that." Her hand went, unconsciously, to the scar on her head. It throbbed a little, and she winced.

"You were eight when we came to Hertfordshire, my dear." Gently, he explained how he and Mrs. Bennet had found her. He patted a small chest he held in front of him. "You have had memories these last ten years, but none ever helped us discover who you are. Yes, Elizabeth, you know that you are not a Bennet by blood. But you are the child of my heart, and I love you dearly. Your mother does, too."

He handed her the chest. "This contains your clothing and the possessions you carried when we found you. There have been no answers all these years. I now pass these treasures to you. Do with them what you will, but know you will always be my child—my dear intelligent Elizabeth. And as my daughter, you are entitled to a dowry. These many years, we have been careful. Investing with Mr. Gardiner, working to improve the yield of the estate... Jane's ten thousand pounds are in the four percents and have been since her eighteenth birthday. Your ten thousand is there now, too. It will grow if you do not marry quickly, but with your wit and vibrancy, I believe it will not be long before some astute gentleman sees your worth."

Elizabeth's thoughts returned to the present. The dowry was the least of Mr. Bennet's gifts. He told her of the day he and Mrs. Bennet found her. She did not know what had happened to her. Indeed, she tried to remember more fervently after that day in the study. The memories were elusive, slipping away from her mind even as she tried to grasp them. It was very frustrating.

"It does not matter," she said aloud. "For all intents and purposes, I am Miss Elizabeth Bennet of Hertfordshire."

Yet her dreams the night before had been more disturbed than they had in years. A man's face haunted her rest—one with a genial smile and fair coloring not unlike Mr. Bingley's. But the features were older, the hair redder, the expression more seasoned by time. Though she could not place him, the resemblance to Mr. Bingley had unsettled her more than she cared to admit.

Other faces had surfaced now and then over the years. She had even taken to drawing so that she could capture likenesses. Unfortunately, she never mastered sketching people and eventually gave up.

There was a lady. She had warm brown eyes and dark curls. Elizabeth often heard her voice singing lullabies in her dreams. There was a boy, too. Younger than her, with sandy blond hair and an infectious laugh. He always giggled when he was tossed in the air by another person. She never saw the man's face, but his deep voice reverberated in her mind. *I love you,* he said.

But those were the pleasant recollections; there were other, darker snippets of memory. These caused her to wake in a cold sweat. When she was younger, her screams had awakened the entire house. Mama had held her as she cried, whispering soothing words in her ears. "It is only a dream, my darling," she said over and over until Elizabeth drifted off to sleep.

Those dreams were never remembered for long. All that remained upon waking was the fear and anxiety that had taken root during the night.

She walked briskly up the slope that led to the top of Oakham Mount. It was merely a prominent hill, but still the highest point for some miles. Elizabeth enjoyed looking out over the fields. During the summer, wheat and other crops swayed gently in the breeze. Now, with the harvest over, the fields sat empty. Even the trees had lost their leaves. Still, there was beauty to be seen.

She crested the summit and turned her gaze toward Netherfield Park. Elizabeth could see it in the distance. The red and white stone glistened in the sunlight. In a distant field, she watched two riders push their mounts into a gallop.

Turning away, she walked a different path back to Longbourn. Feeling calmer, she entered the house and removed her outerwear.

Elizabeth went to her chambers, intending to refresh herself, but soon grew distracted. She knelt on the floor and reached under her bed. The small chest her father had given her was tucked behind a bedpost out of immediate sight. Her younger sisters had thus far respected her privacy, but Elizabeth did not wish to take any chances with this link to her past.

Slowly, she pulled it out and stood to lock the door, then climbed onto the bed, chest in hand. She crossed her legs and set it down before her, rubbing a hand on the smooth surface before opening it.

There was not much inside. A ragged and stained blue dress that the servants had been unable to get clean, a soiled handkerchief that had once been white...and a piece of jewelry.

It was the nicest thing in the entire chest. An ivory crest had been set in gold filigree. There was a clasp on the back that could secure it as a brooch. Elizabeth had always felt that there was something more to the piece. She could make out tiny hinges on the side, indicating that the brooch opened somehow. There was also a tiny hole at the top. It might be decorative, but she thought it looked as though something was missing.

She rubbed her thumb over the surface, marveling at the detail. Once, she had considered taking the brooch to London in hopes of finding out whose crest adorned the surface. Papa had insisted that she not do so. "What if you lose it?" he asked. "Or what if it is stolen? What if someone believes you stole it?" None of her sisters knew the truth about her origins, and Elizabeth could not draw well enough to capture the design. She had allowed his fears to sway her and the token from her past remained locked away beneath her bed.

Now she took it to her desk. Carefully, she sketched the crest on a sheet of paper. The likeness was not perfect, but it was close enough to the original. Two swords crossed behind a shield. The letter 'M' stood out, carved roses climbing the sides of the letter, and the outside edge of the ivory boasted intricate scrolls and ivy. The effect was lovely.

A family crest meant prominence. But what if Elizabeth was only a child thief? What if she sustained her injury when she fled with her purloined treasure?

*Perhaps Papa was right to caution me,* she thought. She tucked the paper into her writing box, burying it beneath a bundle of letters. *You ought to leave it alone,* she scolded herself. *Nothing good can come of your curiosity.*

She put the brooch back into her chest, closing it securely before hiding it under the bed. Determined to think of happier things, she retrieved a favorite novel and made her way to the parlor.

# Chapter Eight

*October 1811*
*Montrose House, London*
*Lady Montrose*

She stared at the fireplace. The flames danced, but she did not feel their warmth. Everything was so cold now. What was the point? It had been two months since Harold had died, and her world had completely shattered.

*How did it come to this?* she thought bitterly. *How am I the last of my family? First Henry, Amelia, and little Harry. Now my only remaining son.* She shuddered, choking back a sob. *What have I left to live for?*

Images of her granddaughter flitted through her thoughts. *Elizabeth.* No. She could not bear it. So many years of searching, leads going cold...*I cannot. My heart will not bear any more.* Standing slowly, she made her way to the table where she kept everything concerning the search for her grandchild. Almost as if in a dream, she gathered the scattered papers into a pile and walked to the fire. She thrust the stack into the flames, watching emotionlessly as they burned.

*Years of searching and nothing to show for it. And today was the final straw.* She let her thoughts go back to earlier in the day when she had received an unexpected caller.

"Madam?" Jameson entered the parlor, a strange look on his face. "There is a gentleman here to see you. He brings a young lady..." her servant trailed off and looked away.

"Well, what do they want?" she asked impatiently.

"The man claims the girl is Miss Montrose," Jameson said solemnly. "His story sounds very convincing, but I am still suspicious."

Her heart leaped, and she sat forward in her chair. "Show them in!" she cried. "Can it possibly be true?"

"My lady, I beg you to be cautious. These years since your husband's death it has been no secret that you seek your granddaughter. And now you are in an especially vulnerable position, given the passing of Master Harold." Jameson knelt at her side, his eyes pleading as he encouraged her to think rationally.

"But what if it is?" she countered. "If it is Elizabeth, then all will be well again. Tell me their story. I am assuming you inquired."

"After interviewing them, I left them waiting in the vestibule with a pair of footmen," Jameson said. "The man's name is Wilbur Roland. He is from Yorkshire and has resided in that county his entire life. The girl has been known as Eliza Montgomery since she came to a foundling home ten miles from your son's residence."

"And her appearance? Does she look like my Elizabeth?"

Jameson nodded. "There is enough resemblance to make me pause, your ladyship. Please *remember that you very recently posted a reward for any information. They could be less than honest and in search of easy coin.*"

Lady Montrose frowned. She knew that her servant spoke sense, but even a vague hope that this girl was Elizabeth Montrose was enough for her to grant the two people waiting in the vestibule an interview. "Show them in," she finally said after a long moment of silence.

Jameson nodded, standing and exiting the room. He returned a few moments later with the man and the girl.

They each greeted her with an obeisance and then stood before her without speaking. *Good,* she thought. *They have sense enough to wait until I address them. Instead of speaking, she took time to observe them.*

The man was middle-aged and not very tall. She guessed he stood only five feet three inches or so. His gray hair still had flecks of brown in it, and he had at least two days of growth on his face. His clothing was that of a common laborer, and he stood with his hands shoved into the pockets of his patched and overly large coat.

The girl stood a little behind the man. Her gown, a dull, brown thing covered in a dirty apron, was made of coarse fabric. Her half boots were worn and scuffed, but still seemed to be in decent condition. Her dark brown hair had been pulled into a knot at the back of her head.

*Not Elizabeth,* she thought. *Her hair is all wrong.* And it was. Elizabeth had naturally curly hair that strained against her braids. This girl's hair was straight and contained.

Lady Montrose turned to address the man. "I see you wish to take advantage of a heartbroken woman," she said sourly. "How very despicable! Did your mother teach you no better?"

"That is hardly fair, your ladyship! We haven't said a word, have we Eliza?" He turned to the girl. "Tell the lady your story." Mr. Roland pulled on the girl's arm and brought her to stand in front of him.

She cleared her throat. "My mother and father and brother were killed. I ran away and went to live at the orphanage ten miles from my home. I've been hiding there all this time until Mr. Roland told me that you were looking for me."

"*It all sounds very rehearsed,*" Lady Montrose said dismissively, waving her hand. "*Those are facts anyone could give. Tell me, what was your mother's favorite color?*"

Eliza gaped. "*Um,*" she said. "*Blue.*"

"*That is a good guess, but wrong.*" Amelia Montrose favored dusty rose colors. "*How much did he pay you to come here and pretend to be my niece?*" Without waiting for a reply, she turned to Mr. Roland. "*How did you even learn what she looked like? I have all the miniatures of my son and his family.*"

Mr. Roland's eyes bulged. "*We will just be going now,*" he said hastily. "*Come on, Eliza. The lady won't be paying us nothing.*"

"*He paid me a half a crown,*" Eliza burst out. "*I didn't think there would be any 'arm in it! But even I can see you are distressed. Forgive me, Lady!*" Mr. Roland pulled her arm again, and she shook him off.

*The girl came forward and knelt next to Lady Montrose's chair. "I do hope you find your girl, madam,*" she whispered. "*I have a family, and you should have one, too.*" Eliza took Lady Montrose's hand and kissed the back.

*Maude tried not to cringe, understanding as she was of the girl's sentiment. "I thank you,*" she said stiffly. "*Pray, do not allow miscreants and malicious men to take advantage of you again.*"

*The ragged girl stood and curtsied sloppily. She turned and left the room, shoving Mr. Roland's hand away from her as she walked by.*

*Jameson showed the pair out before returning to his mistress's side. "Your ladyship?*" he asked quietly.

*Maude sat frozen in her chair, the reality of the unfairness of life crashing down upon her. The rings on her fingers dug into her hands as she clasped them together. "What is left, Jameson?*" she asked.

"Life, madam." He sat on the footstool beside her chair without invitation, but she did not care. He had been her faithful attendant for so long, they were past such things.

"How could anyone seek to take advantage of my sorrow? It is in every way cruel and unfeeling." She swallowed hard, intent on saving her misery for the solitude of her chambers.

"There are many such people in the world, unfortunately. Many take pleasure in other's pain. Still more look for easy ways to secure a fortune. But we must not give up."

"Give up?" she repeated, turning to look at him. "I never thought to. But it is very tempting." So tempting, in fact, that the pull of the idea took root in her chest.

"I believe I shall go to bed now," she said woodenly.

"Shall I have a tray sent to your room, my lady?" Jameson asked. His voice was laced with concern.

"Yes, a little something would be just the thing. Thank you, Jameson."

Her bitter thoughts pressed against her consciousness, and she collapsed. As the tears fell, she did not try to slow them. Face damp, she allowed the despair of so many losses to consume her. But still, something in her demanded that she hold on to hope. Elizabeth had to be alive.

The future of the earldom was uncertain. With her son's death, the title should fall to Elizabeth. But she had been missing for almost twelve years now, and those in power pressured the countess to declare her granddaughter officially dead. She had stubbornly refused. Today, a letter came from the Crown, granting her one year more before the title would be settled on one of her husband's distant cousins. The man had barely reached his majority and lived in Scotland. His great-great-grandfather had been Lord Montrose's great-uncle.

The last of the papers shriveled in the flames as she watched dispassionately. *If I am meant to find Elizabeth, God will have to intervene now,* she reasoned. *I have done all that I can do.*

Hundreds of pounds over the years had gone into the search for the missing Montrose heir. Marks had never wavered, for she paid him handsomely. Eventually, however, he retired and married, settling in a small hamlet outside of London. Jameson, too, had married, but he did not leave. Instead, Lady Montrose asked his wife to be her companion. Mrs. Jameson was pleased to accept the position until the birth of her first child.

The empty house felt oppressive. Resigned to another sleepless night, Lady Montrose readied for bed. As she drifted to sleep with her head resting on goose down pillows, she prayed fervently that her granddaughter would be found.

---

*Bingley*

He woke in a cold sweat, gasping and heaving as he rolled out of bed. *It was a dream,* he thought. *Only a dream.* No—it had been a memory, one he had long buried. Now it had resurfaced with a vengeance.

Bingley padded to the window. He shivered in the cold but welcomed the rejuvenation it brought. How many years since he last had that dream? "It must be at least eight," he said aloud, then returned to his thoughts. It was always the same dream.

*He ran down the street to the Montroses' house. His father had sent him with a note for Mr. Montrose, requesting a meeting later that day. It was early, but Mr. Montrose was always awake at six.*

*Young Charles Bingley knocked on the door, only to have it swing open at his touch. Curious, he crept inside, calling out to announce his presence. The air was eerily still, and it caused his skin to crawl and raised bumps to spring up on his arms. The hair on the back of his neck stood on end, and he crept carefully down the hall. He did not know what urged him to move forward, but he reacted instinctively.*

*He reached the study and pushed the door open. He could see a pair of boots from where he stood in the doorway. Alarmed that Mr. Montrose was hurt and in need of help, he rushed forward.*

*"Sir!" he cried, kneeling and shaking Mr. Montrose's shoulder. "Sir, wake up!" The gentleman was cold to the touch, his eyes closed and his chest unmoving. Charles staggered back, tears falling and breath coming in gasps. He whirled around and bolted from the room. He did not stop running until he reached his home and the safety of his father's arms.*

Charles shook himself from the memory. No one other than his father knew that young Charles Bingley had discovered Mr. Montrose lying in a pool of blood on his study floor. A heavy stone statue lay by his side, clearly the weapon used to deliver the fatal blow. Heaving, he had run from the house and all the way back to his father, babbling incoherently.

The maid-of-all-work and the cook had no idea the residents of the house were dead when they arrived that morning. There was a kitchen entrance, meaning they were not required to venture further into the house until later. Breakfast was at nine, and until alerted, the small staff had no idea what had occurred above stairs. Later, he learned from his father that Mrs. Montrose and little Harry were also victims of the attack. Their daughter Elizabeth was nowhere to be found. Theories and gossip circulated. Some claimed the eight-year-old girl had gone mad, murdered her family, and fled. Others believed that she had been kidnapped after witnessing the entire affair.

Robert Bingley had never been the same after. He worked hard with his other business partner, spending long hours at the factory. Charles and Caroline were sent to school and came home only during the summer months. Then, seven years after the murders, Mr. Bingley sold his shares of the company to Mr. Winters and relocated his family to London, where he turned his attention to new business interests. He found great success in imports and exports and, in time, made his fortune, securing his children's futures.

Caroline took the loss of Mrs. Montrose especially hard, for the lady was her godmother. Elizabeth and Caroline had spent hours in company with Mrs. Montrose, who, though the daughter of a tradesman, had taught them proper comportment and encouraged them to speak as gentlewomen. His younger sister still spoke fondly of the kind, warm lady and her desire to emulate her godmother in all things.

*She was like a second mother,* he thought. *The Montrose family welcomed the Bingleys with open arms and no judgment.* Yes, they had spent many hours together, the children especially. After Mrs. Bingley's death, Mrs. Montrose had often offered to mind Charles and Caroline whilst her husband and their father attended to business at the factory and mill.

He ran a hand through his hair. Harry Montrose had only been four years of age, but already seemed older than his years. Charles recalled giving him rides on his back and galloping around the small parlor. Harry would cling to his shirt, giggling and commanding his 'horsey' to go faster.

They had played with toy soldiers, too. Charles never minded that Harry was so much his junior. He had always wanted a brother and saw the boy as just that.

Father had allowed him to attend the funeral. He could hardly bear to see them lying in repose in the parlor when they had come to pay their final respects, but he knew it was his duty. "You have seen more death than any lad of your age ought to," his father said sadly. Charles agreed.

Caroline wept for days when she learned of Mrs. Montrose's death. "Where is Elizabeth?" the eight-year-old asked. "Why can I not see Elizabeth?"

When he tried to explain that Elizabeth was gone, Caroline only wanted to know when she would return. The idea that no one knew what had become of young Miss Montrose was difficult to grasp.

More memories surfaced as he stood by the window: Mr. Montrose reading from Aristotle; Father telling Mrs. Montrose how much he enjoyed the meal; Caroline throwing her sampler because she could not get a stitch right the first time, and her godmother gently insisting she retrieve the cloth and try again.

Weary from lack of sleep, Charles struggled to push the memories aside. Why now, after nearly twelve years, did he recall those nightmarish events? Something must have stirred them. He knew, of course, what it was, but his sleep-deprived mind resisted acknowledging the source. It was far too dangerous to hope, too reckless to entertain such a notion. It could not be that Elizabeth Bennet had any connection to the missing Elizabeth Montrose. Her resemblance to the late Mrs. Montrose notwithstanding, it was ludicrous to imagine that Mr. Bennet's second daughter could be related to the Montroses.

Still, the similarities between his memories of Caroline's godmother and Miss Elizabeth churned in his thoughts, refusing to let him rest.

At last, in the wee hours of the morning, he called for his valet and dressed for a ride. Bingley made his way to the stables and ordered his most spirited mount to be saddled. Hercules was always good for an intense ride, and the exertion would surely purge these irrational imaginings from Charles's thoughts.

The dark stallion pranced eagerly as his master mounted. Bingley secured his hat and took up his riding crop before urging the horse into a brisk trot. Impatient as he was, he kept Hercules at a canter until the animal was properly warmed, then kicked him into a gallop.

The wind whipped past his face, biting his cheeks and numbing his nose. He did not care. The pounding of hooves on hard ground filled his ears, and he forced himself to concentrate on the path ahead, lest his horse stumble in a hidden hole. He kept Hercules at a gallop for a time before easing him into a trot. Frost crystals clung to the field grass. The horizon brightened, and he knew it would not be long before the sun crept up to melt the glistening, frozen dew.

He was some miles south of Netherfield Park when he caught sight of Longbourn through a break in the trees. The residents of the gray stone structure were likely still abed; no movement could be seen from his vantage point. Then, a figure in a dark cloak slipped away from the house—his instinct told him it was Elizabeth.

*Blast and botheration.* All the purging his ride had afforded him was destroyed in an instant.

# Chapter Nine

*October 1811*
*Lucas Lodge*
*Elizabeth*

Elizabeth smoothed the front of her gown to remove any wrinkles that had gathered during the ride to Lucas Lodge. Sir William hosted a lavish dinner party once a month, inviting all the four-and-twenty genteel families of the neighborhood. A large number of guests filled the lodge that day. Red coats mingled with blues, browns, blacks, and greens, standing in stark contrast to the more muted colors worn by the other gentlemen.

"It is good that Kitty and Lydia are not here." Mary leaned over and whispered conspiratorially into Elizabeth's ear. "They would swoon with so many officers present."

"A man in a red coat may be handsome to look upon, but the life of following the drum certainly holds little attraction." Elizabeth smirked at her younger sister. "Kitty and Lydia like their comfortable situation far too much to succumb to the pull of a scarlet soldier."

"They are young," Jane cut in. "Let them have their fantasies. We certainly had ours."

"Oh, yes, Jane, do remind us what that little poem said. 'Let me compare you to a summer's dawn?'" Mary chuckled and prodded her sister's arm in teasing affection.

"It said nothing of the sort. Besides, that line sounds very much like Shakespeare." Jane sniffed in mock hauteur, then winked. "No, the bard's poetry is far superior to Mr. Wilson's."

Elizabeth laughed with her sisters, remembering the besotted gentleman who had once wished to court Jane. Mr. and Mrs. Bennet had refused him, of course—Jane had been only fifteen at the time. Still, her sister kept the insipid poem to remind her that a poorly written verse could starve any budding affection.

"There you are!" Charlotte looped her arm through Elizabeth's and drew her aside. "Can you believe the crush? I tried to convince my father to limit the guest list, but you know how he is."

"Is there a room on this floor that is not bursting?" Elizabeth asked, fanning herself vigorously.

"Only Papa's study. The servants have opened the other rooms. Papa means to move the furniture in the drawing room for dancing after dinner. There are cards in the parlor, and refreshments will be served in the music room." Charlotte shook her head. "He simply had to invite the officers."

"I noted the plethora of red coats. Mrs. Phillips said they are to be quartered in Meryton for the winter." Elizabeth glanced around the room. Everywhere she looked, another soldier sauntered by.

"It is true. The variety in our little society will be welcome. However, I believe caution is necessary. One cannot be too careful with strangers in our midst."

She nodded in agreement. "Trust you to be sensible, dearest Charlotte," she teased. "Let us hope that all ladies have the same intelligence."

"I have already spoken to my mother about curbing Maria's freedom," her friend confessed. "My sister is a silly flirt. I worry she will end up in a bad way if no one is watching her."

Elizabeth nodded. "I am thankful every day that my parents have kept Kitty and Lydia at home. They are too young to be out."

"Is Thomas here tonight?" Charlotte asked after a brief pause. "I understood from my father that he had returned from university, yet I have not seen him at all."

"Both Bennet gentlemen are here," Elizabeth confirmed. "Mama cajoled and made them feel guilty for abandoning us until they agreed to attend. Thomas hates society as much as Papa, despite being gregarious and friendly."

"It is a curious combination." Charlotte's gaze wandered. Elizabeth watched her friend, wondering for what—or for whom—she searched.

"The Netherfield gentlemen are here," she said, nodding to the doorway. Elizabeth had already noticed them.

"Mr. Darcy looks as stern as he did at the assembly," she observed.

"And Mr. Bingley appears as pleased as ever to be in company. What a pair they make! How do you suppose two such disparate characters became friends?"

"I thought character sketches were my purview, dear Charlotte." Elizabeth swatted her friend playfully, and they laughed.

The announcement of dinner prompted the pair to link arms and move into the dining room. Extra tables had been set up, filling the room to capacity. Charlotte and Elizabeth found seats near the end of one table, relieved that no one had assigned places for the evening.

After three courses, the ladies removed to the drawing room. Lady Lucas called for the pianoforte to be opened and begged Mary to play for them. "It has been some time since we heard you," their hostess said imploringly. "Since you are by far the most accomplished lady here, it would be a pleasure to see you perform."

Mary was, indeed, a very accomplished pianist. Papa had indulged her desire to learn, hiring masters when she was only ten. Now, her playing surpassed that of all the other ladies in and around Meryton, Elizabeth included. She had far too many interests to dedicate the time to become truly proficient.

Mary obliged them, playing two pieces before ceding the instrument to another lady. Elizabeth played at Charlotte's urging, choosing a simple tune she knew she could perform well.

The gentlemen soon rejoined the ladies, and Sir William called for assistance in moving the furniture and rolling up the carpets. "It is a perfect night for dancing," he declared. "Miss Mary has agreed to further indulge us with a few lively tunes."

Mary did not like to dance and preferred to remain behind the instrument. "It is not that dancing is not enjoyable," she tried to explain, "but I find it terribly difficult to make my feet keep time with the music. It is easier to do only one at a time."

Elizabeth remained with Charlotte as couples formed a line down the center of the room. Those who did not wish to dance either sat along the edges or made their way to the parlor for cards. Mary began to play a reel, and the dancing commenced.

"I believe I shall go for some punch," Elizabeth told Charlotte over the din. Her friend nodded. She moved around the perimeter of the room, dodging dancers and seated guests. It was with great relief that she reached the door.

"Miss Eliza!" Sir William called. "Why are you not dancing? See, here is Mr. Darcy. I would wager he is willing to stand up with you. The pair of you looked lovely at the assembly."

"I did not come this way to beg a partner," she protested. "I am merely in need of refreshment."

"Then allow me to accompany you," Mr. Darcy offered. He regarded her steadily, his gaze roving across her face before he looked directly into her eyes. "I, too, am parched."

"Capital, capital," Sir William said. "Well, I shall just return to the card room." He moved away in search of another guest to engage in conversation.

"Shall we?" Mr. Darcy gestured toward the room where a cool beverage awaited. Elizabeth nodded and preceded him inside. He secured a glass of punch for each of them, and they stepped away from the table. This room held fewer people and was, therefore, far more agreeable.

"Are Sir William's parties always so well attended?" Mr. Darcy asked.

Elizabeth chuckled. "That is a polite way of asking if he always invites too many guests. Yes, though tonight is unusually crowded," she answered. "The officers, you see."

"Ah. I suppose it is only polite for us to welcome them to the neighborhood."

"Yes, but Sir William hosts these evenings once a month. He could have invited a few each time. He is fond of company, though, and it is his house."

Mr. Darcy nodded. "That is a good point. Now, I believe we have an unfinished discussion we must see to. What think you of Cowper?"

Elizabeth spent the remainder of the evening pleasantly engaged in stimulating conversation with Mr. Darcy. He was as widely read as she; accordingly, they discussed philosophy, science, history, novels, poetry, and more. He debated her skillfully, and she countered his arguments with observations of her own. On more than one occasion, she took the opposite part simply to see how he would respond.

"If we were fencing, I would declare you the winner, Miss Elizabeth," he said after a particularly vigorous exchange. "I have not enjoyed myself in this manner in years."

"You must spend time with dreadfully dull people," she quipped.

He laughed then, and she marveled at the transformation it lent his countenance. "My cousin is a colonel in the army. He is my usual debate partner, but he has been away for many months. But never has he sparred with me so skillfully, nor with such success. I found myself questioning long-held beliefs."

"And now you know my secret, sir. I am a bluestocking. Whatever will you do with me now?" She quirked an eyebrow and smiled slyly.

"I believe the most prudent approach is to name you a friend and hope that we may enjoy a spirited discussion again very soon." His smile faded, and once more he searched her face. What he sought, she could not say, but his intense gaze made her insides flutter and her heart race.

He cleared his throat and turned away. "Would you like more punch?" he asked.

She nodded, and he stood, taking their glasses to the punch bowl and refilling them.

*Darcy*

*What are you thinking, man?* He scolded himself severely as he filled the delicate punch glasses and made his way back to Miss Elizabeth's side. *You are not some green boy, easily swayed by a pretty face.* Yet, he was making a complete cake of himself, falling all over her as they conversed. What magic did she possess to enthrall him after only two meetings?

"Here you are," he said, offering her a glass. She took it, and he watched—fascinated—as she raised it to her lips and took a sip. He swallowed hard and turned away, downing his own glass in one swift motion.

"Have you any brothers or sisters, sir?" she asked as he stood next to her, staring anywhere but at her lovely face.

"I do." He sat, placing the empty glass on the table next to him. "I have one sister. Her name is Georgiana. She is more than twelve years my junior, having turned sixteen only a few weeks ago."

"Lydia's age," she murmured.

"I beg your pardon?" *Who is Lydia?*

"Oh, forgive me, you would not know. Lydia is my youngest sister. She and Catherine, whom we call Kitty, are home tonight."

Darcy mentally counted. "There are six of you?" he asked, surprised. "I can hardly imagine it. I had a very lonely childhood. My cousin, too, has only his older brother."

Elizabeth laughed. "I imagine it must seem a great number to someone who did not grow up surrounded by children. In truth, I would not trade my brother or my sisters for the world, even when they annoy me." A shadow crossed her face, but it vanished before he could make sense of it.

"I do not believe I have met your brother yet," he said, suppressing his curiosity.

"You are in a fortunate position, then," she replied. "He is there." She nodded toward the door, where a young man with light brown hair had just entered. He looked around the room and grinned when he saw her.

"Lizzy," the young Mr. Bennet greeted his sister. "Who is this?"

The blunt question startled Darcy, but he turned to Elizabeth inquiringly.

"Mr. Darcy, may I introduce my brother, Mr. Thomas Bennet, the second. Thomas, this is Mr. Fitzwilliam Darcy of Pemberley." The gentlemen exchanged cordial greetings before Mr. Bennet turned to his sister.

"I would not have expected you to be hiding in here," he teased. "You are far more social than I."

"It is rather crowded tonight," Elizabeth admitted. "Even I find it a bit much."

Darcy soon found himself in easy conversation with the young man. Elizabeth interjected here and there, but otherwise allowed the gentlemen to speak. Mr. Bennet peppered Darcy with questions about the management of estates, investments, and the future of the landed class.

"Change is coming, I assure you," Mr. Bennet insisted. "More and more common men are making their fortunes through nothing but their own ingenuity. Others will follow, and soon there will be no tenants left to farm our land. I need to diversify my holdings."

"Complete collapse of our way of life is hardly imminent," Darcy countered. "This is how estates have been managed for hundreds of years."

"And yet machines are replacing workers in mills and factories. Tenants are leaving the farms to work in the city because the wages are better." Mr. Bennet nodded firmly and added, "Buying an estate is all well and good, but having another source of income ensures that should the worst occur, one's livelihood will not fail."

"Who taught the pair of you to debate?" Darcy asked at last, throwing up his hands in defeat.

"Our father," Mr. Bennet replied, amused. "He will be the first to tell you that simply presenting your point is not enough. You must be passionate if you hope to win the day."

"And you have enough of that for three men. I know when I am defeated." Darcy smiled, his tone wry. "I confess, I have already sought to diversify my holdings. Pemberley is but one of my estates. Whilst it remains a tenant-managed property, I have raised sheep and livestock on the others. The wool fetches a fair price, especially now that textile mills are springing up everywhere."

"Lizzy could tell you all about textiles," Mr. Bennet said. "She must have read a book once. Do you recall the stories you used to tell, Elizabeth?" He turned to his sister, who flushed and looked down, clearly uncomfortable.

"I am afraid I do not remember," she murmured. "Please excuse me." She stood and moved away, taking a plate from the sideboard and adding a few tarts and biscuits to it.

"She always shies away from her past," Mr. Bennet muttered. "Now Darcy—may I address you as such? Excellent. Let us discuss drainage. Do you have issues in the spring?"

Later, Darcy pondered Elizabeth's response to her brother's remark. Surely, she was not ashamed of her knowledge? Had she not debated him with spirit, then proudly declared herself a bluestocking? Yet something in Bennet's words had unsettled her. After excusing herself, Elizabeth had left the room with her plate of refreshments and had not approached him for the remainder of the evening.

Bingley spoke only of Miss Bennet on the ride back to Netherfield Park, much to Darcy's relief. His friend's strange reaction to Miss Elizabeth had not been present that night. Still, in an unguarded moment, a shadowed look fell upon Bingley's face, and he shifted uncomfortably in his seat. Darcy knew instinctively where his thoughts lay.

# Chapter Ten

*Friday, November 1, 1811*
*Longbourn*
*Bingley*

Charles Bingley had been called many things, but insane had never been amongst them. Yet, as he watched Elizabeth Bennet flitting about the room, he could not help but feel a little mad. It was as if ghosts long dead moved around Longbourn's drawing room, conjuring shadows of the past, and each turn of the lady's head, each smile, caused another pang.

"Mr. Bingley?" Jane Bennet's soft words reclaimed his attention.

"Pray, forgive my woolgathering," he said, forcing a smile. "I find my thoughts wandering this evening. It is abominably rude of me to allow it, especially when the present company is infinitely preferable to my maudlin reflections."

"I am sorry for the nature of your musings." Miss Bennet blushed. "I do hope that I can cheer you. It has never been my preference to dwell on things that make me sad. Elizabeth is very much the same. 'I am not built for unhappiness,' she reminds me often."

Bingley stiffened. How often had he heard Mrs. Montrose utter those very words? *Another coincidence,* he told himself. Turning to face Miss Bennet fully so that her younger sister no longer appeared in his line of sight, he said, "I understand from Miss Lucas that you were very young when your family came to Longbourn."

Miss Bennet smiled. "Yes, we lived in Derbyshire until my tenth year. It was a surprise when Papa inherited, for we never expected it. He had an elder brother, but my Uncle Martin and my grandfather both perished in a carriage accident."

"You look very like your mother," he continued, "as does Miss Mary. Pray, whom do your brother and Miss Elizabeth favor?"

"Thomas is said to resemble Uncle Martin," Miss Bennet replied. She hesitated for a moment before continuing. "Papa says Elizabeth bears a likeness to Mama's mother. I never met her—she died before I was born."

Something about Miss Bennet's tone of voice told Bingley that she was not being entirely honest. She drew a deep breath before continuing.

"In truth, sir, Elizabeth is not my sister. She has been with us since before we came to Hertfordshire. Her parents died in a carriage accident, and we are her nearest kin." Jane looked away. "It is not known here, and my parents treat her as their own child."

He let out a breath he did not know he held. *Elizabeth is their relation,* he said. *She is not a Montrose. Of course, she is not. That would be utterly fantastical.*

"Thank you for confiding in me," he said aloud. "I promise I shall not betray your confidence." He caught a glimpse of Miss Elizabeth out of the corner of his eye and stiffened involuntarily. Though Miss Bennet's words ought to have put his anxieties to rest, something within him still cried out against the notion that the second Miss Bennet could be anyone other than Elizabeth Montrose.

Later, as the carriage returned to Netherfield Park, Darcy cleared his throat. "When did you say your sister and Hurst were to arrive?" he asked.

"Monday." Bingley kept his gaze fixed on the darkness outside the window as he attempted to convince himself that every suspicion he harbored about Elizabeth Bennet was unfounded. It proved rather difficult.

Darcy tried again to make conversation. "I am certain that you will be pleased to see them again."

Bingley made a noncommittal sound, absently nodding in reply.

"What has got into you, man? I thought I was the one prone to brooding, but I have scarcely been able to get two words out of you in as many days!"

Chagrined, Bingley turned to look at him. "I apologize, my friend. I find that heavy thoughts occupy my mind." A pang of remorse struck him. "I promise I shall attempt to be a better host."

"Nonsense! I am more concerned about your state of mind. Do not think me unaware of that ride you took at dawn the other morning." Darcy folded his arms. "If there is anything I can do, I should like to do it, Bingley."

"There is nothing! That is, I do not think I can name a single thing that would help me regain my equilibrium." He sighed heavily and ran a hand through his hair. "Some things never leave us," he murmured. "And it appears they return to haunt our memories when we least expect it."

"Has this something to do with Netherfield?"

Bingley shook his head. "No, I am very pleased with the place. It is everything my father wished for me."

Darcy did not respond, and they continued their journey to Netherfield Park in silence.

---

The next day, Bingley kept himself occupied with estate business. They had no invitations, and he took the opportunity to go over Netherfield's books with the steward and Darcy. Gradually, he began to grasp all that was required to run an estate, and he discovered that the running of a modest property was well within his capabilities. Pemberley, with all its satellite estates, would never be within his reach—nor did he desire that sort of responsibility. Darcy might wear the mantle well, but Bingley preferred to retain some measure of leisure in his life.

"The south field drainage could be improved," Darcy said to the steward, tapping a spot on the map. "Your yields would increase if you did not lose this section here to flooding every year."

The steward, Mr. Gibbs, nodded in agreement. "My master has said as much, but he is at a loss as to how to accomplish it without harming adjoining plots. One of Longbourn's farms borders this area, and if we divert the water in that direction, their field will suffer the brunt of it."

"We might..." Bingley began, but his attention wandered, and he left Darcy and Gibbs to their discussion. His thoughts were more agreeably engaged with the lovely Miss Bennet.

Visions of her blue eyes and blond curls danced before him. Never had he met a lady he admired more—yet her appearance accounted for only part of her charm. Her kindness and unaffected manner made him long to entrust her with his deepest secrets. Though they had been in company only a handful of times, Bingley already knew he wished to call upon her and deepen their acquaintance.

*My sisters will surely approve,* he thought. *She is the daughter of a gentleman and will help elevate our position in society.* Louisa would ask whether she had a dowry. His elder sister had always placed monetary worth and station above all else. That was why she had married Hurst—someone who would elevate her to the gentry. Privately, Bingley thought he had married Louisa simply to avoid waiting for his father's death to gain access to the family funds.

Hurst was an indolent man who enjoyed drink, cards, and sport. Though he was not cruel, neither was he intelligent. He slept after meals, even in company, and did everything in his power to do absolutely nothing. Louisa seemed happy enough, however, and so Bingley did not complain.

Caroline did not have the same pretensions her elder sister exhibited. She wished to marry well and had once tried to win Darcy's favor, but when it became clear that the gentleman had no interest in her, she began to look elsewhere for her happiness, and found it in Sir James.

*She would adore Miss Elizabeth...* he froze. *I meant Miss Bennet. Caroline would adore Miss Bennet. Why did I think of Elizabeth?*

"Bingley, are you even listening?" Darcy frowned. "This is a serious matter, my friend."

Shaking his head, Bingley stood. "Forgive me. I need a breath of fresh air." He left the room without a backward glance.

Sunday passed pleasantly. They attended church, and Bingley admired Miss Bennet from his pew. Her family filled an entire bench with a silver plaque that marked it as their designated seat. Netherfield's bench was just behind it, and so Bingley took a seat from which he could surreptitiously admire the fair angel of Longbourn.

After the service, he and Darcy opted to take a vigorous ride before tea. They spurred their mounts into a gallop, racing across the fallow fields and circling the prominent hill that stood between Netherfield and Longbourn. When they returned, Bingley was in excellent spirits, laughing and jesting with Darcy as they divested themselves of their outerwear.

Sunday night brought more dreams. Even though he retired late, he woke before five o'clock, drenched in sweat and heart racing as fast as Hercules had galloped the day before. The images that had roused him faded at once, leaving him only with panic and fear.

Rising, he went to his window and looked out over the misty grounds. The gardens held no more blooms. Leaves had turned brown in every direction. The world would be asleep for some months. *I shall be glad to see Netherfield in the spring,* he thought. *Surely, it will be awash with color.*

His thoughts turned again to Miss Elizabeth. He attempted, with resentment, to push them away, but they persisted. *Louisa is to come today. Perhaps she will remember...* But no, Louisa was five years Bingley's senior. She had been twelve years old when their father moved them from London to Yorkshire. Their mother had lately died, and Mr. Montrose had offered him a partnership in his business.

Louisa had protested vehemently, and their father had agreed to have her stay with their aging aunt in London. She attended seminary, and the younger children saw her only for several weeks during the summer.

Mrs. Montrose and Mrs. Bingley had been friends as girls. They had never lost touch, exchanging letters every week. As such, Bingley's mother had asked the lady to stand as goddaughter to her daughter Caroline. Mrs. Montrose had accepted the request with alacrity. Mr.

Bingley often remarked that it was likely *her* influence that led to the offer from Mr. Montrose.

Bingley lingered in his chambers for a few hours before calling his valet. Bridger assisted him in dressing and preparing for the day, tying his master's cravat as expertly as he could before bowing out of the room..

"Good morning, Darcy." He went to the sideboard in the breakfast room and began serving himself. Rashers of bacon, eggs, scones, preserves...everything that he loved. "I expect my sister and her husband before tea," he said, sitting next to his friend at the round table. "Hurst will be eager to see what sport can be had here."

"And Mrs. Hurst will be your hostess?" Darcy took a sip from his teacup and turned a questioning look on his friend.

"Yes. That means we can have dinner parties or invite guests for tea."

Darcy grinned. "You have only one guest in mind, I think. I have never seen you so distracted by a lady."

Instantly, Bingley's good mood vanished. Yes, he was distracted, but not *only* by Miss Bennet. Her younger sister occupied far too many of his thoughts. If only he understood how to banish her! "Miss Bennet *is* an angel," he said aloud.

"She smiles too much." Darcy said, cocking an eyebrow challengingly.

"How can anyone smile too much?" Bingley asked in bemusement.

"I suppose I ought to clarify. She smiles at everyone with equal placidity. How is one to know her thoughts?" Darcy shrugged and took a bite of a scone from his plate.

"Young ladies are scarcely at liberty to reveal their feelings openly. Really, Darcy, why must you be so stubbornly against anyone of the fairer sex?" He rolled his eyes and set about putting his egg between the two halves of a scone. Louisa hated it when he did that, but *she* was not there to scold him.

"Merely testing your resolve, my friend." Darcy pushed back from the table. "Be careful. You have not known her for more than a fortnight."

"Do you imagine she is hiding an insane relation in the attic?" Bingley asked sarcastically.

Darcy laughed. "No, no, but you must admit that there is still much for you to learn about her...and she about you. Do not be hasty."

Bingley nodded. Darcy's advice was somewhat out of character. Normally, his staid, proper friend spouted things about duty and honor and marrying to improve social standing. *Is he truly encouraging me to consider my heart?*

Louisa arrived whilst he still partook of breakfast, sweeping into the room as if she were the queen. "Charles!" she cried. "My dear brother." Kissing both cheeks and embracing him, she then stepped back, offering him a charming smile. "Netherfield Park is a most beautiful estate," she continued. "Mrs. Nickens has already shown us our chambers."

"It is Mrs. Nicholls," he said, correcting her gently. "And I did not even hear the carriage. Why was I not alerted to your arrival?"

"Oh, I sent a man ahead and asked that we be allowed to surprise you." Louisa grinned.

"You mean you wished to find me unprepared and then chastise me about the proper way to greet guests," he grumbled. "How very like you, my dear, *older* sister."

Louisa frowned at his stab, but did not reply. "Well, we are here now. Please tell me there is something to do in this backwater."

"We have been invited to dine at Longbourn on Thursday, but I wish to take you to call there before then. I have someone I wish for you to meet."

Louisa sighed. "Already, Charles? Tell me, is she another blond angel? Please say that at the very least, she is a gentleman's daughter with a handsome dowry." She moved to a chair next to his and sat down, her displeasure and disappointment clearly writ upon her face.

"I do not know the nature of her fortune," he admitted. "And I do not mean to find out. Miss Bennet is a lovely young lady, and I am eager for you to meet her."

His sister sighed. "Have a care, Charles. You have come so far. *We* have come so far. We must do all we can to leave our roots as far behind us as possible." She picked at an invisible piece of lint on her skirt, frowning as she smoothed the wrinkles from the fabric.

"And marrying the daughter of a gentleman will help." He stood. "I am my own man, Louisa. If I find that Miss Bennet and I suit, I shall not hesitate to ask for her hand."

Louisa folded her arms and pouted. "Oh, very well. I shall attempt to know her better."

He nodded. "Since you have disregarded both propriety and correct behavior and have already seen your room, I shall see to my estate business. Tomorrow we will go to Longbourn." He turned and left the room without another word, mildly irritated that his sister had acted exactly as he expected. Though they had spent some years apart, she still behaved predictably. Oh, how he wished that for once she would surprise him.

The issue with the drainage once again dominated discussion in the study, and as Darcy and Gibbs debated the merits and deficiencies of each resolution, Bingley wondered if he were truly cut out for such a mundane existence. *Darcy seems to enjoy the intricacies of land management. Perhaps only because I have yet to feel confident in myself.* He struggled to pay attention to the conversation and even offered up a few suggestions. Darcy was kind enough not to roll his eyes at his friend, explaining calmly why each idea would fail to resolve the problem. Mr. Gibbs tried his best to smother a smile, but Bingley could tell that his lack of knowledge amused the man.

"I think we have done all we can do today," Darcy said, rolling up the map and then straightening a stack of papers. "Mr. Gibbs, see to your list and I shall see to mine."

Mr. Gibbs nodded and excused himself, bidding each of the gentlemen a good day.

"Darcy, I cannot learn if you simply discuss things with the steward without involving me. Every suggestion I offered up was dismissed, and whilst I appreciate your patience in explaining the particulars to me, I find that I do not know enough to follow the conversation."

"I do apologize for my manner. I fear taking control and managing others has been my habitual manner for many years now." Darcy replied. "I could offer you a book on drainage if you wish,"

"You know I should not read it even if you did give it to me," Bingley said, laughing. "It is all very boring. I would much rather learn how to raise horses."

"That is still very much an option. Perhaps you might purchase an estate for that purpose. I shall do my best to be a better teacher."

"It has always been difficult for me to learn by discussion alone. Might we ride to the spot in question and discuss the matter there where I can see everything?" He needed a ride anyway.

"That is an excellent idea. I shall bring the map so that you can reference it." Darcy scooped up the rolled paper. "Thirty minutes?"

Grinning broadly, Bingley nodded. He asked a footman to send a note to the stables to prepare their horses. They left the study for their respective chambers and changed into riding clothes. The crisp air prompted Charles to fetch his great coat. It was an old garment, which had once belonged to his father. Though it had long ago lost the late Mr. Bingley's characteristic cologne smell, Bingley still felt close to the man whenever he wore it.

Darcy awaited him in the entrance hall, and they went out to the stables. Hercules neighed upon noting his master, stomping his hooves impatiently. His coat glistened in the afternoon light and he tossed his mane as Bingley approached, palm open, with an apple in the middle. His mount accepted the morsel, snorting as he chewed.

"If you have finished pampering your horse, we can go." Darcy grinned, his expression betraying no risk of giving offense at his words.

"Very well." He patted his horse and mounted him. "Let us go to it."

# Chapter Eleven

*November 5, 1811*
*Longbourn*
*Elizabeth*

Elizabeth stuck the red-threaded needle into her handkerchief. Yesterday she had edged it with lace, and today she meant to embroider a trio of roses into the corner. Green vines would trail along the edge of the cloth, and her initials and more roses would be in the corner opposite the trio of blooms.

She had always liked flowers. Roses, especially, called to her. There were so many colors and varieties—enough to satisfy even the most particular taste. Mama grew at least a dozen varieties in Longbourn's gardens. Elizabeth's favorites were the orange ones with the deep pink edges. When she placed them in a vase in her window, the sun made them look as if they were on fire.

Jane sat at a nearby table with Lydia, with a disassembled bonnet before them. Lydia picked up flowers and ribbons, moving them here and there to create something new. "This color is all wrong for you, Jane," she said, holding up a bright green ribbon. "Your hair is much too fair. This green makes you look positively ill."

"You have the same coloring, sister mine," Jane said, chuckling. "You simply wish to purloin the ribbon."

"Not so!" Lydia placed a hand on her chest in affected innocence. "How could you think such a thing?" They giggled, and Jane offered to let her younger sister keep the ribbon. In gratitude, Lydia offered Jane with a deep blue ribbon that made her eyes stand out.

"If we add some ribbon roses here and maybe a feather or two…"

At the pianoforte, Kitty sat beside Mary. The former had been convinced to turn pages for Mary and the latter focused on the music before her, brow wrinkling in concentration.

Elizabeth smiled to herself. The overall domesticity of the scene pleased her. All that was wanted was Mrs. Bennet seated in her chair, work basket in her lap, to complete the picture. Mama was in Hill's office going over menus.

The front bell rang, and the ladies turned to the door. Mr. Hill appeared, stepping aside to announce their visitors.

"Mr. Bingley, Mr. Darcy, Mr. Hurst, and Mrs. Hurst," he said.

Four people came into the room. "Good day, ladies," Mr. Bingley said cheerfully. "I have brought my sister and her husband to meet you all."

Kitty and Lydia stood and were introduced before leaving the room without complaint. Elizabeth felt a quiet pride that they had not even attempted to linger, though she knew both girls wished to remain. *They have matured,* she mused.

"May I present Mr. Reginald Hurst and Mrs. Louisa Hurst. Mrs. Hurst is my sister." Mr. Bingley spoke mostly to Jane, but Elizabeth did not feel slighted in the least.

She examined the newcomers. Mrs. Hurst was about as tall as Jane. Her dark blond hair had hints of red in it. She was dressed fashionably in a gown far too fine for a morning call, and though her outward expression seemed pleasant, there was something of disdain in her gaze as she regarded Jane.

Her husband, Mr. Hurst, moved directly to Mama's favorite chair and sat in it. He yawned widely and leaned back, closing his eyes and promptly ignoring everyone in the room.

Mr. Darcy came toward her, stopping beside the settee where Elizabeth sat. "May I?" he asked.

At her nod, he sat beside her. "What are you working on?" he asked.

"It is only a handkerchief. Charlotte—Miss Lucas—taught me a new stitch, but I am finding it difficult to master. See? My roses look misshapen."

"They look lovely," he protested.

"That is because you do not know what they are supposed to look like," she chuckled. "Tell me, does Miss Darcy carry linens so poorly embroidered?" She smoothed a hand over the cloth, fingertips lingering on her poor attempts.

"I would not know. I do not recall ever noticing designs on her handkerchiefs. Though she did make this one for me." He pulled a large linen square out of his pocket and displayed it. "Only FD in blue, as she always does."

"Men do not flaunt elaborate handkerchiefs, I suppose," she said, nodding sagely. "Simple initials will work very well."

"I shall have to ask what hers looks like when I next write." A shadow crossed his face, disappearing almost as soon as she noted it.

"Is Miss Darcy in town?"

He nodded. "She stays with my aunt, Lady Matlock. We have arranged to have masters come to her. Georgiana is especially eager to work with a music master. Her skill at the instrument increases daily. She will be as talented as Miss Mary someday, I believe."

"Mary is by far the most dedicated of the Bennet ladies." Elizabeth shook her head ruefully. "I shall never compare. Jane never learned, and the younger girls have shown only passing interest."

"Does your brother play? I know it is not the usual accomplishment for a gentleman. My mother insisted I master an instrument, and I have long believed her views to be anything but the norm in our society."

"Thomas does not play an instrument, but he has a fine singing voice. Pray, tell me, do you also play the piano?" She lifted her gaze from her handkerchief to find him watching her intently. She blushed, wondering what his steady appraisal meant.

"I play the violin," he said finally. "It is a difficult instrument, and I picked it because my cousin said I would never be able to master it."

"Did you prove him wrong?"

His lips curled up into a smile. "I did. I play for Richard whenever we are in company so that he will never forget it."

They laughed together, and Elizabeth reflected that she very much enjoyed his company. The sense of being watched prevailed, and she glanced across the room toward Jane. Mr. Bingley appeared to be paying her sister attention, but as she met his gaze, she knew it was his stares she felt.

"Pray, tell me, have I done something to offend your friend?" she asked hesitantly.

Mr. Darcy's brow furrowed, and he followed her gaze. Mr. Bingley no longer watched them, and he turned an inquiring look to her. "I am not sure what you mean," he said.

"It is only that he stares at me very often," she replied. "His looks are fervent and confused. I worry that I have done something to upset him. If I have, I would make amends. Jane likes him very much, and I would not wish to ruin anything for her."

"He pays your sister a great deal of attention. And I must admit I have noted his peculiar looks in your direction. But I cannot tell you what he may be thinking." Darcy sighed. "I have never known Bingley to be anything other than amiable and considerate to everyone he encounters."

"Then he is very much like Jane in that respect." She shrugged. "I shall not think ill of him unless evidence compels such unfavorable emotions. I am not formed for dwelling in displeasure, unhappiness, or misery, and seek to cast negative sentiments off as soon as I am able."

"Would that I possessed your disposition," he said fervently.

"It is not so very difficult. One must resolve to be of good cheer and then work toward maintaining that manner."

He frowned. "And what of the trials of life? How do you manage to escape dwelling on that which is uncomfortable, unfortunate, or upsetting?" He seemed genuinely curious, and Elizabeth resolved to be as open as she could.

"It is not an easy thing all the time." She paused. "I imagine that for one who has experienced much hardship, it must be difficult to keep a positive outlook on their life, or to see past the misery to the good things. I have always tried to find that for which I can be grateful, because that which upsets and disturbs cannot linger in my thoughts when compared to all the blessings that I have." She glanced meaningfully at her sisters. "I have been raised in a comfortable home and have felt the love of good people. There are many with so much less than I. To be ungrateful would be the height of insult to them and to my family."

She wondered if she had said too much, for his brow creased again, this time in confusion, before he nodded slowly. "Yours is an admirable point of view," he said. "Thank you for sharing it. I shall attempt to apply your lessons in my life. Mayhap I might impart this new understanding to those I love."

Elizabeth wondered if he meant Miss Darcy, for he always seemed a little sad when he spoke of his sister. Uncomfortable, she changed the subject.

"Is Mrs. Hurst always so…" she trailed off, glancing at the lady who sat next to Jane and Mr. Bingley.

"Superior? She does hold a high opinion of herself," Darcy confirmed. "Bingley is not so close to Mrs. Hurst as he is to his younger sister. I understand that the former spent much of her formative years in London attending school and living with an elderly aunt."

"I could not imagine leaving my family behind," she replied vehemently. "How very dreadful to even consider such a thing."

"Many families send their children to school. Did your brother go?"

She nodded. "Yes, Thomas was the exception. Papa would have sent us girls if we had asked, but we never did. We had a governess. Miss Lynd is still here for Kitty and Lydia. And my father always allowed us into his study. His books were ours to peruse, and I assure you, I have read nearly every one of them." Elizabeth raised an eyebrow challengingly.

"Ah, so that is why you excel at the art of debate! Did your brother also master it likewise by reading from your father's library?" Darcy looked impressed, and she smiled.

"Mr. Bennet argued the finer points of every book we read." She shook her head. "He would have us so wrapped in knots that we had quite forgotten our point by the time the debate ended. I have always considered experience to be the best teacher. As we aged, he allowed us to participate when he discussed heavy topics with certain gentlemen in the area. Mr. Phillips, Sir William, Mr. Goulding…those who would help us in our education instead of disparaging our efforts and lack of experience."

"You are very fortunate to have had an excellent teacher." Mr. Darcy glanced across the room, and she followed the movement. Mr. Bingley watched her again. "I begin to see what you mean," he whispered. "Does it make you uncomfortable?"

"I hardly know. I cannot help but think he is looking for something, though I cannot imagine what it is. But, please, let us discuss something else. I would rather ask you about your estate than discuss your friend's peculiar behavior."

Mr. Darcy obliged her and spent the next few minutes telling her everything he could about his estate, Pemberley. She learned that it was in the North near the Peaks, a place she had longed to go for many years.

"The park is ten miles around," he said conversationally. "I ride the acreage at least thrice a week. Some of my tenants are over three miles from the house."

"Are there phaeton paths?" she asked.

"There are a few, but it is easier to reach places on horseback."

She made a face. "I prefer to walk," she clarified when he gave her a questioning look. "Mr. Bennet keeps only one horse for riding. The others work the farm and pull the carriages. Nellie is an old nag and goes slower than I can tolerate. In the time it takes her to go a mile, I could walk two miles in the same time!"

"I suspect you are exaggerating. Perhaps you are only in want of a decent mount to enjoy the exercise. I have a particularly fine stallion called Thor. He is a dapple gray and stands seventeen hands high." Darcy grinned, his gaze distant. No doubt, he pictured the horse in his mind.

"That is such a large beast!" she said in dismay. "If I fell off an animal that tall, I would surely die."

He laughed. "It would hurt, to be certain. For you, I would pick a docile mare of maybe fourteen or fifteen hands." He turned and focused on her, frowning in concentration. "Dark brown or red coat, I think, with white socks and a white blaze on her muzzle."

Her heart sped, and she felt hot. *I wish I had a fan,* she thought. "She sounds lovely," Elizabeth said aloud. "I can almost picture her."

"Georgiana has a mount very similar to the one I just described." He grinned. "She claims Daisy is too docile for her, but I am reluctant to give her a more spirited horse. Maybe a gelding would do in a few years."

"Daisy?"

He laughed. "Do not judge her. She was but ten years old when she named the beast. And everyone knows you cannot change a horse's name once it is bestowed."

"A true tale if I ever heard one."

The call came to an end soon thereafter, and Elizabeth felt regret watching the amiable gentleman leave. She never would have guessed from his arrival at the assembly that he would become a friend. His dour appearance had at first put her off, but now he was all ease and friendliness. *Not at all difficult to converse with,* she reasoned.

Jane was all smiles after meeting Mr. Bingley's sister. "I do think Mrs. Hurst likes me," she said happily. "That is a good sign, is it not?"

"It is!" Mrs. Bennet cried. "Though do not mind so much what Mr. Bingley's relations think. You are marrying him, not his sister. As long as you and he are in love, you will be able to withstand any ill feelings or disapproval thrown in your path."

"Your mother speaks the truth," Mr. Bennet said, chiming in over the top of his paper. "I like the gentleman. His company I can tolerate with equanimity. His friend I have not had much of an opportunity to speak with. No matter, though. Both gentlemen are welcome in Longbourn's drawing room." The paper rustled as he turned a page.

"I have asked Bingley to go shooting tomorrow," Thomas piped up. "He says he is a crack shot. I have my doubts and so we shall have a contest." He grinned arrogantly, and Elizabeth rolled her eyes. Her brother was the least proud man she knew, but he liked the challenge that competition presented.

"Do be careful," Mrs. Bennet cautioned. "No need to play with danger."

"I always am, dear Mama." Thomas patted his mother's hand and grinned. "It will be easy sport. Darcy is from the North and has a country estate. Perhaps he will give me a challenge."

"Mrs. Hurst says her husband is an excellent shot," Jane offered. "Will you attempt to best him as well?"

"If he puts up a challenge, all the better. It has been some time since I had anyone to go up against. All the lads around here know they cannot best me."

"Your arrogance will be your downfall, dear brother," Elizabeth teased. "You had best sight your gun before you go out or you will lose the game for sure."

"Ha!" cried Thomas. "I shall bring you five pheasants, Mama, merely to prove Elizabeth wrong."

Elizabeth smiled, shaking her head at her brother. As silly as he was, she would not trade him for the world.

# Chapter Twelve

*November 12, 1811*
*Longbourn*
*Elizabeth*

Elizabeth started the morning by preparing for a walk. It would not be long before the temperature would drop enough to prevent her from going out early. She preferred to take a stroll before breaking her fast. The activity made her more alert, and her mood was always improved afterward.

The Netherfield party called several times a week. Those visits, combined with other social engagements, meant the ladies of Longbourn were frequently in the company of Mr. Bingley and Mr. Darcy. With each meeting, Jane's affection for Mr. Bingley deepened, whilst Elizabeth's admiration for Mr. Darcy steadily grew.

Mr. Darcy appeared to be everything a gentleman ought to be. He was kind, he listened without condescension, and he treated her like an intelligent woman whose opinions had value. Best of all, he made her feel she was worth more than a pleasing face. Oh, she knew that he would likely offer her no more than friendship. They spoke often enough of his estate, his family, and his responsibilities that she knew he was expected to marry far above her station.

*And what is my station, truly?* she mused. *Can I call myself the daughter of a gentleman when I do not know my parentage?* Mr. Bennet was her father for all intents and purposes, but he was not related to Elizabeth by blood. Neither were her mother, sisters, or brother. Her adopted parents had never told their other children the truth about Elizabeth's origins…as far as she knew. If Jane had been informed, she felt sure her elder sister would have approached her long ago.

How would Mr. Darcy react if he knew she did not know where she came from? She had no people, at least so far as she knew. And if she had not lost her family in a carriage accident, how had she become separated from them? What had caused the wound on her head? And what tragedy had prevented her family from seeking her when she disappeared?

Her hand came up to touch the thick scar on her head. *Perhaps they could not afford to find me,* she reasoned. *Perhaps I am no more than the daughter of a poor tenant.* Yet, Mr. Bennet had remarked about her genteel speech when he told her the truth, suggesting that it likely indicated she had received an education or that her family was gently bred.

*Why do I even consider such things in connection with Mr. Darcy?* she wondered. *He has not expressed any interest in me beyond friendship and will most probably never do so.*

Jane's courtship seemed promising, however. Mr. Bingley paid the eldest Bennet sister much attention. His admiration was plain to see, making it clear to everyone that he preferred that lady's company to any other's. And Jane reciprocated his affection.

Charlotte had pressed Jane to make no secret of her regard. "You had much better secure him," she said one evening at Lucas Lodge. "A man needs a little help to come to the point, and if he has any doubt about your feelings, he will not propose for fear of rejection. They are very sensitive creatures, you know...not suited to disappointment."

The three young ladies laughed together. "How am I to do so whilst still being true to my nature?" Jane asked when their mirth was spent. "It is not proper for a lady to be so forward, and I am naturally reserved."

"Save your best smiles for him," Charlotte advised. "Look at him differently than you do anyone else. I know that you are kind to everyone, Jane. I would wager that if you ever truly disliked anyone, they would never know it."

"I shall try," Jane promised. And she had. Elizabeth's sister's demeanor changed subtly. Her countenance lit up whenever Mr. Bingley came near, and her smiles, though still frequent, were particularly lovely when she bestowed them upon her suitor. In response, the gentleman pursued her more vigorously. The Bennets had every hope that a proposal would be imminent.

Yet one thing troubled Elizabeth. Though his admiration for Jane could not be denied, he still hovered around Elizabeth during gatherings whenever he was not at Jane's side. He listened to her conversations with a furrowed brow, observed her curiously from across the room, and asked strange questions about her childhood.

"Will you tell me where you grew up, Miss Elizabeth?" he asked her one day.

Elizabeth wondered what he could mean. He knew the Bennets had dwelt in Derbyshire until they came to Longbourn. *Could he know I am not truly a Bennet?* She responded vaguely, saying something about spending her formative years traipsing all over Longbourn's fields, but had the impression that he was not satisfied with her answer.

She did not think he had any romantic feelings for her. Indeed, it appeared abundantly clear that he adored *Jane,* not her younger sister. Why, then, did he display such an intense interest in Elizabeth?

She crested the summit of Oakham Mount and turned in the direction of Netherfield Park. The clear, cold morning meant she could see for some distance and the top of the manor house was just visible above the trees. Elizabeth wondered if the occupants of the house had risen yet, or if they kept to town hours.

Movement in the distance drew her attention, and she watched as a large brown horse thundered toward where she stood. She recognized Mr. Darcy, and an involuntary smile spread across her face.

The gentleman slowed to a stop and dismounted before her. "Miss Elizabeth," he greeted, "good morning."

"The same to you, sir!" she replied pleasantly. "And a fine morning it is. Not too cold yet."

"There is certainly a chill in the air, but nothing unbearable," he agreed. "Derbyshire is much colder than Hertfordshire this time of year. Pemberley is amongst the peaks, as we have discussed, and so we see plenty of snow and frost during the colder weather."

"I confess, I adore the snow." Elizabeth gestured to a fallen log and moved to sit. He followed, lowering himself to sit upon the seat beside her whilst keeping the proper distance between them. "Hertfordshire never gets enough to more than frolic in a few drifts. I long for mounds of snow into which I might throw myself and enough to form a few balls to lob at my sisters."

"Yes, you must certainly miss such things from Lambton."

He did not know the effect his words had on her. Elizabeth bit her lip and looked away, unsure of how to reply. In the end, she instead asked him to speak of his favorite winter traditions.

"We have a large sleigh that we use to travel during the winter," he said. "It is red, blue, and cream. The carriage horses are used to pull it, and my sister and I like nothing better than visiting tenants or going to church in the sleigh, listening to the bells tinkling from the horses' harnesses."

"I can almost picture it," Elizabeth replied. "It sounds delightful. What else do you enjoy?"

"We always have a pudding for Christmas, and we have chosen the perfect yule log every year for as long as I can remember. There are Twelfth Night balls, of course."

"What of presents? Not all families exchange gifts during the holy season." The Bennets did, and Elizabeth adored the practice.

Darcy smiled. "We do exchange gifts. It is Georgiana's favorite tradition. She spends hours considering what to give each member of our family, for she wishes what she chooses to have meaning and not simply be a token of familial expectation."

"Your sister has grasped the true spirit of the season, then."

Elizabeth smiled. "I behave the same way. Tokens of affection ought to carry sentiment. I would not give my mama a shawl simply because she likes them. Instead, I would go to the local lady that weaves and request a specific design."

A nearby horse whinnied, and they turned in tandem to see Mr. Bingley dismounting next to where Mr. Darcy's horse stood.

Though she felt disappointed that her conversation with Mr. Darcy had been interrupted, she turned toward Mr. Bingley with a pleasant smile.

"Good morning, sir," she greeted.

"Miss Elizabeth. Darcy." Mr. Bingley tipped his hat and gave a brittle smile that failed to reach his eyes. The turmoil she had witnessed so often when they were in company returned. "It is a cold morning, is it not?"

"Not at all." Mr. Darcy frowned at his friend; his expression perplexed. "It is nearly time for breakfast. I was just about to head back to Netherfield."

"Very good then. I shall accompany you. Miss Elizabeth, until we meet again." His smile seemed more genuine this time, and Elizabeth nodded in reply. She watched both gentlemen mount and turn their horses back toward Netherfield before she stood and made her way down the hill to Longbourn.

---

*Darcy*

"Explain yourself," he ordered Bingley tersely.

Bingley had the temerity to appear confused. "What do you mean?" he asked.

"Your behavior I have thus far ignored or attempted to explain away, but even Miss Elizabeth noted how you greeted her just now. Is there something about the lady that you disapprove of so strongly that you cannot even feign enthusiasm at meeting her upon a walk?"

Bingley gave him a shocked expression. "I do not—that is, I never meant—Dash it all, Darcy, it is more complicated than I can even describe. She unsettles me, and I am no closer to learning answers than I was in October."

"Your attention to her sister is marked, and it is not done to pay court to two ladies at once, Bingley. Miss Bennet is her *dearest* sister! Will you cause a rift between them?" In truth, Darcy did not think Bingley had any interest in Elizabeth in a romantic sense, but he needed to hear his friend say so out loud. *He* was rapidly falling in love with the country miss, despite his best efforts to remind himself what he owed his family, and if Bingley had even a little interest, he did not wish to lose a friend in a competition for a lady's affection.

"*Two ladies at once?*" Bingley repeated, mouth agape. "I am *not* paying court to Miss Elizabeth! It—'tis another matter entirely!"

Darcy sighed, relieved to hear it spoken aloud. "I know you are not. Why, then, do you stare at her so much? Why do you stand near her and listen to conversations?" He shifted in his saddle to regard his friend.

"I had no idea you were so intent on monitoring my movements," Bingley replied sarcastically.

"Blast it, man! You discomfit her!"

Bingley slowed his mount a little until Darcy came up beside him. "How do you know?" he asked quietly.

"She has mentioned it a time or two. Today I could nearly feel her dismay when you barely greeted her civilly. I hate to call you to account for your behavior, my friend, but your manners are sorely lacking where Miss Elizabeth is concerned." Darcy fell silent, giving Bingley time to consider his words. Their mounts walked sedately side by side.

Finally, Bingley spoke. "I have tried to manage it alone, but I can do so no longer. She reminds me of someone I lost long ago. More than one someone. An entire family."

Understanding settled upon Darcy. "Then her presence revives your grief?" He had known such feelings himself. Indeed, for a time, it had pained him to look upon his sister, so like their mother did she appear.

"It is more than that, Darcy. She is like a specter. Memories haunt my dreams, and I am unable to prevent them from coming every night. My very being screams that she is exactly who I think her to be, yet every piece of evidence I have attempted to gather whilst here in Hertfordshire contradicts those suppositions. I hardly know what to do or say around her. How am I to walk up to her and declare, 'Miss Elizabeth, you bear a striking resemblance to a young girl who vanished twelve years ago. Might you be she?' It sounds utterly ridiculous."

"I do not have the liberty of understanding you," Darcy hedged. In truth, everything his friend said only increased his confusion. "You believe Miss Elizabeth is not a Bennet, but some child that disappeared?"

Bingley blew out a breath. "Hearing you say it makes it sound even more ludicrous," he muttered. "But yes, I do. And I do not even know to whom I might inquire—or whom I ought to contact—or anything at all!"

"Has she no family left? This girl, I mean."

He shrugged. "I would have to inquire. The girl—Miss Montrose—her entire family is gone, at least as far as I recall. If she has any living relations, I would not know. That said, would they even wish to meet her? I have never heard of any searches for the missing girl. Most suppose she died, as did her parents and brother."

Darcy frowned. "I sense that you have more of a personal connection to the matter than you have let on. Will you not tell me?"

"I am not ready to share it yet, Darcy. It is still too painful. I thought I had dealt with everything long ago, but Miss Elizabeth's presence has only proved me wrong. I am no more recovered than I was at the age of fifteen—three years after the incident." Bingley slowed his horse before the stables and dismounted, Darcy following suit. They handed their reins to the waiting stable boys and turned toward the house.

"For what it is worth, my friend, I shall work to improve my manner of address. Miss Elizabeth does not deserve to suffer for my ill humor. And if she cannot be comfortable in my company, I shall take myself elsewhere."

"I hardly think that it will be necessary for you to do so," Darcy teased. "Miss Elizabeth seems to accept everyone with the same warmth and kindness. She will forgive you readily and move past whatever discomfort has persisted."

Bingley tucked his hat under his arm as they walked up the stairs leading up to Netherfield's front door. Darcy felt famished and looked forward to having a hearty breakfast.

"Caroline writes to expect her at the end of the month," Bingley said casually. "Sir James will accompany her."

"Has their business in the North concluded to their satisfaction?" Darcy asked. He did not feel ready to see Miss Bingley. Though her constant agreements with his every remark had ceased after he politely informed her that he would not marry her, he still found her company unwelcome.

"It has. Sir James's family approves of her and they have offered to help them find a house in town until they decide where they wish to settle."

"Will he purchase an estate?"

Bingley shrugged. "I believe that he means to, eventually. His reward monies and her dowry are enough to see to the purchase, but it would leave them with little in the way of funds for emergencies and the like. The house in town is meant to help them save and invest so that they can purchase a home in the future."

"It is kind of his family to aid them."

They handed off their mud-splattered greatcoats and retired to their chambers to bathe and change before breakfast. Later that day, they were to dine with the officers in Meryton. Darcy resolved to enjoy the afternoon, even though he would infinitely prefer reading a book in peace.

# Chapter Thirteen

*November 12, 1811*
*London*
*Lady Montrose*

Lady Montrose slammed her bedroom door as hard as she could. "Charlatans!" she cried angrily. "Scheming, devious little pretenders. I ought to have known that putting out a reward for information would bring all manner of riffraff to my door." She collapsed in a chair, putting her elbow on the arm and her face in her hand.

Three this week. Each time, a man escorted a woman into her presence, claiming to have found Elizabeth. People presented all sorts of stories to explain her long absence—fear for a life, kidnapping, and even memory loss. Each girl fell short in some way, from mismatched features to ignorance of her granddaughter's life in Yorkshire.

To make everything worse, the pressure to declare Elizabeth dead mounted. Peers of the realm wished to have a proper heir installed at Marston Hall. Thankfully, Maude had friends in high places. Her friendship with some who were close to the Prince Regent aided her in her quest. However, she learned that even their reach had limits. Marston Hall needed management, and no one thought that she, the mistress of the estate for the better part of three decades, could do it justice.

*It is for the earldom's sake,* they told her. Bah!

Sighing, she stood and moved to her window. It overlooked the gardens and not the street in front of the house. In summer, the garden was a pretty prospect—a riot of blooms and greenery. It was a veritable sanctuary from the grimy streets of London. Now, the plants were stripped of their leaves, and all was dull and brown.

*Am I a fool to keep hoping?* She posed this question to herself often. The answer was always *no*. Lady Montrose felt deep in her heart that if Elizabeth were dead, she would know it. She loved her granddaughter fiercely and had always looked forward to receiving the post, hoping to find one of the little drawings made by the child's hand.

*How much longer can I continue my search? I do not know if I can withstand the repeated disappointment.*

*Elizabeth*

"A note for Miss Bennet." Hill presented a folded piece of paper to Jane, who accepted it with a word of thanks.

"Who is it from, dearest?" Mrs. Bennet looked up curiously, her fork suspended halfway to her mouth.

"It is from Mrs. Hurst." Jane read the letter quickly. "She wishes to invite me to dine today. The gentlemen are out with the officers, and she finds herself in want of company."

"And she did not extend the offer to Lizzy or Mary?" Mrs. Bennet frowned.

"She hardly spoke to us when they called, Mama." Elizabeth sought to placate her mother. Mrs. Bennet despised deliberately rude people, and it would not do for her to have a grudge against Mrs. Hurst when the lady's brother sought Jane's attention so assiduously.

"Oh, if you are certain." She brought her fork to her mouth and consumed the bite of egg. "Jane, you must take the carriage. It appears it may rain."

Jane turned to Mr. Bennet. "Are the horses available?" she asked, with a hopeful smile.

"They are. When shall I call for the carriage?" Mr. Bennet gave his daughter a wink. Everyone in the house felt pleased that Jane had attracted the attention of a wealthy and amiable man—even Mr. Bennet, who did not like the idea of giving the care of his eldest daughter over to any other man.

Jane replied with a time before returning to her meal. Her look of contentment warmed Elizabeth's heart. She found joy in seeing her sister in love.

Thomas spoke from his position next to his father. "I should like to arrange a shooting party with the gentlemen," he said. "I enjoyed the sport with Mr. Bingley and the other gentlemen in residence at Netherfield Park. If we bag enough birds, Mama might host a dinner that very evening."

"That sounds like a lovely idea!" Mrs. Bennet clapped her hands excitedly. "I do like having guests, and we have not had a large party here in some time."

"Very true." Mr. Bennet wiped his mouth with his serviette and pushed back from his chair. "I shall leave the pair of you to plan the affair. Perhaps next week?" He excused himself, likely bound for his study to attend to estate business.

Elizabeth finished her meal and left the breakfast room. Charlotte meant to call later, and she wished to be ready to greet her friend.

The carriage, with Jane safely inside, departed around two o'clock. Elizabeth and Charlotte watched from the window as it trundled down the drive. Heavy gray clouds hung low in the sky, a certain sign that rainfall was imminent.

"He is sure to propose before the month is out," Charlotte predicted.

"I believe you may be correct." Elizabeth smiled and motioned to the settee. "Everything looks promising. He seeks Jane's company whenever they are in the same room, and they ignore everyone else in favor of their private conversations."

Charlotte nodded in agreement. She paused and bit her lip. "And what of the attention he pays you?"

Elizabeth laughed without mirth. "What do you mean?" she prevaricated. That Charlotte had noticed Mr. Bingley's odd behavior regarding her meant that it was real and not something created by her overactive imagination.

"Really, Eliza, do not pretend you have not noticed. His preoccupation has become more pronounced the more often you are in company. What can he mean by courting one sister whilst openly disdaining another?"

"Are you so certain that he disdains me?" she asked weakly. Truthfully, she had feared just that. Would Jane marry only to have her husband forbid her from seeing her dearest sister ever again? It would be his prerogative as her husband.

"I may not be as skilled a judge of character as you, but even I can see Mr. Bingley's looks are not friendly—at best, perplexed; at worst, disapproving."

Elizabeth sighed. "What am I to do about it? I do not seek his attention, and I distance myself from him whenever possible. I am certain I have done nothing to deserve his censure, either. It is not as if I can approach him and ask for understanding. That would be the height of rudeness and presumption."

"I do not envy you your position. Our more astute neighbors will notice, eventually. You know how much everyone loves gossip. I would hate to see you harmed by Mr. Bingley's strange behavior." Charlotte patted her hand affectionately.

Charlotte departed around ten minutes later, leaving her friend alone with her thoughts.

Elizabeth had pondered Mr. Bingley's manner many times since they first met. No explanation seemed plausible, except for one. But even that seemed so outlandish, so as to invite doubt.

*Could he have known me or my kin?* she wondered. It did not seem wholly improbable. The Bennets found her in Derbyshire, and Mr. Bingley was from the North. But 'north' was so broad a description. What were the chances that Elizabeth's place of birth and Mr. Bingley's former home were close enough that they had known each other?

Thunder rumbled, and Elizabeth glanced out the window. Raindrops hit the windowpanes, and she felt glad that Charlotte had departed before the storm began. The drizzle soon turned to a deluge, and the drive outside grew muddy. Little streams of water drained away from the house.

"I am pleased Jane went in the carriage." Mrs. Bennet appeared in the parlor doorway. A shawl was wrapped tightly around her, offering meager protection against the lingering chill of the season.

Elizabeth turned and smiled at her mother. Mrs. Bennet came and stood beside her, and they stared out into the dreary afternoon.

"Do you ever wonder where I came from?" she asked on impulse.

Mrs. Bennet straightened. "I did, once," she finally said. "The horrors you may have faced consumed me for a time, and to maintain my peace, I determined to set aside whatever may have happened and focus only on that which I could control. Whatever life you led before, I could make a better one for you. Have I succeeded, dear Lizzy?"

Elizabeth leaned into her mother's side. "You have," she confirmed. "I have no cause to repine my life here. I would not trade it for anything."

Mrs. Bennet kissed her head. "What makes you contemplate such heavy matters?"

What should she say? She could not speak of the increase in dreams, both benign and frightening, nor could she begin to describe Mr. Bingley's odd behavior. Mrs. Bennet's temperament was, in some ways, akin to Jane's. She saw the best in people and disliked it when people betrayed her trust. Unlike Jane, however, she could detect when someone behaved in a willfully impolite manner.

"It is nothing," she finally murmured. "Perhaps it is the weather that brings forth my musings."

"We love you, Elizabeth." Mrs. Bennet's fervent words went a good way to calming the turmoil in her heart, and Elizabeth nodded.

Jane did not return to Longbourn that night. The rain made the roads impassable, and so she decided to remain at Netherfield until the weather improved and she could make her way home.

Elizabeth retired that night, weary from a day of distressing contemplations and praying earnestly that her dreams would be unmolested by night terrors.

"Catch me, Charlie!" She leapt off the fence post into her friend's arms.

"Careful, Lizzy!" Charlie admonished, the force of Elizabeth's attack causing him to stumble backwards. "You will hurt us both if you are not."

"Auntie Amelia says we should not climb fences." A girl with dark hair and a scowl stood with her hands on her hips. "You will tear your gown, Lizzy."

"I do not mind! Gowns are annoying, anyway. I would much rather wear breeches!"

The girl gasped. "You would not! That sounds very indecent. And I love pretty gowns." She sat daintily on the blanket spread near the offending fence and sighed. "I cannot wait until I can wear grown-up gowns like your mama."

"That is a long way away." Charlie set Elizabeth down and turned to the other girl. "We ought to enjoy being young. We shall have to be responsible sooner than we would like."

"Ladies do not have responsibilities," Elizabeth huffed. "Mama stays home all day with me and Harry."

"Do not be silly, Lizzy." The dark-haired girl chuckled. "Your mama manages the house and her children. That is a chore by itself."

"How difficult could that be?" Elizabeth frowned. "We watch Harry all the time. It is not hard."

Charlie laughed and shook his head. "You will have that discussion with your mother sometime, little Lizzy. I am certain she will tell you all about how hard it is to care for two rambunctious children."

The images faded, and another scene replaced them. A woman with dark brown curls held her tenderly in her arms, a book open in front of them. Elizabeth examined the pictures carefully, tracing the outline of a rabbit and a kitten. She could read the words herself, but having Mama *tell her the story was one of her favorite things. Papa, too, for he used the funniest voices when he read.*

"*It is bedtime, Elizabeth.*" *The woman caressed her hair and kissed the top of her head.*

"*No! Just one more story, please?*" *she begged. Snuggled further into the lady's lap, she pulled an arm tightly around her, hugging it fiercely.* "*Please, Mama? It is not so late yet.*"

"*Harry went to bed an hour ago. We have let you remain up long enough.*" *Elizabeth turned to the doorway. A man stood there; his features obscured by the dim light.* "*Come, my pearl. It is time for sleep.*" *He came towards her, tapping her nose with his finger.*

*She pouted, but allowed him to pick her up and carry her to her bed. He kissed her forehead and patted her cheeks.* "*Sleep well, my little darling.*"

Elizabeth gasped and sat up. Her heart pounded, and she looked around in a daze. The dull light outside signified the coming dawn, and she threw back her covers, ignoring the cold. Climbing out of her bed, she hurried to the window and pushed open the drapes so that she had enough light to see. She must record everything she could remember before the dream faded.

For what felt like the thousandth time, she cursed her inability to draw people. *Who is Charlie?* She wondered about the girl, too. Dark hair, very pretty... She picked up a pencil and a piece of paper and began to hurriedly write the contents of the dream. *Charlie, Harry, Mama, Papa...* Names she somehow knew were connected to her past life. *Who is the girl? And who is Aunt Amelia?*

Her weary mind contemplated the dream after she had it recorded. One name, Charlie, stood out. The idea that Mr. Bingley might have known her in a past life suddenly seemed more plausible. But was her dream the workings of a mind that struggled to understand her neighbor's character, or was it something more? Could this boy in her dream be Mr. Bingley?

Already, the images had begun to fade, and she could not recall the young boy's features. Had he possessed the same reddish-brown hair as the gentleman who now courted Jane?

"It is impossible to know," she murmured aloud. Carefully, she folded the paper and rose from her seat. Kneeling on the frigid floor, cold despite the rug beneath her bed, she drew out her little wooden chest from its hiding place. She opened it and carefully put the folded paper on top of everything else inside. Closing the lid, she slid it back to its hiding place under the bed and then turned, leaning back against the frame and resting her head on the mattress.

*I should try to get more sleep,* she told herself. But now her mind raced, and she felt too restless to sleep. Instead, she stood and went to her wardrobe. A walk seemed to be in order. Perhaps the cold would banish the last of the night's hauntings.

Hastily, she donned a serviceable brown gown and her warmest pelisse. Last, she put on woolen stockings and her half boots. With her winter cloak tucked over her arm, Elizabeth left her chamber and ventured downstairs and out the door.

The cold air bit at her cheeks and her nose and, for a moment, she contemplated returning to the warmth of the house. Eager to be rid of the last of her dream, she pressed forward. A half hour would be all it took to be done with the shadows that taunted her whenever she dared close her eyes.

# Chapter Fourteen

*November 13, 1811*
*Longbourn*
*Elizabeth*

"My dear, it seems Jane has fallen ill."

Mr. Bennet's words froze everyone seated at the table, throwing them into turmoil. Cries for more information created a cacophony, and he raised his hand to settle everyone.

"It is not dire. She seems to have ingested something that disagrees with her. Mr. Bingley writes she is abed, and a maid attends her." He held up the note and read it aloud.

*Your daughter, sir, is very ill, indeed. She cannot keep anything other than tea down, or so her maid reports. Miss Bennet is welcome to stay at Netherfield until she is well enough to travel. May I suggest that one of her sisters comes to aid her in her recovery? Miss Bennet will rest more easily with someone from her family nearby.*

He closed the letter and set it aside. "She will not die, Mrs. Bennet."

"I shall go to Jane, Papa," Elizabeth said at once. "I can leave in an hour."

Mrs. Bennet nodded. "You have always been the best in the sick room, Lizzy. You are the sensible choice to go and tend to her. Oh, I am very glad Jane took the carriage yesterday. Imagine how much worse it would have been if the rain had drenched her, too!"

The carriage was readied to transport Elizabeth to Netherfield. She packed a small valise with her necessities, tucking a few books inside at the last minute. Perhaps she could discuss them with Mr. Darcy. The thought of being able to spend more time in his exclusive company excited her. She liked him very much and anticipated the intellectual stimulation his company always seemed to provide.

She left the house before ten o'clock, eager to be with Jane and to ascertain her sister's condition for herself. The carriage went slowly, ruts and mud in the road hindering their speed. Impatiently, she watched the scenery outside the window, wondering if there would ever be a more convenient method of travel. It seemed ridiculous that a little weather could completely halt their means of transportation.

The carriage turned onto Netherfield's drive, and she sent up a prayer of gratitude. Her anxiety for Jane's health had mounted the closer they had approached, and she eagerly pushed the carriage door open as soon as the conveyance came to a stop. A footman appeared and assisted her down, after which she hurried up the steps.

The butler, Mr. Griggs, welcomed her and took her outerwear. Mrs. Nicholls appeared and led her down the hall to the breakfast room. "The household dines late this morning," she said. "Mrs. Hurst keeps to town hours."

*And as she is the hostess, she has likely ordered the house to her liking.* Elizabeth mentally rolled her eyes. She ought not to judge the lady—after all, they had exchanged but a few words when she called at Longbourn with her brother. Perhaps she was not as high and mighty as it seemed upon their first meeting.

"Miss Elizabeth Bennet, sir." Mrs. Nicholls stepped aside, and Elizabeth entered the room. The gentlemen, save for Mr. Hurst, all stood as she entered. Mr. Darcy smiled broadly and bowed. Mr. Bingley's greeting, whilst more subdued, did not seem to hold the same perplexity and scrutiny as before.

"Good morning, Miss Elizabeth," he said. "I am pleased that you made haste. Miss Bennet rests upstairs."

"May I see her?" she asked.

"Of course. A room has been prepared for you. It connects to your sister's chamber. Wilson, will you show her the way?" Mr. Bingley signaled a footman waiting by the door. The man stepped forward and bowed. Elizabeth recognized him as the son of one of Netherfield's tenants.

"May I inquire where I might find you once I have assessed my sister?" she asked politely.

"I believe we will be in the drawing room. Wilson will show you the way."

She nodded, curtsied, and followed the footman from the room. They climbed the marble staircase and walked the length of the guest hall until they stopped at a door.

"This is Miss Bennet's room," Wilson said. "Yours is to the left."

"Thank you." Elizabeth smiled warmly. "Have my things been brought up?"

"Yes, madam." He bowed and stepped aside, positioning himself to the side of the door.

Elizabeth tapped lightly before pushing the door open and closing it behind her. The curtains were open, and a fire crackled in the fireplace. Jane lay on the large bed, curled on her side and unmoving.

"Dearest?" Elizabeth hurried forward and crouched next to the bed. "Pray, speak to me so I might know how you fare."

"Oh, Lizzy. I have never been so sick in all my life." Jane groaned. "It must have been the fish—it tasted off, and I only had a few bites."

"Did anyone else consume it?" Strange that only Jane had fallen ill.

"No. Mrs. Hurst had it prepared especially for me. I told her I enjoyed fish when she called last week." Jane groaned again, blindly reaching for a chamber pot. Elizabeth retrieved it and offered it to her, holding her sister's hair back as she retched.

"Have you been able to eat anything?" she asked, setting the container aside.

"Only a little tea and broth. I am not hungry, anyway. Please, tell me you will stay until I feel better." Jane reached out and grasped Elizabeth's hand tightly.

"I promise." Elizabeth leaned forward and kissed her sister's golden head affectionately. "I believe I shall send a note to Mr. Jones. He may have a suggestion that could ease your discomfort."

"Hurry back." Jane pulled the coverlet higher around her shoulders. "I shall try to rest whilst you go."

Elizabeth nodded and stood. She left the room and closed the door quietly behind her. "Will you show me the way to the drawing room, Wilson?" she asked the waiting footman.

He obliged, and they took a very direct course to that room. Elizabeth felt she could easily remember the way back to Jane.

Mr. Bingley stood as she entered, as did Mr. Darcy. The Hursts did not even acknowledge Elizabeth's presence.

"How is your sister?" Mr. Bingley's anxiety was plain to see, and he looked eager for an answer.

"Jane is not well at all," she replied. "I believe we ought to send for Mr. Jones. Whilst I know remedies that may help, as the apothecary, he is more likely to provide quicker relief."

"I shall send a note at once." He walked briskly away, seating himself at a little writing desk and penning the note. It was dispatched by a footman.

"Now we must wait." Mr. Bingley said it with distaste.

"You have never been in the habit of waiting." Mrs. Hurst finally spoke from her spot on the settee. "Ever impatient and never seeing the need to proceed with caution."

"I am impulsive, I admit, but I do contemplate decisions before making them. It is hardly a defect of my character that I wish to accomplish things in an expeditious manner. Some might say it is a strength instead of a weakness."

"Impulsivity can have good and bad consequences," Mr. Darcy chimed in. "One could regret hasty decisions as easily as lauding them."

"And which are you, sir?" Elizabeth asked curiously. "You do not strike me as the impulsive type. I would say you contemplate decisions heavily before coming to a conclusion."

"You have taken my measure accurately." Mr. Darcy smiled, his eyes twinkling. He had an air of satisfaction about him, as if Elizabeth's accurate rendering of his character pleased him. "I admit there have been times when I acted in haste and had no cause to repine. But I learned at a young age that my decisions had consequences for more than just myself and have applied caution accordingly."

"Responsibility for others can have that effect." Elizabeth nodded approvingly.

"What of you, Miss Elizabeth?" Darcy looked at her inquiringly. "Where do you fall on the scale of rashness versus meditated choice?"

She cocked her head, frowning as she concentrated. "I must say, I have never given it much thought," she admitted. "In the past, I have made hasty conclusions about people that I have lived to regret. In sketching characters, I believe I have reached a maturity that allows for nuance in behavior. I do not see only the best in everyone, nor do I see only the worst. I have come to the belief that everyone is not at their best all the time, and therefore regard caution as the wisest course when dealing with others."

"But what of decisions?" Mr. Bingley sat forward, putting his elbows on his knees. "Do you rush into situations headlong, or pause to decide the best course of action?"

"That depends almost entirely on the situation. There is a place for rash action. I can assure you, sir, I would run headlong into the flames without a second thought if Longbourn were ablaze, hoping to save my family."

Mr. Bingley chuckled. "I believe most of us would behave in the same manner if the life of a loved one was on the line." Suddenly, his good humor faded, and a tortured look appeared briefly before vanishing. Clearing his throat, Mr. Bingley seemed to be attempting to mask his sudden distress with levity as he continued, "My sisters have ever despaired of my taking life seriously. Louisa would tell you I am just as likely to stay here in the country as to leave it. And she is correct. I could decide at a moment's notice that I wish to be in town and might order the manor closed up on a whim."

"That sort of impulsive behavior is a failing indeed," Elizabeth teased, hoping Mr. Bingley could hear the mirth in her voice. "What a trial that will prove to your future wife! A lady does like a little notice in such situations."

This caused the gentleman to smile broadly. "I have hope that I shall marry a lady with great patience for my ways," he said. "She certainly must, or we shall be miserable."

Elizabeth cheered silently. He most certainly referred to Jane. Oh, her sister would be so happy! Their compatibility was evident, and

Jane's calm nature would perfectly complement Mr. Bingley's impulsiveness.

A reply from Mr. Jones came soon thereafter. He stated he would be at Netherfield Park within the hour, and those in the drawing room waited impatiently for the announcement of his arrival.

"Show me the way, Miss Lizzy," he said upon his arrival and after greetings were out of the way. "Miss Bennet has suffered long enough."

Mr. Jones had been the apothecary for as long as Elizabeth could remember. He was a serious man with a large heart, always willing to help even the less fortunate who could not afford to pay him. He had a special place in his heart for the Bennet ladies. They reminded him of his daughter, who had married and moved to a far distant county some years before.

Elizabeth led the way upstairs to Jane's chamber. She and a maid stood watch as Mr. Jones examined his patient.

"'Tis likely food that caused this, as you suspected." He put his tools back in his bag. "I am certain you already considered peppermint tea. Ginger, too, will help ease the nausea. I encourage rest and as much tea and broth as she can manage. Call for me if her condition declines, though I expect Miss Bennet will be much improved by morning."

"How long must we remain?" Elizabeth did not mind staying, but she did not wish to do so beyond what was proper.

"At least two more days, I should think." He closed his bag and stood, moving toward the door. "I shall speak to Mr. Bingley before I leave."

She followed him back to the drawing room, leaving the maid by Jane's side. Her sister wished to sleep again, and Elizabeth promised to look in on her after a few hours.

Mr. Bingley insisted Elizabeth stay at Netherfield until her sister felt well enough to travel. "I stand by my invitation from earlier, Miss Elizabeth," he said seriously. "Miss Bennet will recover faster under the loving care of a relation, and you are most welcome to stay."

"Thank you, sir," she replied smoothly.

"Darcy and I have some business with the steward before tea. We shall leave you now." The gentlemen departed, leaving Elizabeth and the Hursts alone in the drawing room.

"It is a shame your sister fell ill," Mrs. Hurst said when the men were gone. "But how convenient that she will be here for three whole days! My brother is certainly pleased to have her here."

"I am grateful for Mr. Bingley's hospitality. Jane is very unwell, and it would be foolhardy to move her." *What did Mrs. Hurst mean by 'convenient?'* Such an illness could only be called an inconvenience and a nuisance!

"She will rest very comfortably in her chambers. Netherfield Park is adequate in that way." She sniffed disdainfully before changing the subject. "Dear Jane says that you have an aunt and uncle in town. They reside in Cheapside, I believe?"

"The Gardiners live on Gracechurch Street, *near* Cheapside. My uncle has done very well for himself."

"What is his business?" She said the word like it tasted bitter.

"He works in imports and exports."

Mrs. Hurst bristled. "It is a lucrative enterprise if one can make the right connections," she admitted.

"I believe the Meryton matrons said your brother's fortune came from the same?" Elizabeth watched the lady's expression with amusement. She looked irritated at having been so reminded, but nodded.

"He sold his business. My brother intends to purchase an estate," she said, changing the subject again. "It is uncertain where he means to settle for now. This estate is very close to town; it certainly has that in its favor. Though I would like him to find a house in a neighborhood with more fashionable company."

Elizabeth bristled at the implied insult. "We are a small community," she said aloud. "I do not mind the confined and unvarying society. The common citizens and the gentry alike are kind and courteous. I prefer genuine feeling over fashion. It is far more agreeable to be certain of someone's feelings than to be constantly wondering at their motives, or unsure if their words are true or laced with poison."

She raised an eyebrow, taking some pleasure in Mrs. Hurst's squirming as she comprehended Elizabeth's meaning.

"To each their own, I suppose," the lady finally replied.

"I believe I ought to check on Jane." Elizabeth stood. "Thank you for the enlightening conversation, Mrs. Hurst."

Jane still slept, but Elizabeth stayed in her chambers until tea. The prospect of only having Mrs. Hurst as company did not excite her. She would prefer a book.

# Chapter Fifteen

*November 14, 1811*
*Netherfield Park*
*Elizabeth*

Jane showed little by way of improvement after the first day of her illness. Elizabeth tended to her elder sister diligently, ensuring that she partook of broth and tea regularly. Jane managed to keep liquids down, but could tolerate nothing more.

Whilst Jane rested, Elizabeth spent some of her time in solitary pursuits and some with the others in residence. The gentlemen were kind enough, though Mr. Hurst did little more to contribute than eat or sleep. When he was awake, he spoke of cards, sport, and diversions. He always seemed to be in want of distraction, and never content to simply sit and enjoy company.

His wife showed little interest in those around her. She flattered Darcy, scolded and cajoled her brother, and ignored her husband entirely. Mrs. Hurst carried herself as though merely enduring her time in Hertfordshire, clearly wishing herself elsewhere. Elizabeth knew she would find no friend in that quarter.

Friday morning dawned bright and clear. The rain two days past had left the ground damp, but it was not wet enough to prevent Elizabeth from walking out. She wished for fresh air after being confined indoors for so long—not that she resented staying by Jane's side, but she needed her morning constitutional.

Dressing in a gown she could put on herself, Elizabeth peeked into Jane's chamber to see if her sister stirred. Satisfied that she was still sleeping, Elizabeth closed the door adjoining their chambers and made her way out into the hall.

She nearly collided with Mr. Darcy, and he reached out to steady her by placing his hands on her shoulders.

"I thank you, sir. And I apologize. I was not attending." She smiled and stepped back as he released her.

"There is no harm done," he assured her. "Are you walking out?"

Elizabeth nodded. "The morning beckons. I shall keep close to the house so that I may be called if Jane needs me."

"May I join you?"

Pleased, she nodded. "Shall we?"

They proceeded down the stairs and, after donning their outerwear, left the house through a side door to the gardens. They walked in silence for a time, content to enjoy the brisk air. Their boots crunched against the gravel drive, breaking the morning's silence.

"Netherfield's gardens are lovely in the spring and summer," she ventured to say after they had walked some distance without conversation. "The previous tenant had a daughter my age, and I called here often with my mother and sister."

"When did they give up the lease?"

"Let me see…" she paused, concentrating as she counted. "That would be around four years ago. I was not yet out, but Mama allowed me to come with her when she called here so that Coraline—that was her name—and I could spend time together. Lady Lucas brings Mariah to Longbourn in the same manner so she can visit with Kitty and Lydia."

"What an odd coincidence that Bingley's sister is Caroline! I wonder what you will make of her." Darcy looked speculative as he regarded her, hands clasped behind his back as they strolled.

"I understand she will be here in December and brings her betrothed." She had not known Miss Bingley's given name. Hearing Darcy say it sent an inexplicable shiver up her spine.

"Sir James is a good man. He will make her a fine, caring husband. They are very fond of each other."

She made a noncommittal noise and fell silent. The hush that settled between them did not feel oppressive, but was companionable and easy.

"Mrs. Hurst differs greatly from her brother," she observed after a time. "She does not seem pleased to be here."

"Mr. Hurst wished to come; his wife wanted to stay in town. Mrs. Hurst has lived most of her life in London and dislikes being away from the diversions found there." Darcy frowned. "It is rather ironic. She married an estate owner who spends the summer at his estate. Though I do not know how active Hurst is as a landlord."

Elizabeth chuckled. "He is very attentive to some privileges of owning property," she said teasingly. He laughed along with her, and she felt a thrill at having made him laugh.

"Will you tell me more of your sister?" she asked. "I am aware she loves to ride, and that her favorite Christmas tradition is to exchange gifts. What else interests her?"

Darcy seemed to be considering her question carefully. "She loves music," he said. "She plays the pianoforte very well, though not as well as Miss Mary. In three years, when she is your sister's age, she will have more experience."

"Not many can match Mary in dedication. My sister is zealous when she sets out to accomplish something. Sir William would call her the most accomplished lady in the county, and I shall eagerly second his sentiments."

"Your dedication to your sister does you credit," he said admiringly. "I hope I inspire similar devotion in mine. Georgiana has recently become a mystery to me, however. When she returned home from school in the early spring, she seemed to be an entirely different creature. Her moods shifted wildly—one moment she laughed and sang and then she would descend into tears."

"She is sixteen?" At his nod, she continued. "She is at the most trying age. Her humors are unbalanced—a common occurrence young ladies experience at this time of their life."

"Georgiana is the same in essentials, I suppose." He frowned in concentration. "She seems happier at home studying with the masters rather than at school."

"I am afraid I cannot comment on schooling. As you know, I never had more than a governess. My father oversaw my education and does the same for my youngest sisters now."

"And I know from our past debates that he taught you far more than the typical young lady learns in her life."

Something incomprehensible in his expression perplexed her. "Do you disapprove?"

He turned sharply and looked at her in surprise. "Not at all!" he cried. "Why would you think so?"

"I find it difficult to decipher your thoughts when I have only your countenance to use for a basis. I cannot tell what you are thinking much of the time."

"Habit, I suppose." He shrugged. "If one is too easy to read, one becomes a target for unsavory people. I keep my own counsel and protect those I love. If people know what I love, then they know how to hurt me."

She shook her head. "That is a rather depressing way to look at the world."

"It has proven necessary. I inherited at a very young age—only two-and-twenty. Many considered me an easy mark, someone they could fleece due to inexperience. I was approached by at least four gentlemen in the first months following my father's death, each with absurd investment opportunities. My request to thoroughly research each project before investing surprised them."

"Your father prepared you well, then. That is good."

"He was the best of men. I miss him very much." Darcy appeared downcast and fell silent.

They rounded a bend and arrived at a walled garden. "Roses cover this entire space in the warmer months," Elizabeth said, pushing open an iron gate and walking inside. "The gardeners arrange trellises so the roses may climb and arch above the paths. It is quite lovely."

"It is similar to what my mother did at Pemberley." He spent the next ten minutes detailing every aspect of Lady Anne Darcy's favorite garden. Descriptions of climbing roses in a rainbow of colors entranced her, as did the account of the Italianate fountain she had commissioned for the center, its soft trickle audible above the rustle of blooms. With each word, she could picture a veritable haven, and longed to see it.

As they walked back to the house some time later, Elizabeth knew that if she did not guard her heart, she would soon be in love with Mr. Darcy. *He is not for me,* she told herself. *Even if he were to propose,* he would rescind his offer the moment he knew the truth. And I would never start a life with him based on a lie.

After they had refreshed themselves following their walk, breakfast awaited them in the formal dining room. Elizabeth wondered at the change—they had dined in the breakfast parlor when she first arrived.

"Good morning!" Mr. Bingley stood, grinning from ear to ear. "Come, join me. I have informed Mrs. Nicholls that I wish breakfast to be ready earlier than Louisa prefers. I cannot abide being a slug-a-bed. She can call for a tray when she wakes. We shall return to the breakfast room tomorrow."

Elizabeth thought that a rather sensible solution. She had dreaded being forced to wait until late morning to dine and had already contemplated ordering a tray so that she could maintain her usual country hours.

She and Darcy filled plates from the sideboard and took a seat next to Mr. Bingley.

"I have a letter from Caroline, finalizing her visit." Mr. Bingley produced a sheet of paper and opened it, reading aloud.

*Dear Charlie,*

*We are in a rush to depart, and so I shall be as brief as possible whilst I pen this note. James and I shall leave for London today. We both have business in town that we wish to conclude before coming to you in Hertfordshire. I am very much looking forward to Christmas in the country! Town is so dreary and gray this time of year.*

Bingley paused. "I shall just skip over this next bit," he said, his ears turning red. "She just teases me." He cleared his throat and continued.

*We shall arrive on the first of December. Pray, tell me if you need anything from London and I shall see that we acquire it before we journey thither. I look forward to making the acquaintance of your new friends and neighbors.*

*With love,*
*Caroline*

Elizabeth scarcely registered the majority of the letter, so distracted she was by the salutation. *Charlie,* she thought. Oh, how she wished she could simply ask Mr. Bingley questions! It was impossible, though, because if she did it would reveal her greatest secret: that she was not a Bennet and had no rights to their name or position. To do so would spell disaster, she felt certain. But the curiosity burned. *I only wish to know who I am,* she reassured herself. *But why am I so insistent? I have a family.*

"Miss Elizabeth?" A footman appeared at the door. "Miss Bennet is asking for you."

"Please excuse me, gentlemen." She pushed away from the table, abandoning her partially consumed breakfast so that she could hurry to Jane's side.

Her sister sat in her bed, propped up against a mound of pillows.

"How are you feeling this morning, dearest?" Elizabeth sat next to her, brushing Jane's hair from her pale face.

"A bit better." Jane grimaced. "I would like to try a bit of toast, but I fear the consequences."

"We can attempt it." Elizabeth nodded to the waiting maid, who bobbed a quick curtsey and left to secure a tray. "And if you keep it down, we can try something more later."

Jane nodded. She looked exhausted, despite having slept deeply the night before. Her pale countenance bore witness to her illness, yet rather than detracting from her beauty, it rendered her ethereally lovely.

"Have you had enough to occupy your time?" Jane asked quietly.

"Yes. I went on a walk this morning before breakfast."

"I am pleased to hear it. What of the company? Have you tired of the gentlemen yet?" Jane smiled weakly.

"Never! They have lavished me with flattery and compliments. Why, even Mr. Hurst declared me to be singular!" The remark had come in passing during dinner the previous evening, and if Elizabeth was any judge, it had not been intended as a compliment.

"I am very happy to hear that. What of Mrs. Hurst? Is she agreeable?"

Elizabeth frowned. "We are of very different temperaments," she confessed. "I believe she dislikes being at Netherfield, and I am a reminder that she is to stay here through the winter."

"Before I fell ill, she mentioned she prefers life and society in London. Oh, Lizzy, I do want her to like me! What if she does not and tells Mr. Bingley that I am not suitable? I may love him, you see, and it would break my heart if he decided I could be nothing more to him than a mere acquaintance."

"I do not believe you have anything to fear, dearest." Elizabeth smiled. "I have it on good authority that Mr. Bingley never listens to his elder sister, and his affection for *you* is plain for anyone to see. I shall be very surprised if he does not propose before the end of November. Charlotte agrees with me; we spoke of it the day you fell ill."

"I would not refuse him if he did propose to me. Mr. Bingley is everything a gentleman ought to be. Handsome, amiable, considerate—"

"Do not forget rich. A gentleman ought to have a fortune if he can manage it." Elizabeth gave her sister a wink, and Jane swatted her weakly.

"You know that I do not care for his money," she said. "I have never wished for elaborate clothing or expensive jewels. If he loves me and we have enough for our needs, I shall be satisfied."

"We have always had remarkably similar opinions about marital bliss. I am in agreement. If a man could love me with so modest a dowry, I should be very pleased."

"Ten thousand pounds is hardly a modest sum, Lizzy." Jane shook her head weakly. "It is a respectable dowry, and rather impressive considering our father has five daughters to dower."

"Yes, that is quite a daunting task. Thank goodness our parents were of a similar mind and resolved to do everything they could to save for our futures. Can you imagine if Longbourn did not have an heir?" Elizabeth shuddered.

Jane chuckled. "Mama has ever had an excitable temperament. It would be quite something to see her less settled than she is at present. I imagine her fondness for her nerves would be indulged to such a degree as to astonish us all."

Elizabeth laughed heartily, then tilted her head in consideration. "How would that affect Papa, do you think?"

"I hardly know. Our father is a reasonable man who loves his wife. I have to believe he would make every effort to do what he could to see to his family's comfort. I cannot picture him dismissing our mother's concerns."

The maid finally returned with a light repast for Jane, who proceeded to consume a piece of toast, albeit very slowly. She sighed when she had finished and the maid had collected the tray. "I believe I shall rest now," she told her sister.

Elizabeth stood and kissed Jane's head. "Call for me if you need anything," she said firmly. "I shall be in my chamber." She had no desire to venture far from Jane's side. There was still the question of whether the toast would sit well with her or not.

# Chapter Sixteen

*November 15, 1811*
*Netherfield Park*
*Elizabeth*

**M**ama will be very angry. I should not have taken it. *Elizabeth clutched the pendant to her chest.* I only wanted to see the secret inside. *She pried at the edges and examined her prize closely.* How does Mama do it? *she wondered.* She always opens it so easily. *Still, she could not figure out how to make the clasp open so that she could see the detailed miniatures inside.*

The clock on the mantle chimed the hour, and she jumped. She must return to the nursery. Harry was already asleep—Nurse Nan had put him to bed an hour ago before leaving for her own house. Papa would come searching for her soon, for it was nearly bedtime. He would rock her and hold her close, telling stories in silly voices until she could no longer contain her yawns. Then he would tuck her into her bed, sing her a song, and kiss her softly.

I must return this to Mama's jewel box before she discovers I have taken it. Besides, I left the other piece there. Oh! *Maybe that was the key! Perhaps she could sneak back into her mama's room, retrieve it, and finally unlock the secret.*

*Mama had retired early with a headache and took some powders for the pain. She always slept deeply when she took medicine for her head. It was easy to creep into her chambers and take the brooch. She carefully moved from her sitting position to her hands and knees, ready to crawl out from her hiding spot. A door slammed nearby, and voices came closer. She paused, holding her breath in fear of discovery. Had Papa found her already?*

*Angry voices approached, and she crouched lower in her hiding place beneath Papa's desk. Fear overtook her as two men argued, one shouting angrily as the other responded with indifference.*

*She peeked her head out. One of the men saw her, and he held a finger to his lips, urging her to be quiet. The other man, face wreathed in shadows, came up behind the first.*

"No!" Elizabeth's own shout woke her, and she sat up, chest heaving, perspiration clinging to her skin. She quivered in fear, tossing aside her coverlet and rising from the bed. She padded to the washstand, picked up the ewer, and poured some cold water into the basin, splashing it on her face.

*What was that?* She dreamed often, and the dreams she remembered were vivid and bright. This one felt the opposite. Dark, foreboding, and terrifying. She had no doubt that it was a memory.

She lit a candle and quickly found a pencil and a sheet of paper. Hastily, she scrawled what she could remember. The faces faded, but the feeling of fear and danger persisted. *Oh, that I could capture a likeness! I despair of my inability to draw. I might have had answers long ago if I could do it justice.*

Unable to return to sleep in her present state, and with dawn yet some time off, she resolved to find a book. Having read the three books she had brought from Longbourn, she needed something new to take her mind off the dream and its possible link to her past. *Possible? No, I feel confident that it is a memory. My own mind has locked it away and teases me with it now.*

She slipped on her wrapper, drawing the sash tight to preserve her modesty. No one would be awake, and so she did not bother to change into a gown. Elizabeth stepped into her slippers and crept from the room.

Holding the candle aloft to light her path, she made her way down the stairs and walked the short distance to the library. She opened the door and saw that a fire still blazed in the fireplace. *Strange.*

A figure stirred in the semi-darkness, and she clutched the front of her dressing gown, a sudden, irrational fear stealing her breath. Her long plait fell over one shoulder, and she was keenly aware of the impropriety of being in company in such attire.

"Miss Elizabeth?" Darcy spoke from where he stood near the fire. "Are you well?"

"Mr. Darcy!" She swallowed hard. He had shed his coat and waistcoat and had rolled his sleeves to the elbows. He no longer wore a cravat, exposing his neck. She gazed down at his arms, noticing how strong they appeared, especially in the magical light of the fire. *He is remarkably handsome.*

"I came for a book," she whispered. "Pray, excuse me. I should return to my chambers."

"Miss Elizabeth, you are welcome to search the shelves. Netherfield's library is sadly lacking, though, and since Bingley is no great reader, he did not bother to bring any volumes of his own."

"Then it seems my purpose is for naught." She turned toward the door, disappointed not to have found a book—though she could hardly claim her thoughts were unoccupied now.

"Wait!" Darcy stepped to the table beside the chair he had just vacated and gathered several volumes. He approached, stopping within a foot of her. "These are books from the library at Darcy House—*Robinson Crusoe, Pamela,* and *The Rape of the Lock.* Will one suit your needs?"

Elizabeth could scarcely think; her heart pounded as she stared at him. Somehow, his informal attire rendered him even more handsome. A faint shadow of stubble darkened his chin, and his nearly black hair was tousled, as though he had raked a hand through it repeatedly. Never had she seen a gentleman in such dishabille—not even her father removed his cravat or waistcoat in the presence of his daughters. To behold Mr. Darcy thus thrilled her. Her heart beat wildly, and a longing to be more than mere friends surged within her, threatening to consume her.

"Ah," she said, her voice catching a little. "*Pamela* will do well." She held out her hand to accept the tome.

"Take all three. I have read them twice since coming to Netherfield. Just return them when you are finished, pray."

His ungloved hands touched hers as she accepted the stack of books. Her fingers tingled pleasantly where they met his. "Yes, of course. Thank you," she whispered.

They stood thus, each with a hand on the books, eyes locked and unmoving. A sound from elsewhere in the house broke the spell, and his hands fell away.

"Good night, Miss Elizabeth," Darcy murmured, as she turned on her heel and fled the room. Not until she had returned to her chamber and locked the door behind her did she dare breathe once more.

*Darcy*

He stared at the library door long after Elizabeth rushed from his presence. He could picture her as if she were still standing there: hair in a braid over one shoulder, eyes twinkling in the candlelight, delicate, slippered feet just visible beneath the hem of her nightgown. She wore a dressing gown cinched tightly at the waist, emphasizing her alluring figure.

*I am in a spot of trouble,* he thought, shaking his head as he returned to his chair before the fire. He had come to the library because he could not sleep. Elizabeth Bennet haunted his dreams, and her presence across the hall—two doors down—did nothing to restore his tranquillity.

She had bewitched him from the beginning of their acquaintance, breaking through his sour mood and disinclination for company. He craved her presence—needed it to breathe. Darcy could no longer imagine his life without her, and he knew for certain that it would take very little for him to cast aside his family's expectations and fall to his knees, begging her to be his wife.

*How does one discern between love and infatuation?* He asked himself this at least twice a day, wishing his father were still alive to offer counsel. He had male relations, but none seemed to be the proper person to whom he might turn for guidance. His uncle, the Earl of Matlock, had married Lady Matilda Fitzwilliam in a match arranged by their respective fathers. Theirs was an amiable union, but it lacked both love and passion.

His cousin, Viscount Bramsley, had married a society miss with an impeccable lineage and a dowry to match. They were content with their life and each pursued their own pleasures now that they had an heir and a spare. Darcy's other cousin, Colonel Richard Fitzwilliam, remained unmarried, far too absorbed in his military career. He advanced swiftly through the ranks, owing nothing to his father's influence or that of his well-connected relations.

*I need to clear my head. After Bingley's ball, I shall return to London. I need time to think, and a place to do so where I shall not encounter Elizabeth.*

Would he go? Possibly. He had promised Bingley to remain through Christmas. Could he contrive a reason to return to town? He would need to decide soon. Bingley had announced that once Miss Bennet recovered, he would name the day for the ball—he had no desire to delay until December merely to accommodate his sister's arrival.

He stared into the fire, watching as the flames danced a merry jig about the burning logs. Darcy wondered what his parents would have thought of Miss Elizabeth. Would they have approved? It did not seem likely. He could almost hear his father's voice even now.

*Pemberley is prosperous, but more income never hurts. She is a country miss with only a small dowry! I married the daughter of an earl*, surely *you could secure at least that.* For all his good traits, George Darcy had valued money above love, and security above affection.

*Really, Fitzwilliam,* his mother would say, *I never thought you the sort to let a pretty face turn your head. You are more practical than that. Tell me—what has she done to ensnare you? How did she draw you in?*

His mother, of course, would be more understanding than his father, but even she might not approve of his choice. Could he defy what he knew would be their wish for his future?

*They are not here to stop you,* a wicked little voice in his head reminded him. *You have made your own decisions for five years now. Why not marry where you please? Your life will be much happier if you do.*

The voice made a fair point. How many unhappy ladies and gentlemen had he encountered in society? More than a few, to be sure. Couples like his aunt and uncle, who had grown genuinely fond of each other, were rare indeed.

*Lady Catherine would be furious,* he muttered, offering the little voice yet another reason to resist following his inclinations. *Can you imagine her barging into Darcy House, waving her cane and shouting to be shown to the study at once? She would be on the warpath the moment she found out about my engagement.*

The voice did not care. *Why should it matter?* it asked smugly. *She cannot disinherit you, nor can she take anything you value. She lacks the connections you hold in town. Gossip would do very little harm.*

He knew the voice spoke the desires of his heart. It warred against logic—the sensible part of his mind that insisted marrying Miss Elizabeth Bennet would be both reckless and ruinous.

If only those two organs could be brought into accord, life would be far simpler.

Sighing, he crossed to a table where a decanter and two glasses stood. He poured a measure of amber liquid and drank it down in one gulp. The glass landed with a dull clunk as he set it aside, and he moved to the window. The first vestiges of dawn streaked the horizon with a soft silver light, barely discernible. He stood unmoving, watching as the sky lightened by degrees. The pitch black yielded to vague silhouettes, and at length, color began to tint the horizon.

The fire had died to coals by the time the full sun appeared. Stiff from his vigil by the cold window, Darcy returned to his chair. He took up his banyan and pulled it on, tying the sash firmly at his waist.

He wished to reach his chambers before the household stirred. There remained the chance he might encounter a servant, but that was of little consequence.

Once inside his chamber, he rang for his valet. "Good morning, Morris. Have water brought up for a bath this morning, will you?" He always thought more clearly when he could soak. Removing his banyan, he tossed it over the back of a chair.

Morris proved his worth. He had not waited long before buckets of hot water filled the tub. Darcy disrobed and sank into the steaming bath. The water had been scented with something soothing, and he leaned back, eyes closed. Sleep, long denied, overtook him at last.

Morris woke him some time later. The water had cooled to tepid, and he shivered slightly as he stepped out. After drying himself, he donned the robe Morris held out and crossed to the window, his hair still damp.

His heart gave a jolt—Elizabeth was strolling toward the gardens. A brisk breeze pressed her gown against her legs, tracing the shape of her light and pleasing figure until she paused to tug it free. With one hand holding onto her bonnet, she disappeared around a corner

All the calm of his bath vanished, and his inner turmoil returned with force. Elizabeth's beguiling presence drew him like a moth to a flame, and each day, his will to resist grew weaker.

*I shall conquer this indecision,* he vowed silently. *I shall—I am a Darcy and I can do nothing less.* He had arrived at all manner of difficult decisions before; this would be no different. Whether victory included Elizabeth as his wife remained to be seen.

# Chapter Seventeen

*November 16, 1811*
*Netherfield Park*
*Elizabeth*

"Really, Lizzy, I promise I am well enough to come downstairs this morning! I kept down my dinner last evening, and it was heartier than toast and broth." Jane mock-scowled at Elizabeth, who merely shook her head and chuckled in reply.

"I can do naught but concede in the face of your insistence. I shall call for a maid and order a bath prepared if you wish." She turned to do just that at her sister's urging.

"Will we be able to return home today?" she asked once Jane had bathed and dressed. She ran a comb through her sister's long blond hair, admiring how it glistened in the firelight as it dried.

Jane gave her sister a small pout. "Is it terrible to admit I wish to stay until tomorrow? I know I have been ill, and that is the primary reason for our presence here, but I wish to see Mr. Bingley—and speak with him."

"It would indeed be pleasant to further your intimacy away from the prying eyes of our neighbors," Elizabeth replied. "I caution you, however, that Mrs. Hurst does not appear pleased by our presence. Mrs. Hurst has scarcely spoken to me during my entire stay, and when she does, her words are condescending and judgmental."

"That is a harsh assessment, Lizzy. I have never heard you speak so bitingly of someone with whom you are so slightly acquainted." Jane frowned in disapproval.

"You will see for yourself in time, dear sister." Elizabeth set the brush beside Jane and rose, turning away to pace the room. "I confess, I do not find her company pleasant at all. But it is *you* whom Mr. Bingley admires, and *you* who will have to manage her when you are sisters-in-law."

"Nothing is certain with Mr. Bingley."

"Some things are certain, and your imminent marriage is one of them!" Elizabeth rolled her eyes and dropped back into her chair. "You will have your extra day. I daresay Mr. Bingley will insist upon it. You still appear a bit pale."

Jane nodded and stood. Her now dry hair hung in a silken sheet past her waist. "Will you help me arrange my hair? I do not wish to call for a maid."

Clad in a gown of cornflower-blue muslin, a shawl draped over her shoulders and her hair styled in a simple, yet elegant chignon, Jane left her bedchamber for the first time in three days. Elizabeth followed, filled with equal parts dread and anticipation at the thought of seeing Mr. Darcy after their midnight encounter in the library.

She had not slept a wink after returning to her bed. Nor had she read any of the books Mr. Darcy had so graciously lent her. They had remained in her lap as she curled by the fire, her heart refusing to slow. The image of the handsome gentleman from Derbyshire lingered in her waking thoughts as vividly as in her dreams.

The breakfast room was surprisingly empty, and the look of disappointment on Jane's face made Elizabeth grin. They approached the sideboard, filled their plates, and took their seats at the round table.

Their solitude was soon interrupted by the arrival of the gentlemen. Mr. Bingley's face broke into a broad smile the moment his gaze fell upon Jane. She blushed and returned the smile, her eyes drifting meaningfully to the seat beside her in silent invitation.

Elizabeth observed the exchange with great amusement before turning to meet Mr. Darcy's eyes. They shared a weighty glance, and he inclined his head in greeting before moving to the sideboard to fill his plate. She longed to do as Jane—to invite him to sit at her side—but she dared not. They were not courting, and he had given no indication that his interest in her extended in that direction.

"I am very pleased to see you restored to health, Miss Bennet," said Mr. Bingley. Elizabeth waited, and sure enough, he added, "Though you are still quite pale. Pray, tell me you will remain another day. I must be certain you are entirely well."

Elizabeth nearly choked in an attempt to smother her glee. Jane stepped on her foot beneath the table, which only increased her mirth.

"I believe my sister and I shall accept your kind invitation, sir," Jane replied. "I confess, I do not yet feel equal to the motion of a carriage."

"Wonderful! Excellent. Is there anything you desire that will aid your recovery? Anything in particular that I can request from my cook?" Mr. Bingley looked at her adoringly, his expression earnest and eager to please.

*If he delays a full month complete, I shall eat my bonnet,* Elizabeth thought with wry amusement.

Jane demurred, assuring Mr. Bingley that the fare already provided would more than suffice for her recovery. The happy couple soon fell into easy conversation, leaving Mr. Darcy and Elizabeth largely to themselves.

He made no effort to speak to her, and she wondered whether their encounter the night before had unsettled him. *Perhaps he thinks ill of me now,* she mused with a pang of regret. *Though I did nothing improper beyond leaving my chambers in less than full attire. Still, I cannot understand why he does not speak to me as he has before.*

The meal continued thus, and Elizabeth turned her attention to Jane and Bingley's lively exchange. They were entirely absorbed in one another, and even had she wished to interject, their spirited conversation would scarcely have allowed it. The topics meandered from literature to local society, and with each new turn, their compatibility became more apparent. They shared similar likes and dislikes, and their temperaments—his buoyant, hers composed—seemed to balance one another charmingly. Elizabeth could not help but think they would do very well as husband and wife. Their pleasant breakfast came to an abrupt halt when Mr. and Mrs. Hurst swept into the room.

"Charles, you asked me to be your hostess. Is it not my right to dictate when breakfast is served?" She scowled at her brother as she swept toward the sideboard.

"This is my house, Louisa," Mr. Bingley replied evenly. "If you wish for a later meal, you may call for a tray. It did not seem to vex you these past two days."

"Yes, well..." Her gaze drifted to Jane, and she narrowed her eyes, lips pursed in displeasure.

Jane shifted in her seat, her discomfort evident. Even she understood the meaning behind Mrs. Hurst's glare. The lady did not approve of her brother's attentions to a country nobody, nor would she welcome the idea of a proposal. She had come to breakfast for precisely this reason—to interrupt the growing intimacy between the enamored pair.

Elizabeth looked at Jane and gave a very subtle roll of her eyes. Mrs. Hurst would have very little success if she meant to separate the lovers. *Does she truly believe her influence over her brother so great as to accomplish it?* Elizabeth doubted it very much. Mr. Bingley did not appear in the least concerned by his sister's opinion.

"Will there be any sport today?" Mr. Hurst asked, breaking the tension between the brother and sister.

"I had no such plans," Mr. Bingley replied. "I believe I shall be perfectly content to remain indoors, where it is warm. Perhaps we might enjoy a cup of chocolate later."

"Charles, you ought to go shooting! It is a fine activity for gentlemen. Take Mr. Darcy with you. If you are successful, we might have your birds for dinner."

Mr. Bingley shook his head. "I think not, Louisa. If Hurst wishes to go shooting, he may inform the stables. They will ready the dogs and prepare a mount for him."

"Blasted bore you are turning out to be, Bingley." Hurst deposited a heaping plate upon the table and sank heavily into his chair. "What is the point of having an estate if you do not take advantage of the sport?"

"We have guests, brother." Mr. Bingley said stiffly, his growing impatience betrayed by the tight grip on his utensils.

Ever the peacemaker, Jane rose. "I believe I shall rest for an hour or so," she said with calm grace. "Thank you for the pleasant breakfast." She left the room without a backward glance.

Elizabeth smothered a smile as Mr. Bingley shot his sister a poisonous look. Mrs. Hurst, goal achieved, did not respond—she merely stabbed delicately at a piece of fruit with her fork.

"Will you walk this morning, Miss Elizabeth?"

Mr. Darcy's address startled her, and she jumped. "I had not considered it, but with Jane resting, I believe I shall."

"Pray, allow me to accompany you." Together they rose and left the room, leaving the squabbling brother and sister behind.

They retrieved their outerwear quickly and once more exited the house through the side door. In silence, they followed the main path until they had drawn some distance from the house.

Elizabeth turned to face him. "Forgive me for last night, sir," she said hastily. "I had not meant to intrude upon your privacy."

"There is nothing to forgive," he murmured, his gaze softening as it rested upon her. "You were restless and sought reading material. It is only natural for a devoted reader such as yourself to do so when sleep proves elusive."

"My mother has always encouraged me to stay abed. 'Your body is resting, even if your mind is not,' she often says. But I cannot lie upon my pillows and do nothing when my thoughts are awhirl. I am not one to sit idle during the day, and I cannot do so at night either."

"Your mother's advice may suit some," Darcy replied. "Reading often settles my mind and prepares me for rest. Still, last night, sleep was more elusive than usual."

Elizabeth nodded in sympathy. "May I ask, though I hope it is not too forward, what kept you wakeful?"

A flicker of unease crossed his countenance before it vanished. "My sister," he said at last. "She endured an ordeal this summer. Someone she cared for abused her trust most cruelly. Georgiana has not been the same since. My aunt thought it best to send me away, in hopes that my sister would recover her spirits more swiftly in my absence."

"I would think her most beloved brother's presence would comfort her during such a difficult time." Elizabeth could not be parted from those she loved whilst enduring pain.

"She fears she has disappointed me with her actions," he said softly. "I have assured her that such a thing is not possible, but she does not believe me."

"I am sorry to hear it." Elizabeth moved to a bench and sat, gratified when Mr. Darcy took the place beside her. "We have discussed this trying age. My youngest sister is nearly of an age with yours. She, too, struggles against the norms of life."

"When does it end?" he asked, with something close to desperation.

Chuckling, she patted his arm. "I am afraid your sister will become something of a mix of who she was and who she is now. You will have to learn to know her all over again."

"That does not sound pleasant at all." He pouted, his brow furrowing and his lower lip pushing forward ever so slightly. Elizabeth could picture him as a child with that very expression. She would wager his mother granted him his every desire when he looked so.

"I am pleased that your sister has recovered."

Elizabeth welcomed the change of subject. "Jane has always enjoyed robust health. I do wonder if the fish served the night that she fell ill had been too long out of the water. I have heard one might die from eating improperly aged aquatic vertebrates."

Mr. Darcy raised a brow, a flicker of admiration tugging at the corner of his mouth. *At least he appears amused.* As Mr. Bennet would say, only Elizabeth Bennet would describe spoiled fish in such a manner—and make it sound perfectly natural. "It has been known to happen. I am glad that your sister came through her ordeal with no lasting harm." He paused, then glanced down at her. "It will not be long, I think, before she is no longer Miss Bennet."

Grinning, Elizabeth nodded, her pleasure evident. "Jane is the most deserving person in the entire world. I could not be happier that she has found someone to love who is her match in every way."

"They do seem to share many similarities."

"With just enough differences to keep things…interesting." She tilted her head and smiled. "It is my hope to find the same felicity someday."

*Too bold, Lizzy,* she scolded herself silently.

But he did not draw away in discomfort or disdain. Instead, his gaze dropped to her lips. "I, too, wish to marry for reasons beyond fortune and connection," he murmured.

*He is going to kiss me,* she thought as his head inclined. Her eyes fluttered closed, and she angled her head toward his.

A loud crack echoed across the grounds. Elizabeth and Mr. Darcy pulled apart at once, both turning away. Her cheeks burned with embarrassment. Sanity returned, and she began mentally chastising herself for her foolishness.

"Forgive me," Mr. Darcy said quietly. "Shall we return to the house?"

*Is that all he is going to say?* She felt strangely hurt, a sharp pang of disappointment catching her off guard. He did not appear flustered in the least as he stood and extended his hand to assist her. His eyes, however, twinkled with something she could not name.

She accepted his hand, rising even as she wondered whether the near-kiss had affected him as deeply as it had her. Could she deny the evidence seen in his expression?

They did not speak as they walked back toward the house. Elizabeth kept a proper distance, her arm looped lightly through his, her hand resting gently on his coat, hoping to ease any discomfort he might find in her touch. Not that she understood his feelings, but she dared not risk offending him.

They parted just inside the doors. Elizabeth shed her outerwear with haste, eager for the privacy of her chamber. Once safely within, she chastised herself once more—for daring to hope that a man of Mr. Darcy's standing could ever be hers. Despite the affection that now bloomed in her heart, she had lied to him by omission. He believed her to be the second daughter of a respectable gentleman. He did not know the truth—and she was not at liberty to correct him.

Did she trust him enough to share her secret? Her heart answered with a resounding yes, even as her head protested. To disclose the truth would be foolish—dangerous. It could ruin her reputation entirely.

Perhaps she was destined never to marry, for who could ever want a lady with no past?

# Chapter Eighteen

*November 16, 1811*
*Netherfield Park*
*Bingley*

"I shall call upon you and see how your recovery progresses," Bingley assured Jane as he handed her into the carriage.

"Your call will be most welcome," she replied, her lovely features brightening with pleasure.

Sunday services had concluded, and with the return of the carriage, the Bennet ladies had declared their intention to return to Longbourn. "Jane is well enough to travel, and we would not wish to trespass on your hospitality longer than necessary," Miss Elizabeth had said.

Though her reasoning was sound, Bingley inwardly rebelled at the thought of letting Jane out of his sight. He had no doubt that the moment the carriage departed, Louisa would pounce. Her snide remarks had not gone unnoticed; even Jane had winced at a few, though she was far too well-mannered to return insult for insult.

With his hands clasped behind his back, he watched the carriage roll away. Darcy stood beside him, equally silent. In unison, they turned and mounted the steps to Netherfield's door.

They had scarcely entered the parlor before Louisa swept toward him with a purpose. "Charles, you cannot be serious," she whined. "You could do so much better than the daughter of an insignificant country squire!"

"Whom I choose to marry is no concern of yours. You have wed the gentleman of your choosing and have no cause for complaint."

"Dear brother, every decision you make reflects upon our family. Caroline has secured an excellent match. Her betrothed is not only a knight, but the second son of a prominent landowner. And you would settle for Miss Jane Bennet?"

"Tell me, Louisa," he said dryly, "have you ferreted out the amount of her dowry yet?"

"I have, if you must know." Louisa sniffed disdainfully. "Miss Bennet and all her sisters have ten thousand pounds apiece. A pittance compared to my portion—or to yours."

"That is a respectable amount. He has *five* daughters, you know—and a son, too!" Bingley threw up his hands in exasperation. "You may present whatever argument you wish, sister, but it will not sway me. If Miss Bennet accepts my proposal, she will become your sister by marriage. And *when* that happens, you will treat her with the respect due to my wife—or cease importuning us with your presence."

Louisa gasped in affront and stormed from the room, leaving Bingley alone with Darcy.

"Well, that is over," he muttered, leaning back in his chair with a sigh. "I knew it was coming."

"You handled it well," Darcy said, nodding approvingly. "I am very impressed with your fortitude. And, oddly enough, your sister strongly reminded me of my Aunt Catherine just now."

Bingley chortled. "The Gorgon of Kent? Is that not what the colonel calls her?"

They laughed, and when their mirth subsided, Bingley sobered and turned to his friend. "In truth, Darcy, I should like your opinion. Am I making an error? I have known Miss Bennet for less than four weeks. Am I daft to consider marriage after so brief an acquaintance?"

"Marriages are founded on less every day," his friend replied evenly.

"Arranged marriages, yes, but marriages of affection?" Bingley shook his head incredulously. "Am I a fool? A lovesick one? I cannot imagine life without her, and it pained me to see her ride away in my carriage today. I wanted nothing more than to take her back to her chamber and lock her in."

"A veritable maiden in a tower, hmm?" Darcy chuckled. "Tell me, friend—will you feel the same way in two weeks as you do now?"

"No. I believe I shall feel even more. My admiration for Miss Bennet has grown steadily since our first dance. Each conversation reveals more of her character, and I fall further under her spell with every moment we spend together."

"Then I suppose the only thing left is to decide *when* you will propose." Darcy leaned back and clasped his hands behind his head. "'A happy marriage is possible for any two people who are united,' or so my grandmother once said."

Bingley sat in thoughtful silence for a moment, contemplating his friend's words. Slowly, a broad grin spread across his face. "You have the right of it, Darcy! I meant to host a ball. Let us do it! It shall be in Miss Bennet's honor, and I shall propose that night."

"Congratulations! You will be very happy." Darcy smiled, though something seemed to trouble him; the expression did not quite reach his eyes.

"Are you well?" Bingley asked impulsively. "You are happy for me, are you not?"

"Entirely! I merely wrestle with my own conflicted thoughts. But know that I wish you the very best with Miss Bennet. I believe you are perfectly suited."

Darcy's good opinion meant the world to him, and he thanked him profusely. "I must find Louisa. She will be...*delighted* to host a ball, do you not think?" Chuckling, he rose and left the room.

Louisa was *not* delighted to assist in planning a ball and told her brother so at once.

"Do you doubt your capabilities?" he asked, all innocence. "I had assumed you would have ample experience hosting events of this magnitude by now. Perhaps I was mistaken."

"I have hosted balls in London," she snapped. "An insignificant country gathering will be simple."

"Then why hesitate? Do you not wish to show the denizens of the area what it means to be a truly fashionable hostess?" He knew he had struck the right chord when Louisa's expression shifted from indignation to anticipation—tinged with a familiar, mean-spirited delight.

"I shall show them how a proper London hostess conducts such affairs," she declared. "Very well, brother, you will have your ball. Now go away—I must begin my lists."

Bingley left the room, chortling. Louisa was not difficult to understand. She liked to be praised, valued, and seen as superior to others. He had merely played to her vanity and received precisely what he wanted.

*Darcy*

Darcy remained in his chair long after Bingley left the room. He replayed their conversation, posing to himself the very questions and arguments that he had presented to his friend.

He, too, had only known Miss Elizabeth for only several weeks, yet he found himself irresistibly drawn to her. Her vibrancy lit every room she entered, and each encounter further enthralled him.

Bingley had already begun to contemplate marriage to the lady's sister after the same brief acquaintance. It had been easy to reason on his friend's behalf, but he struggled to apply the same logic to himself.

"Why must life be so blasted complicated?" he complained to the empty room. Rising, he began to pace. With his hands clasped behind his back and his brow furrowed in thought, he returned to the same questions he had earlier asked of Bingley.

*Will I feel the same for Elizabeth in two weeks as I do now? What of a month?* The answer came readily—identical to Bingley's. Already his feelings deepened with every meeting. That would not change.

He posed another question. *Will leaving her side diminish my affection?* He had once considered departing for town after Bingley's ball, hoping distance might clear his mind. But the longer he delayed, the more certain he became that it would serve no purpose. Elizabeth had already taken root in his heart, and the seed of admiration was swiftly growing into love.

He thought of his grandmother's words: A happy marriage is possible for any two people who are united. What he had not told Bingley was that those were the very words his grandmother had used to persuade his mother to wed his father. The former Lady Matlock had insisted upon the match, much to her daughter's displeasure. But her words had proven prophetic, and his parents had shared a contented marriage.

There was truth in the words. Even if his love were to fade, which he greatly doubted, as long as they worked toward common goals, he would be content with Elizabeth.

He had been determined to leave Netherfield Park after the ball, especially following their unexpected encounter in the library. But then came that moment in the garden—when they had nearly kissed. He could not forget it. She had turned her face up to his, clearly inviting the press of his lips against hers. And he had fully intended to do so until some unfortunate interruption forced them apart.

His resolve had fled in that instant. He knew, with absolute clarity, that he could not leave her. He loved her, and he longed to know whether she might return his affection. Running off to London would change nothing. "Semper in absentes felicior aestus amantes," he muttered softly. "Always toward absent lovers love's tide stronger flows." The Roman poet Sextus Propertius knew of what he spoke. Fleeing would likely only deepen his attachment.

*I never imagined that I would find love in Hertfordshire,* he mused. He crossed to the window and looked out. In the distance stood the tree beside the bench where he and Elizabeth had nearly kissed. He wished she were there now, that he might take her on another walk and declare his affections openly.

Since that tender moment, Elizabeth had gone out of her way to avoid him. He wondered whether she felt embarrassed. Perhaps she thought him dishonorable, merely toying with her heart. *I must reassure her that I have only honorable intentions,* he resolved.

Never one to make hasty decisions, he resolved to wait until the ball to discern her feelings. In the meantime, he would continue to court her quietly and would request the supper set the night of Bingley's ball. If possible, he would ease her doubts before then.

Bingley intended to propose to Miss Bennet at the ball. Would he begrudge Darcy the same privilege? Surely not. If nothing else, Darcy could ask permission to court her, or request a private audience with her the following day.

Resolved, he left the room and ascended to his chambers. He had plans to make.

*Elizabeth*

Jane hummed a merry tune as the carriage trundled toward Longbourn. She had regained the color in her cheeks, and she looked the picture of health. This pleased Elizabeth, for she had worried about her sister's welfare.

"Will he wait more than a day to come?" she teased.

Jane turned toward her, rolled her eyes, and looked back out the window. "If he does, I shall be surprised," she replied.

Elizabeth's thoughts drifted to the other unmarried gentleman at Netherfield. She felt ridiculously foolish for having come so close to bestowing favors on Mr. Darcy. *You great ninny,* she scolded herself once more. *What would you have done after he kissed you?*

Mr. Darcy was an honorable man. He would never kiss a lady unless he cared for her—loved her. She knew enough of his character to be certain of that.

And then he would go to Papa—her adopted father—and request permission to court her. Papa would say yes. He would advise to say nothing of her past...and then what? They would begin a marriage based on a lie, and guilt would twist their tender feelings and twist them into something unrecognizable. She would confess—and then Mr. Darcy would hate her.

*But what if he did not?* Her traitorous heart whispered dreams of a rosy future, married to the man she was perilously close to loving. *What if he does not hold your past against you and marries you, anyway? He would keep your secret.*

He would. At least, she hoped he would.

She could not know whether he intended to ask for her hand, but Elizabeth understood she must be prepared to act should he do so.

They were welcomed home with enthusiasm. Mrs. Bennet examined Jane closely, seeking reassurance that her eldest child had returned to full health. She greeted Elizabeth as well, praising her efforts and apologizing for not having called.

"I knew you had it well managed," she said.

Exhausted from all her tumultuous thoughts, Elizabeth excused herself, intending to rest in her chambers for the remainder of the day.

The next morning, Mr. Bennet came to the table looking rather chagrined. "I hope, my dear," he began, "that you have ordered something pleasant for dinner this evening. I expect we shall have a guest."

"Who is it?" Mrs. Bennet asked curiously. "Is it Mr. Bingley?"

"No, it is not Mr. Bingley. Indeed, it is no one that I have ever met in the course of my life. I owe you something of an apology, my dear, for his letter was misplaced amidst the chaos of my desk and I only rediscovered it this morning."

He held up a sheet of paper. "It is from my cousin, Mr. William Collins. He is the heir should anything befall Thomas, or if Thomas fails to produce a son of his own. Somehow, he has learned that the living at Longbourn will come available next summer and wishes to speak to me on the matter."

"If you did not reply to his letter, why do you expect him?" Thomas asked with interest.

"Because he invited himself. Here, read it." Mr. Bennet offered the letter to his son. "Aloud, if you please."

*Dear Sir,*

*The disagreement subsisting between yourself and my late honored father has ever caused me much uneasiness, and since I have had the misfortune of losing him, I have frequently wished to heal the breach; but for some time my own doubts kept me back, fearing it might seem disrespectful to his memory for me to be on good terms with anyone with whom it had always pleased him to be at variance.*

*I recently took orders and have the great honor of holding a living bestowed by none other than the illustrious Lady Catherine de Bourgh. She resides at Rosings Park in Kent, a handsome estate. The Hunsford Parish living falls within her gift, and upon its vacancy last summer, she had the goodness to confer it upon me. I am deeply grateful for her beneficence. Her advice, offered freely and frequently, has impressed upon me the importance of cultivating congenial family relations.*

*And so, having overcome my hesitations and at the urging of my noble patroness, Lady Catherine de Bourgh, I send this letter in the hope that the breach between our branches of the family might at long at be healed.*

*Please expect me no later than four o'clock on the eighteenth of November. It would also afford me great pleasure if, during the course of our reunion, we might discuss the living at Longbourn. As you are my nearest living relation, and the advowson of Longbourn lies with you, I hope we may speak of your bestowing it upon me.*

*Yours, etc,*

*William Collins*

"He sounds ridiculous," Thomas said, handing the letter back to his father.

"His letter intrigues me. I never wrote to deny his coming, and so I expect he will arrive as stated. Mr. Bennet gave a resigned sigh. "I am sorry, Fanny. I know that such short notice is not proper."

"We shall make do, Thomas. I shall go speak with Hill at once."

# Chapter Nineteen

*November 18, 1811*
*Longbourn*
*Elizabeth*

William Collins arrived precisely at four o'clock, clambering from the hired coach that had brought him from Meryton. He straightened at once and smiled broadly at his relations, with no trace of false humility—or, indeed, any self-consciousness—upon his countenance.

Elizabeth observed that he stood close to six feet tall. He appeared fit enough, though he carried a little more weight about the middle than that of most gentlemen of his age she had encountered. He removed his hat and pressed it to his chest, revealing light brown hair tousled from travel.

"My dear cousins," he said by way of introduction. Stepping forward, he bowed low to the assembled Bennets before straightening with evident satisfaction. "I am most pleased to be here. My father spoke of Longbourn's beauty, but I must say his descriptions did not do it justice."

"Mr. Collins, I presume," said Mr. Bennet, stepping forward. "Welcome to Longbourn."

"Delighted." Mr. Collins grinned. "Will your man see to my trunk? I am happy to carry it inside."

"Mr. Hill will see it brought to your chambers. Shall we go inside?"

After the appropriate introductions were made, the family led their guest into the house.

"My, what a superbly appointed room!" Mr. Collins exclaimed upon entering the parlor. He appeared determined to be pleased with everything he saw and complimented the furnishings accordingly. "Tell me, do you pass many evenings here?"

"This is my wife's favorite room," Mr. Bennet replied. "It is ideally situated in the southwest corner of the manor. The placement of the windows ensures we are not too hot in summer nor too cold in winter."

"Our ancestors were wise to arrange it in that manner," Mr. Collins declared solemnly.

Tea arrived, and as Mrs. Bennet began to serve, their guest launched into a series of questions. Once he had satisfied himself as to the size and profitability of the estate, the conversation turned—rather predictably—to the subject of Longbourn's living.

"Is the parish here large?" he asked.

"The church is of moderate size. Much of Meryton and the surrounding estates attend services at Longbourn." Mr. Bennet took a sip from his tea.

"And is it a valuable living?" Mr. Collins leaned forward eagerly.

Mr. Bennet raised his brow, staring at his cousin with studied solemnity. Collins appeared chagrined, looking away awkwardly before he continued in a more subdued tone.

"You know from my missive that I wish to receive the living, Cousin," he said carefully. "I merely hope to learn everything I can of it beforehand."

"Perhaps we ought to reserve such matters for a private discussion—after dinner, perhaps? Thomas will join us. I value his keen insight." Mr. Bennet set his cup down with a slight clatter, the gesture betraying his irritation.

"Yes, that will do nicely. Forgive my impatience. I often find that, once I set my mind on something, the idea consumes me. I cannot rest until I have reached a satisfactory conclusion."

"I understand completely," said Mrs. Bennet, reassuring him. "I am very much the same. My projects and ideas frequently overrun my other concerns."

"And yet you never shirk your responsibilities, my dear." Mr. Bennet said, smiling fondly at his wife.

Elizabeth followed the conversation with interest. Mr. Collins did not appear so foolish as they had imagined. Rather, he seemed eager to please and to be pleased by everything and everyone around him. As her sisters conversed softly, he made his way about the room, inserting himself into various exchanges. They did not mind. He was not intrusive, merely eager to become better acquainted with his cousins.

"That is a lovely bonnet," he said, admiring Lydia's latest creation spread across the table. "And Miss Kitty, what a charming sketch."

"Miss Mary, I find Wordsworth to be excellent reading. Might we discuss your book later?"

"Miss Bennet, have you any suggestions for sights to see whilst I am in Hertfordshire?"

At this, Jane smiled and gestured toward Elizabeth. "My sister would be the far better guide, sir, especially if you are a great walker.

Elizabeth goes wherever her feet carry her and has explored the area extensively."

"Miss Elizabeth?" He turned to her, a question in his eyes.

"Oakham Mount is a favorite excursion," she replied. "I find the paths east and west of Longbourn to be superior as well. They are well trodden and not at all difficult."

"I thank you. I do enjoy walking, though I cannot do so daily whilst I am attending to my parish." He smiled and took a seat beside Thomas, folding his hands in his lap and smiling broadly.

"Will you tell us about your parish?" Jane asked.

"Indeed, if that is your wish. I am most fortunate to have secured a living so early in my career. Lady Catherine is an attentive patroness." He grimaced slightly and looked rather guilty. "May I speak plainly?" he asked, turning to Thomas.

"Of course." Thomas replied, nodding encouragingly. "We shall not judge you for your words."

Mr. Collins sighed. "Lady Catherine is indeed an attentive patroness—*too* attentive. She oversees every aspect of my work with intense scrutiny. I cannot even order meat for my dinner without her remarking at the expense of the cut. I had resigned myself to a life governed thus, when I learned from a friend that Longbourn's living would fall vacant next year."

"I see your purpose." Thomas grinned. "You hope to install a curate at Hunsford and assume the living here yourself. Clever man—escaping the oversight of your patroness whilst retaining the income. I applaud your good sense. My father is not so interfering."

Mr. Collins visibly relaxed and beamed. "I am very pleased that you understand," he said warmly. "I shall leave the remainder of that discussion for later, as your father suggested."

"A perfectly amiable plan. Now, tell us more of yourself." Thomas leaned forward with interest.

Mr. Collins nodded. "What would you wish to know?"

"Everything, sir," Jane responded. "We knew our father had relations, but we know nothing of them. Anything you share is new to us."

"Well," he said slowly, considering his words, "my father dwelt in Essex on a small farm that yielded a modest five hundred pounds per annum. My mother was also raised in the village near there. They had known one another all their lives and married when they came of age. My mother's family has long since passed to their reward, and my father's parents died before he married."

Mr. Collins detailed his upbringing with pride, attributing his education to his father's frugality and his desire that his son live more comfortably than he had. "Upon his death, my father directed me to sell the farm and use the proceeds to take orders," he said. "I am most grateful for his sacrifices. My father was not a well-educated man, though he could read and write."

"The love of a parent for a child is precious," Mary said softly. She had approached as her cousin spoke and taken a seat beside Elizabeth.

"That it is, Miss Mary. And I had a surplus of it."

Mary flushed at his acknowledgement, and Elizabeth exchanged a glance with Jane. Could their younger sister find the parson appealing?

*It would be a sensible match, particularly if Papa grants him the Longbourn living.* One valuable living could support a family in comfort, but two would provide more than ample means—especially if they had a large family. Longbourn's living provided around four hundred pounds a year. Based on Mr. Collins's description of Rosings Park, the Hunsford living must yield at least six hundred.

*A thousand pounds a year and the interest from Mary's dowry would be sufficient,* Elizabeth mused. *And I do not doubt that Papa would help them further.* Yes, it would be ideal—but nothing could be said yet. They had only just made one another's acquaintance, and it would be some time before a decision of that magnitude could be made.

Dinner that evening demonstrated Mrs. Bennet's skill as hostess. With little notice, she ordered three courses of the finest fare their cook could manage. Mr. Collins, thoroughly pleased, consumed two servings of nearly everything—thus accounting for his portly frame.

The following morning, after breakfast, Lydia proposed a walk into Meryton. The weather was clear and fine, with no sign of impending rain on the horizon. Her sisters were quick to agree, though Thomas declined, citing the need to assist his father with repairs to a fence.

Mr. Collins asked hesitantly if he might accompany the ladies. "I have no intention of intruding on your privacy," he said haltingly. "But I should like to see more of the area, and a walk seems ideal."

"Of course you may come!" Mary cried. "I shall take particular delight in showing you our little community." She gave him a broad smile, setting aside her usual shyness.

They departed soon after the meal, donning warm cloaks and pelisses, gloves and walking boots for the journey. The well-maintained lane from Longbourn to Meryton was free of ruts or holes that might cause one to inadvertently trip. Elizabeth and Jane walked behind Kitty and Lydia, keeping a close watch on their youngest sisters, who occasionally wandered off. Mary and Mr. Collins brought up the rear, drifting further behind the others the nearer they approached Meryton.

"Stay close," Jane warned Kitty and Lydia. "I should hate to inform Father that you could not keep to the rules. He would be seriously displeased." A smile belied her seemingly stern words.

"We shall only go to the milliner's," Lydia protested. "Kitty and I will look in the window whilst you retrieve what Mama needs." Their mother had sent a list of errands for the girls to manage during their outing.

"Miss Bennet!" Someone hailed them from across the street, and the group turned to see Mr. Denny approaching from the direction of the bakery. A man in a blue coat followed closely behind.

Elizabeth had never seen a more well-favored man in her life. His dark brown hair curled slightly at his ears and the nape of his neck. His dark eyes sparkled with mischief and, though his smile was charming, it bore a touch of arrogance.

"Mr. Denny," Jane said, curtseying. "How do you do today?"

"I am very well, thank you. I promised my friend that I would introduce him to the neighborhood. Jane nodded, allowing Mr. Denny to proceed with the introduction.

"May I present Mr. George Wickham? I hope to convince him to take a commission with the regiment."

Mr. Wickham bowed and nodded to each of the sisters as Mr. Denny named them.

"This is our cousin, Mr. Collins," Jane added when the introductions concluded. "Our two youngest sisters are just there," she said, gesturing toward the milliner's shop.

The sound of approaching horses drew their attention. Elizabeth felt a thrill as she recognized Mr. Darcy and Mr. Bingley riding closer. Darcy's gaze met hers briefly before scanning the rest of the group—and she noted the moment he saw the newcomer.

His expression darkened at once before smoothing into a mask of polite indifference. He drew up his horse and dismounted.

"Wickham," he said evenly. "Imagine seeing you here, of all places. It has been some months, has it not? My cousin, Colonel Fitzwilliam, asked me to send his regards when we next met."

Elizabeth glanced at Mr. Wickham and saw his expression shift rapidly from amiability to fear. "Yes, well, the colonel is all solicitousness."

She could swear he had paled by at least two shades at the mention of the colonel.

"What brings you to Meryton? Just passing through?" Darcy's words held a subtle bite, as though the question was not truly a question at all. Elizabeth could see he did not like this Wickham fellow, and suspected that he wished to make him uncomfortable—perhaps even encourage him to leave. *He is to join the militia. Will he abandon that plan at Mr. Darcy's urging?*

"Yes, just passing through. I shall depart after I have taken a meal." Wickham swallowed. "Pray, excuse me—I shall just go to the inn now and secure a place on the post coach."

Mr. Denny frowned, clearly confused, and watched as his friend strode off without another word. "He was to join the militia," he muttered, sounding rather dazed. "Colonel Forster promised a fee for every man we brought in."

"You would do well to sever all acquaintance with that man," Darcy said, though Mr. Denny had not addressed him. "I have known Mr. Wickham since his infancy, and though he can make friends easily, he rarely manages to keep them."

Mr. Denny hesitated, then nodded. "I believe I shall return to camp," he said at last. With a bow, he turned and departed.

"Miss Bennet has invited us to Longbourn for tea, Darcy. What say you?" Mr. Bingley grinned. Jane's arm was looped through his, and he patted her hand affectionately.

"That sounds like a marvelous idea. Perhaps we might escort the ladies…" He trailed off, only then seeming to notice Mr. Collins standing nearby.

"Oh, allow me to introduce our cousin to you!" Elizabeth cried. "This is Mr. Collins. He arrived yesterday and will stay with us for a fortnight."

"It is a pleasure," Mr. Bingley said warmly.

Mr. Collins nodded and turned to Mr. Darcy. "Pardon my impertinence, sir, but are you perhaps the Mr. Darcy of Pemberley in Derbyshire?"

Elizabeth saw Mr. Darcy's jaw tightened as he gave a stiff nod.

"What a strange coincidence!" Mr. Collins looked both delighted and somewhat nervous. "I hold the Hunsford living, sir—since last summer."

"Ah." Darcy's manner changed to one of ease. "How do you find Kent, sir?"

"It is truly a lovely county, and I find the area around my parish particularly beautiful."

"May I offer you some well-intentioned advice?" Darcy's lips quirked up in a half-smile. "I am aware that, in doing so, I may seem somewhat interfering."

Elizabeth's cousin swallowed and nodded cautiously.

Darcy continued. "Do not allow my aunt to bully you. She is far too officious for her own good. Remember that she cannot reclaim the living now that it has been bestowed. Act only in *your* own best interest."

Mr. Collins visibly relaxed. Elizabeth wondered if he had feared the nephew might prove very like the aunt and thus did not entirely know how to conduct himself. "I thank you very much, Mr. Darcy. I intend to do just that."

"Let us retrieve Kitty and Lydia and complete Mama's list," Mary chimed in. "I shall be famished by the time we walk back to Longbourn!"

With the youngest girls in hand, the Bennets and their accompanying gentlemen gathered everything on Mrs. Bennet's list before setting off once more. The gentlemen led their horses, choosing to walk beside the ladies. Once again, Kitty and Lydia skipped ahead, whilst Mr. Collins and Mary strolled behind them. Mr. Bingley and Jane came next and, this time, Darcy and Elizabeth brought up the rear.

"I must tell you," Darcy said as they walked, "that I felt great surprise and dismay upon seeing Wickham in Meryton today."

"We had only made his acquaintance when you arrived," she replied. "I confess I am curious about your remarks to the gentleman."

"He is no gentleman," Darcy muttered darkly, his jaw clenched. "He is a libertine and a seducer. His habits are not fit for a lady's ears. Wickham may wear a charming countenance, but he is a snake."

"Your warning to depart seemed to be received with clarity."

"I hope so. I intend to send my man to Meryton tomorrow to make certain he is gone. Wickham leaves debts—and worse than broken hearts—wherever he travels. Meryton would be no different."

She gently squeezed his arm. "I thank you for protecting us," she murmured. "His charm was apparent even in so brief a meeting. I have no doubt he would have employed it to great effect here."

They arrived at Longbourn and joined the family for tea. There, Mr. Bingley presented the Bennets with an invitation to his upcoming ball. It would be held on the twenty-sixth of November. He then requested Jane's hand for the first and supper sets, much to Mrs. Bennet's delight. Jane accepted readily, her face aglow with love and happiness.

Darcy, too, asked Elizabeth for the supper set, with a look so tender and hopeful it warmed her heart. She accepted graciously, bestowing upon him a secret smile she hoped conveyed the depth of her feelings. *I do not care any longer,* she told herself. *I love him, and nothing will stand in the way of my happiness.*

She knew certain truths that might yet stand between them, and she prayed that if he proposed, his affection would prove stronger than the peculiarity of her circumstances.

Mr. Collins requested the first set from Mary, and after explaining—somewhat sheepishly—that he was unfamiliar with the steps, she offered to help him before the appointed evening. Pleased, he accepted, then declared that if he felt sufficiently confident, he would be honored to stand up with Miss Bennet and Miss Elizabeth as well.

When all was concluded, Elizabeth walked Mr. Darcy to the door, then stood at the window and watched as he mounted his horse and rode away, Mr. Bingley close behind.

# Chapter Twenty

*November 26, 1811*
*Longbourn*
*Elizabeth*

D readfully wet weather kept everyone indoors for four days prior to the ball. Elizabeth chafed under the confinement. She abhorred being denied her daily walk. Longbourn lacked both a portrait gallery and a ballroom in which to exercise. Pacing only served to heighten her vexation. At last, the rain ceased the day before the ball, and she eagerly escaped the house to walk out.

It came as no surprise to find Mr. Darcy atop Oakham Mount, his hands clasped behind his back as he looked out over the fields. When she stepped on a fallen branch, the sharp crack prompted him to turn.

"Miss Elizabeth." His voice, warm and low, washed over her, sending a shiver down her spine.

"Good morning, sir," she replied, moving to join him. "Are you as relieved as I to be out of doors again?"

"I share your distaste for being shut up inside," he said agreeably. "I knew you would walk out this morning, even if the paths were muddy."

She laughed merrily. "My maid will be dismayed when she sees the state of my boots and skirt," she admitted. "She is accustomed to it, and I do attempt to tidy myself before she sees my things."

"I am certain she is grateful for your consideration. Many would not take such care."

Elizabeth looked at him with curiosity. "Do you?" she asked. "I confess, I cannot picture you scraping your own boots or brushing your own coat before going indoors."

"My father had a boot scraper placed by nearly every door. And just inside, heavy rugs with stiff bristles were laid to remove the worst of the mud. A wise landlord keeps his servants content–or he risks resentment in his own halls."

Elizabeth nodded, and for a while they stood in companionable silence, their arms nearly brushing. The wind blew the hem of her gown against his legs, and though no words were spoken, the moment felt unexpectedly intimate. She longed to take his hand; her fingers twitched at her side, but she resisted the impulse.

Darcy turned toward her, and she met his gaze. "Elizabeth." Her name left him on a breath, quiet and rough with feeling, as he lifted a hand to her cheek. Slowly, he leaned down, and her eyelids fluttered shut in anticipation of his kiss—

"Ho there! Darcy!"

They sprang apart. "Blast," Darcy cursed under his breath. Then louder: "My apologies for my language, Miss Elizabeth." Turning, he raised a hand in greeting to Mr. Bingley, who had reined in his horse nearby.

"There you are! I thought to ride out with you, but when I woke, you had already gone. Good day, Miss Elizabeth." He tipped his hat, though he did not dismount.

"I shall ride back to Netherfield with you," Darcy replied.

Elizabeth could hear both resignation and regret in his voice. *Interrupted again,* she thought, with wry amusement. "I shall return to Longbourn," she said aloud. "Good day, gentlemen." Turning, she walked back down the hill, wondering whether some unseen force had conspired to ensure she and Mr. Darcy would always be interrupted at the most inconvenient moments.

---

*Darcy*

Riding back to Netherfield, Bingley suddenly demanded, "What are your intentions toward Miss Elizabeth?" He appeared angry, and his reaction confused Darcy.

"I assure you, my intentions are honorable!" he replied, a touch defensively.

"How can you say that? Have you not always spouted nonsense about duty and honor when choosing a bride?" Bingley rolled his eyes. "Do not tell me you have now changed your long-held opinions."

"I have...changed them, that is—at least, I have reconsidered them. My time in Hertfordshire has taught me that there are more important things to weigh when selecting a wife. Miss Elizabeth is...vibrant, and I find I cannot do without her."

Bingley arched a brow. "And does she feel the same?"

"If we ceased getting interrupted, I could answer that." Darcy gave his friend a pointed scowl. "I have been trying to find a private moment, but inevitably someone intrudes before I can declare my sentiments."

"So long as you are not trifling with her affections," Bingley replied, frowning still.

"You seem rather protective of her."

"I am marrying her sister."

Darcy laughed. "You have not even proposed yet! Admirable though your intentions may be, they are a touch premature. You know me, Bingley. Would I behave dishonorably with a lady?"

Bingley sighed. "No, you are a man of honor, especially where ladies are concerned. I cannot fault your conduct." He fell silent, his brow still drawn in thought.

Comprehension dawned. "This is about what we spoke of before, is it not?"

Bingley shrugged. "I do not know—yes, I suppose. I feel protective of Miss Elizabeth. It is not the same as what I feel about her sister. With Miss Elizabeth, it is as though my younger sister is in danger, and I must save her."

Darcy knew precisely what he meant. "I understand, and shall not abuse your trust."

The remainder of that day and the one following were consumed with the menial tasks Bingley wished completed before the evening of the ball. They inspected drainage near the lower fields, discussed crop rotations, and rode out to assess which sections of land might best accommodate future plantings. By the time the hour came to dress for the ball, Darcy felt exhausted. Part of him suspected that Bingley had contrived to keep him occupied—perhaps to prevent him from seeking out Miss Elizabeth.

*He really ought to resolve his feelings where she is concerned,* he thought in amusement. *I shall not tolerate such uncertainty when Elizabeth and I are married.*

He looked forward to their set that evening, and as he bathed, he contemplated the pleasure her fine eyes brought him whenever they turned in his direction. They always sparkled brightly with mirth, cleverness, challenge, or mischief. He could not say which look he most preferred—perhaps the one that seemed to hold a particular warmth meant only for him.

*Careful, man,* he cautioned himself. *You have no assurance that she feels the same. Do not misinterpret the lady's feelings.* He had always struggled in that regard. Unlike Richard, who possessed an easy confidence in society, Darcy found it difficult to catch the tone of conversation or to understand the subtleties woven into drawing room talk. Socializing left him fatigued, and over time, he had developed a decided aversion to it.

*But if she were by my side, it would be no trial. Elizabeth is intelligent enough to manage any barbs or petty slights that might come her way.* Yes, she would be a credit to the Darcy name, even if she did not belong to the first circles of society.

As the guests began to arrive, Darcy cast a final glance at his appearance in the mirror one last time before descending the stairs. Thankful that he was not obliged to stand in the receiving line with Bingley and the Hursts, he positioned himself near the ballroom doors—close enough to observe the arrivals and see the moment Elizabeth arrived.

The Longs, the Gouldings, the Lucases...still no Bennets. Darcy waited, barely suppressing his impatience, as one red coat after another entered the hall, followed by two or three more families. At long last, he caught sight of Jane Bennet on the arm of her brother as they stepped into the room.

Mr. Collins and Miss Mary followed behind, and then—he saw his Elizabeth, her gloved hand resting lightly on her father's arm, Mrs. Bennet on his other. She looked around the room, and Darcy flattered himself that she searched for *him*. When their gazes met and her countenance first relaxed, then brightened, he knew he had the right of it.

Pushing away from the wall, he made his way to their side. "Mr. Bennet, Mrs. Bennet, Miss Elizabeth, how do you do this evening?" He spoke cheerfully, bowing to the trio.

"We are well, sir," Mr. Bennet replied. "We have looked forward to this evening."

"I hope you enjoy it," Darcy said sincerely.

Elizabeth separated from her parents, who drifted toward the Lucases and were quickly engaged in conversation.

"Miss Elizabeth," he said, addressing her. "You look lovely this evening."

"I thank you, sir." She blushed, bit her lip, and cast her eyes briefly aside. "Have you kept busy since we last met?"

"Bingley has kept me more occupied than I would wish. I could not ride to Oakham Mount this morning." He hoped the meaning behind his words was understood.

"I, too, was unable to walk out." Leaning closer, she whispered so only he might hear. "I feared I had left you waiting. I am pleased that was not the case."

His heart gave a sudden leap. *She cares. I knew it.* "I am looking forward to our dance later," he replied.

"Have you secured partners for the rest of your sets?" she asked lightly.

"I have not, though there is no shortage of partners." He nodded toward the crowded room. "Mrs. Hurst saw fit to invite all four-and-twenty prominent families in the area, along with the officers."

"And my neighbors have a surplus of daughters, as I am sure you noticed." She chuckled, the rich sound washing over him and making his heart pound.

"It will be torture to watch you stand up with other gentlemen." His impulsive words he did not regret, for she drew in a breath and dropped her gaze to her slippers. When she lifted her eyes to him, they were alight with feeling—hope, longing, perhaps even desire—tempered by something more elusive. Was it uncertainty? Or fear?

The first set began to form, and John Lucas appeared at her side to claim the set. Darcy watched with barely concealed jealousy as he led her away to take up their positions for the dance.

He looked around frantically, approaching Miss Lucas and requesting her hand. She accepted, and they joined the line two positions down from Elizabeth.

*At least I shall be near her whilst she dances.* But he would make every effort to give Miss Lucas his full attention. It would be abominably rude for him to ignore his partner in favor of another.

And so, the evening wore on until the supper set was announced. Darcy had danced with a number of different ladies, each seemingly gratified by his attention. Thankfully, none sought to flatter him with compliments.

At last, the supper set was called, and he offered his arm to Elizabeth, escorting her to the floor. The slow, stately figures of the dance allowed ample opportunity for conversation, yet neither spoke. Instead, their eyes remained fixed on one another as they moved through each step, looking away only when the movements of the dance made it necessary.

Without uttering a word, they conveyed feelings more than any dialogue could express, and Darcy absorbed every moment. She was, to him, the most captivating woman he had ever known. Her perfectly arranged curls framed her face, drawing attention to her fine cheekbones and her luminous complexion. Her dark eyes held him fast, and he found himself imagining the taste of a kiss placed on her cupid bow lips.

The dance ended, yet it had felt more intimate than any he had known. Darcy had never danced the waltz, but he doubted it could surpass what he had just experienced. With his determination to propose now fully restored, he led Miss Elizabeth to the supper room.

"Jane seems very happy," Elizabeth remarked as they ate white soup.

"Bingley as well. They are a good match." He moved his foot under the table until it came to rest lightly against the side of her slipper.

Elizabeth drew in a soft breath and glanced at him sidelong. She did not withdraw. Instead, she lifted her foot and pressed it gently on the toe of his boot. Darcy's pulse surged, and he took a measured spoonful soup to keep a love-struck grin from taking over his face.

Halfway through the meal, they were obliged to change conversation partners, and Darcy found himself speaking with Mrs. Goulding, the wife of a nearby landowner. She was of an age with Mrs. Bennet, and informed him that she had lived in Meryton all her life, never having ventured even so far as London. He was not required to say much—an occasional nod or murmur of agreement sufficed to satisfy her.

His anticipation to rejoin Elizabeth could scarcely be disguised, and as the ladies rose to excuse themselves, he leaned discreetly toward her. "Will you speak with me on the terrace?"

She nodded. "I shall go there directly."

Darcy waited only until the ladies left the room. He offered a vague excuse, then slipped through a side door. The gentlemen might linger over their port, but he had more urgent business. His lady awaited.

# Chapter Twenty-One

*November 26, 1811*
*Netherfield Ball*
*Elizabeth*

Elizabeth had retrieved a shawl from the retiring room, anticipating the chill of the night air on the terrace. The ladies had withdrawn to the large drawing room and were, even now, displaying their various talents for the assembled guests. Elizabeth slipped away as Mary took her place at the instrument. No one would miss her absence—certainly not when compared to her sister's performance.

"Elizabeth."

She turned as Mr. Darcy approached, pulling the shawl more tightly around her shoulders. He came to her side and, as he had on Oakham Mount, lifted a hand to her cheek. Though he wore gloves, the warmth of his touch reached her, and she leaned into it, grateful for the comfort against the cold. "I do not believe anyone will interrupt us this time," he said, his voice thick with feeling, "but just in case, I shall get straight to the point."

He dropped his hand and took hers instead. Then, before she had time to catch her breath, he sank to one knee. "Dearest Elizabeth, I love you—most ardently. I did not come to Hertfordshire expecting to fall in love, but I have. Your beauty and grace are surpassed only by your wit, vivacity, compassion, and zeal for life. My heart is yours and will belong to no other. Please, I beg you—end my agony and consent to be my wife."

Her heart leapt. Had she not longed for this moment? Had she not rehearsed her reply again and again, all the while hoping he might overcome the strange circumstances of her life and love her still?

"I love you, too," she said with quiet intensity. "And I long to accept your offer. But first, I must acquaint you with my...history, I suppose, is the best word."

His brow furrowed. "Shall we sit?" he suggested. "If you are cold, we might go to the library."

"I would prefer not to be overheard. My story...well, it is best not shared widely." She moved to a stone bench a short distance from the door and sat. He followed, keeping hold of her hand.

"Speak, my dear. I am anxious."

Elizabeth drew a deep breath. "I was not born a Bennet," she said simply. "No, do not speak. Let me tell you everything, and then you may ask questions."

Darcy remained silent as she recounted all that she knew of her past. When she finished, she added softly, "I have tried to remember more, but the recollections are just out of reach."

For a moment, neither spoke. Slowly, he released her hand, and she felt the loss at once, fearing the worst. But then his hand rose to her temple, to the place where the faint scar lay concealed in her hair. He brushed the strands aside and touched it lightly.

"It is difficult to see when my hair is up," she said nervously. "The maids have learned to disguise it as best as they can."

"They do admirable work. I had no idea it was there—and I know your appearance very well." She glanced up and caught the teasing glint in his eyes.

"Then...?" she asked, hardly daring to finish the question.

"This changes nothing," he said fervently. "I care not for fortune and connection—not any longer. You are a Bennet in every way that matters, and they are your family. That is more than enough for me."

"Truly? Oh, Fitzwilliam, I was so afraid. But I could not begin our life based on a lie. I knew I would rather lose you forever than conceal the truth."

He raised his hands to her cheeks, and before she could speak again, he kissed her. Her first kiss was everything she had ever dreamed: tender, gentle, exhilarating. When he drew back, she felt a pang of regret—and a secret wish that he might kiss her once more.

"May I have your answer?" he asked solemnly. "Do I write to my solicitor tomorrow, or no?"

"Yes!" she cried, laughing as she threw her arms around his neck. "Yes, sir, I shall marry you."

A sound interrupted them, and they quickly drew apart. Mr. Bingley stepped onto the terrace, Jane on his arm. At the sight of the pair on the bench, he paused and frowned—though it was only mock disapproval.

"I believe Miss Elizabeth ought to be returned to her mother," he said seriously. "I have something to discuss with Miss Bennet."

Darcy rose and assisted Elizabeth to her feet. "We shall leave you to it," he replied with equal gravity. As they walked inside, he leaned down and whispered, "At least this time, we were not interrupted."

Elizabeth laughed softly. "It was a near thing. Let us give them their moment. We can announce our engagement tomorrow."

Darcy agreed. Just before the dancing resumed, Mr. Bingley and Jane shared their own happy news. Their betrothal was met with cheers and heartfelt congratulations. Mrs. Bennet dabbed at her eyes. "Oh, Mr. Bennet," she sighed, "God has been very good to us."

"He has indeed, my dear," her husband replied warmly. "They will be very happy. Of that I am certain."

By the time the Bennet's carriage rumbled off toward Longbourn, the sky had begun to lighten. The mood within was subdued, but content. Everyone was exhausted, and Jane, yawning frequently, could not suppress her smile.

Elizabeth fell into bed, dreaming of her own happiness. Soon, her own story would begin—a life with a gentleman who not only offered her security despite her uncertain past, but who loved her deeply. And she loved him. *Life*, she thought drowsily, *could not be any more perfect.*

---

*Darcy*

Darcy slept fitfully. Snippets of conversation mingled with Elizabeth's story about her origins, drifting through his dreams. As his mind worked over the fragments, something shifted into place. He sat up abruptly, gasping for breath.

"Not a Bennet!" he cried. "Elizabeth is not a Bennet." Did Bingley have it right all along?

The sun was already high, and one glance at the clock confirmed it was past eleven. He knew at once that he could not delay. Bingley needed to hear this.

Without bothering to dress, he threw on his banyan and slippers and left his chamber in haste. Crossing to the family wing, he banged on Bingley's door. "Open the door, Charles!" he called urgently. "I need to speak with you at once."

Bingley opened it, looking every bit as disheveled as Darcy. His hair was unkempt, and his tone was cross..

"Confound it, Darcy!" he said irritably. "We were not abed until nearly dawn. What is so important it cannot wait a few hours more?"

"She is not a Bennet," Darcy said in a low, fervent voice, leaning closer to avoid being overheard.

Bingley froze, his mouth falling open. "Come in," he said, stepping aside. Closing the door, he led Darcy to a pair of chairs before the hearth. "Explain."

"I proposed to Elizabeth last night. She would not accept until she had told me about her past. Bingley, she is not a Bennet. They found her in Derbyshire, very near to the Yorkshire border. She had a head wound and remembered nothing but her name, and that she was eight years old."

Bingley stared at him, stupefied. "Is that all? It is not enough to prove anything."

"She has a box of her belongings. I have not seen it myself, but she says it contains a brooch bearing a family crest."

He watched as Bingley buried his face in his hands, a shuddering breath shaking his shoulders. "It seems impossible," he said, voice thick with emotion. "But if she is Elizabeth Montrose...well, then a terrifying chapter of both our lives may finally come to an end."

Darcy leaned forward anxiously. "Will you tell me the whole of it?" he asked.

"It is a grisly story, Darcy. My father was one of Mr. Montrose's business partners. I spent a great deal of time with the family. Our mothers were dearest friends, and after Mama died, Mrs. Montrose tried her best to offer herself as a substitute. 'Never a replacement,' she often said."

He drew another unsteady breath. "And then it ended. The entire family was found dead, murdered in their beds—except for Mr. Montrose. The culprit struck him down in his study." Gasping, he choked back sob. "I found him, Darcy. I have never been able to forget what I saw. Their daughter, Elizabeth, was the only one not discovered in the house. If Miss Elizabeth Bennet *is* Elizabeth Montrose..."

"A blow to the head could explain her lack of memory," Darcy pondered.

"How could anyone do such a thing? And to children? Poor Harry." Overcome with emotion, Bingley stood abruptly and crossed to the window. "Should I tell her what I know?" he asked. "Does she not deserve the truth, even if she chooses to do nothing with it? And she has a grandmother still living. I sent out inquiries after our last discussion."

"Montrose. Surely you do not mean Lady Maude Montrose?" Darcy recollected the name. His father had spoken of the family more than once, usually during lectures on the importance of duty. Lord Montrose had disowned his younger son when he chose to enter trade. His elder son, Viscount Marston, remained a dutiful heir and served as an example of proper conduct.

"Lord Montrose—the son, not the father—died recently," Bingley continued. "I have not read the papers since, but I learned that the Dowager Countess Lady Montrose has offered a reward for information regarding her granddaughter. She was discreet, made no public spectacle of it, and so I never knew until..." He shrugged helplessly. "What am I to do? And Caroline is coming! She and Elizabeth were the best of friends."

"You must tell Elizabeth," Darcy advised. "As you said, she deserves to know. If she wishes to seek more information, we may be able to assist."

Bingley nodded, his resolve appearing to solidify. "Well, I am awake now. Would it be improper to call upon my betrothed so soon after such a late night?"

Darcy chuckled. "Miss Bennet will be pleased by the attention. Have you a gift to bring her?"

"As a matter of fact, I do." Bingley padded to his bedside table and opened a drawer. "I found this hair comb in Meryton. I shall take it to Jane directly."

Scarcely an hour later, the gentlemen mounted their horses and made their way to Longbourn. Darcy, too, bore a gift for Elizabeth—though it was but a trifle: a note expressing the sentiments he had not yet spoken aloud. He intended to send to Pemberley for a selection of jewels he thought would suit her. His grandmother's betrothal ring would look perfect on her hand.

When they arrived, the family had already gathered in the parlor. Bingley went directly to Jane and greeted her with a kiss upon the back of her hand. Darcy caught Elizabeth's eye and gave her a subtle wink, but turned first to her father. "May I have a word in your study, sir?" he asked.

Mr. Bennet startled, but nodded. They stood and withdrew. Once within the privacy of his study, Mr. Bennet gestured toward a pair of chairs arranged before the hearth, where a low fire crackled gently. "Come, Mr. Darcy—sit. What is it you wish to say?"

"What I must tell you is somewhat complex," he hedged. "First, your daughter, Miss Elizabeth, accepted an offer of marriage from me last evening. She did so after she confided her past to me."

Mr. Bennet blanched and sank heavily into his chair. "She told you and yet you still want her?" he asked hoarsely. "I have feared this moment since the day we found her. Tell me, Mr. Darcy, what could have befallen a child that rendered her memory void?"

"That is the more complex part I spoke of." Darcy hesitated. "Bingley believes he knows her true identity."

Mr. Bennet gaped at him. "Does he mean to expose all that we have kept hidden?" he whispered, his face awash with agony. We never intended deceit, only protected her as best we could. She is our daughter and holds the same place in our hearts as every one of our own."

"Rest easy, sir. Neither of us wishes to rob you of your daughter. But we both feel she has the right to know the truth, and to do with that knowledge as she sees fit. Her history is more tragic than you may imagine." He paused. "And she has a grandmother still living."

"Does she? And has this lady searched for her grandchild? We have heard nothing here." Mr. Bennet sat straighter, his tone edged with unease.

"Bingley assures me the circumstances are unusual. I do not know the details, but Lady Montrose *has* been looking for her granddaughter."

A peer, then. Mr. Bennet slumped back into his chair, face drawn. "I could not bear it if she took my Lizzy."

"I cannot begin to speculate what Lady Montrose may do should she acknowledge Elizabeth. But surely, sir, do we not owe it to your daughter to offer her this piece of herself?"

Shuddering, Mr. Bennet nodded slowly. He tugged the bellpull; when a footman appeared, he bid him summon Elizabeth and Mr. Bingley.

The pair arrived a moment later—Elizabeth looking bemused and Bingley appearing grave.

"Have a seat. This may take a while." Mr. Bennet indicated a table near the window, arranged more suitably for group conversation. Darcy remained standing but stepped to Elizabeth's side and placed a hand on her shoulder.

"Sir, I have not yet given you my consent to marry my daughter, and until such time as I do, I expect you to behave with proper decorum." Darcy blanched and withdrew his hand at once.

"Papa!" Elizabeth cried, nudging him with her elbow.

Mr. Darcy inclined his head. "Well, sir? May we hope for your blessing?"

Mr. Bennet cast them both a long, pointed look. "And you, Lizzy... Are you not out of your senses to be accepting this man?"

"No, Papa," she laughed, nudging him once more. "I am honored by his proposal. I know we will be so very happy together."

Mr. Bennet sighed in resignation. "Very well. Let me be the first to wish you joy. I own myself surprised, but I am gratified that my Lizzy has chosen a respectable gentleman...even if he is a trifle stiff." That earned a round of laughter.

"Now, returning to the other matter, Mr. Darcy, why do you not tell Elizabeth what you told me? And Mr. Bingley, you may speak when his knowledge fails."

Darcy spoke plainly, recounting Bingley's strange behavior since his introduction to Elizabeth. He described the epiphany he had experienced that very morning; and then his friend took over.

"I believe you are Elizabeth Montrose," Bingley said, his tone firm. "You resemble your mother...a second mama to me after mine died." He fell silent and swallowed. Darcy was certain his friend was struggling not to reach up and tug at his cravat. After a moment, Bingley said gently, "There is no easy way to tell you, Miss Elizabeth. Your family was murdered; everyone in the house was killed. You vanished that same night. From what Darcy has told me, I suspect you were meant to be amongst them."

Elizabeth gasped, her hand rising to her hidden scar. Her gaze darted to Darcy. "You told him?" she asked incredulously, strangling a sob. "That was shared in confidence, sir."

"Pray, forgive me, Miss Elizabeth. I did—but only because I believed it might help bring clarity to the questions that have long plagued you. I meant no betrayal, only to aid in the discovery of who you truly are."

"Who... Did they ever find the culprit?"

"No. I...my father was never the same, and we left Yorkshire a few years later. Darcy says you have evidence...something that would identify you."

Elizabeth nodded, her wide-eyed confusion softening her features, rendering her younger than her twenty years. "Could it be?" she asked. "You could be mistaken. Why has my family not searched for me?"

She rose. "I shall fetch the box." Elizabeth hurried from the room.

The gentlemen sat in strained silence until her return a few minutes later. She crossed to her father's desk, placed the small chest upon it, and lifted the lid. After moving aside several folded papers, she drew forth a stained blue gown and something wrapped in a handkerchief. Slowly, she unfolded the gown. It was small, a silent testament to her slight frame, even in childhood. Then, with careful hands, she removed the linen covering to reveal a finely wrought cameo brooch. She cradled it in her palm and turned it toward them.

"M for Montrose," Bingley choked, eyes shining as he blinked rapidly, unmistakably near tears. "Oh, Elizabeth, I thought I would never see you again."

# Chapter Twenty-Two

*November 27, 1811*
*Longbourn*
*Elizabeth*

She ignored the informality; it felt strangely *right* to hear Mr. Bingley use her given name so freely.

"I have seen that before," Mr. Bingley said, once he had regained his composure. "Aunt Amelia wore it nearly every day. It was a gift from her mother-in-law, the only Montrose who would speak with her husband after the...their marriage. I understand that, though Viscount Marston kept his distance, he disapproved of his father's harshness and sought to remain in contact with his Montrose family through his mother."

"Is it a brooch then?" Elizabeth asked. "I confess, it has puzzled me exceedingly. See the hinges there? And yet there is a clasp on the back."

"I cannot say. Though I recall Mrs. Montrose wearing it, I do not remember whether she wore it as a brooch or something more. The crest, though, is unmistakable. Mr. Montrose kept a coat of arms in his study—a reminder, he called it, of where he came from, and that being born to privilege did not ensure kindness." Mr. Bingley smiled faintly.

"And now we come to the crux of the matter," Papa said, leaning forward. "Mr. Bingley informed Mr. Darcy that you have family living; a grandmother who, from the name I was given, is a member of the peerage. It may be, Lizzy, that your hand is no longer mine to give."

"The Dowager Countess Lady Maude Montrose, wife of the late Arthur Montrose, Earl of Montrose." Darcy spoke matter-of-factly, his features devoid of expression. "Bingley says she has been searching for you."

"The choice is yours, my dear. If you wish to pursue this hidden chapter of your life, I shall stand by your decision. I only ask that you not forget your old papa and the family you have here." His eyes appeared damp, and he turned away, patting his pocket in search of a handkerchief.

Elizabeth did not know what to say. She remained silent, weighing each thought as she began to tally the advantages and drawbacks of meeting this unknown paternal grandmother. A part of her longed to meet her. Through her, she might learn who she had been before becoming Elizabeth Bennet. "If I were to pursue knowledge," she began, "how would we proceed?"

"We have not yet settled on a plan," Mr. Darcy said. "I suppose with Miss Bennet soon to marry, you might accompany her to town to purchase her wedding clothes."

"That is an idea, her father agreed. You could stay with the Gardiners. They are coming in December for Christmas. I shall write to your uncle Gardiner directly, informing him of our discovery and asking that he make discreet inquiries." He paused, his eyes meeting his daughter's. "I should like to have one more Christmas with my girls," he added quietly.

"Miss Bennet—Jane—and I have not spoken of a date for our wedding, though I imagine it will be March before we say our vows." Mr. Bingely smiled. No doubt his thoughts had turned to his betrothed, who waited for them in the other room.

"And what of my own betrothal?" she asked. "What does this mean for us?"

Darcy moved to kneel beside her. "As far as I am concerned, we will be man and wife—the only question is timing." I do not think your grandmother will have any cause to object to our match. Marston Hall lies not far from Pemberley. She will be pleased to have you so near, I am certain. Still, it may be prudent to keep our happy news quiet for now."

Elizabeth gazed adoringly into his eyes, her heart full. "That sounds delightful," she murmured.

Mr. Bennet cleared his throat. "I propose we depart before Twelfth Night. Bingley, have you any acquaintance with Lady Montrose?"

"I have never met her, but my father did. I can use that as a pretext to request an audience." Bingley nodded with resolve. "It is not an easy subject. I can only hope she will."

Darcy nodded and rose. "Then we have our course. We shall depart for London after Christmas. The ladies will stay with the Gardiners, pending their invitation and permission. Bingley will arrange for an introduction between Elizabeth and her grandmother."

"And once the introduction has been made?" Elizabeth asked. "What if she will not allow me to see anyone I love again?" Her voice trembled, and panic crept in at the thought.

"We shall address that *if* it ever comes to pass," Darcy assured her. "From all I have heard, Lady Montrose is known for fairness and good sense."

Feeling a little of the tightness in her chest ease, she nodded.

"Off with you, now," Mr. Bennet waved his hand at them dismissively. "No doubt Jane wonders what is keeping you, Bingley. As for you two," giving the newly engaged couple another pointed look, you may walk out in the garden. I dare say Lizzy is in more need of fresh air to restore her spirits than my delightful company."

"Thank you, Papa." Elizabeth rose and carefully placed her treasures back into the chest. In haste, she carried it to her chambers, secreting it once more beneath the bed frame. Only as she fastened her pelisse did she realize she might show the drawings from her dreams to Mr. Bingley. Perhaps he could say whether they were memories or mere imaginings.

Joining Darcy at the front door, she took his hand and led him outside to the small wilderness that bordered Longbourn's gardens. They walked to the farthest wall and settled upon an intricately carved bench beneath the wide, bare branches of an old oak tree.

"How do you feel, my love?" Darcy wrapped an arm around her, and she leaned into his chest, relishing the sense of security she felt in his embrace. "You have had quite an upheaval today."

"I hardly know what I ought to feel," she admitted. "I suppose I should be grateful that the mystery surrounding my abandonment has, at least in part, been solved. Yet I have some trepidation, for Mr. Bingley said the culprit was never found. Ought I to fear for my life?"

"It is more likely that the assailant, whoever he was, is long gone." He ran his hand slowly up and down her arm. "We may never learn his motives, or what drove him to descend to such cruelty."

"The whole affair is dreadful. Though Mr. Bingley did not linger on the details, I could see that it weighed heavily upon him."

"He once confided in me...he was the one that found your father. That would be distressing for any man, but Bingley was only twelve-years-old at the time."

Elizabeth drew in a sharp breath. "Poor Mr. Bingley," she whispered. "No wonder he seemed so deeply affected. And yet he spoke of it only with concern for me. I cannot begin to imagine the horror of such a discovery." She paused, then added quietly, "I hope I shall find a way to express to him what that means to me—that he carried the burden of such a memory, and still welcomed the idea of my return."

Darcy nodded, pressing his lips to her temple. "He remembers you fondly."

"I am more eager than ever to meet Miss Bingley," she said after a moment. "Will she recall me, do you think?"

"Bingley says you and Caroline were the best of friends. Whether she recognizes you remains to be seen, but she is expected to arrive on the first of December, if I am not mistaken."

"And her brother will waste no time dragging her to Longbourn—just as he did with Mrs. Hurst."

Darcy laughed, giving her shoulder a light squeeze. "I dare say your reception will be warmer this time. Miss Bingley is not so entirely wrapped up in herself." Darcy tightened his hold on her and placed a kiss upon the side of her head. "I intend to act every bit the besotted betrothed, come what may," he said with a low growl near her ear. "These weeks of torment must end, and it can only be so if I am permitted the full rights and privileges of a man desperately in love with a beautiful woman."

"I look forward to it," she replied saucily, pulling away just enough to meet his eyes. "Thank you."

"For what?" He wrinkled his brow in confusion.

"For loving me even in the most uncertain of circumstances. For refusing to be driven away by all that remains unknown." She beamed and reached up to caress his face. "I love you very much."

"And I love you, dearest Elizabeth." The kiss they shared exceeded anything Elizabeth had ever experienced. She knew without a doubt that whatever was to come, everything would turn out right in the end.

*We can face anything together,* she told herself. *Even an uncertain future.*

---

*Mr. Bennet*

Thomas Bennet sank into his chair once the door to his study had closed behind the three young people. His worst fears were coming to pass, and he could do little but yield to the unforeseen turn of events. Who could have imagined that the new tenant of Netherfield Park would carry the past in his wake?

He and Fanny had often discussed what they might do, should anyone come forward to claim Elizabeth. He knew that she would be devastated to learn that their adopted child's true identity had at last been discovered. From the very beginning, she had taken Elizabeth under her wing, coaxing her into good humor when shadows disturbed her peace, instructing her carefully in all that a young woman ought to know to become a well-respected woman, a good wife and mother, and more besides.

Fanny had taken it almost as a personal affront that anyone could so mistreat a helpless little girl, and she had made it her duty to ensure Elizabeth never felt deprived of love again. None of the other children suffered from the addition of one more to the nursery. They had welcomed her with open arms, readily accepting their new sister and the account their parents had given of her origins. Elizabeth herself had never bothered to challenge the tale. Even Jane knew nothing of the truth. Thomas had long believed it was because dwelling on the past brought Elizabeth only distress.

*And now I must tell Fanny that, after Christmas, Elizabeth's grandmother may take her away. And if the lady forbids the marriage, we may never see our girl again.* He did not believe Lady Montrose would object to Mr. Darcy. Indeed, who could? Though he bore no title, he was, by every account, a wealthy man of excellent character and connections. Someone had once remarked he was the grandson of an earl. That would make him equal to Elizabeth in station.

Sighing, he rose slowly and left his study. He walked to the parlor and paused in the doorway, taking a moment to admire the familiar scene of domestic contentment. Kitty and Lydia sat bent over a game of spillikins, both focused intently. His youngest daughter had ever possessed a competitive spirit and was not above bending the rules in pursuit of victory. By the window, Mary and Collins conversed earnestly over Wordsworth. Jane and her betrothed were nowhere to be seen, and he hoped that his son had accompanied the happy couple as chaperone.

"Mrs. Bennet," he said quietly, "will you come with me? There is something I must tell you." His wife looked up from her needlework, blinking owlishly.

"Very well," she murmured.

He saw the worry settle on her features, and, not for the first time, marveled that he had married a woman who understood him so well. Of course, more than twenty years of marriage had afforded her ample opportunity. She set her work aside and went directly to him.

He took her hand tenderly, lifted it to his lips, and kissed it. Without letting go, he led her down the hall and into his study. Holding her hand was such a simple gesture, yet the light brush of their ungloved fingers still sent a thrill through him, even after all these years.

Closing the door, he crossed to a large armchair by the fire. Sinking into its deep cushions, he drew his wife into his lap. She nestled against his chest, pulled his arms securely around her.

"What is wrong, Thomas?" she asked at length, after they sat in silence for a time.

He drew in a deep breath and let it out in a long exhale. "We have had an...interesting turn of events." Waiting for a moment to delay the true subject, he added, "Mr. Darcy has proposed to our Lizzy. She has accepted."

"Oh, that is wonderful!" She turned to face him, her face alight with joy. "I knew she would do well."

He smiled, though there was sadness in it, and patted the hand resting on his chest. "Yes, she is as beautiful as Jane and twice as clever as Thomas. But there is more. It seems Mr. Bingley and Mr. Darcy have discovered her identity."

Mrs. Bennet stilled. "You mean her true identity, do you not?" she asked, her voice suddenly subdued. "Oh, Mr. Bennet! What will happen now?"

He felt her begin to tremble and held her more tightly, pressing a kiss on her cheek. Fanny had always been excitable, but over the years she had learned to temper her natural boisterousness. Having the security of a settled home had done much to soothe her nerves. Her father had not been a wealthy man, and money had too often been a source of worry in her youth.

"It will be well, my love," he murmured. "We have formed a plan. You see, she has relations who have missed her." Quickly, he related all that he, the gentlemen—and Elizabeth—had discussed.

"But what if we never see her again?" Mrs. Bennet's lips trembled, and tears gathered in her eyes. "This relation did not want her then. Why must they take her now?"

"Dearest, we do not yet know what is to come. Bingley says that Lady Montrose has been seeking information about her for some time. Is it right to withhold the truth from someone who may love Elizabeth as dearly as we do?" He kissed her once more, hoping it might calm her rising distress.

It did, and after a moment, she grew quieter. "You are right, of course," she said sadly. "It is a comfort to know that she was loved before the tragedy. I have often been haunted by thoughts of what might have caused Lizzy to be wandering the road that day. It is a sad tale, but at least she knew love before she came to us."

"You have raised her beautifully, my dearest Fanny. Her grandmother can have no cause to repine. I am certain she will offer her gratitude rather than grief, and instead of depriving Elizabeth of the family she has known—and depriving us of *her*—she will wish to preserve the connection. Besides, our Lizzy would be leaving us soon in any case, even without this revelation."

Fanny groaned. "Yes, and Derbyshire is so far away! I can console myself knowing that Jane will be nearby—for the nonce." Shifting into a more comfortable position, she turned a stubborn gaze upon her husband. "I shall be going to London," she declared. "And I shall be part of whatever scheme is afoot to reunite Elizabeth with Lady Montrose."

"I never once considered leaving you behind. As it stands, you must assist Jane with her wedding clothes. I would be quite useless surrounded by lace, bits, and baubles." They chuckled and held one another a little closer.

Content to take comfort in each other's presence, they remained in the study until Elizabeth came in search of them. The gentlemen had taken their leave, promising to return the next morning. Mr. Bingley had intended to go to town on business but resolved to delay his departure until they were all removed to town at the end of December.

Later that same day, Mr. Collins knocked lightly at his cousin's door. At Mr. Bennet's call, he entered, shifting from foot to foot with nervous energy. "Cousin," he began, "the time draws near for my return to Kent. I should like to speak with you regarding the Longbourn living before I depart. I do apologize for the delay."

"You have been rather distracted." Mr. Bennet replied with a wry smile. "My Mary appears to enjoy your company well enough."

Mr. Collins flushed and stared at his shoes. "Yes—and I like her very much indeed. But it is too soon to ask for more than a formal courtship. We are still becoming acquainted."

"So, tell me then, what is this conversation about, sir? My daughter or the living in my preferment?" Mr. Bennet gestured to a chair, and his cousin took a seat.

"Both, really. I do wish to court Miss Mary, but I also desire the living. Kent has its advantages, to be sure, but I chafe under my patroness's...domineering manner. If I can secure the Longbourn living, I shall hire a curate to tend Hunsford, and perhaps remove to Hertfordshire once your current incumbent retires in the summer."

Mr. Bennet had observed his cousin closely during his visit. Though long-winded, he did not seem to be a fool, and Bennet trusted that the man would make a respectable clergyman. "I see no reason to deny you the living," he said at length. "As for Mary, let us ask what she wants, hmm?"

Mary was summoned, and when her father inquired whether she would be willing to enter into a formal courtship, she agreed with marked enthusiasm.

"That is settled, then." The happy couple left the room, and Mr. Bennet leaned back in his chair with a heavy sigh. "I pray that no one else comes to take my Kitty away. I do not think I can bear losing another daughter today." Though he felt no small measure of joy in seeing his dear girls so well provided for, Mr. Bennet could not deny that the prospect of their leaving—one by one—brought him sadness.

# Chapter
# Twenty-Three

*December 1, 1811*
*Netherfield Park*
*Elizabeth*

Elizabeth adjusted her gown, her fingers lingering on the Montrose brooch that secured her fichu. The carriage had just arrived at Netherfield. When the door opened, a footman assisted Jane down first. Elizabeth followed, drawing a deep breath as she ascended the steps.

Today, Caroline and her betrothed were expected. It had been agreed that their first meeting should take place at Netherfield, where any potential shock on Caroline's part might be more easily contained. Elizabeth had argued that the lady might not recognize her, but Charles, as he had asked her to call him, had laughed and insisted his sister would know her at once.

In the days following the discovery of her origins, the household had been filled with discussion. On the evening of the twenty-seventh of November, Elizabeth had at last confided in Jane. Her sister had been suitably shocked and distressed, embracing her warmly and kissing her cheek. Mama and Papa had informed Mary and Thomas, though they decided to wait before telling the two youngest daughters until matters had settled somewhat.

Elizabeth had also shared her dreams with Bingley, and confirmed that they were, indeed, memories. "You were a rambunctious child," he had chortled. "Caroline thought you would break your neck climbing fences."

And now, the moment had come. Today, she would meet the lady who had, by Bingley's account, once been her dearest friend.

"Good morning, my dear!" Bingley stepped forward and took Jane's hand. "You look lovely."

Jane blushed. "Thank you, sir. If you continue to flatter me so each day, I shall come to think far too well of myself."

Darcy greeted Elizabeth in a like manner, and the four soon settled on two settees arranged before the fire. The ladies' maid, Sally, sat quietly in a distant corner, doing her utmost to remain unobtrusive.

"When is Miss Bingley expected?" Elizabeth asked when they were comfortable before the roaring blaze.

"She said they would arrive before tea. It cannot be more than half an hour now." Mr. Bingley glanced at his pocket watch. "Yes, they intended to leave London early. They must be very near."

"Shall I ask Mrs. Nicholls to prepare tea?" Jane smiled, though it was somewhat strained. After Mrs. Hurst's cold reception, she worried that Miss Bingley would likewise find her wanting. The Hursts had kept to their rooms whenever the Bennets called, and Elizabeth wondered whether their manners might improve were she introduced as the granddaughter of an earl.

"Yes, by all means. It will be your right and duty soon enough." He grinned and kissed Jane's hand, catching it as she rose to give the orders.

"Have you written to Miss Darcy?" Elizabeth asked her betrothed.

"I have. I did not mention the news. Instead, I teased her and said I had something of great importance to tell her when next we meet. I imagine I shall have an express demanding information before the week is out."

They chuckled together. "You are so serious most of the time, sir, I had begun to wonder whether you possessed a sense of humor. I am pleased to see that it exists. Has it rusted from disuse, perhaps?" She raised a brow with mock severity, relishing the thrill of his answering grin.

"I have had much cause to be dismal in recent years. I should still be so, were it not for you."

"Careful, sir. With such praise, I may begin to believe I am quite without fault." She gave him a saucy wink, delighted by the depth of his love.

"Then you will be in the same situation as your sister. I have no intention of ceasing my efforts to praise you, and Bingley will do the same with Miss Bennet. You had best grow accustomed to it."

"That will not prove difficult." In truth, she had known love from her Bennet family for a long time, but this was something altogether different. Darcy's love completed her—made her feel truly whole, save for the small corner of her heart still left unfulfilled until the past was at last resolved.

"A carriage is coming up the drive, sir." Mr. Griggs bowed as he spoke, then withdrew to await the arrival of guests at the front door.

"I had best go greet them." Bingley stood and left the room.

Elizabeth's nerves grew with every delicate tick of the gilt clock on the mantelpiece.. She grasped Darcy's hand and took comfort in his steady touch.

At last, the door to the drawing room opened, and Bingley entered, followed by a handsome, dark-haired gentleman with a beautiful woman on his arm. Elizabeth at once noted a resemblance to Charles. Dressed in a fashionable travel gown that accentuated her trim figure, Miss Caroline Bingley carried herself with confidence and poise.

*This was my dearest friend?* Elizabeth could scarcely fathom it.

"You know Darcy, of course." Bingley had begun introductions, and Elizabeth realized she had missed part of them whilst she was woolgathering.

"My betrothed, Miss Jane Bennet." He took Jane's hand and drew her gently forward. Elizabeth remained partially concealed behind Darcy. Miss Bingley's attention had fixed upon Jane, and she greeted her future sister-in-law with an enthusiastic smile.

"And this is Jane's younger sister, Miss Elizabeth." Darcy stepped aside as Bingley made the introduction. Miss Bingley turned—and froze. Whatever greeting she had intended to offer died on her lips. The color drained from her face, and she gave a sharp cry before collapsing into a dead faint. Her betrothed, whose name Elizabeth had missed, caught her just in time.

"If we had wagered, Elizabeth, I should have won." Bingley looked both smug and a little chagrined.

"What is the meaning of this?" the gentleman demanded, cradling Miss Bingley's in his arms as he carried her to a nearby chaise and laid her upon it with great care.

"Sir James, I apologize. I ought to have arranged the introduction more delicately. I knew Caroline might be startled, but I never imagined—"

"Just who is this 'Miss Elizabeth'?" Sir James turned a dark look on her. "Something out of a nightmare I should say, judging by Caroline's reaction just now."

"Have a care how you address my betrothed, sir," Darcy said coldly, stepping forward and placing a steadying hand on Elizabeth's back. "If you would allow us but a moment to explain—"

A low moan interrupted him. Caroline stirred and put a hand to her head. "What happened?" she asked weakly.

"You had a fright, my dear. Pray, take care as you sit up." Sir James assisted her, one hand at her back to support her, just as Darcy had done for Elizabeth.

"Charlie?" Miss Bingley looked about and caught sight of her brother. "Aunt Amelia? Is it possible?"

"I am very sorry, sister, for not giving you warning. We needed to see your honest reaction." Chuckling, he shook his head. "You did not disappoint."

He beckoned Elizabeth forward and stepped aside. "Look who I found in the wilds of Hertfordshire."

Miss Bingley's gaze lingered on Elizabeth's face, then dropped to the brooch fastening her fichu. "Can it be so?" She pushed herself up to stand and came within half a foot of her. "How very like your mother you look." A sob escaped her, and she promptly threw her arms around her long-lost friend.

Uncertain how to respond, Elizabeth tentatively put her arms around Miss Bingley, remaining thus until Caroline broke the embrace. Tears glistened on her cheeks as she placed her hands gently on Elizabeth's shoulders.

"Let me look at you! I never thought to see you again—and here you are. Why did you never write?"

"It is a long story, Caroline. Shall we sit? Jane has ordered tea." Bingley motioned to the chairs gathered around the fire. He took his betrothed's hand and led her there.

Caroline did not leave Elizabeth's side as they followed. When they were all settled, the entire tale was told once more, including Elizabeth's loss of memory.

"You see, Miss Bingley, I did not know who I was until very recently." Elizabeth gave a little shrug and bit into a biscuit.

"There will be none of that. You were Lizzy to me for eight years and so you will remain. And I beg you to call me Caroline, as you did before." She grinned, her pleasure unmistakable. Then she turned to Darcy. "I see you have at last succumbed to the charms of a lady. Nothing could please me more than to know my dearest friend will be well settled."

"I thank you, Miss Bingley." Darcy shifted slightly, as though her informal address made him uncomfortable. "Elizabeth and I are very happy."

"I am pleased to hear it. I must host everyone at my brother's house in town whilst you pursue the matter of Elizabeth's grandmother. That is, of course, if Charlie agrees." She cast a pleading look at her brother.

"It would hardly be proper, Caroline—with you in residence, they may come to call as often as they like." Bingley turned to Jane, lifting her hand and pressing another kiss to her knuckles.

"Save your displays of affection for when I am not in the room, dear brother." Mrs. Hurst appeared in the doorway, her husband trailing behind her. "Welcome, Caroline."

"Good day, Louisa." The sisters' greetings were painfully formal. It was clear that their relationship was strained and distant. Elizabeth felt a pang of sorrow for them. Her own bond with her sisters and brother was amongst the dearest things she possessed. Only Darcy held a closer place in her heart.

"You have only just arrived," Mrs. Hurst continued. "And already you speak of going back to town?"

"Caroline has offered to be my hostess when Jane goes to London for her wedding clothes." Bingley spoke in a rush, forestalling Caroline's reply—they had agreed to keep the full truth from the Hursts until all matters were properly sorted.

"And when is this wedding? Have you even set a date?" Mrs. Hurst flounced to a nearby chair and seated herself, folding her hands with deliberate poise.

"We plan to marry in March," Jane said, beaming at her betrothed.

"Well, I suppose it is wise to order your gowns before the season's rush. I could introduce you to my modiste, if you like. Madame Pierre is very fashionable and highly sought after."

"I thank you for the offer, however my aunt's modiste, Madame Dubois, will be making my wedding clothes."

Mrs. Hurst gaped. "Your aunt…the one from Cheapside? *She* is one of Madame Dubois's clients?" Her expression mingled doubt and disbelief, and it took all of Elizabeth's self-command not to laugh aloud..

"Yes. She has made our family's clothing for years," Jane replied evenly. She spoke the truth. Mrs. Bennet had secured the appointment quite by chance after encountering Madame Dubois in Hyde Park. Impressed by her efforts at clothing and raising five daughters, the modiste had offered her services. Though her clientele was exclusive, she had taken a liking to the family and made room for them. They paid handsomely, of course, but their gowns were modest in design, making the cost manageable. The connection to their Aunt Gardiner had been revealed later.

"Well, then." Mrs. Hurst muttered, adjusting a fold in her skirt. "When is this little excursion to take place?"

"We shall leave before Twelfth Night," Bingley cut in. "Darcy's sister will be in town, and he plans to accompany us. Mrs. Bennet and Miss Elizabeth will go as well."

"Well, what will Hurst and I do?" Mrs. Hurst huffed, folding her arms like a sulky child. "We have come all the way to Hertfordshire and now you mean to abandon us?"

"You may come to London or remain here." Bingley said with an indifferent shrug. "If you choose to stay, Mrs. Nicholls will see that you have everything you require. And you have met enough people in Meryton and the surrounds that you should not want for invitations. I am sure I could persuade young Master Bennet to go shooting with you, Hurst."

"A capital idea," Hurst exclaimed, his florid face lighting with enthusiasm. "Cracking good shot, that boy. Gave me quite the challenge last time."

Mrs. Hurst looked ready to protest, but thought better of it. She pursed her lips into a thin line and fixed her eyes on her clasped hands.

"We must have a celebration dinner, in honor of your engagement." Caroline clapped her hands in delight. "James, do you not agree?"

"I would agree to anything that brings you pleasure, my love," he replied, gazing at her with unabashed affection.

"Wonderful! When shall we have it?" Caroline's excitement was infectious, and Jane and Elizabeth exchanged bright smiles.

Louisa interjected, frowning. "I am the hostess here, Caro."

"Then you will know the best day to hold a dinner. Jane, Elizabeth, do you know your mother's schedule?"

"We have no fixed engagements until the week of Christmas," Jane answered. "Our uncle and aunt will come then. Longbourn always hosts a Christmas Eve soirée for the neighborhood."

"Then next week, it shall be!" Caroline turned to her brother for confirmation, ignoring Louisa's irritated huff.

"We shall send round an invitation," Charles agreed with a smile.

Jane and Elizabeth did not linger at Netherfield much longer. Caroline and her betrothed walked them to the door, trailing behind the two happy couples. Before Elizabeth stepped into the carriage, Caroline gave her another tight embrace.

"I shall call and share every memory I can recall," she promised. "And we shall never be parted again, not even when we marry, for we will exchange letters five times a week."

Elizabeth laughed. "That seems a little excessive," she replied, but I shall do my best." Yet even as she smiled, a small doubt stirred within her. Caroline's zeal to resume their former closeness as if nothing had ever happened gave her pause. What if Caroline Bingley disliked the woman Elizabeth Montrose had become? What if she expected Elizabeth should act as the girl she once knew—not as her current self? It did not bear dwelling on, and Elizabeth resolved to act only in the manner most likely to secure her own happiness.

# Chapter Twenty-Four

*December 24, 1811*
*Longbourn*
*Elizabeth*

Longbourn's public rooms brimmed with guests. Mrs. Bennet had outdone herself in the matter of refreshments, dinner, and entertainment. The large parlor offered ample seating and a well-laden table of delectable confections and savories for the enjoyment of ladies and gentlemen alike. Mr. Bennet had the drawing room rug rolled up, and the furniture moved to make room for dancing, whilst the sitting room held card tables, a chessboard, and other games of quiet amusement.

The ladies had festooned Longbourn with garlands of greenery and brightly colored ribbons. Lydia helped Kitty fashion five kissing boughs, which now hung throughout the house in conspicuous, yet conveniently secluded, locations. The youngest Bennet had asked Jane where she most wished to kiss her betrothed, then promptly hung one in that very spot. Jane bore the teasing with good humor, unashamed in her anticipation of that particular Christmas custom.

Elizabeth had grown more pensive as the year's end approached. Each passing day brought her nearer to meeting her grandmother and uncovering the remainder of her story. A nameless dread weighed upon her—an irrational yet persistent fear that the great lady might dismiss her without a second thought. For years, Elizabeth had wondered whether her family had abandoned her. The idea that such fear could be justified disturbed both her waking hours and her dreams.

But she put on a brave face. Her courage always rose with any attempt to intimidate her. Darcy's presence helped. His quiet support steadied her and filled her with hope, for even if Lady Montrose should reject her, she would still have a future with her dearest Fitzwilliam.

Amongst the guests at Longbourn that evening were several officers of the militia. They frequently attended gatherings at other houses with young ladies to admire. Since the elder the Bennet sisters were now spoken for, the officers did not call often. Still, Mrs. Bennet felt compelled to invite them, and so scarlet once more adorned the rooms of her house.

"I never asked whether Mr. Wickham left the area," she said to Darcy as she observed the men mingling amongst the other guests.

"He is gone. My man confirmed it the following day. I am sorry—I ought to have told you." He patted her hand in reassurance. "It will be too soon if I ever lay eyes on that man again."

"He has done you much harm. Anyone can see that." She disliked Mr. Wickham on principle because he had wounded her betrothed.

"His sins are far greater than I can describe here. Suffice it to say, he has hurt me, and those closest to me, more often than I can forgive. My good opinion once lost is lost forever, and he had the distinction of losing my esteem long ago." Darcy grimaced and shook his head. "Let us not speak of him now. I wish to enjoy the season without spoiling my stomach."

Elizabeth laughed. "Very well. Tell me what your sister is doing for Christmas. Did she ever reply to your letter?"

"I have been a lax suitor! I did not even tell you when she answered my teasing note." Darcy turned to her with pleading eyes. "Forgive me, my love?"

"Always. But now you *must* tell me what she said!"

He obliged. "Georgiana declared she would not wait for my return to town and threatened to take the post coach to Meryton herself if I did not tell her the news at once. Naturally, I replied I had met a lady—dark hair, handsome features, excellent walker... He paused, his eyes twinkling. She replied by asking whether I had stolen Miss Bingley from her betrothed."

Elizabeth laughed again, delighted to learn that her future sister had a playful streak. "And is this banter still ongoing?"

"It is—and I am very grateful for it. She has not been herself since the summer." The same dark look he sported whenever his thoughts included Mr. Wickham appeared, and she wondered, not for the first time, what the blackguard had done to wound Miss Darcy so deeply.

"Georgiana will spend Christmas with my aunt and uncle. They are in town. She writes forgiving my absence but insists I bring you to call at Matlock House when we arrive in town."

"I shall be very pleased to meet Miss Darcy," Elizabeth said with enthusiasm. "We are kindred spirits, I think."

"How do you feel about gaining yet another sister?" Darcy asked. His gaze shifted to Mary, seated near a window, gazing out with a touch of longing, before turning to nod at Jane and Bingley. That couple had just slipped back into the room through a side door. Bingley's rumpled cravat and a loose pin hanging behind Jane's ear betrayed their activities.

Darcy leaned down and whispered in her ear. "I think I prefer Bingley's ideas to cards."

Her heart raced as she turned. Their faces were but inches apart. "Pray, excuse me... I must go assist Jane," she murmured. "She will be quite embarrassed if anyone notices. Then, perhaps, we might go in search of...diversion."

She cast him a saucy wink and slipped away, tugging Jane aside before she and Bingley reached the cluster of guests in the center of the room.

"You have a pin loose," she said, tucking the offending object neatly back into place. "Now, in payment for my services, you must tell me where that kissing bough is."

Jane flushed from her neckline to the tips of her ears. "Lydia hung it in the doorway at the back of the drawing room," she whispered.

Ingenious. That particular doorway was partially obscured by a folding screen and led into a smaller room where the pianoforte stood. Thanking her sister with a squeeze to her hands, Elizabeth returned to Darcy's side, took his hand, and began leading him along the edge of the room. They left the parlor through the same door Jane and Bingley had used moments before.

The hallway beyond felt pleasantly cool and was largely empty. A few guests stood conversing in lowered voices, punch glasses in hand. Darcy and Elizabeth passed them, nodding in greeting but not stopping to talk.

The adjoining parlor was less crowded, but they still kept to the perimeter, unwilling to be stopped. At last, they reached the screen—and slipped behind it together.

Smirking, she looked up into his eyes and whispered, "You are very tall. The screen will not hide you." His ears flushed red, and the corners of her mouth twitched with satisfaction.

Slowly, he bent and captured her lips with his own. "Minx," he murmured huskily as he drew back, though their lips were barely touching. She did not move as he reached up and plucked one white berry from the kissing bough. Glancing up, he grinned.

"There are still more berries. Tell me, is it permitted for a man to claim more than one kiss, and one berry, from a single bough?" The roguish glint in his eye made her insides flutter.

"If such a rule exists, I am unaware of it," she replied, breathless

"Then I shall take this opportunity to kiss you again." He did, gently at first, but with a fervency that made her heart race and her head spin. When he broke away, she could scarcely think, and he looked every bit undone.

"I can see now why Jane lost a hairpin," she said with a warm breath of laughter. One of her own pins had come loose, and she reached up to secure it as Darcy claimed another berry.

"We had best return before your father comes looking." His look of regret drew another laugh from her. She left first, mingling amongst the guests as she waited for Darcy to emerge. When he did, he joined her and the Gardiners.

"I understand you are to accompany Jane to London next week." Mr. Gardiner's knowing look told her that Papa had apprised him of the situation.

"Yes," Elizabeth confirmed.

"I am certain you will find everything you need in town," Mrs. Gardiner replied. "We are happy to have you, your parents, and your sister at Gracechurch Street."

"Are you sure, Aunt? We would not wish to be an inconvenience." Elizabeth bit her lip. The Gardiners lived modestly.

"We shall always have room for our loved ones, my dear." Aunt Gardiner patted her hand soothingly.

"If it becomes too much, madam, I shall be pleased to host the Bennets at Darcy House." Darcy offered courteously.

"Did we not refuse Bingley because he had no hostess?" Elizabeth asked, puzzled.

"We did, but we have arrived at a solution. It would not do to house Bingley's betrothed beneath the same roof. Nor would it be proper for *mine* to stay at Darcy House. If need be, Miss Bennet and Mrs. Bennet can remain with me, and you and Mr. Bennet can stay at Bingley's."

"You think of everything, sir, do you not?" Elizabeth's eyes sparkled as she smiled.

"Be that as it may, sir," Mr. Gardiner interjected, "my relations will stay at Gracechurch Street until matters are resolved. I have inquiries concerning Lady Montrose, Mr. Darcy. As it happens, her house stands three doors from yours. Should she agree to receive Elizabeth, I expect my sister and her family will descend upon Darcy House to be nearer to Lizzy." His tone brooked no argument.

"As you like," Darcy agreed. "It is a fine plan, and I shall abide by your wishes—and those of the Bennets."

The party from Netherfield returned to Longbourn following church services the next day. Servants had laid out a generous repast of cold meats, fruit, bread, cheeses, and preserves. The cheerful group served themselves and took seats where they pleased, their conversation muted and companionable.

Later, Darcy and Elizabeth donned their outerwear and strode to the garden. "I have a gift for you," he said quietly. "I should like you to wear this." He withdrew a small blue box from his coat and opened it.

Inside, nestled in dark velvet, lay a ring of gold, set with a striking blue gem. The band, delicately wrought, bore intricate flowers and curling vines on either side of the stone, which then merged into a braid that encircled it. "Such rings may no longer be fashionable, but seeing it on your finger will declare to all that you are taken, even if they do not know by whom."

"It is lovely," she breathed.

"It belonged to my mother, and now to you. We can have it reset if you prefer." He pulled off her glove and slipped the ring onto the third finger of her left hand.

"Never! It is perfect just as it is. I shall wear it always."

"At least until I give you a wedding ring. And my grandmother's. Oh, and my mother's collection. Those were her favorite pieces."

"Shall I be expected to change rings often?" she asked, bemused. "I thought one wore their wedding ring at all times."

"As long as you have something on that finger declaring to all the world that you are mine, I care not which bauble it is." He lifted her hand, pressing a kiss first to the ring, then to each of her fingertips. "Will your glove fit over it?" he asked.

"I suppose we shall find out."

It did not, and after several failed attempts, Elizabeth finally gave up, tugging off her other glove and tucking both into the pocket of her pelisse.

"I have a gift for you as well." She reached into her other pocket and stretched out her hand to him to reveal a small parcel. "It is not much; merely a few handkerchiefs."

He unwrapped the package with care and lovingly ran his fingers over the embroidery. She had joined their initials together in an elegant design, encircled by roses and ivy—mirroring the motif of her brooch.

"You are very accomplished," he said. "I shall carry one with me always." He kissed her warmly, and they returned to the house.

"There you are!" Caroline appeared with hands planted firmly on her hips. "I have something to show Elizabeth. It arrived from London late last night. I had thought to wait until our return to town, but I simply could not resist!" She settled beside Elizabeth and held out a bundle wrapped in oilcloth.

Elizabeth accepted it, her curiosity piqued, and untied the twine securing the parcel. She peeled back the oilcloth to reveal a swathe of rich velvet within. Carefully, she unfolded the softer layer—and gasped. Reverently, her fingers traced the edge of a gilded frame.

"Is this...?" she whispered, lifting the miniature to examine it more closely.

"This is my godmother, Amelia Montrose. You can see now why I swooned when I first laid eyes on you. She gave it to me for my eighth birthday."

Indeed, Elizabeth could see. The resemblance was striking, from the delicate curve of the nose to the dark curls. It was as though she were gazing upon a mirror of herself.

"No painter ever quite captured her eyes," Caroline added with a tinge of wistfulness. "I am thankful God saw fit to preserve them in her daughter."

Tears welled in Eliabeth's eyes. "It is a gift beyond measure to see my mother's likeness. Thank you, Caroline."

"I have already arranged to commission a copy in London. When it is completed, the original shall be yours." Caroline reached out and clasped Elizabeth's arm with quiet affection.

"I shall be content with the copy if you would prefer to keep the original," Elizabeth demurred.

"It is of no consequence. The same artist will paint the copy, so it will be as though I, too, have the original work."

Elizabeth cradled the miniature with care. Caroline and Darcy sat without speaking, as she studied her mother's visage. As she did, memories forced their way to the present, a sudden, sharp pain pierced her head. Struggling to catch a breath, she lowered the portrait to her lap and pressed her fingers to the scar at her temple.

"My love?" Darcy leaned forward, his concern evident. The warmth of his nearness touched her heart, and the pain eased. "Are you well?"

"It is nothing," she said, attempting to reassure him. "At least, I believe it is nothing. Though there are times when my head hurts—usually without warning."

"Do you need to retire?"

His concern was apparent, and he touched her arm as though to be certain she was well.

"Was it the portrait?" Caroline asked anxiously. "I am very sorry if it caused your upset."

"No, no. You are both needlessly worried! I shall be quite well."

The matter was allowed to rest, and Elizabeth endeavored to enjoy the rest of the evening. That night, she dreamed of her mother. Amelia Montrose rocked her gently, singing a soft lullaby until sleep enfolded her once more.

# Chapter Twenty-Five

*December 30, 1811*
*London*
*Bingley*

Caroline had been speaking nonstop since they left Hertfordshire. Elizabeth and Jane did not seem to mind. The former listened raptly, as if she hoped Caroline's tales would unlock the memories hidden away in her mind. For Charles Bingley, the memories were soothing but also unsettling, for they reminded him of the worst day of his life. And so, he breathed a sigh of relief when the Bennet sisters had been deposited at Gracechurch Street.

Mr. and Mrs. Bennet had taken their own carriage. The Gardiners, with their children, followed in their conveyance. Darcy rode with Bingley, but his own carriage transported his belongings and his valet. His horse plodded along behind, slowing the pace. They would stop briefly at his townhouse to deliver Caroline and her things before continuing to Darcy House—and hopefully, a meeting with Lady Montrose.

"I believe I shall have a rest," Caroline said as she climbed out of the carriage and made her way to the front door. "I am very tired."

"You spoke enough to earn it," he said good-naturedly. "I shall see you at dinner." The carriage door closed and lurched forward. Both gentlemen stayed silent for the rest of the journey. When they arrived at Darcy House, a servant showed Bingley to a room to wash the road dust away. He had no plans to rest. Montrose House stood only a few doors away, and he meant to see Lady Montrose without delay. The sooner the interview was behind him, the sooner he might find peace.

Almost before he realized it—before he had fully composed himself—he found himself standing on her threshold. Summoning his courage, he knocked on the door and waited. A moment later, it swung open to reveal a rather severe-looking butler. "Yes?" the man intoned.

"Mr. Charles Bingley, to see Lady Montrose on a matter of great importance." He prayed the man could not detect the strain in his voice.

"You will wait here." The butler stepped aside and motioned to a chair. "I shall see whether her ladyship will accept your card."

Bingley waited for ten interminable minutes before the butler returned. "Her ladyship will receive you," he said. "Keep your remarks brief. Lady Montrose has no patience for idle chatter."

Bingley inclined his head, and the butler relieved him of his hat and gloves. Following a few paces behind the silent servant, he used the opportunity to examine his surroundings. The house bore signs it had been recently redecorated. Everything had been masterfully redone with colors to welcome and soothe the onlooker.

The butler stopped before a pair of polished doors and pushed one open. "Mr. Bingley, your ladyship," he said.

"Thank you, Morton," came the clipped reply.

Bingley entered. The room was dim, but welcoming, the fire crackling cheerfully and several candelabras casting golden pools of light. Lady Montrose sat in a high-backed chair near the hearth, her features wreathed in shadow.

"Well, come here," she snapped.

He obeyed at once, halting a few feet from her chair.

"You bear the likeness of your father," she remarked. "I can see the resemblance, despite having met but once. I have a good eye for faces."

"You honor me, ma'am," he said, bowing in response.

"State your business then." She did not invite him to sit.

He hesitated. "I scarcely know how to begin. I have taken a lease in Hertfordshire, and whilst residing there, I believe I discovered your granddaughter."

Of a sudden, her countenance hardened, cold and immovable. Slowly, she rose. Lady Montrose was not tall, but looked every inch the formidable woman, and were he a lesser man, Bingley might well have quaked beneath her commanding presence.

"Enough. I shall not endure another word. Where is this woman? Was she too cowardly to come herself? I am weary of charlatans and fortune hunters. Tell me, have you squandered your inheritance and now seek to wring coin from an old woman's sentiments? Are you so dishonorable?"

"No! I swear to you, your ladyship, I have found Elizabeth. The proof is undeniable!"

"Then why has my granddaughter not contacted me herself? My Elizabeth wrote every week."

She faltered slightly, and Bingley thought he saw her lip quiver. He pressed on. "She suffered a head injury. She has no memories from...before."

"And why, then, should I believe this woman is my granddaughter if there is no evidence?"

"There is! She has—"

"No! I shall not hear it—not one more false claim. Jameson! Milton!" Two liveried footmen appeared at the door. "Remove this man. I shall not endure another disappointment." She sank into her chair, her face hidden in her hands as her servants moved to either side of Bingley. He allowed himself to be guided from the room, his limbs leaden.

Dejected, Bingley took his hat and his coat. "But she has the brooch," he murmured as the door opened.

"Sir! What did you say?" asked Jameson, stepping forward.

"The brooch—with Mr. Montrose's personal crest. I recognized it. And she is the very image of Aunt Amelia."

Jameson's brow furrowed. "I shall do what I can, sir. Her ladyship places her trust in me, though I can promise nothing. Might I have your direction, sir?"

Bingley withdrew a card from his pocketbook and handed it over without delay. "Why did she cast me out without a proper hearing?" he asked quietly.

"Lady Montrose has been inundated with pretenders," he revealed. "She is weary of the charade. I do not doubt she is, even now, penning letters to have her granddaughter declared dead."

"But she is not!" Bingley's breath caught. This could not be happening—not after everything. He had promised!

"I shall do my best to forestall any rash actions. Watch for a note. I shall advise you how to proceed."

Bingley donned his hat, and turning to face the servant directly, asked "Why are you helping me?" he asked.

Jameson stilled. "Because my mistress has suffered enough sorrow. I wish only to see her smile again."

Satisfied, Bingley gave him a solemn nod and took his leave, fervently hoping Jameson would send word soon. He could not conceal this encounter from the interested parties for long.

# Chapter Twenty-Six

*January 1812*
*Bloomsbury Street, London*
*Winters Winters*

"Come," Winters called. His man entered. Jarvis's cunning and stealth were unmatched and impossible to replicate. He bowed to his master.

"The Bingley whelp visited Lady Montrose today," he said in his coarse accent. "My sources say he has found the brat."

Winters sat forward. "Impossible. We have looked everywhere."

"And yet he found her by chance. In Hertfordshire."

"This changes everything. If her grandmother recognizes little Miss Montrose, we may secure the business shares." Winters grinned. Yes, all would go splendidly. He could satisfy his debtors and continue as he always had, leaving the management of his company to lesser men whilst he enjoyed the profits.

"How do you reckon that? The old bird has refused to sell. She be the trustee, and coulda done it years ago." Jarvis folded his arms and frowned.

"Lady Montrose will not want her precious grandchild entangled in trade. Henry told me often enough that his family disapproved. Though his mother kept in touch, she did not visit more than once a year." By his estimation, the girl had not yet reached her majority, either. Her grandmother would still make all the decisions.

"Then why'd she keep it so long?"

"People are odd when they mourn. I imagine she held on to it because surrendering it would be admitting defeat. We must confirm whether Bingley's son has truly found Elizabeth Montrose. Then we wait for the right moment. We must time it perfectly. The girl must be acknowledged publicly before we approach."

"I'll keep me eye on 'em," Jarvis promised.

"You have done well." Winters tossed him a bag of coins. "For expenses." Jarvis weighed it in his hand and nodded, satisfied. With a short bow, he tucked it into his pocket and departed.

"Twelve years," Winters said to the empty room. "Twelve years of waiting, and soon it will all be mine."

He had plagued the lady in countless ways over the years—sending false reports, hiring strangers to approach her with claims of being her lost granddaughter. He had never expected any of them to succeed. He had wanted to break her spirit. Once she abandoned hope, she would declare her granddaughter dead. Montrose's will had been explicit: should no family remain, his partners would gain control of his business interests.

*There must be thousands of pounds by now.* And soon, it would belong to him.

*January 2, 1812*
*London*
*Bingley*

*Dear Sir,*

*My mistress refuses to see reason. I have delayed sending her letters for now, but I cannot do so for long without discovery. Lady M. plans to attend the theater on Twelfth Night. Her box is number five and overlooks the stage. Secure a seat nearby, and ensure that Elizabeth is wearing the brooch. I shall arrange for both you and her to meet my mistress during the intermission.*

*Jameson*

"Well, we have a way forward." Thankfully, Jane, Elizabeth, and Darcy had joined him and Caroline that morning. Bingley had told them all, including what he had learned from Jameson.

"That poor woman!" Caroline cried, aghast. "How could someone take advantage of another in such a way?"

"It happens all too often," Darcy replied gravely. "I have fallen victim to such schemes myself."

"How would your parents feel about attending the theater?" he asked Jane. "It is short notice. I am uncertain whether we shall secure seats."

"My box is available. And it is very near box five—close enough that Lady Montrose will be able to see everyone inside." Darcy took Elizabeth's hand. "If this fails, shall we continue to try?" he asked.

Elizabeth shook her head. "No. I shall have my happiness, even if Lady Montrose does not recognize me." She gave his hand a gentle squeeze and offered him a sad smile.

"Then let us prepare."

A note was sent to the Bennets, and they agreed to attend the theater three nights hence. Now, all they could do was wait.

Bingley lacked patience. He paced endlessly when Jane was not present to distract him. He pored over old letters, once more questioning who had sought to eliminate the entire Montrose family. Could it have been a relation, eager to advance in the line of succession? Yet, no new heir had ever been declared. The Montrose earldom remained without an earl.

Could it have been something else? His father had never been the same after that night—ever wary, always glancing over his shoulder. Perhaps a business associate had arranged the deaths, some affront by Montrose having provoked their wrath.

"It sounds like a gothic novel," he muttered aloud. Still, he forced himself to consider it. The idea that revealing Elizabeth's existence might yet endanger her continued to haunt him.

He blamed himself for their deaths. There—it was admitted. Foolish though it might be to shoulder the guilt, he could not cast it off. Had he arrived earlier, he might have interrupted the tragedy. Perhaps he would have stopped Elizabeth before she wandered away.

Bingley could only hope that, once all was settled, he might at last be free of the irrational shame that had followed him for half of his life.

*Elizabeth*

Three nights later, Bingley's carriage conveyed him, Caroline, and Sir James to the theater, where Darcy and the Bennets awaited them just inside the entrance.

After exchanging greetings, they made their way to the Darcy box. "We must not allow her to see Elizabeth too soon," Darcy explained. "She may cry foul and depart."

Elizabeth took the seat beside Darcy, with Jane on her other side and Bingley beyond her. Mr. and Mrs. Bennet were seated just behind them in the second row.

"Elizabeth, take these." Darcy handed her a pair of lorgnettes. "I know you. You will be more interested in the stage than in the audience."

"Why ever would I be interested in *them?*" she asked with a touch of incredulity.

He chuckled and leaned in to murmur. "Because people come to the theater to see and be seen. Though you have never been of their ilk."

"*Much Ado About Nothing* is one of my favorite plays by the Bard. I do not intend to miss a moment of it."

A signal was given, and the performance began. Elizabeth watched, wholly absorbed until Darcy nudged her gently. He gestured toward a box slightly behind and to the left of theirs. "That is Lady Montrose," he murmured.

Elizabeth raised the lorgnettes to her eyes to examine the lady more closely. "She is very elegant," she whispered. Lady Montrose's hair was white—had it once been blond? She appeared only a little older than

Mr. Bennet, who still had color in his locks. Faint lines marked her face, and an unmistakable air of sadness and resignation clung to her. She lowered the lorgnettes, her eyes stinging with sudden emotion.

*Do I belong to your family?* she asked the lady in her mind. Some part of her longed to cry out, *I only wish to know who I am!* Yet she *did* know. She was Elizabeth Bennet, the second daughter of Thomas and Fanny Bennet of Longbourn. She had a loving family and an idyllic childhood. Truly, she had no cause to repine. Still, until the mystery of her past was resolved, she could never feel fully at peace. There would always be a gaping void in her heart—and in her thoughts—where memories ought to dwell.

The intermission arrived far too soon. Darcy rose without hesitation, intent on accompanying her. "You will be more likely to gain entrance if you go in my stead," he advised. Bingley remained in the box.

Jameson met them outside. The man stared openly at Elizabeth. "He was not exaggerating," he murmured, astonished. "Where is Mr. Bingley?"

"We thought it wiser that I escort Miss Elizabeth." Darcy answered smoothly, his tone both courteous and firm. "Fitzwilliam Darcy, to see Lady Montrose."

At the name, Jameson straightened and nodded with eager approval. "Come, I shall escort you, sir. Miss."

They stepped into the corridor, and Elizabeth remained close behind Darcy, irrational fear thrumming through her veins. In mere moments, she would know—without a doubt—whether the lady would receive her.

"Mr. Darcy to see you, ma'am."

"Darcy? George Darcy's boy? Well, I suppose I ought to greet him. Show him in, Jameson."

At the servant's bidding, Darcy stepped forward, drawing Elizabeth with him. They parted the curtain, and there she was.

Lady Montrose did not rise, nor did she turn; she waited for them to approach. As they neared her seat, a delicate fragrance reached Elizabeth's senses—citrus, jasmine, and rose. She gasped as pain exploded in her head. Clutching her scar, she cried out—then everything went black.

When she came to, she found herself in Darcy's arms. Her hair had come loose from its pins, and she drew in a sharp breath as she attempted to sit up. Jameson had drawn the curtain to afford them privacy.

"Easy, Elizabeth. You suffered a fall."

Blinking, she touched her temple. "What...?"

"You bear a striking resemblance to my late daughter-in-law", came Lady Montrose's calm observation. "None of the others looked even remotely like her." Elizabeth turned and met her gaze. The lady sat in a chair now positioned to face the spot where she had fallen.

Elizabeth made another attempt to rise, and this time, Darcy allowed it. Her shawl lay crumpled on the floor, and she bent to retrieve it.

"Who hired you?" the Dowager Countess asked bluntly.

"I shall not be called a liar, madam," Elizabeth replied sharply. "I came to you with good intentions, hoping to solve the mystery of my past. If, in so doing, I might ease your sorrow, then so much the better."

"You are a very good actress. Have you considered the stage?" Lady Montrose pulled her reticule open and drew out a small bottle. She began removing her gloves, one finger at a time, her eyes remaining fixed on Elizabeth.

"I was raised as the daughter of a gentleman. I would never." Elizabeth held her gaze steady until Lady Montrose looked away.

Stepping to Elizabeth's side and touching her arm with subtle assurance, Darcy said, "I have remained silent until now, but you will not insult Elizabeth further."

"I never imagined a Darcy would take part in such a deception," Lady Montrose replied with cold detachment. "Your father and I were acquaintances, though I have never met *you*. What would he say if his son sullied the family name by putting forward little upstarts?"

Though the words were cutting, Elizabeth glimpsed something beneath the surface—an undercurrent of emotion—the barest shred of hope. Still, her heart ached from the insult, and she longed to leave.

"Enough." She placed a hand against Darcy's chest. "I do not require her approval to be happy. I have *you*, my love." She gathered her shawl, but as she adjusted it, the brooch slipped into view—directly within Lady Montrose's line of sight.

"Wait," the lady said as Elizabeth turned to go. "Where did you get that?"

"My adoptive parents saved it for me. I was clutching it in my hand when I was found." Elizabeth placed a hand over the brooch as if to protect it.

Lady Montrose gasped. She fumbled with the bottle from her reticule, uncapped it, and dabbed a little on her hands. The scent wafted toward Elizabeth—and with it, a memory surfaced.

"Citrus, jasmine, rose," she murmured. "I once soaked a handkerchief in it. Mama was livid and scolded me endlessly, but I kept it under my pillow...so I could remember you when you were away."

Elizabeth blinked rapidly, her vision blurring, then fixed her gaze on her grandmother. Lady Montrose had risen, the bottle still in hand, her reticule falling to the floor. "May I?" she asked, gesturing to the brooch. Elizabeth nodded and unpinned, the brooch, placing it into the lady's outstretched hand.

"I gave it to Amelia," she said, voice thick with memory. "On the birth of her son. Our line felt secure when Harry was born." She handed the bottle of oil to Jameson and then reached into the cluster of necklaces at her throat, selecting one. "I never take this off," she murmured, fastening her fingers around it. "So that I may always remember my family."

Suspended from the end of the chain was what appeared to be a key. Its top bore the intricate design typical of such, but the bottom resembled a pin. Notches marked it in odd places, and another memory stirred in Elizabeth's mind.

"A locket," she murmured. "It is a locket. And I could never open it because I left the chain with the key in Mama's room."

Without hesitation, Lady Montrose lifted the chain from her neck and handed it to Elizabeth. She took it and promptly fitted the pin into the small hole at the top of the brooch. Pressing down gently, she felt it click. The front of the brooch sprang open, revealing two finely painted miniatures. On the left were a man and a woman; on the right, a little girl cradling a baby.

"My dear Elizabeth!" Lady Montrose cried. "Oh, my darling girl!" She pulled Elizabeth into her arms, and the two clung together, tears falling freely.

"You must come to my home at once! I shall not rest until you do. Please, say that you will."

Darcy cleared his throat. "May I suggest we rejoin the rest of my party after the performance? If we remain in our boxes until the crowd has dispersed, it may help prevent gossip before we are prepared to address it."

"And what part have you in this, Mr. Darcy?" Lady Montrose asked, arching a brow.

"Charles Bingley is my closest friend. I was with him in Hertfordshire."

Lady Montrose frowned. "Do not think I failed to notice the familiar way in which you held my granddaughter."

"He is my betrothed, your ladyship," Elizabeth said hurriedly.

"None of that. *Your ladyship* indeed," she replied, waving a dismissive hand. "I am your *grandmother*, or *grandmama*. As for you, Darcy, I shall not say I am entirely pleased to know Elizabeth's heart is already spoken for, though I ought to have known. She is a rare beauty."

Her features softened. "Still, it is a comfort to learn Marston Hall lies but twenty miles from Pemberley. We shall settle the particulars later. Jameson! Open the curtain!"

Elizabeth and her grandmother spoke through the last hour of the play. Darcy departed long enough to inform those in his box of what had transpired and how they ought to proceed, then returned promptly to his betrothed's side.

When the theater had emptied but for a few stragglers, Bingley and the Bennets came to Lady Montrose's box. Bingley lingered at the threshold, uncertain—fearing another reprimand. To his astonishment, Lady Montrose came directly to him and kissed him on both cheeks. "Thank you," she said fervently. "I am in your debt."

"It was Darcy who put the pieces together," Bingley mumbled. Then he brightened. "I am so relieved, your ladyship. When the curtain of your box opened following the intermission, and I observed you and Elizabeth speaking so warmly, I could scarcely contain myself."

"And who is this?" Lady Montrose turned to Jane. "Oh, you are a pretty girl!"

"This is my sister, Jane," Elizabeth said. "She is betrothed to Mr. Bingley. And here are my mama and my papa. They saved me."

Mrs. Bennet stepped forward, her nervousness evident as she curtsied and twisted her handkerchief in her hands. "Your ladyship," she murmured.

Lady Montrose took her hand. "I cannot thank you enough," she whispered with great emotion. "You are truly the best of women and mothers. I do not know it all, but my Elizabeth assures me you and Mr. Bennet raised her as your own. I shall not forget that."

"Will we see her again?" Mrs. Bennet blurted. "It is only…we love her so dearly." Tears filled her eyes, and she dabbed at them with a handkerchief.

"I know what it means to be separated from those I love. I would never subject another to such pain." Lady Montrose next addressed Mr. Bennet. "Elizabeth has no need of a dowry now," she said kindly. "If it would benefit you or your other daughters, you may use it elsewhere."

"It is hers," Mr. Bennet replied firmly. "Ten thousand pounds—the same as Jane and all my girls."

"She is heir to the earldom," Lady Montrose revealed, raising a brow. Gasps of astonishment sounded around the box. "Her father's business holdings are hers as well. Our Elizabeth is a very wealthy woman. I suppose I ought to be grateful to Mr. Darcy for securing her affections. It will save me the trouble of turning away fortune hunters."

"If it pleases everyone," Darcy interjected, "I propose we move to Darcy House. Elizabeth's trunks might be sent for and discreetly deposited at Montrose House. From there, we may consider how best to proceed."

All having agreed, they departed. Darcy sent the Bennets and Bingley in his own carriage. Caroline and Sir James had already departed in Bingley's conveyance—they would make Lady Montrose's acquaintance at a later time. Darcy accompanied Lady Montrose, Jameson, and Elizabeth in her ladyship's carriage, and together they made their way to Mayfair and Darcy House.

# Chapter Twenty-Seven

*January 12, 1812*
*Montrose House*
*Elizabeth*

"You sent me this drawing just before..." Lady Montrose trailed off, handing Elizabeth a sheet of paper.

Elizabeth laughed. "Harry said it looked like a donkey—and he was right!" It had been an attempt at a portrait, though when it was finished, it resembled a monster more than a person. "I am sad to report that my drawing skills have not improved over the years."

"And here is this one." Grandmother handed her another page. "You pressed a flower and sent it to me."

"Roses," she whispered. "They have always been a favorite."

"Oh, Elizabeth, I have missed so much of your life! It cannot be undone, but believe me when I say I shall support you however I can—even after you marry Darcy."

"We have not set a date. Jane and Charles are to marry in March. We have long dreamed of sharing our wedding day, but..."

"Do not concern yourself on my account. I shall be there when you marry, and then, after you have had a little time to yourselves, I shall descend upon Pemberley so that I may be near you once more." Her grandmother reached out and gave Elizabeth's hand a gentle squeeze. "You will come of age in March, after all."

"You know my true birthday!" Elizabeth turned eagerly and continued. "We celebrated it on the eighth of March at Longbourn."

"You were very close. Your birthday is on the fourteenth of March. I remember your father found it rather amusing to have a child born on that day—he had a fondness for mathematics and called you his *'pi child.'*"

Elizabeth laughed. "That is a pet name I shall always hold dear."

Lady Montrose wasted no time in announcing Elizabeth's return. Once she notified those who had sought to name another heir and presented the irrefutable evidence of Elizabeth's identity, they withdrew their claims without protest. One gentleman, who had met Elizabeth's mother and had seen Elizabeth as a girl, asserted without hesitation that she was the very image of Amelia Montrose.

The Bennets resided three doors down at Darcy House and visited daily. Bingley often brought Caroline and Sir James with him. On one such day, Caroline shared a *now* fond memory of an encounter she had with Lady Montrose as a child.

"She frightened me to death! I had sneaked a biscuit, and she came up behind me, asking if I had one for her. Naturally, I broke it in half and shared." Caroline laughed, as shook her head. "I fully expected to be scolded."

"Every child sneaks biscuits," Lady Montrose said, smiling. "They always forget to share the spoils."

Mrs. Bennet grew more at ease in Lady Montrose's company with each passing day. She came to see that the lady harbored no intention of taking Elizabeth away from the only family she had ever clearly known.

And Elizabeth's memories were returning. Bit by bit, small recollections resurfaced with the scent of her mother's perfume…her father's favorite book. She remembered her little brother breaking her cherished doll and the punishment she received for striking him in return. And she remembered the house.

"It sits empty," her grandmother told her. "I had all that belonged to your parents moved to Marston Hall, but I never sold the house itself. Now, I think it may be time—only if you wish it."

The most astonishing revelation of all was that Elizabeth would not be merely *Miss Montrose*. With the death of her uncle, she had unknowingly become the suo jure Countess of Montrose. At last, and with unfeigned pleasure, her grandmother happily embraced her new role as the Dowager Lady Montrose.

At that moment, Jameson entered the room. "Mr. Silas Winters is downstairs. He says he has come to pay his respects to Lady Montrose."

The Dowager Countess frowned. "Show him in." Then, turning to Elizabeth, she added, "That man tried to have you declared dead. He wants your father's share of the company."

"I am not averse to selling the shares," Elizabeth said calmly. "What use have I for them? I possess more than enough and am to marry a wealthy man."

"Now is not the time to be hasty," her grandmother warned. "Let us hear what he has to say. I would wager the matter will arise before the call is through."

A man of advancing years entered the drawing room. His hair was stark white, and though he appeared friendly as he bowed and greeted the ladies, there was an indefinable air about him, one that

Elizabeth attributed to certain dissolute habits. Despite his outward cheer, something in his voice caused her heart to stutter painfully. A shiver of dread settled in her limbs, and she struggled to maintain her composure.

"You are the picture of your mother," he said to Elizabeth. "She would be proud of the lady you have become."

"I understand you were my father's business partner." Elizabeth offered a thin smile, hoping he did not perceive her discomfort.

"Yes. Such a tragedy when…well." He paused, then added with false solemnity, "Have they ever discovered the miscreant?" Mr. Winters looked curious, but not nearly grieved enough by his partner's death.

"No, the Runners made no progress," Lady Montrose replied, reaching out to take Elizabeth's hand. "It appears to be a crime of passion or a burglary gone awry. I fear we shall never know."

"I was thrilled when I read the announcement in the papers," Winters said. "With Miss Montrose as your heir, she will no doubt wish to sell her father's shares. I stand ready to offer a fair price."

Mr. Winter's misuse of her honorific did not go unnoticed. He had clearly not heard the latest.

He named a figure that sounded absurdly low to Elizabeth's ear. "I thank you for the offer," she replied with polite composure. "I shall consult my uncle, who is far more versed in such matters, and will contact you in due course."

"Very good. Your man has my direction." As he turned to leave, Winters paused at the door. "A shame that Robert Bingley died before you were found. He was never quite the same after it all happened—seemed rather guilty, if you ask me."

And with that, he left the room, giving neither lady a chance to say another word.

"Do you think it is possible?" she asked her grandmother. "I cannot see it. I do not remember Charlie's father well, but he was no murderer. Could an evil man have raised two such good-hearted children?" Elizabeth deliberately excluded Mrs. Hurst. She was not at all pleasant.

"I hardly know, Elizabeth. I suppose we never shall have the answers we wish."

*Winters*

"I've news, sir." Jarvis entered the room so silently that Winters startled, nearly upsetting his chair.

"Confound it, man! Must you be so…stealthy?" He scowled as he mopped up the brandy he had spilled in his agitation.

"I wouldn't be 'alf so good at me job if I weren't." Jarvis replied, dropping into a chair and propping his feet on the table with deliberate insolence.

"Out with it." Winters waved an impatient hand. His books beckoned.

"The brat's engaged already."

He froze. No. No, that was not good at all. "Are you certain?" he asked, barely above a whisper.

"'Eard it from a maid who 'eard it from a maid at Bingley's 'ouse. She's set to marry that Darcy fella in March, so's it said."

"This could ruin everything. Elizabeth Montrose owns her father's business only so as long as she is *Miss* Montrose. Once she weds, her husband will have full control of her assets."

"The Darcy bloke is already flush—wager 'e'll give it up rather than deal with the stink of trade."

Jarvis's reasoning was sound, but he could not risk it. "We must separate them. Or..."

His man's face split into a wide grin. "Or finish wot was begun twelve years ago," he said maliciously.

Winters shuddered. "I would rather not go so far if we can avoid it." The first time had been an accident, or so he had long told himself. He had not meant to... "No. We will begin with division. The Montrose name is old and respected. Lady Montrose will never allow her granddaughter to marry a man with a sullied reputation. Here is what you will do..."

# Chapter Twenty-Eight

*February 3, 1812*
*Montrose House, London*
*Elizabeth*

"Oh, dear." Grandmother frowned as she read the paper. "This is not at all what I expected."

Elizabeth waited for her to expound, but when she did not, she cleared her throat. "Grandmother? Of what are you talking?"

"Darcy's name has made into the tattle sheets." She tut-tutted and handed the paper to Elizabeth.

She accepted it and read where Lady Montrose indicated.

*Dear Reader,*

*After so many generations of dull—though very wealthy gentlemen from Derbyshire—one has managed to shock this writer. His actions may shake the very foundations of the* ton *for years to come! Mr. F. D. was seen leaving the theater last night with an unknown woman. Fear not, for I have learned her identity. The mysterious beauty is a new courtesan, found in the wilds of the North. Her raven hair and flawless complexion would tempt any man. That she has managed to* ensnare *the illusive F. D. testifies to her arts and allurements.*

*What will come of the mesalliance, I wonder! Lady Featherdown will discover it all.*

Elizabeth could not suppress a laugh. "Who could believe such ridiculous drivel?" she asked, still chuckling.

"You do not?" Lady Montrose peered at her over the rim of her spectacles, her lips pinched in disapproval. "How can you be so sure? You have scarcely known Darcy for more than six months."

"Grandmother, he was *here* last night."

"Oh." Lady Montrose looked momentarily abashed. "I ought to have remembered that."

"Even had he not been, I should never have believed it. Darcy is the best of men; the most honorable man I have ever known. I only wish we might announce our engagement."

"When you are properly introduced to the *ton* as my granddaughter, I shall give my consent to announce it. I am a selfish creature—I shall not have much time with you as it is, darling!"

After speaking at length with Jane and the Bennets, Elizabeth and Darcy had decided they would not marry in March. At Lady Montrose's request, they had agreed to delay the wedding until after the Season on the condition that they be permitted to exchange their vows at Longbourn Church. They would return to Meryton for a few days in March to celebrate Jane's nuptials, after which Lady Montrose intended to host a grand ball in honor of Elizabeth's birthday, There, she would be formally introduced to society, and her engagement to Mr. Darcy would be announced.

Jameson stepped into the breakfast room. "Mr. Darcy, my lady."

"Show him in." She turned to Elizabeth with a knowing look. "He has likely seen that rag and seeks to reassure you of his love."

Darcy came in, a harried look in his eyes. "Elizabeth," he said, scarcely acknowledging her ladyship, "I swear, it is not so."

She laughed softly, extending her hand. He dropped to one knee as he took it. "What amuses you?" he asked, clearly bewildered by her response.

"You were *here* last night, you silly man! Do you truly think me so foolish as to credit a baseless rumor that paints you as dishonorable? Never."

He exhaled, and bowed his head, visibly relieved. "I ought to have known you would not cast me aside at so little provocation."

"I would not call rumors of a mistress *little* provocation," Lady Montrose interjected, raising a stern brow. "If you harm her in any way..." She left the threat hanging in the air.

"On my honor, Lady Montrose, there is no one for me but Elizabeth. She is my world, and I would *never* dishonor her in such a disgraceful manner." Darcy spoke earnestly, and his complete lack of guile warmed Elizabeth's heart.

"Very well, I shall believe you. But what prompted this strange bit of gossip?" Lady Montrose frowned again. "It cannot be a coincidence."

"You are seeing demons where there are none," Elizabeth said soothingly. "Why would anyone target Darcy now? What motive could they have? What would they hope to achieve?"

Her grandmother shuddered. "I cannot help but think this has something to do with *you*, my dear. Could someone have connected Darcy's name with yours and now wishes to separate you?"

Elizabeth felt a tremor of unease but pushed it aside. "It cannot be. Why would anyone do it? If someone wished to win my affection, attacking Darcy is hardly the best-conceived plan. There is no guarantee I would choose that person, even if I gave up my love. As my happiness rests so firmly on Darcy, that sort of ploy would be doomed from the outset."

Lady Montrose did not appear convinced. She rose from the table with quiet resolve. "We have callers coming," she told Elizabeth, changing the subject. "Many are my friends, and all hold considerable influence in society. They will speak of you to their children, and from there, word will spread through the circles of the *ton*."

"Will they speak favorably of Elizabeth?" Darcy asked with concern.

"I chose the guests with care. You may be assured their reports will be favorable." Lady Montrose replied with a resolute nod.

Elizabeth rose to accompany her grandmother whilst Darcy prepared to take his leave. He had several meetings of business to attend and was due back at Darcy House. "I shall call later," he promised.

The Bennets and Jane had returned to Longbourn three days prior. Elizabeth missed them dreadfully, though she was content enough in her grandmother's house. Having Darcy near was a balm to her aching heart. Lady Montrose had offered to hire an express rider solely for the delivery of letters between London and Longbourn. Elizabeth had demurred, for now, but admitted she might avail herself of the luxury in the future.

The first callers soon arrived, and Lady Montrose received them with warm enthusiasm. Amongst them was Mrs. Eva Harrington, accompanied by her daughter. "Lady Montrose," the Dowager Countess said with gracious formality, "may I present my friend, Mrs. Eva Harrington, and her daughter, Mrs. Anna Norton."

The ladies curtsied, Mrs. Norton offered a warm smile. "It is a pleasure to meet you, Lady Montrose. And to see your grandmother smiling once more, though I suspect society will require time to adjust to having two Lady Montroses."

Elizabeth's brows lifted slightly at her grandmother's use of her new title, but she understood—it must be so from now on.

"Have you long known my grandmother?" Elizabeth asked with polite interest.

"Oh, yes, quite some time—two decades or more," Mrs. Norton replied, casting a fond glance toward the Dowager Countess. "She and my mother met at Almack's. I was ten years old at the time, I believe." Mrs. Norton accepted a cup of tea and settled beside Mrs. Harrington. "You have quite stirred the *ton*, your ladyship. I cannot have a single gathering without being peppered with questions. Your grandmother is wise to keep you to herself for a time."

"There were many matters that required our attention," Elizabeth replied carefully. Unable to discern her tone, Elizabeth was not certain whether Mrs. Norton meant to chide or merely make small talk.

"Oh, certainly! I understand there was much to arrange—your inheritance, the move to Montrose House... No, I do not blame you in the slightest for hiding yourself these past four weeks."

"I hardly hid. My...the Bennets stayed very near, and we saw one another often." Elizabeth felt a prickle of defensiveness—if this lady dared to speak ill of her adopted family...

"How lovely! And generous of them, truly, to have taken in a child of no relation." Mrs. Norton's smile seemed sincere, and Elizabeth allowed herself to relax—just a little.

"We were shopping for my sister's wedding clothes," she said, steering the subject elsewhere. "Jane is to marry Mr. Charles Bingley." *No need to say that it was the same man who discovered her in Hertfordshire.*

"I know the name." Mrs. Norton tapped her chin. "Oh, yes...his sister is marrying Sir James Blackwell, is she not? The Blackwells are not of the first circles, but are a respectable family. Her marriage will benefit the whole Bingley connection!"

"Beyond his pedigree, Sir James is a kind and attentive man."

Mrs. Norton nodded. "Yes, that is certainly a factor for some. Well, I am happy for them. And for you."

Mrs. Harrington and Mrs. Norton took their leave a short while later. They had barely a moment to reflect before more guests were announced. And so, the morning progressed. One lady followed another, each bringing polite curiosity and carefully phrased questions, and Elizabeth answered as best she could. None behaved with false politeness, at least so far as she could tell, and though she felt entirely worn out by the end of calling hours, she was quietly pleased that the day had gone so well.

Lady Montrose took Elizabeth on calls or to other small, private gatherings every day the following week. Darcy called regularly during the day and occasionally dined at Montrose House. One afternoon, he brought his sister to meet Elizabeth, and she could not have been more pleased with the young lady.

Georgiana Darcy was a kind, quiet girl. Though her round cheeks betrayed her youth, there was a seriousness in her manner that made her seem older than her years. Elizabeth tried several topics to encourage the conversation before settling on music, which at last inspired Miss Darcy to speak with animation of her favorite composers.

"I play the pianoforte and the harp," she said shyly, "but as the pianoforte is more often found in company, I have grown more practiced with it."

Elizabeth smiled and shook her head. "I also play the pianoforte, but I have never become truly proficient. That distinction belongs to my sister, Mary."

"My brother says you play very well."

"Then he has perjured himself thoroughly! Darcy, did you not mean my sister when you offered such praise?" Elizabeth laughed as her betrothed's ears flushed.

"I shall stand by my statement. You play very well, and nothing has given me greater pleasure than hearing you perform." His gaze warmed her from within.

"Have I performed a great many times in your presence?" she asked lightly.

"Yes. Remember, we dined in company many times, and the hostesses almost always called for exhibitions." He reached out and took her hand.

Georgiana cleared her throat delicately, causing Elizabeth to blush. "Perhaps you and Lady Montrose will be available to come to Darcy House for tea next week," she said hopefully.

"I shall ask my grandmother. I do not foresee any obstacle. We have no fixed engagements that I recall. Pray, do send round the invitation."

---

*Winters*

"Well, that ploy failed," he groaned. "Darcy and the girl are still keeping company. I would have expected Lady Montrose to cut the acquaintance."

"Them rich types rarely make sense." Jarvis fingered his knife, his feet up on the table. Winters hated it when he put his disgusting boots where they ate.

"Want I should take care of yer problem, sir?" the hired man asked, smiling with relish.

Winter's stomach churned. He did not want to kill her—nor have someone else do it. Standing, he crossed the room to his writing desk and retrieved the letter that had come only an hour before. A boy had brought it. All his post went to another location before reaching him. He remained ever cautious about being discovered.

*Dear Sir,*

*After speaking with knowledgeable sources and investigating the state of my niece's company, I present a counteroffer for you to consider. Lady Montrose* will accept *a sum of one hundred thousand pounds in exchange for her father's controlling shares of the company, the warehouses still in his name located in Yorkshire, and even his* house, *if it is your desire.*

*I believe this compensation to be more than equitable and look forward to your letter.*

*Yours, etc.,*

*Edward Gardiner*

He scoffed in disgust. Winters would not even dignify the missive with a response. "What do you know about this man?" He tossed the letter at Jarvis. "You investigated Miss Montrose's adopted relations." He should have known Lady Montrose would stick her nose in his business.

"Gardiner's in imports an' exports. Owns warehouses in Cheapside—done well fer 'imself. Very good 'ead for business. You ain't gonna talk 'im down. I wager 'e already offered you a bargain."

"I am very aware of what my company is worth!" But he did not have the assets to purchase Montrose's share—not at that price. The amount he had offered Miss Montrose was less than half the value of everything listed in Gardiner's letter.

"The only way to get yer 'ands on it now is to—" Jarvis made a slicing motion across his throat.

Winters sighed and sat down. "I had hoped it would not come to this." Not again.

"The girl walks in the park every day. Takes a footman with 'er, but I can deal wit 'im easily. Quick grab 'n the job'll be done. You'll get yer business, and I'll get me cut."

"Of course, of course." Sighing heavily, he waved a hand. "Do what you must. But do not get caught."

"Got an idea, I think. There's a bounder turned up when I looked into our problem. 'Ad some kind o' fallin' out with Darcy years ago. Down on 'is luck now. Let's see if we can get 'im to do the dirty work fer us."

Winters nodded in agreement. Best to keep their hands as clean as possible and let someone else take the risk. "Give him whatever he wants in the way of compensation—within reason, of course."

Jarvis grinned wickedly, and Winters sighed in resignation. He knew that if Jarvis had any say in the matter, his mark would not see a farthing. More likely, he would end up taking a permanent dip in the Thames.

He did not acknowledge Jarvis's departure. Instead, he took his seat before the fire and stared into the flames in stony silence. Time was running out. Dangerous men waited to collect on his debts, and he could not put them off much longer. Even now, he hid within his house, afraid to step outside for fear that they would find him and take what they were owed—out of his hide, if necessary.

He had no doubt Jarvis would succeed. The man was *terribly* persuasive. Winters had met him by chance whilst traveling. What he had done before entering Winters's service was a mystery, though he suspected that Jarvis had run with smugglers. He operated with stealth and cunning and would do anything his master required—so long as he was paid.

Of course, he wanted half the business profits in time, but Winters had no intention of keeping him that long. Jarvis believed him soft. But even he did not know what Winters was capable of. No one did. No one alive, at any rate. And he meant to keep it that way. *I suppose it is inevitable that the girl be dealt with,* he thought.

The door opened a few hours later. "Did you accomplish your aims?" Winters asked without turning to look at the newcomer.

"O'course I did—said yes straight off. Seems 'is grudge against that wealthy nob goes deep." There came the sound of movement as Jarvis rummaged about. He came to Winters's side with a decanter and two glasses. He watched as Jarvis set them down and then filled them nearly to the brim. Then he raised his glass and toasted: "To fat profits." Winters took the offered glass and took a sip. It was cheap wine, but he savored the bitter flavor before swallowing. "To our future, indeed," he muttered, raising his glass to Jarvis. "May it come sooner rather than later."

# Chapter Twenty-Nine

*February 14, 1812*
*Darcy House, London*
*Darcy*

He grinned, reassured by Elizabeth's playful words. Whatever had pulled him away, she did not hold it against him. Glancing at the clock, he grimaced. He had three hours to wait before his meeting. Wickham had insisted upon discretion, and Darcy would honor the request, unpleasant as it was.

*He likely wants money for whatever information he has to give.* Darcy would do anything to protect Elizabeth, and so went to his safe and withdrew a bag of guineas. He held a veritable fortune in his hand for a man of Wickham's status. Whatever the blackguard had to say had best be worth every bit.

Georgiana played the pianoforte for an hour, and though he listened with fondness, his mind wandered. He tried to read but abandoned the book, turning instead to estate business. Nothing held his attention. Anxiety pressed against his chest. What danger now threatened the woman he loved...after all she had already endured?

The hour finally came to depart, and he donned his outerwear, patted his pocket to make sure Wickham's *'fee'* was secure and left the house. Hyde Park was close, but he would not go there directly. Instead, he circled the block and entered the park by a lesser-used gate, the sort the *ton* seldom frequented. He slipped inside, glancing around as he did. Darcy continued through with casual ease, resisting the urge to look over his shoulder. He hoped no one followed. He strolled down the path, swinging his walking stick as though he had no care in the world.

When the path split, he veered left and wandered down toward the pond. Idly, he watched the ducks for a moment before moving on. A few more turns brought him to the grove—a quiet corner of the park where he and Wickham had played as children. Darcy's governess had often brought them whilst Mr. Darcy handled business.

As he stepped deeper into the trees, he caught movement behind a stand of shrubbery. A moment later, Wickham emerged, peering about before stepping into view.

"I half-expected you would burn my letter and never come," he said, relief evident in his tone. "Were you followed?"

"I saw no one," Darcy said curtly. "Now, out with it. What danger threatens Lady Montrose?"

Wickham swallowed, and Darcy sighed. "How much?" he asked.

"I need enough to see me hidden. The man who approached me seems a rough sort. He will likely kill me for giving you warning." Wickham looked genuinely distressed. Darcy had not seen such fear on his former friend's face in a long time.

"I have plenty to meet your needs. Speak now, or I shall depart." He leaned lightly on his walking stick.

Wickham glanced about, then lowered his voice. "Someone wants Lady Montrose dead. Only—he called her Miss Montrose. He does not seem to know about her title."

"How do *you*—never mind. It was in the announcement." Darcy recalled it had been printed in small type at the bottom. Elizabeth had not wanted it to draw attention. "Did this man give you a name?"

"No. He found me in a public house in the Rookery—filthy place, filled with thieves and the worst sort. He knew far too much of both you and me—he did his research thoroughly. The man offered me a sum to help him dispose of Lady Montrose. Said his master had a vested interest in seeing her dead. I agreed, of course. He is not the sort one refuses." Wickham cast another anxious glance around the grove. He was tense and seemed ready to bolt.

"And you thought you would be a good Samaritan, and come warn me. Really, Wickham, how stupid do you take me for?"

"I shall admit to less-than-altruistic motives—I am in a desperate position, and you know it. I also knew you would pay more for the information than the man's mystery puppet master! Please, Darcy, I have told you everything I know." He practically danced on the balls of his feet, eager to be gone.

Darcy slowly pulled out the bag of guineas from his coat pocket. "If I hand you this, you will go directly to the docks and board a ship out of England," he said firmly. "It is enough to establish yourself anywhere else. I hear the Americas are full of opportunities for an intrepid young man *such as yourself*."

"Agreed." Wickham lunged for the bag, but Darcy stepped back.

"If you *ever* return to England," he said coldly, "I shall call in every marker of yours I possess and see you locked in Marshalsea for the rest of your life. Am I understood?"

Wickham had always known a good bargain when he heard one, and he nodded.

"Come to the mews at Darcy House in an hour. My man will be waiting to take you to the docks. You will receive your money then."

"That will give me time to collect my belongings." Wickham muttered with a grimace. "What is left of them, anyway. I have had to sell practically everything since—"

"Since your plans this summer were thwarted? Do not test my patience, Wickham. Be at Darcy House in an hour. Every minute you are late, I shall remove a guinea from this bag." He tucked the pouch back into his pocket and walked away, praying Wickham would do as he promised.

He strolled through the park, taking a circuitous route to once more ensure no one had followed him before returning at last to Darcy House. Once safely inside his study, he added several carefully folded banknotes to the pouch—easier to conceal, and far lighter than gold. They would serve Wickham just as well, and cost Darcy little effort. The information he had offered was invaluable, and much as he loathed to give his wayward friend more funds, if this payment allowed Wickham to start afresh in a new land, it was a price worth paying…in gratitude for helping him keep Elizabeth safe. With this final act, Darcy intended to wash his hands of the man forever.

Wickham arrived at the kitchen door, where Darcy met him and handed him a satchel. "Food and drink for the day," he said. "Your payment is inside. Have a care and do not part with the bag under any circumstance."

He accepted it and slung the strap across his chest, tucking it beneath his greatcoat. He buttoned it securely, hiding the satchel from view. Then he lifted a sack containing the remnants of his possessions and nodded once at Darcy. Without another word, he turned and walked away, leaving his former friend standing in the doorway, watching him go.

When that business had concluded, Darcy went to his chamber to change for dinner and gather the gifts he had prepared for the Ladies Montrose. He was still uncertain how he felt knowing that his future wife now held a title in her own right—an earldom. One day, their eldest son would inherit it. Darcy had always imagined his firstborn son would inherit Pemberley. There would be plenty of time to sort that out later. For now, he wished only to see Elizabeth with his own eyes and be assured that she was safe.

He knocked awkwardly on the door to Montrose House, roses in one hand and the box of sweetmeats under his arm. The jeweled comb, fashioned in the shape of the Montrose crest, was in his coat pocket.

Morton answered the door and stepped aside to let Darcy enter. He accepted the roses and the sweets with a nod and waited as Darcy removed his coat and handed it to a footman. Darcy retrieved his parcels from Morton and followed him down the hall. The doors to the family sitting room opened from within, and he was shown in.

"There you are!" Elizabeth exclaimed from her seat beside her grandmother. "I thought you would never arrive!"

"Nothing could keep me from your side, dearest Elizabeth." He bowed slightly, then turned to the Dowager Countess. "Lady Montrose, I have brought you something for your sweet tooth." He offered her the box and flashed her a charming smile. Each sweetmeat had been shaped and wrapped in delicate paper. "The finest in London," Darcy assured her.

"I suppose I cannot tease you now," she replied, accepting the package with pleasure. "It was kind of you to bring them."

"And these are for you, my dear." He handed Elizabeth the roses, and she lifted them to her nose and inhaled with evident pleasure.

"And this." Darcy pulled the jewel box from his pocket and opened it. "For your presentation ball." Nestled within, a comb gleamed in the candlelight, with an arrangement of gold filigree and small gems shaped into a cluster of tiny roses and trailing ivy leaves surrounding her family's crest.

Elizabeth gasped. "Oh, Fitzwilliam, it is perfect!" She ran her fingers lightly over the jeweled comb. "Thank you."

She presented Darcy with a rare first-edition book he had not read, and he exclaimed over the fine leather binding. "I look forward to reading it. Thank you, Elizabeth."

When they had settled themselves and awaited the summons to supper, Darcy turned to Lady Montrose and Elizabeth, his countenance grave. "I bring news, and it is not good." Without delay, he told them of the plot against Elizabeth. Lady Montrose blanched and clutched her granddaughter's hand.

"You must hire additional footmen!" she cried. "We cannot allow anything to happen. No! Pray, I could not bear it."

"Grandmother, I am well." Elizabeth trembled, though her tone remained composed. "Darcy will not permit any harm to befall me."

"No, indeed. I believe further protection is essential. We must take care not to tip our hand. Those who conspire against you must not know that we are aware of their plot." Darcy took Elizabeth's free hand and pressed a soft kiss upon it.

"What do you propose?" Lady Montrose asked, her voice quivering.

"I have several acquaintances who may be of service—men capable of vanishing when it suits them. It is a rare talent, and one they have employed on my behalf more than once. You and Elizabeth must conduct yourselves as though nothing is amiss. We shall uncover the one who hired Wickham and, through him, learn who desires the extinction of the Montrose line." Darcy spoke with confidence, concealing the dread he harbored for his betrothed's safety.

"Will it succeed?" Elizabeth turned to him, her gaze pleading for reassurance.

"I can promise nothing, but we stand a better chance if we take the initiative and bolster our defenses so that we may act, not merely respond. My cousin might be persuaded to escort you about town. As I have been seen often enough in your company, it would not appear strange for Richard to take my place."

Lady Montrose narrowed her eyes. "Who is Richard?" she asked.

"Colonel Richard Fitzwilliam, second son of the Earl of Matlock," Darcy replied.

"Ah. I have not seen the earl or his wife in some time. I had forgotten one of their sons joined the army. Is he proficient, or is he one of those sons of peers who purchased his rank?" Lady Montrose frowned, clearly disapproving.

"My uncle bought him a commission as an ensign. Richard earned the rank of colonel through his own merit." Darcy's tone held quiet pride as he spoke in defense of his favorite cousin.

"At ease, both of you," Elizabeth said firmly, breaking the tension between them. "Jameson, would you suggest anything else?"

Jameson stepped forward and bowed. "I do not believe it wise to add staff to the household—unless they come under the recommendation of Colonel Fitzwilliam or Mr. Darcy. Any sudden additions would rouse suspicion. Lady Montrose has now been in residence with my lady for nearly six weeks, and no new servants have been engaged in that time. However, it would be prudent for either Morton or myself to know Lady Montrose's whereabouts at all times."

Darcy grimaced. Ever independent, Elizabeth would chafe against constant supervision. He glanced at her, and she gave a nod, though the set of her jaw made her displeasure plain.

"Promise me you will comply until we can put an end to this conspiracy against your life," her grandmother pleaded. She still clung to Elizabeth's hand, and her face looked more drawn and anxious than it had been since their reunion.

With a sigh, Elizabeth gave her word. "That does not mean I must be pleased with the arrangement," she added, her tone light. "Mr. Darcy, I shall count on you to visit me daily and see to it that I do not fall into a stupor from boredom."

"On my honor. Richard and I shall escort you to Bond Street, Hyde Park, Vauxhall, the theater..."

She laughed, as he intended. "Very well. You have made your point. Now, is dinner nearly served? I am ravenous."

As if on cue, the doors opened, and Morton stepped in. "Dinner is ready, your ladyship," he said solemnly. Darcy rose and assisted both ladies to their feet, offering his arm. As they made their way to the dining room, he silently prayed the matter would soon be brought to a close.

# Chapter Thirty

*February 20, 1812*
*Bloomsbury Street, London*
*Winters*

"It is as I suspected. Wickham's done a bunk." Jarvis kept his tone even, but Winters, who knew him well, could hear the anger simmering beneath the surface.

"Blast!" Winters slammed his hand on the table. "Now we have a loose end." He stood and began pacing the room, his hands clasped tightly behind his back, jaw tight. If Wickam talked, he could lose everything.

"Don't worry, Jarvis said, eyes narrowing. "I'll find 'im—and when I do, 'e'll pay for what 'e's done." His glare would have made a lesser man flinch, but Winters did not scare easily. He never had. Life had always bent to his will, and he had no intention of letting that change now.

"Handle it yourself," Winters snapped. "We cannot afford another complication."

Jarvis gave a slow nod, something like pleasure flickering across his face. "Gimme two weeks. I gotta learn 'er 'abits."

"Do whatever it takes." He needed this handled quickly. His creditors had given him until April and time was running short.

With an exaggerated bow, Jarvis turned and left. At least the man did not waste time.

---

*Jarvis*

The shadows had ever been his ally. Raised in the slums of London, Jarvis learned young how to pick pockets and lift wares unnoticed. As he grew, his skills drew the attention of smugglers, who soon recruited him into their fold. The entire crew had eventually been arrested, but not Jarvis. No, he had sensed something was wrong as he neared their hideout. He could not have said what warned him, only that something felt off, and he had lingered in the shadows to wait.

And before the night ended, the entire hideout had been raided, the smugglers taken, and their goods seized. Jarvis had watched it all unfold from the darkness. After that, he realized it was time to seek more profitable—and safer—employment.

He worked only for himself. True, Winters might believe he had Jarvis's loyalty, but that mistake would be his undoing. The man had offered the largest share he had ever been promised—half the proceeds once he controlled every share of the Montrose business.

Jarvis knew about the creditors. Winters fretted over being seen and rarely left his house, as though secrecy were protection enough. The fool did not realize his enemies already knew where he was. They had even employed Jarvis. He would play both sides—collect payment for keeping an eye on Winters and remove obstacles that kept him from seizing the business outright.

Everyone would win. The creditors would have their money, and Jarvis his share. Even Winters would be free of his debts. But the only way forward was to remove the Montrose brat from the picture.

Dressed like a common laborer, Jarvis loitered in Mayfair with the air of a man who belonged there. He kept his head down and eyes sharp, watching Montrose House at all hours. Days passed. Then, near the end of February, an opportunity presented itself.

Perched on a garden wall, half-concealed by a tree, he aimed for the front steps of Montrose House. Every morning at ten, the girl and the old woman left the house together, accompanied by a single servant. Predictable. Foolish.

The door opened, and *she* stepped outside. Jarvis drew a steady breath and took aim. He squeezed the trigger. The crack of the shot rang through the street, the noise bouncing off stone walls. Screams followed. Someone pulled the girl inside. He had missed.

Cursing under his breath, Jarvis dropped from the wall and fled into the alley. Another chance to finish the job would be nigh impossible.

---

*Darcy*

"I am well, I assure you!" Elizabeth patted her grandmother's arm reassuringly. "See? Not a scratch anywhere."

"There is a bullet hole in our door frame, Elizabeth." Lady Montrose's voice quavered. "That was too close for comfort. Darcy, what have your men to say for themselves?"

"Browning reports they are tracking the man now. He believes he escaped cleanly, but my men remain on his trail."

"How long before this is over?" Lady Montrose sighed and pressed her face into her hand, elbow resting on the chair's arm.

"Soon, we hope. Let us remain at home today. We can send our regrets to Mrs. Hiddleston." Darcy's bearing remained composed, but Elizabeth saw through the calm—beneath it, he trembled with fear.

Jameson entered. "Browning has more news."

"Show him in," Elizabeth said at once.

Darcy's man stepped into the drawing room. Brown-haired and bearded, he bore the air of quiet confidence. Though his eyes held a spark of dry humor, his manner now was all business..

"He has holed up in Seven Dials, sir," he said. "We will not reach him there. He must come to us."

"What do you mean?" Elizabeth asked.

"I propose we set a trap. I know his type. He will alter his appearance and return. In his arrogance, he will strike again, believing we have relaxed our guard. You plan to leave for Hertfordshire in March, do you not?"

"Yes, we shall only be gone a few days. My sister is marrying." Elizabeth's face brightened briefly before settling again into solemnity.

"Very good." Browning cast a purposeful glance about the room. "Encourage the servants to speak of the wedding. He is receiving information from somewhere, and your staff are the most likely source. They mean no harm, your ladyships," he added quickly, noting their dismay. "You may lecture them on discretion later. For now, we need them to chatter. Once he hears of your plans to leave London, he will do just as I expect."

"And what is that?" the Dowager Countess asked sharply.

"He will make another attempt on the North Road—mark my words. There are countless places where he may lie in wait. My men will continue to shadow him, and once he settles, we shall tighten the noose."

"Do you require extra men?" Darcy asked. Richard had offered a few of his soldiers, but Browning, who operated under cover, had declined. Military men, he claimed, stood out—they were too stiff, too precise.

"I have more than enough to meet our needs, sir," Browning replied with a polite nod. "I had best be off. I have lingered too long already." He departed with Jameson, no doubt heading to the kitchens to slip out through the mews unnoticed.

"Has he truly been watching us for a week?" Elizabeth asked, wonder in her voice.

"He has. Browning is a master at avoiding detection. I have entrusted him with delicate matters in the past, and he has never failed me. And he is no rogue, either, which recommends him further. A thief will betray his employer when it suits him." Darcy knew from experience that a man who would raise a weapon against an innocent woman could not be trusted to keep faith with anyone.

They remained at Montrose House the rest of the day. The next morning, at Darcy's encouragement, Elizabeth and the dowager resumed their usual activities. His dear betrothed did so with courage, though Darcy could see that she concealed her fear for her grandmother's sake.

*I can only pray this is over soon,* he thought, drawing Elizabeth a little nearer as they walked down Bond Street.

Though their engagement had not been formally announced, word had already begun to circulate. Whispers reached their ears from more than one quarter of the *ton,* suggesting a match was in the making. The gentlemen at Darcy's club hounded him whenever he appeared, so he was determined to stay away for the present. Richard reported that the betting books were filled with wagers, and more than one fellow had called Darcy a fortunate dog. All wondered how he had managed to win the *suo jure* Countess of Montrose before anyone knew she existed. He would tell the tale someday—once the danger had passed.

*Jarvis*

Jarvis tugged at the too-tight stolen livery, and took up a post beside a wall, doing his best to appear as though he belonged. His scruffy beard was gone—he had even bathed. His once-greasy hair had been slicked back and hidden beneath a powdered wig. White gloves covered his hands, and he wore shoes so impractical he could hardly walk in them. Still, he stood across the street from Montrose House, the picture of a liveried servant.

After lying low for several days, he had devised a new approach. One more day, and he had secured all he required. Now he waited for information. Had the ladies resumed their habits? Or were they cowering in their grand mansion, hoping he had vanished? They had hired additional guards, as far as he could tell. *Fools.*

A group of giggling girls passed by, trailed by a stern woman and a footman. Then came a pair of gentlemen and a dog. He waited. Time dragged. At last, two maids appeared, baskets in hand, chattering freely as they walked—just what he had hoped for.

"They be leaving London for a few days," one said. "I'll be able to go home and see Mother."

The second maid scowled. "Old Lady Montrose gave you permission, did she? I never thought to 'ear it from her. That 'ouse ain't got no joy. You ain't never been given leave before."

"'Tis much better now," the first insisted. "What with the new young lady, Madam seems quite 'appy."

"If you say so. When're they goin'?"

The first maid smiled. "First of March. They'll be gone for a week or somethin'. I have two days' leave before I'm to return."

"Mama will be excited. I shall see if I can change my 'alf day. Then we might surprise 'er together."

Their voices faded, and Jarvis forced himself to remain still. He could not afford to leave his post. It would draw the wrong sort of notice. After a quarter of an hour, he glanced at his *borrowed* watch, then waited five more minutes for the hour to strike. At last, he stepped away from his station and slipped through a garden gate he had unlocked earlier. It need only appear that he returned to the house.

Once in the shelter of the garden, which was still far too cold this time of year for its occupants, he stripped off the livery and shoved the garments into a burlap sack. The powdered wig came next. He had half a mind to grind it into the dirt, but prudence prevailed; it, too, went into the bag, just in case it was needed. He freed his hair from the tie and tousled it to restore his usual appearance. Then he watched the street, waiting for a chance to slip away unnoticed.

Two days later, Jarvis walked the North Road with a sack over his shoulder, scouting for a place to lie in wait. His rifle had been stashed beneath a hedgerow, the spot marked by a discreet 'X' carved into a tree—visible to only him.

At length, he came upon a broad oak near the roadside and studied it. The trunk was solid, the branches thick and sturdy. Though bare of leaves, it would provide ample concealment. His coarse clothing, all brown and gray, would blend with bark and shadow. It was the perfect vantage from which to carry out his evil doings.

Jarvis retrieved the rifle and climbed into the tree. The night would be long, but he needed to be in position before the Montrose carriage passed. The shot would prove more difficult than the one he had taken outside Montrose House, and he cursed his luck. Never before had his aim failed him. Now, it must not. If he judged it well, he could put a bullet through a carriage window—and if fortune smiled, he might strike Darcy or the old woman as well, reloading whilst they screamed.

He drew a blanket from his sack and wrapped it around his shoulders. His greatcoat provided some warmth, but the blanket helped to stave off the cold. Closing his eyes, he settled back against the tree and tried to rest until his moment came.

Morning arrived swiftly. At first light, Jarvis climbed into position. The rifle rested neatly between a forked branch, angled toward the road. At last, the carriage appeared in the distance. Closing one eye, he squinted down the barrel and waited—steady and still. He held his breath.

A sudden crack rang out—and a sharp bolt of pain shot through his hand. He looked down, staring in disbelief as a patch of red bloomed across his knuckles. *What had happened?* Dazed and with pain surging through his arm, he scrambled down the rear side of the tree—only to be struck from behind. He hit the ground hard, his arms wrenched back, and a hood thrown over his head. Panic surged through him, and he wondered what he had done to upset his employers.

"Not a word," someone growled in his ear. Rough hands hauled him to his feet and dragged him away. A carriage door opened, and he was thrown inside without ceremony. No one spoke as the door was closed. A rap on the roof and the conveyance began to move.

"Keep him there," the first voice commanded.

"Should have locked him in the boot," growled another. "The floor's too good for the likes of him."

A boot pressed down between his shoulders, resting there as though he were a footrest. "I do not believe our friend will give us any trouble," the first man replied. "But if he does, his lot will be worse when we arrive."

Jarvis clenched his jaw. He would escape—he must. He would bide his time until they neared their destination—and then he would find a way out.

# Chapter Thirty-One

*March 1, 1812*
*Netherfield Park*
*Darcy*

"He's in the stables, sir," Browning reported as soon as the prisoner had been secured. Richard grinned beside him. Colonel Fitzwilliam had insisted upon accompanying his cousin once he learned of the plan—his skill in interrogation would be invaluable.

"Has he said anything?" Darcy asked.

"No. Hood's still on. I doubt he even knows where he is." Browning allowed himself a wicked grin. "He never saw our faces, either."

"Let us have done with it immediately, then." Darcy rose. "The Ladies Montrose are at Longbourn. They do not yet know we have captured their assailant. I shall inform them once we understand the full nature of the threat."

The three men left the house and crossed to the stables. At the rear, in a storage room far from the horses and out of earshot, their prisoner waited. Darcy entered first, Richard close behind. Browning positioned himself behind the man, out of his line of sight, and pulled off the sack.

"Greetings." Richard said smoothly, stepping forward with a smile that did not reach his eyes. "Thank you for joining us. Your name, if you please?"

The man clenched his jaw and turned away. Browning seized a handful of hair and yanked his head back, forcing him to meet their gazes.

"It will go easier on you if you cooperate. Transportation is your best hope, though the destination remains negotiable. I hear Van Diemen's Land is a fine place. Snakes, spiders, larger reptiles...perfect punishment for a would-be murderer."

"I ain't sayin' nothin'."

Richard dragged a chair forward and swung it around, seating himself astride it with his arms resting on the back. He met the prisoner's eyes, unflinching. "No? Why is that? Loyalty to your masters? I doubt it. Fear then? You need not fear, for they will not find you where you are going."

Beads of sweat formed on the man's upper lip. From the doorway, Darcy watched in silence, arms folded, his jaw set in a hard line. He had promised Richard he would stay out of it, but the urge to plant his fist in the man's face had not lessened.

"Don't matter then. Ye can toss me aboard a ship bound for anywhere. What I say won't make no difference." His rough speech grated on Darcy's ears.

"But it does." Richard leaned forward. "If you would rather spend your journey swimming in bilge water, say nothing. More comfortable accommodations await those who cooperate."

Richard stood. "We shall leave you to consider your options." At his nod, Browning replaced the hood. The three men exited the windowless room, leaving their prisoner tied to the chair and alone in the dark.

"Keep watch," Richard ordered. "Do not allow him to escape. He has been searched, I trust?"

"Yes, sir," Browning replied with a nod. "We found four blades and a pistol on him."

"Let us hope he has nothing more hidden."

Darcy scoffed. "I am more interested in hoping he speaks."

"He will, Darcy. Men like him place their own skin above all else. He will talk—if only to save it."

"He has already resolved to say nothing. He knows he will be transported regardless."

"That remains to be seen. I suspect a more...fitting punishment may be arranged. If he will not speak, I believe Marshalsea would be an appropriate destination."

They left the stables, two guards posted at the door behind them. Darcy's patience wore thin. *When will this end?*

*Jarvis*

Jarvis caught every word they spoke, though they likely believed themselves well out of range. Jarvis had always had good hearing, and it served him well now. Marshalsea or transportation? The latter held more appeal, certainly. His former masters had men in the prison—he would not last more than a day in there. He would have to give the nobs something—anything—to keep himself out of the place.

But what? Of those who had hired him, Silas Winters was the lesser threat. He could give up the location of the townhouse and, if Winters managed to slip away, claim he had been hired off the street and had no name. No names—just a house number and a location. It might be enough to keep him alive and get out of England. Once abroad, he could start again. His trade travelled well——there were always thieves and smugglers somewhere in the world.

His face dripped with sweat. Despite the spring air, the small room had grown stifling, especially under the hood. His breathing grew labored in the heat. After what felt like hours, he heard the door open. Three sets of boots crossed the floor. He sensed movement behind him, then the hood was pulled away. Cool air touched his skin, and he drew a deep breath.

"I do hope you have given my offer proper consideration," said the red-coated officer. "I have been more than generous, you know."

Jarvis swallowed. "Yeah, I thought on it. I'll tell ye what I know. It ain't much." He swallowed again, throat dry.

"Speak." The officer pulled up a chair and sat.

"Don't know no names. I was hired off the street to do a job." He shrugged. "Not out o' the usual for me."

"You are often hired to kill young ladies?" the redcoat asked, sharp-eyed.

Jarvis stiffened. "That ain't what I meant! I get hired fer odd jobs is all."

"You, sir, are a liar. If it comforts you to believe your target was your first, cling to that thought. But give me the information I seek, or you will lose your chance to negotiate."

Darcy stood by the door, silent until now. Yet Jarvis could sense the anger radiating from him—sharp and unmistakable. "There's a house on Bloomsbury Street," he said, his voice unsteady. "Number five. Got my orders there." *Let Winters face what was coming.*

"Thank you," Richard replied coolly. "Make yourself comfortable. We will verify your claims before proceeding." The hood came down once more, plunging Jarvis into the darkness. Muffled voices followed just beyond the door.

"Send a rider at once." Darcy's commanding voice—firm and unyielding—brooked no argument.

"Even if he rides hard, it may be hours before we have word. And subtlety is required. They must proceed with care. Go to your lady, Darcy. I shall remain here."

Jarvis leaned back in the chair. His discomfort and the pain in his hand would keep him from resting, but he had best make the attempt.

---

*Winters*

Ten days. It had been ten days, and not a word. Jarvis had never stayed away so long. He kept chambers in the house and favored his soft bed. Fearing the worst, Silas began to gather any incriminating papers. If Jarvis had been caught, he had no doubt the sneak-thief would offer up his employer to save himself.

Years of detritus littered the house. Silas burned every item that might reveal his involvement, taking care to destroy anything bearing his name. He left Jarvis's rooms untouched. If anyone came for him, they would find his belongings and assume he had lived there alone.

*Where would he go now?* Silas frowned. There was a boarding house across the street. He could stay there and watch his own front door. If anyone arrived, he would know he had been betrayed. He packed a small trunk with essentials and whatever valuables remained. A purse of coin tucked into his coat, he slipped out the rear door and made his way across the street.

The proprietress had a room available, and he secured it at once. Fortunately, it overlooked the street. He paid for the week in advance, then settled at the window with a book. From there, he could easily see his front door.

Nothing happened for two days. Passersby came and went. The noise and bustle of the street, so familiar from within his home, now felt strange when viewed from the other side. Silas passed the hours with books, cards, and small amusements. By the third day, he began to believe he had misjudged Jarvis—that perhaps the man had succeeded, and all would proceed as planned.

On the fourth day, soldiers arrived at his front door. They did not trouble themselves with knocking; instead, they broke down his finely carved entrance and stormed inside. Silas' face darkened with fury. Jarvis had betrayed him. *If the man is anywhere in England, I shall find him.* He glared out the window toward his house, and though he could not see what passed within, he imagined it clearly—his furnishings cut open, every drawer and wardrobe turned out, every scrap of paper examined.

An hour later, two men left the house, leaving three within. Silas paced and fumed, calculating his next move. Returning home was out of the question. He might flee to Yorkshire, but his creditors would find him there soon enough. He picked up a decanter he had brought from the house and drank directly from the mouth. The spirits dulled his edge, and he drifted into a restless doze.

Memories stirred in the haze. A small girl, seated beside her prone father, his hand clutched in hers. Her tear-streaked face turning toward him. Her crumpled form as he...

He jolted upright. *If you want something done properly, you must do it yourself,* he thought grimly. Snatching up the newspaper, he scanned the pages until he found what he sought.

*Lady Maude Montrose, now the Dowager Countess of Montrose, plans to present her granddaughter, the suo jure Countess of Montrose, to the ton. The lavish ball is scheduled for the fourteenth of March, the young countess's birthday and the day on which she reaches her majority.*

"This," he murmured aloud. "This is my chance." It would likely be his last opportunity to rid himself of the wretched girl. He could not fail again.

---

*Darcy*

"No sign of an accomplice?" he asked, incredulous. "Were we played for fools?"

"I do not believe so. The hearth showed traces of burnt paper—our man must have known we were coming and destroyed whatever might have implicated him. We did find a room in the house that appears to have belonged to our prisoner." Richard shook his head. "He knew whoever hired him more than he let on."

"So, he lied to us. I suppose I ought not to be surprised. So, the danger to Elizabeth is still out there."

"You cannot hide her away forever, Darcy. Keep your men alert and go about your business. Bingley and Miss Bennet are to marry in two days' time. Go, attend the festivities—socialize with the family and be with your Elizabeth." Richard clapped him on the shoulder.

"Will you accompany me? The invitation included you." He wanted Richard close; an extra pair of eyes.

"I shall join you at Longbourn once I see to it that our guest in the stables is on his way to London," his cousin assured him. "Browning will see him aboard a ship bound for Australia. I am half-tempted to send orders that he be stowed with the cargo…or the bilge."

"So long as he is gone, and no longer a threat to Elizabeth." Darcy rose. "I believe I shall ride to Longbourn now."

The Ladies Montrose had chosen to remain with the Bennets. Though the accommodations were humbler than Netherfield, Elizabeth wished to be near her dearest sister in the days before the wedding, and the Dowager Countess had no desire to be separated from her granddaughter. Darcy continued to reside at Netherfield Park with Bingley and his family.

Miss Bingley and Sir James had arrived the day before; the Hursts were already in residence, having remained through the winter. The dismal state of Bingley's wine cellar stirred his indignation, and he announced to his relations they must depart promptly after the wedding.

Darcy called for a fresh horse. Bingley and his sister were likely already at Longbourn, as they went near daily. Miss Bingley busied herself with the wedding preparations, and her brother hovered devotedly at his *angel's* side.

In truth, Darcy envied him. Though he understood why he and Elizabeth were forced to wait, he did not like it. He longed to begin their life together in Derbyshire—far from danger, far from prying eyes—where he could have Elizabeth all to himself.

Lord and Lady Matlock had encountered Elizabeth at several events. His aunt had speculated about his connection to the newly discovered countess, but he had offered no information that might be passed along through the *ton*. Lady Matlock, unfortunately, had a penchant for gossip. She would learn the truth, along with the rest of society, when the engagement was announced at Elizabeth's ball.

Eager to see her, Darcy mounted the horse and urged it into a gallop. As the hooves thundered across the fields, each stride carried him nearer to her side. One vigorous ride later, he dismounted, handed the reins to a waiting servant, and hastened to the door.

It swung open before he could knock. Mr. Collins nearly collided with him on his way out.

"Oh! Forgive me, sir, I was not attending." He beamed and bowed. Miss Mary came up behind him, resting a light hand on his arm.

"I had no idea you had returned to Hertfordshire," Darcy said, offering a polite smile. He had not come to know the parson well, but he appeared steady; responsible and eager to be of use.

"I came for my dear cousin's wedding…and for unfinished business." He glanced bashfully at Miss Mary, who looked equally shy.

"Then you must go to it." Darcy grinned and stepped aside. The couple hurried toward the gardens, and he watched them go, recalling his own proposal. *Mrs. Bennet will be pleased,* he mused. *Three daughters married. That is no small feat.*

He stepped inside, where Hill greeted him and took his coat and hat. The old servant lingered, as though he wished to speak. Darcy nodded, granting permission.

"I just want to thank you, sir, for taking care of our Miss Lizzy," Hill said respectfully. "I remember when she first came to the Bennets. She is one of theirs, and we never saw her as anything else." He cleared his throat and turned away.

"You are most welcome," Darcy replied. "She is easy to love."

"That she is, sir. That she is."

Darcy followed the sound of conversation to the parlor. Bingley sat with Mr. Bennet and Thomas, engaged in a lively debate. He turned instead toward his betrothed. She sat amongst her female relations, deep in discussion of wedding details. Miss Bingley was with them, speaking animatedly to Jane as they reviewed a list of final tasks.

"Ladies," he greeted them. "Is everything prepared for the wedding?"

"It is," Elizabeth replied. "Have you resolved your business?" She spoke vaguely, glancing at her adopted mother and giving a subtle shake of her head.

*The Bennets do not know, then.* He would honor Elizabeth's choice to keep them unaware. Heaven knew they had worries enough already.

# Chapter Thirty-Two

*March 5, 1812*
*Longbourn*
*Elizabeth*

Elizabeth waited quietly for her turn to walk down the aisle. Jane had gone ahead on their father's arm, looking resplendent in a gown of cornflower blue. Her bouquet, a delicate arrangement of early spring blossoms, complemented her angelic countenance—now made lovelier still by joy. Elizabeth followed her sister and took her place across from Darcy. He stood up with his friend, just as she did for Jane.

"Dearly beloved, we are gathered here today in the sight of God to join together this man and this woman in holy matrimony..."

Darcy met her gaze, and for the rest of the ceremony, they only looked at one another. Elizabeth imagined his thoughts mirrored her own. She pictured their wedding day; trees dressed in green, and flowers blooming everywhere. June felt far away. Part of her longed to elope, if only to bring this long wait to an end.

The ceremony concluded, and the bride and groom signed the register. Elizabeth took Darcy's arm and followed them from the church.

The wedding breakfast would be held at Netherfield, and so thither they would go.

Darcy handed Elizabeth into her grandmother's carriage and then climbed in beside her. He had arrived with Charles and had sensibly yielded the bridal carriage to the married couple. Caroline rode with the Hursts and Sir James. Privately, Elizabeth wondered how her friend could endure even a brief ride in the Hursts' presence.

They had warmed considerably toward Jane, and indeed toward the Bennets generally—Elizabeth included—after the Dowager Lady Montrose had arrived. Somehow, they had either missed the announcement in the London papers, or failed to connect Elizabeth Bennet with Elizabeth Montrose. Whatever the case, as soon as her connection to the Dowager became known, Mrs. Hurst promptly determined that Elizabeth must be her closest friend. Now it seemed there was no escaping the association—her dearest sister had married the brother of that most tiresome woman.

Mrs. Bennet's hostess skills were on full display for the residents of Meryton and its environs. Longbourn's cook collaborated with Netherfield's to create a sumptuous feast worthy of an advantageous marriage. Elizabeth enjoyed the fare immensely and spoke with animation to her grandmother and Darcy throughout the meal.

When it came time for Charles and Jane to depart, the guests gathered on the front steps and waved them off. Carriages soon began to arrive to convey the remaining guests to their homes.

The Gardiners, having come from London, joined Elizabeth in the drawing room. Mrs. Bennet conversed with Mrs. Nicholls, ensuring that the manor returned to good order. Several of Longbourn's servants had come to assist, easing the burden upon Netherfield's staff.

"Have you heard from Mr. Winters regarding our offer?" Elizabeth asked her uncle.

"I have not. Are you so eager to be rid of your father's assets? Holding on to a profitable concern is often the more prudent choice, even if your husband possesses a vast estate and considerable wealth." Mr. Gardiner picked up a glass of port and sipped thoughtfully.

"Your uncle offers sound advice." Darcy seated himself beside Elizabeth and took her hand. "If Mr. Winters has not responded by now, I would wager he does not intend to pursue the purchase. If that is the case, perhaps we ought to consider buying him out. I could engage a manager to oversee its operation. It would serve as an additional source of revenue."

Lady Montrose nodded. "My husband was a fool, but even then, Henry perceived that times were changing and wished to be a part of it. Common men are amassing fortunes that rival, or surpass, those of earls and barons."

Elizabeth ran her thumb gently across Darcy's hand. "Will you prepare a proposal for Mr. Winters, Uncle?"

"I shall." Mr. Gardiner replied with a smile. "And I thank you for allowing me to remain a part of your life. You are a great lady now, Lizzy—far too grand for the likes of me."

"You and Aunt Gardiner are two of my favorite people. I shall never be 'too grand' for you. Or for my little cousins."

Lady Montrose chuckled. "Let us delay any meeting with Mr. Winters until after your ball," she said. "You will have more than enough to occupy you in preparation."

She made a face. "I never thought to have a come-out, let alone be paraded before the entire *ton*. If I had my way, I would hide away in my chambers instead."

"Then it is a good thing that I shall have *my* way." Grandmother patted her hand gently. "It is not so terrible, Elizabeth. And once it is over, everyone will know that you are betrothed. That alone will spare you a great deal of unwelcome attention, particularly from gentlemen."

"And just think you will be able to reassure Georgiana that the ordeal is not so fearsome as she imagines. My sister does not wish to come out, being of a shy and retiring nature." Darcy grinned and gave Elizabeth's hand a gentle squeeze.

"Oh, very well. You have managed to persuade me." Elizabeth huffed in playful resignation. "I suppose the thought of my gown is enough to excite me." Her grandmother had purchased an entirely new wardrobe, but the gown chosen for the ball was especially exquisite. It was a soft butter yellow, trimmed at the high waist with sky-blue ribbon. The square neckline dipped daringly low, though still within the bounds of modesty. The sheer sleeves of a fine silk net, worked with gold thread, came to her elbows. They completed the ensemble and gave the gown a regal finish, making Elizabeth feel like a princess.

"I am eager to see it," Darcy said huskily, causing Elizabeth to glance up at him through her eyelashes. The look of love in his eyes said more than words could convey, and she felt her heart beat faster.

"When will you return to London, your ladyship?" Mr. Gardiner asked, drawing her attention back to the conversation.

"Elizabeth wished to visit with the Bennets for several days," Lady Montrose replied. "We shall return on the ninth to see to the final preparations for the ball. There is still so much to be done! The ballroom has not been used in an age. I set the servants to cleaning it before we left, but I expect we shall return to a list of repairs and adjustments before that night."

Her grandmother launched into her plans for the ball, and the Gardiners listened attentively. Darcy gave Elizabeth's hand a light tug, and they rose, quietly slipping from the room with none the wiser.

Darcy led her to the library. A cheerful fire crackled in the grate, keeping the spring chill at bay. Since no one had used the room all day, she knew he must have arranged it just for them. They crossed to the settee, and he drew her down beside him, wrapping her in his arms and pressing a kiss to the top of her head. "Alone at last," he murmured.

"Be careful, sir, lest your words summon company down upon us!" Was that not what always seemed to happen? Having been interrupted so many times in the past, she would rather not tempt fate.

His chest rumbled with laughter as he pulled her closer. "If anyone claims compromise, I shall gladly purchase a common license and marry you tomorrow."

They were silent for a time, simply content with each other's company. "Any news from your men?" she asked idly, lacing her fingers through his and placing his hand into her lap.

"None. There has been no movement at the house. If fortune favors us, the man responsible has fled."

"But you do not think that." She turned to look at him. He met her gaze briefly, then gave a slight shake of the head. Disappointment settled in her chest, and she turned back toward the fire, resting her head lightly against his chest. "You do not believe I am safe," she whispered.

"I do not. Elizabeth, someone wanted you dead twelve years ago. Now that you have been found, they intend to finish what they began. Who knows what drives such a villain? Your fortune alone might tempt someone, but with the earldom involved..."

"Could this have something to do with my inheritance?" she asked, more serious now. "I mean the earldom. Could someone have murdered my family to prevent my father from inheriting?"

"He had an elder brother. I do not know who would have stood to inherit if all of Lady Montrose's immediate relations were gone, but it seems unlikely that the title itself set all this in motion." He stroked her arm, sending shivers down her spine, and she breathed deeply, taking in his citrus and sandalwood scent.

"So now what are we to do?" Elizabeth had no wish to live in fear, always watching and wondering when something might happen. She wanted to move about freely, to travel as she pleased without the worry that something would befall her. And what of the future? If she had children, would that fear become dread, knowing it was not only her life at risk?

She felt safe in Darcy's arms and never wished to be away from him. But alas, after a blissful hour in quiet companionship, they were discovered. Lady Montrose was highly amused as she observed them.

"Comfortable?" she asked archly. "I wondered where you had gone. Naughty children, sneaking off to the library."

"We have done nothing but sit, Grandmother," Elizabeth replied in mock affront. "Sit, and talk, and watch the fire."

"Very well, I believe you. Darcy is an honorable man. He would not dare betray my trust. Now, it is time to be off. Your mother has called for the carriages, and the servants have the clearing up well in hand." Lady Montrose turned and departed, glancing over her shoulder to ensure the couple followed her.

Darcy withdrew his arm from around Elizabeth and rose. He turned and extended his hand, helping her to her feet. She adjusted her shawl, then tucked her arm through his. Together, they went to the entrance hall, where she retrieved her outerwear.

Mrs. Bennet bustled into view. "Mr. Darcy!" she exclaimed, beaming. "I trust you will join us for Lizzy's birthday celebration on the eighth? Miss Bingley and Sir James are welcome, too."

Elizabeth smiled. The Bennets would not attend her ball. Though they wished her every happiness, they believed it best for her prospects if they were not present. Moreover, though Mrs. Bennet delighted in society, she had no desire to field prying questions about her adopted daughter.

"I should be honored, madam," Darcy replied with a respectful bow. I shall extend the invitation to Miss Bingley and Sir James. They intended to return to town, though I am uncertain when they mean to leave Hertfordshire." Darcy turned to Elizabeth and took her hand, raising it to his lips in a gentle kiss. "The view from the mount must be spectacular in the morning," he murmured.

She caught his meaning at once and gave a small nod. "Yes. I have often walked there. I believe I might enjoy it again."

He leaned a little closer. "Bring a footman," he said beseechingly. "And take care."

"Of course. At dawn?" He inclined his head. "Dawn."

"Come, Elizabeth!" Lady Montrose called, her walking stick tapping smartly against the marble floor. "The carriage is waiting. I am not as young as I once was, and I need to rest."

Elizabeth stepped forward and offered her grandmother her arm. Together, they descended the steps and climbed into the waiting carriage. She settled on the rear-facing seat opposite her grandmother, leaned into the plush squabs, and closing her eyes, she breathed deeply. The gentle motion of the carriage soothed her as they trundled away toward Longbourn.

Worrying over the identity of her assailant would only bring added anxiety, and so Elizabeth resolved to put it from her mind. Her past had been marked by fear and uncertainty; now she longed for a future shaped by security and peace. In Darcy, she would find both. His steady presence calmed her troubled heart, and she felt deeply grateful that her grandmother would remain a constant part of her life. Lady Montrose had become as dear to her as any of the Bennets.

Life would change considerably after her presentation at court. There was still much to learn about her role as countess, but Darcy would guide her. His uncle was an earl, after all, and he himself oversaw a vast estate; who better to assist her in learning her new responsibilities? All would unfold as Providence intended. What must be, would be; and no one could stand in the way of it.

Jane had married, too, bringing further change to Elizabeth's life. And Mary was betrothed to Mr. Collins. Her heart ached, just a little, for the simple days of her girlhood, even as she rejoiced in the happiness that these changes had brought to those she loved.

Change was inevitable. She would embrace it and live her life to the fullest.

Early the next morning, Elizabeth awoke and selected a simple gown from her wardrobe. It was nothing compared to the garments her grandmother had bestowed upon her, but its plainness pleased her. She could dress herself without the assistance of a lady's maid. After tying her hair in a modest knot at the nape of her neck, she took up her cloak and slipped quietly to her chambers.

Jameson awaited her in the vestibule. She ought not to be surprised. Her grandmother's faithful servant had taken her safety as his personal responsibility. Once her father's valet, Jameson had shared many stories of her father with her that she would otherwise never have known—some, he claimed, that even her grandmother did not know. A second footman stood ready to accompany them, ensuring she would not go unguarded.

She walked briskly, hoping the exercise would soon drive away the morning chill. Though spring had arrived, the air still carried a bite, and whilst her cloak and pelisse were too warm, neither alone seemed quite sufficient. No matter. At the end of her walk, Darcy would be waiting, and she would find warmth in his embrace.

As Oakham Mount rose into view, she quickened her pace. Her escorts trailed behind, their labored breathing testifying that they could benefit from more vigorous exertion. The mount, little more than a hill, truth be told, ought not to have posed such a challenge. Yet they huffed and puffed as they trudged after her. The slope gradually evened out, and she slowed as she crested the summit.

He waited for her. Darcy sat on a fallen log, elbows resting on his knees, his head bowed. At the sound of her approach, he looked up and smiled. Rising, he opened his arms. Elizabeth slipped her hands inside his greatcoat and wrapped them around his waist, sighing as his warmth surrounded her.

"It is colder this morning than I expected," she murmured, burying her face in his lawn shirt. "It is not fair that gentlemen may wear breeches or trousers. Surely, they must be warmer than a gown."

"I cannot say, and I have no intention of donning a gown to find out." His teasing made her giggle, and he chuckled in reply.

"I cannot picture you in one," she said, her smile spreading ear to ear. "What a sight it would be! I shall ask Georgiana to sketch the image I have in mind."

"Do not dare! My sister would never let me forget it." He affected a scowl and kissed her nose as she looked up at him.

Sighing, she stepped back and moved to the log. She sat, and he joined her. "June seems so far away," she said quietly. "I only want everything to be over…to have it all made right again."

"That is no small wish. Life offers trials and misfortunes, and you have known more than your share of both. And though I do not doubt there will be more ahead, I believe the worst of your troubles is nearly behind you."

"You have more faith than I," she muttered.

"Dearest Elizabeth, I have your love. That alone gives me cause for hope." He took her hand and pressed a kiss to it, then lifted his other hand to her cheek and kissed her gently. "In a few short months, I shall carry you off to Derbyshire, and we shall hide ourselves away at Pemberley for a month. The knocker will be down, and every visitor will be turned away at the door."

"That sounds delightful." He kissed her again, and they remained agreeably engaged for several quiet moments in one another's arms. Then something caught his attention, and Darcy broke their embrace.

"She is rising," he said, nodding toward the horizon. Together, they stood and watched as the glowing orb climbed steadily into the sky, bathing its warmth and light across the landscape.

"It is impossible to despair in the face of such beauty," she said softly. "Thank you for sharing it with me."

"So it is…though I find the view beside me far more distracting. I shall join you for every sunrise when we are married." He turned toward her and waggled his brow. "Though we may choose to stay abed a little later once we have achieved that happy state."

She laughed and swatted him playfully. "Are sunsets in Derbyshire as pleasing as sunrises?" she asked. "Perhaps we shall watch those instead."

"They are both beautiful, but neither compares to you." He kissed her once more, then turned to untie his horse from a nearby tree. "I shall call later, my love."

She watched him mount and ride away before making her way back down the hill. Her escorts emerged from amongst the trees and followed at a respectful distance as she returned to Longbourn. With only a few more days remaining before her return to town, Elizabeth had plans to visit the neighborhood. Charlotte and her family were already in London—she had their direction from Lydia, who had written to Maria. She would see her friend upon her arrival.

# Chapter Thirty-Three

*March 9, 1812*
*Montrose House*
*Elizabeth*

Lady Montrose descended wearily from the carriage, and Elizabeth followed close behind. She, too, felt the strain of the journey. They had stopped only once to refresh the horses before continuing on to London. The coachman had pushed the horses to maintain a brisk pace. The weather remained a touch too cold for comfortable travel and all aboard had longed to reach town as swiftly as possible.

They arrived at Montrose House before tea, to Elizabeth's relief and quiet delight. Much as she loved Longbourn, the cook in her new home possessed rare skill, and she had missed his delectable dishes. Once they changed out of their travel-worn garments, Elizabeth and her grandmother retreated to the drawing room and rang for tea.

When it arrived, Elizabeth poured for them both, adding a generous amount of sugar and cream to her own. She inhaled the aroma of the house blend with contentment before taking a sip.

Darcy had returned to town ahead of them, having left Netherfield early that morning on horseback. He had told Lady Montrose that he had business with his solicitor, but Elizabeth knew he meant to meet with Mr. Browning regarding their situation. She hoped he would have news to share when he next called.

She slept soundly that night, her head resting on a feather pillow, and buried beneath her now-familiar coverlet. By morning, her grandmother's strength would be restored, and together they would visit Bond Street for gown fittings. Then would come meetings with the florists, the cook, the housekeeper…the list was long. The very thought of it made her tired.

After breakfast, they left the house. Jameson accompanied them, ostensibly to carry packages. He also carried a pistol, however, should any protection be required. They went directly to Madame Dubois's modiste shop, where one of the attendants quickly led them to the fitting room.

"It turned out perfectly, my dear." Lady Montrose stood at Elizabeth's shoulder, their reflections side by side in the mirror. "I have never seen a gown more suited to a young lady."

"You are required to say so, because I am your granddaughter," Elizabeth teased.

"I assure you, child, if you put on something wholly unsuitable, I shall not hesitate to tell you." Lady Montrose gave a dignified sniff, then smiled and slipped an arm around Elizabeth's waist. She rested her head against her granddaughter's shoulder. With Elizabeth standing on the pedestal, the gesture was easily made, and Elizabeth leaned into her in return.

"I believe the sleeves need to be gathered here, and here." Madame Dubois appeared with pins in hand, expertly adjusting the fabric until the sleeves lay more smoothly and the puffed shape was gently reduced. "A little fullness at the shoulder is all this gown needs. The embroidery is exquisite, is it not?"

"Yes, it is absolutely lovely. Could we add a gold ribbon at the sleeve hem? Lady Montrose asked, gently fingering the spot. "It may help the line lie better." Lady Montrose fingered the spot and turned inquiringly to the modiste.

"Indeed, your ladyship, that is quite possible. I shall see it done and deliver the finished gown for a final fitting in two days. Will that be acceptable?"

Elizabeth listened with only half her attention. Her thoughts had drifted to Darcy, and she imagined him seeing her in this gown—the heated look that would appear in his eyes drew her in. Never before had she felt so beautiful, nor so truly part of the world into which she had been cast. Jewels and other accoutrements would complete the ensemble, but Lady Montrose had kept those a surprise. She meant to present them to Elizabeth on the night of the ball.

The rest of their busy errands were completed, and upon returning home, they collapsed in the parlor and called for refreshments. Thankfully, the morrow promised a day of rest. Elizabeth knew she needed it.

When Wednesday arrived, they remained at home to receive callers. Elizabeth would rather have hidden in her chambers, but she dutifully joined Lady Montrose in the parlor during calling hours.

Ladies trickled in and out, each staying no more than fifteen minutes and saying nothing of consequence. Mrs. Norton called, and Elizabeth conversed with her amiably for half an hour. The lady seemed genuine, and Elizabeth thought a friendship might be possible there.

Just as the hour drew to a close, another guest arrived. Elizabeth suppressed a groan and summoned a polite smile as Morton showed the lady in.

"Jane!" Her smile broadened at once and became genuine. She rose and embraced her sister warmly. Stepping back, Elizabeth examined her. "You are positively glowing!" "Marriage agrees with you. I did not expect to see you until June!"

"Surprise!" Jane laughed. "Lady Montrose arranged it all. Charles and I are to attend your ball. You could not possibly face the *ton* without someone from your family!"

Elizabeth turned to her grandmother, choking back a sob. Lady Montrose wore a smug grin which turned into a fond smile as her beloved Elizabeth hugged her tightly. "This is the best surprise I have ever had. Thank you so much."

"Caroline and Sir James will attend as well, though she was not free to call with me today. Tell me, have you been much occupied with preparations?"

"More occupied than I should like." Elizabeth huffed and crossed her arms. "Do you know, I have not read a single book in a month?"

Jane gasped in mock horror. "No! That is not like you at all. No wonder you are at your wit's end." They both laughed, and Elizabeth silently vowed to read something—anything—the moment all the chaos ended.

"This ball makes me wonder whether I am suited to society," Elizabeth admitted quietly. "How am I to manage a lifetime of this if one event exhausts me so?"

"This is hardly a small affair, my dear. I have invited everyone of note. Even Prinny received an invitation, though it remains uncertain whether he will attend. Once you are Mrs. Darcy, you may host as many guests as you please. Many ladies hold only one or two large events each year and keep the rest of their engagements small with intimate guest lists." Lady Montrose patted her arm in reassurance. "It is rather a lot, I confess. But never fear. In two days, it will all be behind you."

It brought her little comfort, but she smiled and thanked her grandmother all the same.

Jane departed, reminding Elizabeth that she and Bingley were just a few minutes away on Charles Street should she need anything.

After her sister's departure, Elizabeth found herself stewing, wondering why she felt so out of sorts. At last, she realized the cause. It was Wednesday, and she had not seen Darcy since their arrival in town two days prior. She missed him…and the quiet strength he always brought.

"You are rather dull this evening, my dear," Lady Montrose observed after the meal. "Tell me, you would not be meditating on a tall, handsome gentleman from the North, would you?"

Biting her lip, Elizabeth nodded.

"Well then, write to him! You are betrothed, after all. I had assumed you understood you were free to exchange letters. Go on—invite him to dine tomorrow. You will need cheering after your fitting. I have never known a lady so disinclined to purchasing new gowns."

"It is not the new clothing I mind; it is being forced to stand still and wait to be stuck with a pin." Elizabeth rose at once and crossed to the writing desk to pen Darcy a note.

*Dearest Love,*

*My, that sounds rather silly, does it not? No matter, for you are my dearest love, and I must be certain you know it. I miss you so! Though it has been but two days, I long for your presence. I know that business has occupied you, and I hope to hear all about it when you come for dinner tomorrow.*

*My grandmother bids me extend the invitation, and so I shall. Pray, bring Georgiana. I have not seen her in an age. We shall be a small party, but I do not repine at that. Intimate gatherings are my preference.*

*Send a reply with Jameson.*

*Yours,*

*Elizabeth*

The note was dispatched to Darcy House, and not ten minutes later, she held his reply in her hand.

*My dearest Elizabeth,*

*I have neglected you most shamefully, and shall rectify that at once. Georgiana and I are pleased to accept your invitation to dine on the morrow. I shall call a little early with her, that we might discuss the business which has kept me so engaged these last weeks.*

*Visions of you fill my dreams, and I long for the day when we shall never be parted unless we choose it. You are everything to me, and I thank Heaven for the day we met, for never did I imagine I would be so fortunate to win your regard. All else pales beside it.*

*I know you are anxious for answers. I beg you to wait just a little longer, and we shall speak of all in person.*

*Yours in love and affection,*

*F. D.*

Her heart warmed, and a sense of peace settled over her. She could wait a little longer for answers...and for him.

The following afternoon, Madame Dubois arrived for the final gown fitting, her assistant in tow. Elizabeth stood before the large bedroom mirror and gazed admiringly at the exquisite creation. The women in the room all breathed admiringly at once, prompting a round of giggles from Elizabeth and the assistant.

"*C'est magnifique,*" Madame Dubois said with satisfaction. "Mark my words, ladies all over London will be clamoring for a gown in this style."

"It is a work of art," Elizabeth agreed. "There are no words to express how pleased I am."

The gown was carefully removed and hung in the wardrobe before Madame Dubois and her assistant took their leave. Elizabeth looked at the time and groaned. Darcy would not arrive for nearly an hour.

The time passed quickly, however, and the Darcys arrived just before four. They would stay through the evening, and Elizabeth was determined to savor every moment in their company.

Georgiana made her way to the pianoforte at once and began to play after receiving a pointed look from her brother. He then joined the ladies, prepared to speak of his '*business.*'

"Browning has had no success locating our man," he said grimly. "No one enters or leaves the house, and we still have no idea who we are even looking for. The guilty party could be any number of people."

"Let us set it aside until after the ball," Elizabeth said sensibly. "We shall take proper precautions, and I shall be quite safe."

"And then we can put the entire matter behind us," Lady Montrose added. "Perhaps by then, Mr. Gardiner's offer will have reached Mr. Winters, and we can turn our attention to more pleasant matters."

After dinner and tea, Elizabeth bade a reluctant farewell to Darcy and Georgiana, wishing she and her betrothed might have had more privacy so that he could bestow something more than a kiss to her hand.

That night, dreams of a happy future danced in her mind as she slept. Though she had not yet seen Pemberley, Darcy's descriptions had painted a vivid picture of the house and its grounds. She imagined long walks on his arm, and quiet evenings spent in his company.

Georgiana would, of course, reside with them, but there would be ample time for themselves. Their suite of rooms, he had said, would be perfect for hiding from the world. And should they ever desire more privacy, they might retreat to Marston Hall, another ideal location—and just twenty miles away.

*Soon,* she thought as she drifted into slumber. *It will not be long now.*

<hr />

*Winters*

He had evening attire prepared, purchased hastily since he could not go to his house. The Montrose Ball was the most talked-of event in town. In various disguises, Silas had visited his club, Bond Street, Gunter's, and other establishments, gathering gossip. Everyone spoke of Lady Elizabeth Montrose. *Lady!* How had he failed to learn she had inherited everything? It was not fair. She no longer needed the business now, so why demand such an exorbitant sum for its purchase?

Donning his waistcoat, Winters selected a fine gold watch and fob, secured them, and reached for his coat. It hung a little loose—necessary since he did not have a valet. He pulled on his polished boots, and settled his hat upon his head.

For fortitude, he drank as much brandy as he dared. He could not afford to lose his faculties. The alcohol lent him courage, and he added a full flask to his pocket.

His plan was simple. He would sneak into the house through another door, eliminating any who stood in his way. All the servants would be occupied with the evening's preparations, so he was confident that he could slip inside unnoticed. Once within, he would mingle with the crowd, remaining hidden in plain sight whilst he waited for his moment to strike. Yes, tonight would be a night to remember.

# Chapter Thirty-Four

*March 14, 1812*
*Montrose House*
*Elizabeth*

Tonight would indeed be memorable. Elizabeth's grandmother had sent her to her rooms at noon to begin preparations, a full six hours before the guests were due to arrive. Her maids bathed, brushed, and perfumed her until she felt like a pampered princess. Then, dressed in her nightgown and robe, she took tea and light refreshments before the next ordeal began. Two maids worked on her hair, curling, twisting, pinning and poking for what felt like hours. At last, they helped her into her gown, with only an hour to spare before she was needed downstairs.

"You look beautiful," her grandmother said as she entered the room, two jewel cases in her hands. "Now, for the finishing touches." She opened the first case and drew out a heavy gold necklace. A deep blue stone, set in gold, hung from the center of the chain, with matching stones spaced evenly along either side. She fastened it around Elizabeth's neck.

It felt cold and heavy against her skin, but not unpleasantly so. "It is beautiful," she whispered in awe.

"It is from my personal collection," her grandmother replied. "It is yours now. I have not worn it in years, and this piece deserves better than to sit hidden in a safe. There is also this." She opened the second case and revealed a tiara, gold and set with the same rich blue gems.

Now Elizabeth understood why no jeweled pins had been placed in her hair. Lady Montrose gently lowered the tiara onto her granddaughter's head and made sure it was secure. "You are ready," she said reverently.

Elizabeth did not feel ready. Yet instead of protesting, she took her blue silk wrap from one of the maids. Together, she and her grandmother went to meet their guests.

Darcy met her on the stairs, his steady presence soothing her nerves and providing comfort. "You look ravishing," he murmured, his gaze moving from the tiara to her slippers. She saw admiration in his eyes, but more than that—love. Wonderful man that he was, Darcy remained at her side in the receiving line. Lady after lady, gentleman after gentleman, they welcomed each arrival in turn. At last, the guests began to move into the ballroom. The lack of declined invitations meant the space was filled to capacity. The first set was called, and Darcy offered his arm. He had claimed her for the first, supper, and final sets, a declaration to all that she would soon be Mrs. Darcy.

The evening passed more swiftly than she could have imagined. Elizabeth had just enough time to greet Jane and Charles before Lady Montrose whisked her away once more. Supper followed, then the evening's entertainment. At last, one of the musicians broke a string, and she was able to rest for a moment.

Darcy went in search of punch, and Elizabeth slipped out onto the terrace. The night air held a chill, but after the warmth of the ballroom, it felt wonderfully refreshing.

"You look lovely, Lady Montrose."

Elizabeth turned, surprised to see a man standing in the shadows. Something niggled the back of her mind. She knew that face. As he swayed slightly, a wave of recognition washed over her. Suddenly, she was no longer at Montrose House, but hiding next to the desk in her papa's study, watching as this man argued with him. "You." she whispered. "It was *you*."

"Do not tell me you remember *now*. I had so looked forward to helping you along." He stepped forward and caught her around the waist, clamping a hand over her mouth. "Come along, my dear. We had best take our meeting to a quieter place."

She struggled, but his strength seemed unnatural. Her wrap slipped from her shoulders, and one slipper came off as he dragged her down the short flight of terrace steps and out through the garden gate.

The gate, hidden at the back of Montrose House's garden, opened near Hyde Park. He took her there. Elizabeth fought with every step, praying that Darcy would soon notice her absence. Rocks and twigs dug into her bare foot and she lost her second slipper when she tried once more to pull away.

They reached a small grove set back from the main path. Still holding her firmly, he drew a rope from his pocket. "Scream, and I shall take extreme measures," he hissed. Dropping his hand from her mouth, he seized her wrists and bound them together so tightly that the rope bit into her skin. Her gloves offered some protection, but not enough.

Once her hands were secured, he pushed her roughly to the ground. Turning away, Mr. Winters took a flask from his pocket and drank deeply.

"This is all your fault. You could not stay dead. Everything would be fine if you were dead." He chuckled, low and dark. "And so you will be—very soon. The *ton* will revel in the tragedy. As much as they have celebrated your discovery, they will mourn your death twice as much. And why should they not? Your tale is so very gothic."

"Why?" she cried. "I do not understand."

"I want Henry's company. All of it. I have debts, you see, and what I can withdraw from the business without harming it is not enough. But if I had access to your father's shares, and the funds accumulating in the trust, it would solve everything."

"I offered to sell it!"

"A hundred thousand pounds?" He scoffed. "What right have you to demand so much? You have had no hand in managing *my* business. I have done everything!"

Elizabeth trembled as he leaned over her. The smell of spirits was strong on his breath and, and she turned her face away in revulsion. He grabbed her chin and forced her to meet his eyes.

"You are the very image of your mother." He shuddered and shoved her back to the ground. "I did not mean to, you know. That night, when I met Henry, I was in my cups. He had discovered my gambling debts and the embezzlement I used to conceal them." Winters shook his head slowly. "Henry was very disappointed, but he refused to listen to reason. My memories after that are unclear. But you...you would know all about that, would you not?"

He took another drink. Elizabeth knew if she could keep him talking, it might buy her a few precious moments. The tiara dug into her scalp, and she longed to remove it. The necklace pressed against her throat, and she shifted slightly, allowing the gem to fall to the side so she could breathe more easily.

Mr. Winters turned back to her. "I awoke before dawn, still in your father's study. There he was... In a stupor, I wandered the house. First, I found your brother. And then Amelia." He choked out a sob. "She, who had never spoken an unkind word to me—and I had done that to her. But you...you were nowhere to be found. I looked everywhere. The door stood ajar, and I realized you had wandered off. There was nothing to be done. I slipped away and returned home, pretending I had been there all night."

He took a long, shuddering breath and looked at her once more. "All would have gone well if your dear grandmother had not poked her nose where it was not wanted. She refused to declare you dead. Your father's will left his shares equally to me and Bingley if his family were gone. I knew I could persuade Bingley to sell. He would not want to remain in Yorkshire without *his dearest friend*. But I could not touch anything else unless your death became official. Instead, I was forced to place your father's income into a trust. Lady Montrose sent funds for expenses, and I managed to convince her of my need for more. But it was never enough."

"Why did you not leave her alone once she refused?" Elizabeth asked desperately. He seemed to be reaching the end of his wretched tale, and she needed more time. *Oh, Fitzwilliam, where are you? Her mind cried out into the darkness, hoping he would find her in time. Surely someone must hear. Can the park truly be so empty at this hour? How had no one heard her?*

"I needed the money!" he screamed, kicking her leg. She cried out, and he swung to kick her again, but in his inebriated state, he was thrown off balance. "The men I owe are dangerous," he spat. "I sent those people to your aunt, pretending they had found you. I hoped she would give in to despair and declare you dead. And I might have succeeded, if not for that meddling whelp of Bingley's. His timing was dreadful."

Winters took another long swig from the flask. If he was not foxed upon entering the park, he certainly was now. "Enough," he muttered. "It is time to end this."

He grabbed her arm and dragged her from the grove. Elizabeth stumbled beside him, silent tears slipping down her cheeks as she prayed for help. When they reached a fountain, her heart sank.

"Not long now," he muttered. He dropped her at the edge of the stone basin, then shrugged out of his coat and let it fall to the ground. Rolling his shoulders, he reached for her. Elizabeth scrambled to her feet. She would not just lie down and die. Not without a fight. If he wanted to kill her, she would not make it easy. Hands still bound in front of her, she turned and ran, trying her best to stay upright and not trip over her skirts.

He caught her easily, clamping an arm around her waist yet again. "No, no, little bird," he snarled. "It is time to clip your wings." His breath was hot against her neck, making her skin crawl. With a cry of rage, she threw her head back and struck his nose. The satisfying sound of a crunch made her gasp. He cursed and released her. She ran again, ducking into the bushes, forcing her way through the branches as she tried to escape him. Brambles tore at her gown, and the delicate fabric ripped in several places, but she did not stop.

"Elizabeth!" Darcy's voice rang out across the park and she collapsed in relief. Curling up at the base of a tree, she did not dare cry out. Winters was too close. Twigs snapped as he came closer, but she remained silent lest he find her.

"There you are!" He grabbed her by the hair and yanked her to her feet. "Enough!" He ripped the tiara from her head and tossed it aside. Her necklace followed, pulled from her neck. She closed her eyes against the pain and tried once more to resist, but her legs did not support her. This was it. She was going to die and there was nothing she could do. Her captor held her in complete control.

Suddenly, he released her. She opened her eyes to see Darcy tearing Winters away from her and striking him—squarely in the face. Mr. Browning and two other men appeared and seized Winters by the arms.

"We have it from here, sir," Browning said.

"Not on your life!" Winters bellowed, blood pouring from his nose. He thrashed violently, elbowing one man as he broke free. Darcy pulled Elizabeth close, shielding her as the struggle became heated, both on guard as they watched.

Winters staggered back and drew a pistol and leveled it at Elizabeth. A single crack split the air, but it was not his weapon that fired.

Colonel Fitzwilliam stepped from the shadows, smoke rising from the barrel of his pistol as Winters dropped to the ground. "Death was too good for him," he muttered grimly.

Browning's men stood, both groaning. One bore a lump upon his head; the other's nose bled. Elizabeth took it all in with a strange sense of detachment.

"Dearest?" Darcy whispered in her ear. She whimpered, then burst into tears, burying her face against his chest. He tightened his hold, murmuring soothing words as his hands moved to untie the ropes about her wrists.

"We must get her home."

"Are you mad, Darcy? Montrose House is full of guests." Colonel Fitzwilliam shook his head. "Take her to Darcy House. I shall speak with Lady Montrose and contrive an excuse for your lady's absence. The ball is nearly at an end. Perhaps a headache?" He bent to retrieve the fallen jewels, sticking them into his pocket. "Browning, see to that loathsome carcass, will you?"

Elizabeth felt herself lifted into Darcy's arms. She still trembled, fear and relief warring within her. Shock set in, and as she drifted in and out of consciousness, someone began tugging on her gloves. Panic seized her, and she thrashed, crying out in terror.

"It is I, dearest." Jane touched her hand and Elizabeth's vision cleared enough to recognize her sister. "All is well. Come, let us remove this gown." The gloves came off, and Jane undid the buttons of her gown. Elizabeth sat motionless, half her hair falling from its pins, whilst Jane gently guided her this way and that, removing the soiled garments and bathing her wounds with a warm cloth.

A nightgown was drawn down over her head, and Elizabeth flinched anew. Soon, though, Jane led her to the bed, tucked her in and handed her a cup of tea. She tasted the laudanum and drank eagerly, anticipating the dreamless sleep it would bring.

She awoke the next day, sore from head to toe. A large bruise marred her leg where Winters had kicked her; her feet were cut and swollen. Her wrists, though covered by gloves, had not been spared—the delicate skin was bruised and chafed from the tight ropes.

"How do you feel?" Lady Montrose stood in the doorway, looking far older than her years. The worry for Elizabeth had clearly worn on her.

"I believe I look worse than I feel." In truth, Elizabeth felt much improved. Her heart no longer raced, and though the memories would surely haunt her dreams, she knew Winters was now dead and he could no longer harm her.

Grandmother came forward and folded Elizabeth into an embrace. "It is over," she wept. "It is over."

# Chapter Thirty-Five

*June 30, 1812*
*Yorkshire*
*Elizabeth*

She never expected recovery to be easy. The memories plagued her by night, filling her dreams with panic and terror. Grandmother could not soothe her, and after one particularly harrowing night, sent for Darcy. In his arms, she found rest at last.

In consequence, she and Darcy traveled to Meryton and secured a common license. They married quietly in Longbourn Church, with the Bennets, the Bingleys, and Lady Montrose in attendance. Returning to London for their honeymoon, they secluded themselves at Darcy House until her wounds had healed.

Lady Montrose's excuse that Elizabeth had taken to her bed with a megrim was accepted without question. The Dowager Countess politely declined calls in the days following the ball, the servants informing callers that Elizabeth had taken ill. The knocker was kept down to afford the two ladies some reprieve.

After another month, their wedding announcement appeared in every London paper. Well-wishers descended upon Darcy House, and

Elizabeth endured hours of callers when she would far rather have remained in quiet company with her husband.

In May, Charlotte called at Darcy House to share news of her betrothal. Sir William's final efforts to see his daughter married had borne fruit: Charlotte was engaged to a parson with a respectable family living in Cheshire. She would reside in a county bordering Derbyshire and would be able to visit Elizabeth often.

In June, the season drew to a close. All matters concerning her father's business had been resolved. She inherited Mr. Winter's shares, and all documents pertaining to the Yorkshire mills were sent north for her attention upon arrival at Pemberley. In the pocket of Winters's coat, they had found a letter directed to him at a boarding house on Bloomsbury Street, which led them to the rented rooms he had taken. They surmised he had taken lodgings across from his own house once Jarvis had been apprehended.

Amongst his possessions was a worn journal, within which they discovered a full confession to the murders. He claimed he did not remember his deeds, having been in his cups, though he knew he had committed the murders in Yorkshire. It would have sufficed to see him hanged, had he lived.

The Darcys departed London on the twenty-fifth of June. Lady Montrose followed in her own conveyance, and together they made quite a procession: the Darcy coach, the Montrose carriage, and an additional vehicle bearing their servants and trunks.

Before traveling on to Pemberley, and after they had stopped at Longbourn to farewell the Bennets, they had one final stop to make. Late on the last day of June, the carriages pulled up before a modest house in a small town in Yorkshire. A hazy fog hung in the air—vapours from the mills, Darcy explained—which made Elizabeth cough.

Grandmother joined her and drew a key from her reticule. She inserted it into the lock of the green-painted door and turned it. The mechanism creaked, and Elizabeth heard the dull clunk of stiff tumblers. The door groaned on its hinges as it opened.

Elizabeth stepped inside, her husband and grandmother lingering just behind. The last rays of the sun streamed through a narrow gap in the drapes. Motes danced in the beam of light. She drew in a deep breath and moved further into the house.

She remembered. "Papa's study is through there," she gestured. "Mama's parlor lies that way. Our chambers were upstairs." Her limbs trembled, and she sank to her knees, burying her face in her hands.

Darcy came to her at once and helped her rise. He embraced her, gently. "We need not go any further," he said quietly.

She shook her head and stepped back. "No, I must see it all," she replied. "I must see it so that I may let it go."

"Then we shall go together." He took her hand and pressed it tenderly. Lady Montrose moved to her other side and clasped her other hand. Together, the three of them walked through the house. All signs of the past devastation that had occurred there were erased. Every room stood bare, stripped of adornment; many contained no furniture at all. The warm, cheerful home she barely remembered no longer existed.

After an hour, they departed. "I am ready to sell it now," she said firmly. "It is time."

Lady Montrose embraced Elizabeth before parting ways. "It has been far too long since I visited Marston," she said with a touch of regret. "Come to me in the autumn. I shall show you where we laid your family to rest."

After bidding her grandmother a fond farewell, Elizabeth climbed into the carriage and settled close beside Darcy. They would reach

Pemberley before nightfall. Georgiana would arrive with the Matlocks in a fortnight.

"Are you well, my love?" Darcy kissed her brow and slipped an arm around her.

"I am," she promised. "I feel lighter, somehow—as though that chapter of my life has truly closed. It is time for us to build a future together. We shall raise our children to love their family and to appreciate all that this world has to offer. And with your help, I shall overcome any lingering fears that may arise."

"Your strength is admirable," he said, with abiding love. "If only everyone possessed a tenth of your courage!"

The sun had begun to set when their carriage crested a hill overlooking Pemberley. The golden light struck the stone façade, causing it to gleam like a thousand diamonds. They alighted and stood hand in hand, gazing upon the handsome prospect.

"It is beautiful." Never had she seen a place more happily situated. The land had been left to grow in harmony with nature, unspoiled overzealous landscaping. The wild beauty of the surrounding countryside blended effortlessly with the cultivated gardens, creating the prettiest picture Elizabeth had ever beheld.

"And it is ours." He squeezed her hand. "Are you ready to see it?"

"Yes. Let us go at once."

Instead of clambering back into the carriage, Elizabeth convinced Darcy to walk with her. In no time at all, they were in front of the manor house. She could swear there were a hundred servants lining the steps, awaiting their new mistress. Each curtsied or bowed deeply in turn as they greeted Lady Elizabeth Montrose-Darcy.

Much later, as Mr. and Mrs. Darcy dined privately in their chambers, they spoke with quiet delight of the future. Everything appeared brighter. The shadows of the past had lifted, and their life together now stretched out before them.

# Epilogue

The Darcys welcomed a son one year after their marriage. Henry Thomas Darcy, Viscount Marston, would inherit the earldom one day. He was a cheerful child and bore a marked resemblance to Elizabeth. The Dowager Countess of Montrose insisted he looked like his grandfather and could not be persuaded otherwise.

Three more children arrived over the next seven years. Another son joined his brother in the nursery. Bennet James Darcy favoured his father in both looks and temperament, and was ever mindful that the Darcy estate came to him only because his elder brother had inherited the Montrose earldom. Like all Darcys before him, he became an honorable master who ensured Pemberley prospered under his careful stewardship.

Jane and Charles likewise welcomed an heir two months after Henry's birth. They did not renew the lease on Netherfield Park, choosing instead to purchase an estate in Derbyshire, twenty miles southwest of Pemberley. Two more children, a boy and a girl, were added to their nursery. They were frequent guests at Pemberley, where their children were raised in close company with their Darcy cousins.

The Collinses left Kent as soon as possible. Lady Catherine's displeasure at her parson's decision to appoint a curate made their situation at Hunsford untenable. Each new curate departed within half a year—beginning a pattern of appointing a man, only to have Lady

Catherine drive him away within six months. Mr. Collins ensured each curate was well compensated, but no inducement could persuade any to remain long. The pattern continued until her death.

Georgiana was presented at court and married in her first season. She fell in love with a handsome viscount from a southern shire. Though Darcy initially disliked the idea that Viscount Wilton would take his sister so far away, he approved the match and gave his blessing. They had two children, a son and a daughter.

Caroline and Sir James married in July. Their wedding was elaborate and quite grand. They settled into a handsome townhouse and became frequent visitors at Darcy House and Montrose House when the families were in town. After many years of hoping for a child, God finally sent them a son, whom they loved and adored. Years later, to their great surprise, a daughter followed. Caroline's fondest wish, to share her life with a daughter, was fulfilled.

Elizabeth renamed her father's company to Montrose Mill and Textiles, which became the most desirable place for employment in Yorkshire. Fair masters and improved working conditions attracted laborers from afar. The business flourished, and Mr. Gardiner, through his import and export connections, supplied the mill with cotton and wool. As Elizabeth's profits grew, so did his, benefiting both their families handsomely.

Mr. and Mrs. Bennet lived long and comfortably into their later years. Elizabeth remained ever close to them, visiting at least once a year and encouraging them to travel north as often as they pleased. The prospect of Pemberley's library proved irresistible to Mr. Bennet, who twice annually dragged his wife with him to Derbyshire.

Master Thomas Bennet assumed management of Longbourn from his father upon his twenty-fifth birthday. He married one of Mrs. Long's nieces and their union proved a happy one. The entail ended upon his majority, but he need not have worried. He and his wife, the former Miss Harriet Long, had four sons and one daughter, a neat reversal of his parents' family. The remaining Bennet sisters also married well: Lydia, to a minor country gentleman from a neighboring county, and Kitty to a solicitor from Stevenage. They wrote often to their adopted sister and remained close.

Elizabeth's curious tale became the fodder for gossip in Meryton. Wild theories abounded, but none ever discovered the truth of how the unassuming Elizabeth Bennet became not only a countess, but the wife of one of the wealthiest men in England.

She did nothing to gratify their curiosity, instead choosing to focus on her happy past, never allowing the shadows to take hold. "Today is a gift," she said. "That is why we call it the present." And no one could disagree.

---

I hope you enjoyed *Shadows of the Past*. It was an adventure to explore this alternate path for our dear couple. Be sure to check out my other books. I have a soft spot for redemption stories, so if that's a favorite trope of yours, take a look at my other books! Find them at Amazon.com!

<u>MJ Stratton Books</u>
Thank you for reading!

# Other Books by MJ Stratton

*Note: Books with an asterisk are redemption stories*

**Darcy and Lizzy Variations:**

A Far Better Prospect**

When Given Good Principles**

No Less Than Any Other

The Lake House at Ramsgate

Thwarted

To Marry for Love

Love Unfeigned

**Other Stories:**

The Redemption of Lydia Wickham**

Catherine Called Kitty**

Mary, Marry? Quite Contrary!**

Charmed

Charming Caroline**

From Another Perspective

Crossroads

**Variations from Jane Austen's other works**

What Ought to Have Been**

Thank you for reading!

# Acknowledgements

Thank you to everyone (betas, editors, ARC participants) who helped me along with this book. A special thanks to Gratia, Kim, Debbie, Christie, Ruth, Sunny, and Shannon for your efforts to help make this book free of error.

Many thanks to Marie. I cannot fully express how deeply I appreciate your unwavering support and patience. Your guidance and insight have been an invaluable gift, and I will always be grateful for everything you've done to help me. More than anything, I treasure your friendship—it means the world to me. Thank you, from the bottom of my heart.

Thank you to Pemberley Darcy for the spectacular cover design! You are very patient with my particular ways. This cover is everything I wanted for this book—practically perfect in every way!

And, as always, thank you to my darling husband, who has supported me through it all, especially when it came to finding time to write whilst still being a wife and mom. This book was your idea in the first place, and I think it turned out very well. Keep feeding me great ideas!!

# About The Author

MJ Stratton's love affair with Jane Austen began at sixteen, thanks to a much-beloved aunt who introduced her to *Pride and Prejudice*. That fateful moment led to an insatiable passion for Austenesque fiction, sealing her destiny as both a reader and a writer. After nearly a decade of beta reading and editing for others, MJ took the plunge into publishing her own works in 2022.

A lifelong enthusiast of reading, learning, and all things bookish, MJ balances her time between crafting Regency tales, tending to her garden, and sewing her way through creative projects. She shares her small-town life with her husband, four lively children, and cats who firmly believes they are the true masters of the household.

When she's not writing or wrangling her feline overlords, MJ can usually be found lost in a book, researching obscure historical facts, or daydreaming about her next story.

Printed in Great Britain
by Amazon